Also by Eric Brown

PENUMBRA

ERIC BROWN

First published in Great Britain in 1999 by
Millennium
An imprint of Orion Books Ltd
Orion House, 5 Upper St Martin's Lane,
London WC2H 9EA

To receive information on the Millennium list, e-mail us at:
smy@orionbooks.co.uk

A CIP catalogue record for this book
is available from the British Library

ISBN 1 85798 592 3

Typeset at The Spartan Press Ltd,
Lymington, Hants
Printed in Great Britain by
Clays Ltd, St Ives plc

For
Emilie Rachel Dunnett
With Love

1

Bennett's last shift began with the late arrival of his co-pilot and ended with a near-fatal collision between his Viper tug and a colony liner. In between, he learned a little about Bhao Khet Buddhism.

He crawled through the umbilical and strapped himself into the pilot's couch. The cabin was a cramped, darkened wedge that stank with the sweat of a thousand previous pilots. The narrow, mock-leather couches were so low-slung that he operated almost horizontally, staring down the length of his body through the acutely angled view-screen.

After ten days aboard Redwood Station, piloting his tug two shifts a day, Bennett was looking forward to his leave period on Earth. Lately he had come to hate his job. What years ago had seemed to him a life of excitement and glamour had turned into nothing more than mind-numbing routine.

He jacked the leads into his helmet and got through to Control. 'Bennett here. Any sign of my co-pilot?' They should have been sealing up and splitting five minutes ago.

'Ah . . . check, Bennett. She's on her way.'

He settled back and magnified the viewscreen. There were times, even after fifteen years, when he was struck anew by the visual majesty of so many colossal orbital structures. His tug adhered to the skin of the station like

1

some minuscule parasite to the flank of a basking cet-
acean. Beyond the station, strung out in a vast parabolic
archipelago, industrial orbitals and habitats, labs and
factories scintillated in the raw light of the sun. Tiny
vessels, reduced to the size of gnats by comparison,
shuttled between the orbitals. Occasionally, bigger tugs
set off at right angles from the shimmering necklace,
heading for the mining depots out on the asteroid belt.

As Bennett watched, a colony ship detached itself from
an orbital transit terminal, turned with the colossal
languor of all vessels its size, and moved to a phase point
well away from the orbitals.

The sight of these interstellar colony ships embarking
for the stars never failed to stir in Bennett a sense of
venture quashed, of opportunities missed. For how many
years had he promised himself that, one day, he would
leave Earth and relocate to one of the colony worlds? He
had dozens of downloads and holo-cubes back at his
dome advertising holidays and resettlement on a hundred exotic planets.

He wondered whether it was the coward in him that
shied away from the challenge of new experiences,
contenting himself with the mind-numbing routine of
work in the high orbitals.

The systems analyst appeared in the hatch and swam
through. 'Sorry I'm late,' she said as she floated past,
elbowing him in the chest. He noticed that she was
barefoot, an increasing trend aboard the station.

She was a tiny woman in a bright scarlet flight-suit,
black-skinned and shaven-skulled. There was something
severely Oriental about her features, the slanting eyes set
flush in the sheer fall of her cheeks, at once childlike yet
knowing.

He tried to guess at her age. She might have been
anything from fifteen to thirty.

She pulled on her helmet. The bulbous headgear on so slight a figure appeared ridiculously top-heavy and ant-like. She was having difficulty with the chin strap, frowning as she tried to snap the catch.

Bennett thought of Ella, his dead sister, and the face she had made when trying to buckle her cycling helmet, and he had to stop himself from reaching out to give assistance.

She strapped herself in and analysed the computer systems, going through the checks with a swift professionalism, small hands darting around the console housing, lips moving as she talked to herself.

The name-tag stitched on to her upper arm said: TEN LEE THENEKA.

'Josh Bennett,' he said. 'Where you from, Ten?'

She closed her eyes briefly with a mixture of impatience and disdain. 'Bhao Khet, Rigel VII. Was Rocastle's World five years ago, before the War of Independence.'

'I know it.' From the brochures. 'Vietnamese?'

'Principally Viet-Zambian.'

He nodded. That explained her jet skin.

'Now, Joshua, if the geography lesson's over for the day, do you think you might get this ship up and running? It's over to the ICI Industrial for routine ferry work, then up to phase point with supplies for the liners. She's all yours.'

Bennett gave the command to disengage and through the sidescreen the excoriated skin of the station seemed to drift away. At the required distance from the dock, the engines cut in and they banked and followed the long curving line of the orbitals.

'Been on the station long?' Bennett asked.

Ten Lee sighed, staring at him. 'As a matter of fact, one week.'

'Settling in okay?'

3

She flashed him a glance. 'Why all the questions?'

'Hey – I'm sorry.' He looked at her, surprised at the tone of her voice.

He hesitated. Outside, hulking orbitals flashed by.

'It's just that you're new here. I was curious, that's all. We don't get many colonial spacers through this way. They're all from the academy on Mars.'

He realised he was shooting off, trying to win her over.

'I don't like much personal contact, okay?' she said. 'Where I come from, we realise the danger of emotion. We try to distance ourselves from the illusions of senti-ment, to avoid the suffering that is a consequence of living too much in this world. It is all maya – things that are impermanent and therefore illusory.'

Bennett nodded. She sounded like one of the many religious fanatics he came across these days. 'Isn't that some kind of Buddhism?'

She regarded him, nodded minimally. 'The Bhao Khet code of the philosophy. We've taken it further even than the Avatamsaka school. One of the tenets of my belief is the attainment of sunyata, of nothingness. I do not need the petty distractions of your society.'

He shrugged. 'Sorry if I offended you.'

Ten Lee smiled and flipped down the visor screen of her helmet.

They came to the sunlit vastness of the ICI Industrial and approached a cantilevered shelf marked with the stark black numeral 65. Bennett took control of the tug, turned it about and backed on to the shelf stacked with containers.

Ten Lee ran a hand across a touch-pad, instructing the tug's grabs to engage with the containers. Contact and engagement rang through the tug as if it were a struck bell. Bennett lowered the visor on his helmet and monitored the pick-up on the integral screen, less out of necessity than for something to watch during the hour it took to load up.

He had often wondered why this class of tug had been named Viper; Squid would have been more appropriate. With its tapering nose-cone and multiple trailing grabs, it resembled nothing so much as that many-tentacled creature of the deep.

'Ease forward, Joshua,' Ten Lee said.

Bennett touched the tug forward ten metres and the vessel shook as more grabs snaked from its stern and contacted with the containers. This procedure was repeated for the next fifty minutes until Ten Lee gave the thumbs up. On his helmet screen, the nose-cone of the tug was dwarfed by the bulk of the two dozen containers looming aft.

Bennett eased the tug from the shelf and set course for a slow traverse of the inner curve of the serried orbitals. With the computer running things, he flipped up his visor, lay back and watched Ten Lee.

She lifted her visor, frowned down at the monitor and shook her encephalic, helmeted head.

'Something wrong?' he asked.

'I . . . don't know. Yes, but not so serious, I think. We're scheduled to pick up a load from the Burgess manufactory bound for the phase point, but the pre-programmed route takes us past the interstellar terminal.'

'Shouldn't we go via station?'

'Of course. But there's a hitch in the pre-programming.'

'Think you'd better check it with Control?'

'I'll put a query in, but it could take hours to locate the operator. I could rewrite the sub-routine . . .' She regarded Bennett, her expression blank as she considered her options. 'Hokay, I'll contact Control, explain the situation and request clearance to do the rewrite.'

She tapped her visor down and linked with Control.

'Systems analyst Theneka here. Viper-class code 45/7a. We have a problem, Control . . .' She outlined the situation while Bennett watched the orbital archipelago drift by.

Minutes later Ten Lee lifted her visor. 'Control's okayed the rewrite.'

She pulled the com-screen down from a padded recess above her and ran quick fingers over the touch controls, rewriting the program.

Bennett considered the potential disaster the systems glitch might have caused. In years of working in high orbit, the closest he'd come to a possible life-threatening situation himself was when a micro-meteorite impacted with an air tank and cut off the supply. For an hour it had been touch and go as to whether he could get back to station before his existing air gave out. He'd made it, but only just.

He'd considered himself lucky. Every year saw the loss of at least one tug crew. More often than not the fatalities were the result of human error – both on the part of pilots and engineers – sloppy workmanship caused by apathy and complacency, the it'll-never-happen-to-me ethos that was bound to affect crews who had worked in space for years without mishap.

Ten Lee pushed the com-screen back into the ceiling. 'Control have vetted and passed the rewrite, Joshua.'

They slowed on the approach to Terminal 2, a great silver-ringed construction the periphery of which consisted of a hundred docking bays. Ground-to-orbit ships drifted across the hole in the middle of the doughnut, collecting goods manufactured in orbit to deliver to the cities of Earth. It was the most spectacular sight in space, Bennett thought. Twenty-four hours a day, cargo ships came and went like so many bees at a hive, a constant sunlit flux of arrival and departure. Way below the station, dwindling into the vortex, the ships were no more than tiny specks of scintillating dust; up close, the cargo ships manoeuvring and docking inside the ring-station could be seen for what they really were, vast streamlined shuttles the size of towerblocks. For the first five years of his tenure with the Redwood Corporation, Bennett had piloted these leviathans on their journeys to and from Earth, before the repetition had become monotonous and he'd requested a transfer to inter-orbital work.

He turned the tug and backed towards the delivery bay. Ten Lee directed the operation of unloading the containers, each one disappearing into the terminal to be loaded on to a cargo vessel. One hour later she gave the thumbs up and Bennett eased the tug from the terminal.

As they moved away, he asked Ten Lee about her name.

A brief sigh was the extent of her protest. 'It doesn't *mean* anything, Joshua. My mother wasn't very imaginative – she ran out of names for her children after the first five, so the rest were called Six, Seven, Eight, Nine . . . I was her tenth.'

Josh peered at Ten Lee in the gloom of the cabin, but her expression was serious as she stared at the passing station.

'My mother was religious, so I got Joshua,' he offered. 'Christian fundamentalist.' She had died when Bennett was seventeen, three years after the death of her daughter. She had never recovered from the shock of losing Ella.

'My mother,' Ten Lee responded, surprising him, 'worked all her life to overthrow the government of Rocastle's World. She was a writer. She wrote political pamphlets exhorting revolution. When the change came, she taught Buddhism. I trained at the Bhao Khet Space Academy and piloted sub-orbital freighters for ten years before coming to Earth.'

'Ten years?' He shook his head. 'How old are you now?'

'Thirty-two.'

'Hell, I had you down as twenty.'

'If that's meant as a compliment, save it for the girls on the station.'

Bennett lifted his hands in a gesture of helpless innocence.

'Age is an irrelevance,' Ten Lee went on matter-of-factly. 'What is important is experience, and how one interprets and uses that experience in this incarnation.'

'In *this* incarnation?' Bennett said.

She stretched out her stick-thin arms and yawned. 'This is my final incarnation in the physical. Upon my death I attain the void. This life is merely a means to prepare myself for that state.'

Bennett fell silent for a time. To change the subject he said: 'Why did you come to Earth?'

'I needed new experience. My Rimpoche – my teacher – suggested that my fate was elsewhere. I should follow an outward path. Outward even beyond Earth.'

Bennett nodded. He had met many colonists in his years on the station, most conforming to character types and belief systems prevalent on Earth. Occasionally he came across humans so strange that they seemed almost alien in their idiosyncrasies.

The Viper banked around the curve of the orbitals on automatic. Bennett closed his eyes and contemplated the end of the shift and his three-day leave.

He would visit his father in hospital in Mojave Town, more a courtesy call to salve his conscience than a genuine display of sympathy or concern. Every leave he made the short journey to the private clinic that had been his father's home now for the past year. He was not so much ill as merely old. He was over a hundred, and it seemed that everything was failing at once. Expensive and expert medical care kept his vital organs ticking over, but the quality of his life was diminishing fast. He spent most of his time hooked up to some mindless virtual reality entertainment, and seemed to resent his son's intrusion. Bennett never looked forward to their futile, stilted dialogue. They had nothing in common other than a mutual experience of resentment.

His father had waited until his retirement before starting a family – an afterthought to his major concern of amassing wealth. Even then, he had spent much of his time immersed in business matters, regarding his son and daughter as a distraction from the more serious matter of accumulating saleable assets. The laughable irony was that his father had lost most of his savings with the collapse of a string of dubious financial investments months before his final hospitalisation. Now the old bastard was fading fast after a life of futility, and the hell of it was that Bennett could not help but feel guilty for his lack of concern.

After visiting his father he would call on Julia, and try to assess the current state of their relationship.

He opened his eyes as the Viper altered course. They dropped from the plane of the orbitals, the radiant white light of the Earth, spinning hugely to starboard, filling the tug with unaccustomed illumination. The Burgess manufactory was situated below the orbital chain, an ugly silver rectangle producing the catering supplies for the interstellar liners. Five minutes later they docked and began the loading process.

Bennett watched Ten Lee as she stared at the read-outs on her helmet screen. She was washed in the stark light of Earth, and he was made aware again of her diminutive size and frailty. Involuntarily, he recalled the image of his sister, her thin body wasted by the lymphatic cancer that finally killed her.

The pick-up was through in twenty minutes. They

collected ten containers and moved slowly away from the manufactory. They climbed past the orbitals and Redwood Station, and headed 'up' towards the phase point. Bennett stretched, savouring the thought that soon he would be in his berth on the station, showering before taking the ferry to Earth.

'Joshua . . .' Ten Lee said.

At the same time, Control spoke in his headset. 'Bennett. What the hell's happening out there?'

'Joshua,' Ten said again. She was sitting up on her couch, frantically running fingers across a touch-pad on her lap, staring intently into the screen of her visor.

'What is it?' Bennett said, a sick feeling in his stomach.

'I don't understand this,' Ten Lee said. 'The Viper has reverted to the original program.'

Control's shout almost deafened Bennett. 'Jesus Christ, man! Watch out for that bastard liner!'

He stared through the viewscreen, the improbability of what was happening slowing his reaction time. He felt a stab of disbelief – this was surely impossible.

A starship was moving slowly through space towards phase point, and the tug's flight-path was taking it on a collision course. Bennett grabbed the controls and yelled at Ten Lee to abort the pre-program. She was already cutting the link. Thanks to her quick work, no sooner had Bennett gained manual override than he felt the tug respond.

The liner swelled before them. Bennett watched a knot of passengers gathered by a viewscreen, gaping out like fish in an aquarium. Their collective reaction mirrored his own sense of panic: they fell to the floor or fled as the tug hurtled towards them.

Bennett cried out and pushed on the controls, sending the Viper into a steep dive. The liner seemed to bob up and out of view, and for a split second Bennett almost allowed himself a sigh of relief. Then he saw before him, and impossible to avoid, a forest of antennae and guidance probes bristling from the underbelly of the starship.

They scythed through them, a series of sickening thumps conducted through the cabin. The tug yawed wildly, spinning out of control and hurtling towards the swollen cargo blister on the rear underbelly of the liner. For all their speed, the silver blister seemed to approach in slow motion, expanding before the Viper like a blown bubble. Bennett dragged on the controls, less from intent than sheer blind hope, and miraculously the liner vanished.

He was about to congratulate himself when something hit the Viper. One second they were drifting in the welcome void of space, and the next they were swatted by a terrifying and powerful force.

Bennett swore and stared through the viewscreen above his head, hardly able to believe what he was seeing.

The starship had phased out, washing the Viper in the molten backblast of its ion-engines. The temperature in the cabin was climbing alarmingly and Bennett felt his skin beginning to burn. The tug swirled out of control like a leaf in a hurricane, the jets incinerating the vessel's paintwork and melting the viewscreen.

'Get the suits, Ten!' Bennett screamed, expecting the viewscreen to crack and the tug to depressurise at any second – and then the alarm sounded, an ugly, pulsing double note that almost deafened Bennett. The tug was floating, becalmed. The viewscreen held, a blurred mess of scorched plasti-glass.

The alarm dinned in his head and Bennett fought to control his breathing. He fumbled at the controls, trying to kill the noise.

Ten was scrambling around in the confines of the tug, attempting to find the suits.

11

Control was yelling: 'What the hell were you doing, both of you?'

'The Viper rejected the rewritten flight-path!' Bennett yelled back.

The alarm cut off, to be replaced by the Viper's calm, synthesised voice: 'Cabin depressurisation. Advise immediate evacuation.'

Bennett felt his pulse quicken. 'Ten! Those suits!'

'You were slow, Bennett!' Control went on. 'You should have seen the liner long before you did, taken evasive action.'

'We were on an original flight-path, okayed by you! I wasn't exactly expecting company!'

'That's not the point—'

'And fuck you!' Bennett shouted. He turned to Ten Lee. 'Where the hell are those suits?'

She was floating, twisted, behind the seats. She stared at him with a calm expression which, in the circumstances, he found maddening. She indicated the empty suit storage unit. 'They aren't here.'

'Jesus Christ . . .' Bennett said.

'Repeat: cabin depressurisation. Advise immediate evacuation.'

Ten Lee resumed her seat and regarded the monitor. 'We have seven minutes before the tug breaks up, Bennett.'

His visor screen flared. He blinked and made out the hunched head and shoulders of Matheson, the flight manager.

'Hope you both enjoyed that little roller-coaster ride. I want a full report and systems analysis in my terminal in six hours, got that?'

'It was a program error,' Bennett began. 'And what the hell are you doing to get us out?'

'I'm not bothered what the hell you *think* it was, Bennett. I need to find out what went wrong out there.'

12

'Hey – and who equipped this fucking pile of junk?' he began, but Matheson had cut the connection.

Ten, professional to the last, was reporting a list of damages back to Control. Bennett stared at her. She seemed calm, composed. Her voice was even, her expression neutral.

He closed his eyes and concentrated on not spilling the contents of his stomach.

'Major functions damage,' Ten Lee said. 'The tug is inoperable. Control's sending out a salvage ship.'

Bennett stared at her. 'Christ, Ten, we've got five minutes to live and you don't even bat an eyelid.'

She shrugged, regarding the screen of her visor.

'Okay, I know. You don't fear death, right? You're past all such fear . . . Well, just between you and me, I've yet to learn that lesson and I'm shit scared.'

He was aware of the tremor in his voice and shut up.

'Repeat: advise immediate evacuation.'

'How long before that damned tug gets here?' he said.

Ten Lee glanced at him and smiled, something mocking in the regard of her slanting eyes. 'Calm down, Joshua. Panic can benefit no one.' She raised a small hand and pointed. 'Look, the salvage ship is here.'

Bennett stared through the damaged viewscreen and made out the hulking silver blur of the salvage vessel as it slowly approached.

His visor flared and Matheson stared out at him. 'Bennett, Theneka,' he said, something ominous in his tone. 'This is just to tell you that you're both suspended for ten days until we get to the bottom of this. Out.'

Ten Lee raised a hand, forestalling Bennett's protest. 'We have nothing to worry about. It was a systems error, after all. Calm down.'

Bennett lay back in his couch, closed his eyes and awaited the pick-up.

13

2

Rana Rao crossed the crowded foyer of the Calcutta police headquarters and paused before the plate-glass door. In the second before it swished open, she caught a glimpse of her reflection. The sight of herself in the trim khaki uniform often caught her unawares. She saw the girl she had been in her surprised eyes and thin face, and the woman she was now in her lieutenant's uniform, and she found it hard to reconcile the two images. She sometimes felt guilty at the privilege conferred by the uniform; she wanted to tell people that she was nothing special, that she too had once been the lowest of the low.

She stepped through the glass door and stood beneath the red-and-white-striped polycarbon awning. Rain lashed down, drumming on the awning, bouncing off the slick tarmac of the busy road. The monsoon clouds piled over the city had brought a premature twilight to the afternoon. All along the wide pavements paan sellers, fortune tellers and laser beauticians switched on their orange glow-tubes and huddled beneath stolen scraps of polycarbon.

Rana looked up and down the street for her car. No doubt it was stuck in the traffic. Her driver was old and slow, which she didn't mind most of the time. But today she had a meeting with a street-kid she was helping; she had arranged to meet her at a certain time and a certain place, and she knew from experience that street-kids didn't wait around. When the whole city is your home, you move from place to place in search of the necessities of life: food and baksheesh.

'Rana-ji! Over here!'

The gnarled head of her driver emerged from the side-window of the battered patrol car, lodged in a line of stalled traffic ten metres away.

Rana was about to make a dash for the car when her communicator clicked in her inner ear. She twitched her lower jaw to activate the connection and snapped, 'Yes? Lieutenant Rao here. Who is this?'

'Commissioner Singh.' The voice, weighted with for-bearance, sounded in her ear. 'Have you set off yet, Lieutenant Rao?'

'Not yet, Commissioner.' She peered along the line of traffic to her driver and waved that she would be with him shortly.

'Jolly good. I will come with you today, ah-cha?'

'Ah-cha, Commissioner. I'm just outside the building. Please hurry. My driver's waiting.'

Commissioner Singh cleared his throat with censure and cut the connection. Rana cursed the fat, pompous pig. He liked to 'get his hands dirty', as he said, from time to time. See how his men were coping on the front line. Rana could have done without his ignorant presence today. He would frighten the kids away. She had worked hard to gain their trust over the years, to show them that she was an exception to their generally correct assump-tion that all cops were corrupt.

A minute later Commissioner Singh stepped through the sliding doors. He was not alone, Rana saw with dismay. In his wake shuffled a subservient private, tur-baned like Singh himself.

The commissioner nodded. 'Lieutenant Rao, Private Khosla.'

Khosla nodded. She knew the tall, gangling private. He was a file-shuffler in the computer division, one of a few young men who resented Rana her position of lieutenant and showed it by jibing her whenever they met. Not today, though; Khosla was on his best behaviour, toadying up to the commissioner. She wondered why he was coming out with them on this patrol.

The introductions over, Singh looked imperiously up and down the street. 'Where is your car, Lieutenant?'

'Over here.' Rana led the way, dodging through traffic to where her driver had leapt from the car and opened the passenger door. He had seen the commissioner and was working for his tip. 'Thank you, buba.' Rana smiled with feigned grace and slipped into the passenger seat.

Her driver goggled, then quickly whipped open a rear door. 'Please, sir . . .'

Singh slumped heavily on to the back seat, leaned forward and tapped Rana on the shoulder. 'So what is your agenda today, Lieutenant?'

The car started up and inched down the street.

'I'm going over to Howrah to talk to a group of children who live beneath the bridge,' she replied. 'They've formed a co-operative: shoe-shining, tailoring, tattooing . . . This sort of enterprise is to be encouraged.'

'Ah-cha, but what about the Choudry girl?'

Shiva! So that was why the fat pig was with her today. Vandita Choudry had run away from home three weeks ago, a home where, Rana knew, she was being beaten by her father. She had fallen in with the group of children who lived beneath the Howrah bridge. It was Vandita who had first suggested the co-operative, and Rana had helped them get it started. Of course, she should have picked up Vandita Choudry and returned her to her father, but Rana didn't play by the book. The kids knew this and respected her.

Rajiv Choudry was a Brahmin and a big-shot in engineering, and he was no doubt putting pressure on Commissioner Singh to find his daughter.

They crawled through the jhuggis to the south of the city, kilometre after kilometre of drab slums, dilapidated polycarbon and polythene shacks little bigger than comscreen kiosks housing entire families. Overhead, bright ad-screens hovered like giant butterflies beneath helium-filled dirigibles, their gaudy images offering the poor glimpses of an unattainable other world.

Amid the blare of horns and tangle of metal that was the usual congestion of traffic by the Howrah bridge, Rana's driver slowed and indicated to turn off down a track to the wharf. Rana caught a glimpse of a gaggle of kids, Vandita among them, beside the water. The Choudry girl saw her, waved and ran towards the car.

'Keep straight on, buba,' Rana told her driver. 'Not this side of the bridge, the other.'

The car accelerated, turned on to the bridge, and Rana began to breathe again. She stared back at the commissioner; he had suspected nothing. He probably wouldn't have recognised Vandita from any other street-kid, anyway. It was amazing how even a Brahmin girl, with plaited hair, Chanel perfume and expensive shoes, could soon discard all the meretricious trappings of wealth and blend in with her barefoot peers.

They crawled across the bridge in a procession of slow-moving traffic. The space not taken by vehicles was packed with pedestrians, a surging crowd of humanity making its way back and forth across the bridge in a never-ending flow.

They turned off the bridge and Rana told her driver to pull up on the bank of the Ganges. She climbed out and walked to the edge of the wide river, Singh and Khosla joining her. A gang of kids, Dullits by the look of them, bathed their skinny brown bodies in the filthy shallows.

Khosla was shaking his head. 'These days it seems there are more kids than ever,' he said. 'It is an insurmountable problem.'

Rana stared at him, doing nothing to conceal her dislike.

'You are right, Private,' she said, emphasising his rank, 'it *seems* there are more street-kids than ever. But at monsoon time each year this is always the case. You see,' she went on, as if explaining the obvious to a simpleton, 'many children have nowhere to live other than in the storm drains. So when the rain falls, the monsoon drains fill up, driving the children out and on to the streets. When the monsoon stops, they will return to their homes.'

She fell silent, staring at a young boy dunking himself repeatedly in the brown water.

'And as to your claim that it is an "insurmountable problem",' she continued after a short while, 'I would dispute, first, that it is a problem, and then whether it – whatever "it" is – is insurmountable. The only people the kids pose a problem to are the rich, who don't like to be reminded of their guilt, and the tourists, who can go to hell. The children provide the means for a thriving economy to flourish. If you talk to the kids, you will find that in most cases they're perfectly happy living on the streets. As for it being an insurmountable problem, well, if the government were to invest in more schools and jobs . . . but then these kids are only kids, aren't they? They have no power, no vote.'

She stared at Khosla until he looked away. She caught the superior smile that played on his lips. She knew what some people said about her back at headquarters, that she loved street-kids because she had never known the love of

18

a man. Well, she might never have known the love of a man, but that wasn't the reason why she felt compassion for these children.

Commissioner Singh cleared his throat. 'That is all very well, Lieutenant, but I am more concerned with the runaways, the children who leave good homes and families to live on the streets. It is all very tragic for their families.'

Rana felt a tightness within her chest. 'It's also tragic for the children that they feel they have to run away in the first place.' She glanced at the commissioner. 'They have a lack of love and affection in their lives.'

Khosla looked at her with an expression that said, What do you know about love?

Not much, Rana admitted to herself, staring across the river to the lights of the ad-screens floating above the city, but I know something about the lack of it.

She pulled a sheaf of pix from the hip pocket of her trousers and walked towards the kids dancing about on the muddy river bank to get dry.

'Can I talk to you?' she said to them in Hindi. 'I'm Rana and I'm looking for this girl. I wonder if you'd be able to help? Look, these pix can buy you food.'

She passed a dozen pix of Vandita Choudry to the gaggle of kids bustling around her to get a closer look. The pix showed a version of Vandita that bore no resemblance to what she looked like today: she was prim in a red Western-style dress, short white socks and plaited hair tied with ribbons. The kids were more bothered about the promise on the reverse of the pix: each one could be exchanged for *behl puri* at certain stalls along the Howrah bridge.

When Rana returned to Singh and Khosla, Singh said: 'Where are the co-operative kids? I thought we were going to question them, Lieutenant?'

'I was going to *talk* to them,' she said. 'But they seem to have disappeared. Well, they have better things to do than talk to me. Maybe another day.'

She was going to suggest they return to the car when a tiny figure squeezed from the press of humanity flowing from the bridge and ran across to her. Rana glanced at Singh and Khosla, but they were watching the antics of the Dullit kids who were playing kabbadi, with the pix as prizes.

Rana hurried across to the girl. 'Vandita,' she hissed in Hindi. 'I'm with my boss today. We can't speak.'

Disappointment showed in the brown eyes of the twelve-year-old.

Rana glanced back at the commissioner. He was watching her, but clearly didn't recognise Vandita. The girl had traded her red dress for a torn brown smock, was barefoot, and wore her hair long and tangled. In just two weeks Rana had watched Vandita turn from an unhappy little rich girl into a happy, confident child revered by the children she helped to look after.

'Ah-cha. We can talk for two minutes, but no more. They're looking for you. Your picture's all over.'

Vandita laughed. 'I've seen it. They'll never find me.'

'How's work?' Vandita and another girl cleaned cars and bicycles for ten rupees a time. Rana was trying to get them to spend a little of their earnings on school classes set up by private foundations around the city.

'Lieutenant!' Singh called impatiently in English. 'When you can spare the time . . .'

'Run!' Rana said. 'I'll see you tomorrow or the next day. Be careful.' She watched Vandita turn and squirm through the crowd surging across the bridge.

Rana returned to the car. Singh was examining the mud on his boots, and when he looked up his gaze suggested that Rana was responsible. 'Very well . . . I have seen enough here. Do you have your com-board, Lieutenant?'

Rana slipped it from her belt. 'I am due to visit the City Children's home at six to give a talk on road safety, and at seven—'

'Ah-cha, enough. Give the board to Khosla – he will be taking over now.'

'Why? I mean—'

'Don't argue, Lieutenant.' Singh turned and spoke to the driver. 'Back to headquarters. Then take Private Khosla to the City Children's home.'

This time Singh appropriated the front seat for himself. Rana sat in the back and passed her board to Khosla without meeting his glance, wondering what all this was about. Was she being relieved of duty for good, or just for this shift? She wondered if word had got back to Singh about Vandita and the other rich kids she'd helped.

She watched the city teem by as the car carried them towards the police headquarters. So this was why Singh had come out with her, along with Khosla, to strip her of her post and charge her with dereliction of duty . . .

Ten minutes later she climbed out and hurried after Singh as he crossed the pavement and entered the crumbling Victorian building. The interior was as modern and comfortable as the exterior was ancient. Rana sometimes felt guilty that she worked in such luxury, while outside so many citizens lived in squalor.

She shared the clanking elevator with the commissioner in silence, alighted on the tenth floor and followed him along the corridor to his office, as cowed as a beaten puppy. She wondered where her insubordinate spirit had vanished to now, when she needed it most.

'Take a seat.' Singh indicated an uncomfortable-looking upright chair and seated himself like a maharaja, pulling

21

up his padded swivel chair so that his swelling belly butted the edge of the desk.

Rana sat down, her stomach churning.

Singh scrolled through something on his computer screen, the blue reflection giving him the colouration of an overweight Krishna. He tapped his lips with a plump forefinger, clearly delighting in keeping Rana in suspense.

'I've been going through your records of late,' he said at last. He left it there.

Rana merely nodded. She felt cold sweat trickling over her ribs.

'You joined the academy at the age of fifteen.'

A silence followed. He tapped his lips judiciously.

'You had no formal education, but you passed the entrance exams with flying colours.'

She closed her eyes briefly, feeling sick. Singh had found out about her past. He was not here to reprimand her about her most recent conduct, but to accuse her of falsification of records, of lying to gain admittance to the academy.

And she knew the penalty for that sin was automatic expulsion.

'Very interesting . . . You came in off the streets, applied for a place on the examination rota and gained a pass mark of ninety-five per cent, one of the highest passes for the past ten years.' He paused again to regard the screen.

Rana wished she was out on patrol, talking to the kids, helping them make the best of a corrupt, uncaring world.

'Your achievement was noted by the then commissioner, and he kept tabs on your files and records.'

So this was it. Now he would come out with the evidence against her.

'He commended you to me when he retired. He had you marked out for great things. I took his advice and followed your career. I must admit that I have been quietly impressed over the years.'

It was all the worse because she knew what he was doing: building her up for the fall. Praising her, cataloguing her achievements, only to hit her with the fact of her duplicity.

'Your work with the street-kids is truly impressive. The instituting of work schemes and co-operatives, self-education and health programmes.' He shook his head. 'Exceptional.' Then he pierced her with his gaze. 'What have you got to say for yourself?'

She opened her mouth to speak. At last the words came. 'I . . . I was only doing my duty, sir. I volunteered for the position at Child Welfare, to work with the under-privileged, and saw that the scheme as it stood was lacking—' She stopped herself. It was no good trying to justify what she had done if Singh intended to accuse her of dereliction of duty.

He was nodding. 'As I said, I've been watching your progress for some years, and in my opinion the time has arrived for me to act on my predecessor's recommendations. You are wasted working with the street-kids. Your talents for organisation and problem-solving can be used to greater effect in a different department.'

He went on, but Rana hardly heard a word. She had expected the worst, and he was offering her promotion, a move away from her work with the street-kids – and the idea filled her with horror.

'. . . so as of now, Lieutenant, you are officially a part of the homicide team working under Investigating Officer Vishwanath.'

He beamed at her, slivers of gold glinting between his big paan-stained teeth.

'Well, do you have a tongue in your head, Lieutenant?'

'I . . .' She shook her head. 'I'm sorry. I . . . I can't

accept. I don't want to work at Homicide. My place is with the children. I think that my skills can be utilised to greater effect at a grass-roots level with those who find themselves at the bottom of society . . .' She realised that she was rattling off the line she used when high-caste acquaintances scoffed at her work with the kids.

Singh was having none of it. 'My dear Rana, I run a police force here, the biggest law enforcement agency in India, not some welfare scheme for Dullits, beggars and pick-pockets.'

'I like working with children, sir. I wouldn't be happy anywhere else.'

'Your skills are needed elsewhere, Lieutenant.'

'Are you saying that if I were less skilled at my job, then I would still be able to work with the kids?' The thought appalled her.

'I am saying, Lieutenant, that the department's work with the homeless children of Calcutta is low-priority.'

'But it's necessary work, sir! Much of what I've done has given these kids jobs and security, kept them from prostitution and thieving.'

'Lieutenant, your work will be carried on. I am not eradicating the post you held.'

'Who?' Rana asked. She stared at him. 'You can't mean Khosla? I thought he was only taking over temporarily?'

'He's a young, intelligent and ambitious officer.'

'Ambitious for promotion, maybe,' she said. 'But he doesn't know the first thing about the kids. You heard him today. He's ignorant and dangerous. He has not the slightest sympathy with them.'

'Then perhaps, Lieutenant, a year or two in the post will educate and enlighten him.'

They stared at each other for what seemed like long minutes, opponents who would not concede defeat and back down.

24

'What if I refuse the promotion?' Rana asked at last.

'Then I will be forced, with great reluctance, to ask for your resignation.'

She shook her head. Was he calling her bluff?

Commissioner Singh gave an indulgent laugh. 'I've heard a lot about your unconventional spirit, Lieutenant. My predecessor called you a wild cat. I think he was understating the case.'

Rana felt tears prickle her eyes as she realised what she had to do. Ah-cha, so she might not be able to work officially with the kids any more, but she could still see them in her own time. She would continue helping them, try to counter the mess Khosla would make of his posting.

'When do I start, sir?' she asked at last.

'Good. I'm glad you've seen sense. You can go and clear your desk immediately. Vishwanath's department is on the eighth floor. You'll find him a good man and a hard-working boss. I hope you do as well in Homicide as you have done in Child Welfare, Lieutenant. Well done.'

She stood, saluted, wheeled around and left the room. In a daze she made her way back to her office on the second floor.

An efficient fan turned on the ceiling, disturbing what little paperwork sat on her desk. Her com-screen glowed with a dozen files she could no longer call her own. She stared at the windowless walls. One was filled entirely with the pix of young boys and girls, gazing out at her with eyes made tired by experience.

Her screen flashed. It was Singh. 'Oh, Lieutenant. I forgot to mention a couple of things. Firstly, you'll be moving into a new apartment near the river. Also, you'll be receiving a pay rise. I'll download the information right away.'

Seconds later Rana was staring at her new contract. She read the clause detailing her yearly salary. Either her pay as the Child Welfare officer had truly represented the law enforcement agency's contempt of the post, or the officers at Homicide were grossly overpaid. She would be earning three times the amount she'd been paid in Welfare.

She considered all she would have been able to achieve if the money had been directed at her office, and not at the fat cats upstairs. Then again, she supposed, someone had to catch the killers.

She read through the details of her new apartment overlooking Nehru park. It sounded fantastic: three air-conditioned rooms, fully furnished, the building patrolled by security guards. It was a far cry from the sultry, one-room apartment she had now in a poor district of the city prone to burglary. She considered the luxury of a three-room apartment, and then felt a sudden pang of guilt.

She began the quick job of clearing her effects from the desk. They filled a small plastic bag: a stylus and an antique biro pen, an old softscreen recording from her childhood and an effigy of Ganesh, the elephant god, which her mother had given her years ago. She no longer believed in anything like that, but it was her only reminder of her mother. She decided to keep these things at her new apartment, now that she could be assured of security.

She stood and looked around the room. One thing caught her eye. She walked over to the wall and knelt to examine the pix. A small girl with jet-black bangs and frightened eyes stared out at her. On the tag-line beneath the pix was the computer code and a name: Sita Mackendrick.

Rana slipped the pix into her pocket and took the elevator to the eighth floor.

26

3

After ten days in space, enduring cramped living conditions and consuming recycled food and drink, a leave period on Earth was like parole in paradise.

Bennett drove from the spaceport on the perimeter of Los Angeles and took the highway into the desert. The shuttle had touched down in the early hours, and it was still a couple of hours until dawn. The road stretched away beneath the swollen lantern of the full moon, the tarmac laced with luminescents so that it glowed green in the night. In an age of draconian energy conservation, luminous road surfaces were a means of doing away with the expensive street-lighting of old. Seen from space, as the terminator swept across the Americas, the rising sun illuminated the roads that crossed the western seaboard like the veins on the brow of an old but healthy patriarch.

Bennett accelerated, enjoying the cool air on his face. He sipped occasionally from a carton of fresh orange juice and thought about the near miss in orbit. All things considered, his extended leave would compensate for the carpeting and/or fine he could expect on his return to the station in ten days. As he drove, he considered renegotiating his contract in favour of more leave on Earth. He even entertained the fantasy of changing jobs, looking for something a little more varied.

Two hours later he passed Mojave Town, where his father was hospitalised and Julia worked as a landscape

27

designer. Constructed piecemeal at the end of the last century by eco-freaks dreaming of an environmentally friendly society, its population had been augmented over the years by an exodus of well-to-do home-workers, artists, computer specialists and on-line business people. In the light of the moon, multi-level domes glistened like agglomerated soap bubbles, interspersed with oasis gardens, trees and lakes, and tall masts bearing solar arrays.

Bennett's habitat dome was situated twenty kilometres further along the highway. From the veranda of his dome, Mojave Town was a blur in the distance, and his nearest neighbour was ten kays away. He was surrounded by the soothing silence of the desert, his only company the occasional patrolling condor or scavenging jackal.

He pulled off the highway, trundled the final three kilometres along the rough track, and parked in the tropical garden that shaded his dome, patio and swimming pool.

The habitat came to life as he climbed the interior steps to the main lounge. Lights turned themselves on; he was greeted by a selection of his favourite music – mood-jazz from one of the colony worlds. Beside the sliding door to the veranda, his com-screen flared into life.

He took a beer from the cooler and sat in the swivel chair before the screen. One quarter of the screen displayed a head-and-shoulders shot of Julia, frozen mid-smile, another quarter someone Bennett had never seen before, a silver-haired man in his seventies. The upper half of the screen listed e-mail shots that had come in during his absence.

He regarded the pix of Julia, short dark hair parenthesising a calm, oval ballerina's face. She was attractive and intelligent, and he never ceased to be amazed that their relationship had lasted so long – coming up to a year, now. They had met when he'd hired her to redesign his garden, began talking and never stopped. He'd been attracted to her sophistication – an attribute rarely found among the women on Redwood Station – and he assumed that she had found appealing the fact that he was a pilot and well off.

Their first rift, a couple of months later, had come about because Bennett had been fool enough to tell her this. She had been hectoring him for some declaration of commitment, a vow of his love for her. 'Why?' he had responded. 'You don't love me. I'm just a rich high-orbit pilot to show off to your friends.' She had just stared at him, shocked. 'You bastard, Josh. If that's what you think I see in you . . .' and, unable to go on, she had hurried from the dome. A day later she had downloaded a vis-link to his com-screen. She had cried and told him that she loved him *despite* the fact that he was a privileged, arrogant bastard and a pilot.

Shame, mixed with something akin to fear that she might be telling the truth, had stopped him contacting her for a few days. Then he had left a message to say that he was sorry, he knew what a shallow fool he was, and could they meet for dinner somewhere?

From then on things had never been the same. It seemed that his admission of blame gave Julia *carte blanche* to snipe away at his faults, psychologically reduce him to nothing more than a textbook example of adverse childhood conditioning. He wondered if it was the thought of being without her companionship that made him endure her hostility. Having someone, even someone who seemed to dislike him so much of the time, was preferable to being alone.

He brushed the back of his hand against Julia's face, and instantly the smile unfroze. 'Josh. I'm calling Sunday – you're due back Tuesday, aren't you?'

She moved away from the screen, touching her throat

in the gesture he knew meant she was considering what to say next. She paused in the middle of her lounge, surrounded by baskets of hanging flowers. From there she looked back at the screen, as if to distance herself from what she had to say next.

'Josh . . . I've been giving things serious consideration lately. I've been considering my life, where I am . . .' This was typical of Julia, her tortured verbal circumlocutions and pained analysis. 'I've been thinking about us, Josh. I wonder . . . when you get back Tuesday, could we meet for lunch? Say around one, at Nova Luna? Call if you can't make it, okay?' She gave a final, sad smile. 'Bye, Josh.'

The image froze, dissolved. Josh sat staring at the emptied quarter of the screen, sipping his beer and trying to work out his reaction to what Julia had said.

It was over, at last, just as for months he had known it would be. He had never expected Julia to be the one to end it, and he had declined to do so because during the short periods he had spent on Earth he had enjoyed her company, had felt a genuine affection for her. But . . . what was it that Julia had called a man's declaration of genuine affection? 'Nothing more than a euphemism for "You'll do until I find something better."'

He finished his beer. He would meet her at the restaurant later today, chat over old times, agree that they were going nowhere, and part on civil terms. He just prayed that she wouldn't create a scene, accuse him of being a cold emotionless bastard, as she had done publicly more than once in the past.

He touched the second quarter of the screen, activating the face of the well-dressed stranger. The man sat side-saddle on the edge of a desk, like an executive giving an informal pep-talk to a team of salesmen.

'Joshua Bennett? I'm sorry to have called when you're away. I'm Dr Samuels, consultant geriatrician at the Oasis

Medical Centre in Mojave. Your father is under my care. I understand that you are returning on the twenty-second. If you could contact my secretary and arrange a meeting on that day, or whenever is convenient for you . . .'

Dr Samuels paused, and Bennett wondered what was coming next.

'Mr Bennett, your father has requested the option of voluntary euthanasia. As his doctor, my consent is mandatory, and I was wondering how you, as his only next of kin, felt about the issue. As I've said, if you could contact me as soon as possible I'd be grateful. Thank you, Mr Bennett.'

Euthanasia . . . Bennett had never expected it to come to this. He wondered why he was so shocked: because of the imminence of his father's extinction, or the fact that he had chosen this way to go? He had always expected to be informed of his father's death in his absence, had reconciled himself to the fact and rehearsed what little grief he might feel. But euthanasia . . . He realised he was shocked because his father's option of euthanasia would include himself, Bennett, in the process of his going. He would have to face his father last time, discuss with him his reasons, exhibit sympathy for someone he did not and never had loved.

Not for the first time, he cursed his father for being so inconsiderate as to start a family at such an advanced age. Hell, there had been a certain affection between them, at times, he thought; and after all, he was – is – my father. Bennett knew what Julia might have to say about that affection.

He pushed himself from the swivel chair and stepped out on to the veranda. Dawn was rushing in over the desert, turning the sky to the west a burnished, blue-tinged aluminium and washing the stars from the night overhead. He had slept on the shuttle, eaten just before

31

touchdown. He could not sleep now, especially after the message from Dr Samuels.

On impulse he took the steps from the veranda to the garden and climbed into his car. He drove away from the dome along a rough track, passing sentinel cacti like overgrown candelabra. Fifteen minutes later he made out the low-slung dome in the distance, to the right of the track. He pulled up beside the overgrown and neglected garden, the sight of the abandoned dome bringing back a slew of unwelcome memories.

He climbed out and approached the dome along a lichen-carpeted path, batting aside encroaching fronds and palm leaves. The dome stood in the dawn light like some abandoned habitat on an alien world. Seeds had worked their way inside and filled the main cupola with riotous growth so that it resembled a steaming arboretum. The habitat had been empty a year now, ever since his father's hospitalisation. Bennett had grown up here, with his stern and pious mother, his often absent father, and Ella.

He moved around the dome and stepped into the enclosed garden at the rear, aware of the pounding of his heart.

His relationship with Ella had been unlike the usual elder brother–little sister confrontation. Excluded from the affection of their elderly parents, they had sought companionship and succour in each other. She might have been four years his junior, but she was his equal in terms of intellect and understanding. Being the elder, and a boy, he had often incurred the brunt of his mother's temper, and rather than gloat as little sisters were wont to do, Ella did her best to cheer him. She had been more like an elder sister in her apprehension of his pain.

And then at the age of ten she had fallen ill. She had spent long periods in hospital, during which time Bennett was never told of the true seriousness of her illness. He had watched her waste away, never truly understanding what was taking place. Then, the day before Ella was due home for the very last time, his father took him to one side and explained, with a brutality that struck him at the time as cruel, but which later he came to understand was an inability to articulate his feelings, that Ella was dying. 'I'm afraid she is very ill, Joshua. The medics have told me that there's no hope.'

He had always assumed she would get better. To be told that Ella would soon die had filled Bennett with a sense of disbelief and, later, anger.

Two days later Ella had died, with Bennett and his parents at her bedside, and with her impossible death something within Bennett seemed to vacate him, leaving in its place a vast and terrible emptiness.

A week after the funeral, his father had interrupted his com-screen lessons. He had done his best to avoid his parents since Ella's death; he felt a residual resentment at being kept in the dark for so long, and had no desire to see his grief mirrored in theirs. Now his father said: 'We've decided to establish a memorial to Ella, Joshua, in the garden where you played together.' And he had told his son what it was.

He had avoided going into the garden for a long time after Ella's death. He did not want to be reminded of his loss. The memorial seemed to him a crass memento of someone once so vital and alive. Later he wondered why people with the Christian beliefs of his parents had erected such a tawdry icon, and came to understand that it was merely their way of coping with a grief just as real and painful as his own.

Perhaps a year after her death, Josh realised that he could no longer hear Ella's voice in his head. He had forgotten the sound of her confiding words, her excited chatter, and that terrified him. One afternoon, after ensuring that his parents were away from the dome, he had stepped with trepidation and curiosity into the enclosed garden.

Now Bennett pushed open the rusty iron gate to the memorial garden. A riot of untended blooms, frangipani and rude bougainvillaea, crowded the paved enclosure like unwelcome guests at a party. He quickly crossed the garden, his throat tight and sore, swept away fallen leaves from the mock-timber bench and sat down. A high voice asked, 'Hi, Josh, how's things in space these days?'

The dark-haired little girl in a blue dress crouched before Bennett, tanned arms wrapped about tanned legs. Her blue eyes, so treacherously alive, stared at him with delight.

He came almost every leave to the memorial garden, and every time the sight of Ella struck him a painful blow in the solar plexus.

'Oh, fine . . . you know, it's a job.'

'Anything exciting happened?'

She stood and moved to an overhanging branch, reached up, grasped it and swung back and forth. She was perhaps a metre from him, as visually substantial as the bench on which he sat. He stared at the brown straining muscles of her arms, her impishly pretty face and long black hair. He wanted suddenly to reach out, take her in his arms and crush her to him, and the desire brought tears to his eyes.

'I was in a close shave yesterday, Ella,' he said. He told her about the accident, enjoying her open-mouthed, wide-eyed reaction, her little girl exclamations.

As they chatted, the pain abated. He enjoyed the company of this ersatz sister, this companion ghost of many years. She might only have been a fabulously intricate simulated identity hologram, a genie conjured by state-of-the-art logic circuits, and no more real or sentient than the com-screen back at his dome, but the illusion satisfied some deep need within him. She salved his pain, briefly; she fuelled his memories.

'Ella, you know I told you that Daddy was ill last time?'

She nodded, suddenly serious. 'How is he?'

He shrugged. 'I don't know. I mean, not good. He's just so old – over a hundred now.'

Ninety years older than you were when you died, Ella. There was no justice in the world.

'Does he still tell you off?'

Bennett smiled. What a little girl thing to say! It was what he loved about his hologram sister. It was just what Ella would have said.

'No, not any more, Ella. He's still . . . I don't know, censorious – I mean critical. Still finding fault in every-thing I do. I'd like to win his respect,' he said, and hated himself for the admission. He shrugged. 'He's very old and frail now, but inside he's still the same person he always was.'

'Why do you mention him, Josh?'

There were times when the program was just too advanced, Bennett thought. Would Ella have asked him that?

'His doctor contacted me yesterday. Dad wants to exercise his right to undergo euthanasia.'

Ella frowned. She was seated cross-legged on the ground now, her hands placed primly on her bare knees. 'What's eutha— whatever?'

'It means he wants to die. He wants to take a drug that'll end his life. I've got to go and see him today. Talk it over.' He stared into her big, unblinking eyes. 'You don't understand, do you?'

35

She pursed her lips, then nodded. 'I think I do, Josh. You feel guilty.'

The program running the simulated identity hologram had a learning facility. Over the years it had integrated everything Bennett had said to Ella, analysed and interpreted his pronouncements for meaning.

'It's just . . .' He shook his head. 'I don't want to do this, Ella. I can't face him about this. I don't want him to see that I understand his life's been a terrible failure.' After so long being so distant from his father, he realised, the time was coming when they would have to share an unaccustomed emotional proximity. Perhaps it was just that he didn't want his father to see that he really cared.

Ella was smiling at him. 'You'll do okay, Josh,' she said. 'You know what you always tell me?'

'What?'

She pulled her pretty, thinking-cap face. 'What is it – something like, reality is never as bad as you expect it to be.'

He laughed. 'I'll remember that, Ella. Thanks.'

They stared at each other for a long time.

At last she said, 'Josh,' and slowly, watching him, she reached out a slim brown arm, fingers outstretched towards him.

He reached too, staying his hand so that his finger-tips were millimetres from her own, so as not to spoil the illusion. Like this, he told himself, in the long silence there was some kind of contact happening that could not be quantified by logic.

He dropped his hand. 'I must be going, Ella.'

Still seated, she gave a quick wave in the air. 'Come back soon, okay, Josh?'

'I'll be back.' He stood, and the image of his sister disappeared before his eyes.

4

It was almost ten when Bennett reached Mojave Town.

Automobiles were not allowed within the city limits, so he parked in the small lot on the perimeter. Rather than take an electric bus, he walked the two kilometres to the town centre.

He shared the wide streets with citizens out jogging or strolling, cleaning-drones that seemed to have very little to clean, and children on scooters. The habitats on either side of the streets occupied spacious, abundant gardens, an eclectic collection of the latest domes, mock-timber A-frames and more conventional carbon-fibre houses. The high foliage of a thousand evergreens shaded the town, and power was provided by tall masts which pierced the canopy and opened petal-like energy panels to the burning desert sun.

The Oasis Medical Centre occupied extensive grounds in the centre of town, over two dozen polycarbon units linked by a warren of diaphanous passages set in rolling landscaped gardens. Bennett strolled across the avenue and into the hospital. He found reception and was directed down long corridors to the consultancy rooms of Dr Samuels.

The door opened automatically at his approach, forestalling his attempt to knock. He stepped inside.

'Mr Bennett, I'm glad you could make it. If you'd care to take a seat.'

Samuels, as informal in person as he had appeared on

the vis-link that morning, moved from his desk and sat on the window-seat overlooking the rolling greenery. Bennett took the offered swivel seat and turned to face the doctor.

'Mr Bennett, I appreciate how you must be feeling—'

Bennett heard himself saying: 'My father's been ill for over a year now. I've had time to consider the inevitable.'

Samuels nodded. 'I know it's always a hard decision for loved ones to make. I don't know how you stand, ethically, on the issue of euthanasia, but if you'd like me to run through the legal side of things . . .'

Bennett shook his head. 'I followed the state rulings when the bill was passed,' he said. He paused. 'I've nothing against euthanasia. If it's really what my father wants . . .' He hoped he didn't sound too perfunctory.

Samuels was nodding. 'Your father is bed-ridden, unable to feed himself, and in occasional pain. We administer the most effective analgesics, but there is only so much we can do to relieve his discomfort. Your father is failing on many fronts; the side-effects of the drugs he is on are becoming as difficult to treat as the primary complaints. In my opinion he is sound of mind. He has stated daily for the past week that he wishes to die, and in my opinion his quality of life is so severely reduced that euthanasia would be a mercy.'

'Can I talk it over with him?'

'By all means. I'll take you to his room immediately.' Samuels hesitated. 'Are you aware that your father spends much of his time in VR?'

Bennett nodded. 'I see him every couple of months.'

Samuels rose from the window-seat and gestured to the door. 'Please, this way.'

As they passed down a series of corridors, Bennett experiencing a mounting sense of apprehension. Samuels cleared his throat. 'The actual apparatus of euthanasia is ready to utilise almost immediately,' he said, 'should you decide to sign the usual legal forms and waivers.'

Bennett nodded, finding it hard to accept that they were talking about the termination of a life. It was more like a business transaction. 'How soon? I mean—'

'That is entirely up to your father. As long as it takes him to compose himself.'

'And I can be with him?'

'Of course. Here we are.' Samuels paused before a white door and turned to Bennett. 'Lately your father has refused to exit the VR site. He finds it . . . comforting. He will only see visitors in the net.'

Bennett stared at the doctor. 'And you say he's of sound mind?'

'In my opinion, yes, Mr Bennett. His retreat to the VR site is his way of . . . of coping with his decision to die. As you will see for yourself.'

Bennett stepped into a sunlit room occupied by a narrow bed, banks of medical apparatus, a VR module and a chair.

His father lay on the bed. He had always been tall, somewhat martial, but near death, laid out as if in preparation for his exit, he seemed elongated, whittled down to a wasted minimum of flesh and bone, stripped of dignity. He wore a grey one-piece VR suit and wrap-around glasses. So many leads issued from the suit that Bennett was unable to discern the VR links from the tubes pumping blood, plasma and drugs into the hundred-and-three-year-old body. His mouth was open and drooling. Occasionally his limbs twitched in reaction to some event in the make-believe VR world, giving lie to the notion that he had already died. Beside the bed a cardiogram bleeped with his feeble heartbeat.

Bennett sat down. 'He's so wasted . . .' he began.

'He's been refusing food, so we've had to feed him intravenously.' Samuels passed him a pair of VR glasses.

'If you'd care to put these on, I'll patch you into your father's site.'

Bennett slipped the glasses over his eyes. The room went dark and the ear-pieces muffled all sound.

He waited, unsure whether to be grateful he was being spared a real-world confrontation with his father, or fearful of what was to follow.

He was jolted by a sudden flare of colour. His vision adjusted and he stared out across a vast expanse of rolling grassland, dotted here and there with sumptuous habitat domes. He was surprised by the clarity of the vision: the panorama of greensward and cloudless blue sky was as real as the latest holographic images. He felt as if he could reach out and actually touch the grass before him. His father had obviously gone to some expense to obtain the very best programming software.

'Joshua! Is that you, boy?'

His father's voice – recognisably his father's voice, but changed, deeper of timbre, confident – sounded in the ear-piece of the glasses, coming from behind him. His heart set up a steady pounding.

He turned and stared, shocked, at the image of his father. He was no longer the skeletal old man on the bed – not that Bennett had expected him to be. But, also, he had not expected to see this apparition from the past. The image of his father was as he had been thirty years ago, in his seventies. Tall and balding, thin-faced and stern, he stood with his hands behind his back, staring at his son with unspoken censure.

'Joshua, answer me for mercy's sake!'

He found his voice at last. 'Dad.'

His father peered at him. 'It's sometimes hard to tell who's wearing those damned glasses. They're supposed to scan a likeness of the user's face direct to the site, but they're none too accurate. The rest of the programming works like a dream, though.' He gestured around him at the rolling greensward. 'What do you think, Joshua?'

'It's great, really great.' Seeing his father here like this, an apparition from his boyhood, Bennett felt like a six-year-old again, dominated by the presence of the man he had always secretly feared.

'I'm pleased you decided to visit at last. Where the hell have you been, boy?'

'I've been working, Dad. I work, remember?' He stared at the face of his miraculously rejuvenated father, and the memories flooded back.

'I suppose that smarmy creep Samuels has filled you in?'

Bennett nodded. 'That's why I'm here.'

His father gave him an intimidating glare. 'And I take it you have no objections to granting your consent.'

Bennett swallowed. 'No. No, of course not.'

His father sniffed. 'Thought not,' he said, and then, more to himself: 'You always were amenable to reason.' He gestured Bennett to follow him as he set off at a brisk pace across the grass.

Bennett recalled how to use the VR glasses and tipped his head forward. His vision seemed to float across the ground in the wake of his father.

'I have something to show you, Joshua,' he said over his shoulder. 'Over here.'

They approached the nearest dome and paused before the semi-circular plinth of steps at its base. His father lodged a foot on the bottom step and regarded Bennett.

'Do you know where we are, boy?'

Bennett stared at the dome. 'I don't recognise it . . .' The dome was like hundreds of others he saw every day when on Earth.

'I don't mean the dome, you numbskull. This!' He flung out a hand at the greensward. 'This site. Do you know where we are?'

41

Bennett shook his head. 'I give in,' he said. 'Tell me.'

His father gave a broad grin. 'This is Heaven, boy. Take a good look round at Heaven.'

His mouth was suddenly dry. He could only stare at his father. He wondered why he should be so shocked that, this close to the end, his father had finally lost his reason.

'What do you think, Joshua?' he laughed. 'Now just you wait until you see who I've got . . .' And he turned and shouted into the dome. 'Mother! Come out here – look who's come visiting!'

As Bennett stared, the hatch opened and his mother – or rather a version of his mother in her fifties – stepped from the dome. She peered down at Bennett, her face scoured of pleasure by years of fundamentalist belief, and shook her head. 'Josh? It doesn't look like Josh to me.'

'How did you do that, Dad?' Bennett asked.

His father laughed. 'A simple bit of programming, boy. A simulacra circuit built up from all the vid-film and holograms I took of mother over the years.' He paused, then called again: 'Hey, Ella. Look who's out here.'

'No . . .' Bennett said to himself. 'Please, no.'

As the diminutive figure of his sister skipped from the dome and sketched a wave his way, Bennett felt a sudden pang of jealousy. Over the years he'd had Ella to himself in the memorial garden, had built a relationship that was as exclusive and private as it had been in reality all those years ago.

'Hi, Josh. I've been playing rockets in the lounge. Want to come and join me?'

He found his tongue. 'Some other time, Ella, okay?'

She beamed. 'Sure,' she said, smiling down at him.

'Had the simulated identity hologram from the memorial garden copied years ago,' his father explained. 'Always intended to use it in my VR module, just never got round to it till now. Still, better late than never.' He laughed. 'Cute, eh?'

Bennett stared up at the image of his sister, aware that this copy could have no memory of their conversations over the years. This version of Ella's ghost was a cheap imitation, with no knowledge of him and his pain.

He shook his head, as if to clear it. They're just programs, he told himself – all of them, just expensive holographic projections and complex memory banks.

'So you see, Josh, you see what I'm going to when I finally shuffle off this mortal coil!'

'Praise be to God,' his mother carolled.

'Amen to that!' Ella responded.

Bennett closed his eyes, blanking out the tawdry concoction of his father's private Heaven.

'Now Josh and me need a few private minutes together, mother. Joshua . . .'

When Bennett opened his eyes, his father was beckoning him away from the dome. Compliant, eager to get the conversation over with so that he could re-enter the real world, Bennett followed.

His father halted and turned to him. 'I'm glad you've agreed to let me die, Josh. I'm an old man and I've had enough. I just want out. You've seen what's awaiting me . . .' He stared back at the dome, and a smile softened his features; then his gaze snapped back to Bennett. 'When you get back, tell Samuels to go ahead with the process. And tell him – this is important, boy – tell him that I want to stay in here while he's administering the drug. You got that? I don't want to be dragged back to that antiseptic room and the wreck of my shrivelled body. Do you understand, Josh? Tell Samuels that I want to die with dignity.'

Bennett nodded. 'I'll tell him.'

'I knew you would, Joshua.' His father nodded. 'Goodbye, son.'

Bennett regarded his father, wanting to say something

43

final and fitting, but the words were impossible to find. He reached out a hand, intending to shake, before remembering that he wasn't equipped for tactile sensation in VR. His father just stared at him, realising his son's mistake. The impasse seemed fittingly symbolic of their life-long relationship. Bennett sketched an embarrassed, inadequate wave, and quickly ejected himself from Heaven by pulling the VR glasses from his face.

The sunlight in the small hospital room dazzled him, and when his eyes adjusted he found himself staring at the shrunken body of his father. In the drawn, collapsed face beneath the glasses he saw the merest lineaments of the man he'd spoken to in the VR world. From time to time the thin hands fluttered, and his lips twitched in a grotesque parody as his father smiled in Heaven.

'Mr Bennett?'

He looked up. Samuels was staring down at him.

'I know, it must have come as something of a shock.'

Bennett shook his head, clearing it of the visions. 'I told him I agreed with his wishes,' he said. 'Are there forms I need to fill in?'

For the next couple of hours, as medics prepared the apparatus to administer the lethal injection, Bennett was introduced to his father's legal representative and chaplain, who murmured platitudinous condolences and assured him that it was for the best. He signed a raft of various release forms, waivers and other legal documents, including arrangements for the funeral, and was finally left alone in the room with his father.

He considered switching off the VR module, trying to talk to his father as he had been unable to do so in the ersatz Heaven. He decided that he had little to say to the old man; he would let him pass his last few minutes in the Heaven bought with the money he had managed to save from his creditors.

At noon, Dr Samuels and two medics, his father's representative and the chaplain, entered the room and gathered around the bed.

Bennett recalled his father's wish to die while still in the VR site. 'Dr Samuels, my father wanted to remain linked to the module.'

Samuels frowned and glanced at the legal representative. 'State law dictates that a patient's death must be monitored free from the artificial stimulus of VR linkages or similar,' Samuels explained.

'But surely it won't make any difference? It was his last wish.'

'Mr Bennett, I'll ensure that your father is so sedated that he will have no way of knowing that he no longer occupies the site. If you'd care to tell me when . . .'

Bennett pulled the chair towards the bed and took his father's hand. It was already cold, as if death was claiming him piecemeal. He nodded to Dr Samuels.

A medic slipped the glasses from his father's face, and to his relief Bennett saw that his eyes were closed. Another medic deactivated the VR module. Dr Samuels nodded to Bennett and pressed a touch-pad on a monitor behind the bed.

As his father died, Bennett experienced a sudden and involuntary rush of images – a compendium of incidents from their shared time together – and wished that somehow it might all have been different.

He squeezed the cold hand in his, and at that second his father opened his eyes briefly and stared at him. Bennett could sense, from long and bitter experiences of his father's moods, the old man's silent articulation of betrayal.

Then his father's eyes fluttered shut, and the cardiogram flatlined with a high, monotone note, and the chaplain at the foot of the bed began a hushed prayer.

5

Bennett left the hospital just before one o'clock and boarded an electric shuttle to meet Julia at the Nova Luna restaurant.

He arrived early and sat at an outside table overlooking the lake. He ordered a beer and watched the swans upending themselves in the water. He was in no mood to face Julia, her complaints and criticisms. He decided he would make his excuses and get away as soon as possible.

He was on his second beer when Julia approached from around the lake. She smiled and waved, but Bennett knew from experience that her apparent good mood was no indication of what to expect: on every occasion in the past, when their meetings had descended into a minutely detailed catalogue of his faults, she had deployed a gambit of good cheer to hide her intent.

She ordered a coffee from the bar and carried it carefully across the lawn, a tall, tanned woman in her early thirties wearing a long red dress. She was barefoot, and Bennett wondered why this fact should nag at his memory. Then he remembered: Ten Lee Theneka went barefoot also. It was, he thought, the only similarity between the two women. Julia was a hard-headed pragmatist who believed exclusively in the here and now. At least she and Bennett had that much in common.

She sat across from him, meeting his gaze with a slight nod. 'Josh.'

'I'm afraid I've already eaten, Julia. Go ahead and order – I'm okay with this.' He lifted his beer.

She ordered something called an Acapulco salad from the waiter.

'So,' she said, between minute sips of cappuccino, 'how were things in high orbit?'

He shrugged. 'As ever. No, I tell a lie. Perhaps even more monotonous than ever.' He paused, then said: 'Anyway, I'm seriously considering a change.' As soon as he'd said it, he wondered why.

Something in her gaze, outwardly friendly so far, hardened. 'And how many times have I heard that?'

'No, I mean it this time. I was almost involved in an accident up there. I'm not happy with the safety standards.'

'What did you tell me last time, or was it the time before that? Weren't you up for promotion, some kind of liner job out of Mars?'

'I didn't get it, but I was shortlisted.' The lie came easily, surprising him.

She sipped her coffee, eyeing him judiciously over the chocolate-sprinkled froth. 'So, what are your plans?'

He lowered his gaze. 'I haven't got that far yet.'

Her salad arrived, and from her indulgent expression he guessed that she was calling a truce. She forked cubes of avocado and chewed, watching him. 'How's your father keeping, Josh? Have you had time to visit him yet?'

He nodded. There was no way he could talk to Julia about the morning's events. 'You know how he is.'

He ordered another beer, his third. Already he was feeling light-headed, abstracted from this ridiculous little scene with someone he could no longer bring himself to regard with any degree of affection whatsoever.

Julia paused, brie-loaded fork halfway to her lips. 'Josh,

you've visited Ella's hologram since you've been back, haven't you?'

He shrugged, surprised by the turn of conversation. 'What if I have?' he said, then: 'How do you know?'

'Because you're always so . . . I don't know, melancholy, I suppose, after visiting the SIH.'

Referring to Ella's image as the SIH was Julia's way of ridiculing his time spent in the memorial garden.

He nodded. 'We talked. It was good to see her again. I haven't seen her for over a month.'

'It's not a "her", Josh, for Christ's sake. It's a computer program, a projection.'

'I know that.' He stared at her. 'But apart from my memories, that's all I've got of Ella.'

'You should make do with your memories then, like most grieving people.'

'But memories aren't enough, Julia. I need more. I feel I have a relationship with her.'

Julia dropped her fork, theatrically, into her salad. 'Jesus Christ.'

Bennett felt anger rise within him. 'I do. I feel—'

'Josh, you can't have a "relationship" with a damned machine!'

'I don't know. I think I can. I relate to her. I respond. She responds to me.'

'Let me put you right, Josh.' She picked up her fork and used it to point at him. 'A relationship is a two-way thing between two human beings. A transaction of feelings, emotion, concern. But of course you wouldn't know anything about that, would you? A machine is about all you're able to feel anything for.'

His voice cracking, he said, 'The program learns, stores what I say, remembers our conversation. It's like talking with a real person, Julia, except that it's impossible to touch.'

Julia was silent for a while, staring at him. She leaned forward and whispered with vehemence, 'But you'd like that, wouldn't you?'

'What do you mean?'

'You'd like to touch her, wouldn't you?' Her gaze was relentless. 'Or let me put it another way: you'd like to fuck her.'

'You bitch.'

He was overcome with the sudden urge to hit her, wipe the smug expression from her face. Then he thought he should walk away, just leave. But both options, he realised, would be craven.

'I'm serious, Josh. I don't know what went wrong after Ella died, but it screwed you up. It warped you so that you couldn't relate.'

'What crap!'

'No? Look at the girlfriends you've had over the years – not many, I must say, but a reasonable enough sample to trace a definite trend. What did all those women have in common, Josh?'

She waited, watching him.

'I'll tell you. They were all tall, dark, dominant, pretty, younger than you. They were all grown-up versions of Ella, Josh. Ella as she might have been had she lived. You're trying to find in us something of Ella, and when you fail to do so you close up. No wonder we can't relate.'

He finished his beer and gestured to the waiter for another.

Surprising himself, he leaned across the table and said, 'You're so full of shit! If you spent half your time applying your half-baked psychology to yourself, you might learn something.'

He was aware of the other diners, watching him.

Julia was half-smiling at him. 'Such as?'

He leaned back, suddenly weary and ashamed. He shook his head. 'I don't know. Forget it.'

He fell silent. He stared around the outside tables, suddenly aware of the other diners. They shied away from his regard and spoke in lowered tones, embarrassed.

After a while, he said, 'Why did you want to see me? Is there someone else?'

She sighed. 'I don't know. There might be. I just had to tell you that it isn't working. I owed you that, at least.'

He nodded, kept on nodding at the inevitability of what she had said. Julia finished her salad, slowly picking through the debris of endive and watercress.

Bennett drank his beer. When she looked up, he said, 'You might think I'm a cold bastard, Julia, but we've had some good times.'

She was good enough not to contradict him. 'I hope you find whatever it is you're looking for, Josh. I really do.'

'Julia,' he began. He almost reached across the table to take her hand, but stopped himself in time.

She stood and strode from the table, paid her bill at the bar and hurried away through the trees. Bennett watched her go, filled with that strange mixture of regret and relief he knew so well from all the other partings in the past.

He drank steadily during the afternoon, feeling the unaccustomed effect of the beer dull his senses. On Redwood Station he hardly socialised, and drank only occasionally. He pushed the thought of the station from his mind. He sat and watched the swans, their antics at once comic and undignified: they tipped themselves upside down, rubber-looking orange feet flapping, soiled scuts waggling.

He considered what Julia had said. He wondered if he was really looking for some mature version of Ella, the

50

only person he had ever really loved. He found that the hardest thing in the world was to look into himself and attempt to determine the truth, so wrapped up as it was with the deception of self-interest and vanity. The thought that his actions as an adult might have been conditioned by events in his childhood filled him with fear, a terrible sense of not being in control of his motivation, and therefore his destiny.

He finished his beer and walked back through Mojave to his car. He drove slowly through the shimmering heat of late afternoon, aware of the effects of the alcohol. He arrived at his dome with the grateful sense of having gained refuge.

Mood-jazz began a gentle syncopation as he entered the lounge. He turned it off. The com-screen came on and the picture divided into small squares, each bearing a frozen face. He wondered why he should have been bombarded by so many calls. As he sat down in his swivel chair, he understood: these people were all friends or business associates of his father. He cycled through the messages of condolence, the dispiriting repetition of inadequate sentiments: 'Your father was a fine, God-fearing gentle-man, Joshua. He'll be missed by everyone at the Church'; 'I'm calling to offer my condolences, Mr Bennett . . .' Others were evidence of a side of his father's character that he had managed to keep hidden from Bennett: 'I was saddened to hear of your father's passing. I worked with him back in ninety-five and I never met a more caring and compassionate man'; 'Your father helped me out in a time of need back in the fifties, Mr Bennett. I've never forgotten him for his kindness.'

Rather than sit through them all and then reply individually, he set his screen to record, and said: 'Joshua Bennett . . . Thanks for calling. Sorry I was unable to speak to you personally. You're welcome to

51

attend my father's funeral, on the twenty-sixth at three p.m. at the Mojave Grave Gardens. Thank you again.' He sent the recording as a one-off shot to all the callers, then sat back.

He hadn't eaten since early that morning, but he didn't feel all that hungry. He was about to take a cold beer out on to the veranda when the screen chimed with an incoming call.

Another of his father's acquaintances? Or perhaps Julia, calling to initiate a second round of abuse? He pressed the SECRECY decal on the touch-pad and the image of a uniformed man in his forties flooded the screen. Belatedly, Bennett recognised Matheson, the flight manager up at Redwood. Only then did he remember his promise to get a report on the accident to Control.

He accepted the call and sat up.

'Bennett?' Matheson stared out at him, his expression uncompromising.

'Bennett here. About the report – I know, but I've had a few personal matters to sort out down here.'

'Forget the report, Bennett. As of now you're on indefinite suspension. I want you up here in four days, noon western seaboard time, to face disciplinary charges.'

The effects of the beer slowed his response. 'Disciplinary charges? What the hell . . . ?'

'Don't look so goddamned surprised, Bennett.' Matheson leaned forward, staring at him. 'The Viper débâcle, remember? The accident? The starship you nearly decommissioned?'

Bennett shook his head. 'Hey, hold on there. We weren't at fault. It was a glitch in the Viper's sub-routine. The ship rejected Ten Lee's rewrite and—'

'Listen up, Bennett. Your reaction time was sloppy, no matter what your excuses. Have you any idea how much your incompetence cost Redwood? The bill for the repair

52

of the Viper and the starship? You're lucky we can't sue you for it. You've no damned excuses.'

'But—'

'I'll see you at noon on the twenty-sixth, Bennett. Out.'

The screen died. The twenty-sixth was the day of his father's funeral.

He sat back, angry at the injustice. Suspension without pay, a fine or demotion at best. He wondered if Redwood had enough evidence of incompetence to fire him. But Ten Lee had been running systems checks constantly that flight, and the rejection of her rewrite should not have happened.

The screen chimed again, this time with an incoming pre-recorded message.

Bennett pressed ACCEPT.

A chunky, belligerent-faced man with grey curling hair began a fast, rapid-fire delivery. Bennett watched in a daze, catching none of it. The man was sitting behind a desk, a logo on the wall to his right: a stylised letter M shot through with an arrow. Encircling the logo was the legend MACKENDRICK FOUNDATION.

He played the message again from the beginning.

'Mackendrick here, Bennett. I'm a busy man and I can't waste time chatting one to one, hence this shot. Heard about your little bust up with Redwood – don't worry about it, pal. You know what those Vipers are – pieces of shit. It was a systems error the Viper should've picked up, and we all know that. Look, I won't waste your time or mine: I'm in LA tomorrow and recruiting. I need good pilots for an upcoming project. Don't worry about the bastards at Redwood – I'll sort them out. I'll be in my offices at the shipyards from noon. See you then, pal.'

The screen went blank.

Bennett replayed the message, doing his best to assimilate what Mackendrick was telling him.

He was being exonerated from blame by a stranger – Mackendrick of the Mackendrick Foundation – told to forget Redwood, and offered a possible job on some 'future project'.

He wondered if this was someone's idea of a joke.

He reached for the touch-pad and accessed GlobaLink. He typed in 'Mackendrick Foundation', and two seconds later the message flashed up on the screen: 'Three thousand articles re. Mackendrick Foundation. State specific area of interest.'

He typed 'Mackendrick Foundation: summary'.

Seconds later text filled the screen: 'Mackendrick Foundation, formed 2102. Extra-Expansion exploration company. Primarily concerned with discovery and exploration of new worlds beyond already charted space. [See: worlds discovered.] Fourth largest such company in Expansion. [See: business prospects.] Director: Charles Mackendrick. [See: Mackendrick: biography.]'

There was more, but Bennett had seen enough for the moment.

He fetched a beer from the cooler, stepped out on to the veranda, and watched the sun going down over the desert.

6

Ezekiel Klien stood before the wraparound screen of the security tower and stared out across the simmering expanse of Calcutta spaceport.

As the chief of security at the port, and king of his domain, Klien felt invincible. He had been at the port for thirteen years now, thirteen lucky years, working his way up from lowly security officer to his present lofty position.

His communicator buzzed. 'The captain of the freighter is in the interrogation room, sir.'

'I told you I wanted his name and the name of his ship, Frazer.'

'Yes, sir!'

For the past five years, as chief of security, he had ruled with absolute and unwavering authority. He knew that his team hated him, but this only served to assure him that he was doing his job with clinical efficiency. His orders had to be obeyed to the letter and anyone who showed less than one hundred per cent dedication to Klien and his objectives would find themselves out of work.

'Ah . . .' Frazer said, 'he's Vitaly Kozinsky and his ship is the . . .' Klien could almost sense Frazer's panic as he checked his com-board. 'The *Petrograd*.'

'Very good. I'll be down immediately.'

He cut the connection and stared through the

viewscreen at the squat, toad-like shape of the Russian freighter sitting on the tarmac. The ship had violated Indian airspace, phasing in without warning or clearance and claiming main drive failure. Klien had authorised landing and scrambled his team. In all likelihood the captain's claim was genuine and the ship was damaged, but Klien was taking no risks.

He stepped into the elevator and rode to the ground floor. He smiled at his reflection in the polished steel door. Physically and facially he bore little resemblance to the young man who had left the world of Homefall almost fourteen years ago. He had lived indulgently over the years, dined well and overfed himself with the express purpose of gaining weight and radically changing his appearance. His face was padded with fat and he wore his hair in black, shoulder-length ringlets. He had taken bromides for the past ten years, both to suppress his sexual urges and so allow ultimate concentration on what was important in his life, and to change his appearance further. His team called him the Eunuch. He knew this because he had planted surveillance devices in their changing rooms. There was very little that happened at the port of which Ezekiel Klien was not aware.

Frazer was waiting for him outside the interrogation room.

'Have you got the crew out of the ship?'

Frazer nodded. 'They're waiting in quarantine, sir.'

'Good. Keep them there until I say so. And get the team aboard the *Petrograd*. I want the ship stripped and a full report in my terminal in one hour. Also, I want the flight program examined and relayed to me. That will be all.'

'Yes, sir.' Frazer saluted, something like fear and hatred in his eyes.

Klien's draconian regime had paid dividends over the years. Security at the port was the envy of business organisations and governments. National and even colonial concerns had tried to lure him away from the job, tempting him with talk of fabulous wealth, but he had refused all offers. He had joined the port security staff with one aim in mind, and he did not intend to be distracted from that aim.

He touched the sensor on the door and stepped into the interrogation room.

Kozinsky was a big man in scarred radiation silvers. His hair was dishevelled and his face unshaven, and he stank. It was the peculiar body odour of men in a failing ship, the rank stench of fear and unwashed flesh.

'Klien, chief of security.'

Kozinsky stood quickly and held out a hand. 'Vitaly Kozinsky, captain of the *Petrograd*.'

Klien ignored the hand. 'Sit down, Captain.'

Kozinsky nodded, sat down uncomfortably. He was fidgety after too long in space. Klien could tell that he wanted to stand and stride about. Intuition told him that the man was almost certainly genuine, and not the ringleader of some anti-Indian faction out to bomb the port.

But Klien was not about to trust intuition. He remained standing, maintaining a psychological advantage over the seated spacer, and for the next hour fired a barrage of questions at the bemused Russian.

Kozinsky was a freelance spacer who would take any in-system job between the planets if the price was right; he was paid well to fly tubs that no other self-respecting spacer would go anywhere near. The *Petrograd* was an Earth–Mars cargo freighter of the Cosmoflot Line, on the return leg to Kazakhstan from Mars with a hold full of iron ore.

'Why did you choose to come down here, Captain? Surely you could have made it to Kazakhstan?'

'I tried, but there was no way we could have lasted.'

'Auxiliary engine failure?'

Kozinsky looked up. 'No – main drive dysfunction.'

Klien smiled to himself. 'And you came down on the auxiliaries?'

The captain nodded. 'But we had trouble with those, too. I decided to land at the first port.'

Klien stared at the man, considering. 'What we'll do, Captain,' he said at last, 'is contact Cosmoflot and arrange payment for repairs to the ship. You'll be accommodated here in the meantime at your employer's expense.'

He nodded briefly and left the room.

From time to time he liked to take a look around the ships himself, less to check the diligence of his team than to reacquaint himself with the interior of a void-going vessel. He left the tower and walked across the tarmac to the damaged *Petrograd*. A ramp gave access to a foul-smelling interior. More than just the drive had failed: the air system and ventilation had laboured to keep the atmosphere clean and breathable.

He made his way to the flight-deck and watched Frazer and the team at work, sensing their unease at his presence. He touched the back of the worn command couch, his gaze moving over the control console. Technology had moved on a lot over the years, since he had piloted the scout ship away from Homefall to Madrigal. He would be unable to pilot these more modern vessels, though he daily dreamed of returning to the planet of his birth, of appropriating a void-ship and heading away from the corruption and filth that was the Expansion.

He smiled to himself. A man needed his dreams.

'Frazer?'

The officer turned from examining the ship's flight program, saluted. 'Sir.'

'Your findings?'

'The system shows a routine Earth–Mars run, sir. Nothing untoward at all. There was a main drive dysfunction picked up by the on-board computers on initial orbital approach. The main drive shut down and they came in on the auxiliary system.'

Klien nodded. 'Contact Cosmoflot for credit rating and have the crew transferred to temporary lodging.'

Klien left his team and crossed the tarmac to the security tower. Once back in his office he went through the flight programs of the many other ships occupying the holding berths and blast-pads across the port. Shortly after his appointment as chief of security, he had ordered the installation of a computer system that would enable him to check on the flight programs of every ship that used the port; he had also arranged a reciprocal facility with Security at Los Angeles spaceport, so that he could check on their ships too.

There was always the chance that his home planet had sent another ship after his own. He had to be ready for his fellow colonists in the event of their arrival, either to eliminate the crew should they be from the opposition, or to greet fellow members of the Council of Elders.

He had been waiting for such a long time now that he had almost given up hope. He had come to accept that he was stranded on Earth, an Earth corrupt beyond his ability to accept or to change.

For the rest of the afternoon, Klien processed routine security matters and studied Frazer's report on the *Petrograd*. The ship was given a clean status and engineers were assigned to make the repairs. He filed a report to the director of the spaceport and considered his meeting with Ali Bhakor that night.

At four he got through to Bhakor, using the voice-only facility on his com-screen.

'Smith here,' Klien said. 'I'm calling to finalise the arrangements.'

The screen showed Bhakor's big face, beaded with perspiration in the heat of the day. 'Why can't I see you?' he rapped.

'I'm calling from a public kiosk,' Klien said. 'It's been vandalised.'

He had only ever met Bhakor once in the flesh, to give him the sample of the drug called slash in the hope that the dealer would want more. Then Klien had been effectively disguised.

Bhakor said, 'Have you got the stuff?'

'A kilo of prime grade,' Klien assured him.

'Ah-cha. Where and when?'

'Tonight at eight. I've booked a room in your name at the Hindustan Plaza hotel. I'll see you then.'

Bhakor nodded. 'Ah-cha, Smith. I'll be there.'

Klien cut the connection and sat back, exhaling with relief. He realised that his hands were shaking. His mouth was dry. He poured himself a glass of iced water and worked to control his breathing.

Days like today – and there had been many others in the past – were what made his life on Earth worthwhile – along with opera, of course. This evening, after he had dealt with Bhakor, he would take his box at the National Indian Opera Company and lose himself in the sublimity of Puccini. It would be his reward for making the world a safer place.

At six thirty he took the elevator down to the suite of rooms he used when he had to work a double shift. He showered and changed, wearing as always on these occasions the black suit he had bought on Madrigal fifteen years ago. It was tailored from sabline, the most expensive and exclusive suiting material in the entire Expansion, and looked as stylish now as it had on the day

60

of its purchase. He had worn it at his confrontation with Quineau, all those years ago, and on every special occasion since.

He unlocked the wall-safe and collected the equipment he would be needing tonight, then left the tower and climbed into his Mercedes two-seater. He drove along the northern sector of the great Calcutta ring road with care and consideration for his fellow road users. That day's monsoon downpour had been and gone, leaving the roads slick and shimmering. The sun was going down over the distant bay and the lights of the city were coming on. The great ad-screens moved across the dusk sky like aerial cinemas.

Just after seven he braked in the car-park of the Hindustan Plaza and met the manager and head of security in the foyer. They were courteous to the point of servility; it was not every day that Ezekiel Klien consented to advise a hotel on the maintenance of its security systems.

'Has the equipment been delivered?' he asked as he rode the elevator up to the third-floor conference room.

The manager nodded. 'It's set up and ready,' he said. 'I can't begin to tell you how delighted I am that you agreed—'

Klien turned him out. He might refuse commissions from world governments to advise them on security matters, but if an offer came along which he might turn to his own advantage, then he would graciously agree to lecture, even going so far as to donate his usual fee to charity.

The security and communications company Inter-Tech had offered him fabulous sums to promote their latest range of computer communication devices. Klien had initially turned down their offer, and then had seen a way he might benefit from the deal.

61

The hotel's security team had followed his instructions to the letter. In a small room next to the conference room, accessible by a door which could be locked, a com-screen had been set up. The other was in the conference room itself.

Klien watched the room fill up with about thirty men and women from various companies in the city, along with the hotel's own security staff. He smiled to himself. As well as supplying himself with a foolproof alibi tonight, he could be assured that the security team was otherwise engaged.

He was introduced by the manager and stood as applause filled the room.

'Thank you . . . please . . . As you know, I don't usually accept invitations to endorse company products, but Inter-Tech's latest range is in my opinion something very special . . . and I'd heard it rumoured that the hotel has one of the finest cellars in the sub-continent. To your good health.'

He raised his glass and sipped as polite laughter greeted his quip.

'Tonight I'd like to talk about the Inter-Tech Arrow 200 com-screen.'

For the next thirty minutes he sang the praises of the Arrow 200's design features and technical specifications, the screen's reliability and range, peppering the advertisement with anecdotes and personal accounts of his experience with other screens over the years. The audience listened with genuine interest.

At one point he glanced at his watch. It was just after eight. Ali Bhakor would be waiting for him on the fourth floor, room 180. It was time he was moving.

'But enough of the talk,' he said now. 'I think it's time for me actually to show the Arrow 200 in action. If you'll bear with me for one moment . . .'

He left the stage and moved into the adjoining room, quietly locking the door behind him. He approached the com-screen and loaded the recording he had made the day before. He switched on the screen. In the conference room, he could hear his relayed voice saying: 'Thank you for your patience. Now, I think you will agree with me that the clarity of both sound and vision . . .'

Heart hammering with the thrill of the risk, Klien pulled the fine net of fibre-optic capillaries from the inside pocket of his suit and drew the device over his head. In the same pocket was the activator. He fingered the touch-pad. Instantly he was aware of a haze of light in his vision. Seconds later his eyes adjusted, and he quickly slipped through the door to the corridor. To any casual observer he would no longer resemble Ezekiel Klien, but a man in his sixties with a hatchet-thin face and silver hair. The capillary net was, officially, still in its design stage. As chief of security at the spaceport, he had contacted a local software company and sponsored its manufacture. It was making his work a lot easier.

He hurried along the corridor to the elevator and ascended to the fourth floor. His heart was pounding at a rate he only ever experienced on nights such as these. He tried to calculate the risk. The only possible danger was if the recording on the com-screen developed a hitch – and what an irony that would be! The pre-recorded disc would last fifteen minutes, allowing him what he considered to be more than enough time to get to the fourth floor, deal with Bhakor, and return.

He knocked on the door of room 180, and seconds later it opened fractionally. A sliver of Bhakor's dark face appeared. A blood-shot eye blinked at him. 'Smith. Ah-cha. You have the slash?'

'Don't worry,' Klien said, slipping into the room. He crossed the lounge and sat down.

Bhakor returned from closing the door and lowered himself into the opposite armchair.

Klien watched the man as he leaned forward nervously. It was always his main regret that he could not, before he despatched his victims, lecture them on the error of their ways, explain to them just why they had to die.

Bhakor was impatient. 'You have the slash?'

Klien nodded. 'Have you had a good life, Bhakor?' he said.

Bhakor blinked. 'What? What do you—'

'Are you ready to meet the judgement of your god?'

Before Bhakor could react, Klien pulled the laser pistol from his inside pocket and fired at point-black range, the blast charcoaling the right side of the drug dealer's head. He slumped back into the chair with a posthumous grunt. The flesh of his cheek was blackened and cracked and the stench of singed hair and pomade filled the room.

Klien stood and pulled a razor from his pocket. Carefully, with almost loving exactitude, he sliced a crucifix in the plump flesh of the dead man's left cheek. Then he hurried from the room, filled with an exultation and joy at the knowledge that he was doing God's duty and sanitising this terrible world.

Two minutes later he entered the small room on the third floor, pulled off his capillary net and waited five minutes for the recording to finish. He heard his voice from the next room: '. . . as I think you'll agree. Thank you.'

He pocketed the disc, unlocked the door and stepped through to stirring applause. He took his place on the stage, faced the audience and smiled.

'Thank you. I can honestly say that I think that little display went very well. I, at least, am very pleased with the performance.'

He wound down the talk, replying to a few predictable

questions and thanking all present for being a know-ledgeable and appreciative audience.

He stayed behind briefly for drinks with the security team and selected guests. He made an appointment to visit the team and go through a few of the latest systems. He had to suppress a smile as he arranged a date with the head of security. He would certainly enjoy telling them what they should do in future to ensure that their guests were not murdered in their rooms. Surveillance cameras would, he thought, be a good start.

Thirty minutes later Klien excused himself, left the hotel and drove into Calcutta city centre. He parked outside the opera house five minutes before the performance was due to begin, ordered a drink from the bar and slipped into the comfortable seat of his private box high above the stage.

For the next two hours he put aside his consideration of the state of the planet and enjoyed the music. He had often wondered if his love of opera and his ability to kill were somehow linked. He thought that they might be. He was, after all, doing God's bidding here on Earth, and it was as if his appreciation of the beauty of classical music was a gift from God, a reward, as it were, for services rendered.

As the music swelled, Klien smiled to himself.

Later that night, at home, he suffered another episode of his recurrent nightmare. He was back in a cavern far below ground and tall, grotesque aliens were performing their terrible ritual. This time, they were accompanied by the strains of Puccini's *La Bohème*.

Klien sat up with a startled cry and fumbled for the light pad. The images vanished, along with the terrible sense of evil that always accompanied the dream, and his breathing gradually returned to normal.

Unable to sleep, he dressed and moved to his study. On

the desk was the pile of pix he had left out the night before. He picked them up and stepped out on to the balcony. Spotlights in the garden illuminated the white cladding of his dwelling. Five years ago he had moved to one of the most exclusive areas of the city and bought a luxurious polycarbon house on Allahabad Marg – a scaled-down version of the Sydney Opera House. Kitsch, he knew, but at the same time appealing.

He sat on the lounger and shuffled through the pix. The first three showed a young Indian girl in a blue dress. She was perhaps eight or nine years old. The other three pix were computer-generated images, showing Sita Mackendrick as she might appear today, aged twenty-three.

He laid the pix aside with a sigh. He had come to Earth from Homefall almost fourteen years ago on a mission more important to him than his own existence, and so far he had failed.

His one hope, now, was if he could find the woman who was Sita Mackendrick.

7

Bennett stood before the plate-glass window of the observation gallery and watched the activity on the apron far below. After all his years in space, his experience piloting ships to orbit, there was still something about the sight of vessels blasting off from Los Angeles spaceport that filled him with excitement.

He suspected it had something to do with childhood. As a kid he'd taken the coach from Mojave, against his father's express instructions, to spend long afternoons watching ships lighting out for the stars. He had even brought Ella here once, his joy at the experience heightened by his sister's obvious delight. He smiled to himself. It seemed a long time ago since he had dreamed of being a pilot; if only his younger self could have known that one day his dream would come true. He felt a twinge of sadness at the thought of how dreams fulfilled never satisfied the expectations of the dreamer. It had taught him never to dream, never to look too far into the future.

The spaceport was a vast concrete plain that stretched away in every direction as far as the eye could see. Every half-kilometre the surface was pocked by a blast crater, a sunken collar of steel flanges in which the ships and shuttles squatted preparatory to take-off. Many of the vessels in the immediate vicinity of the observation gallery were ground-to-orbit ships, bulbous bell-shaped tubs squatting on powerful, flexed stanchions. There were only four big companies now, competing to win the stars. There'd been dozens during his childhood, and he'd meticulously memorised the livery of every shipping line.

He watched as a supply shuttle rose from a nearby berth, and the thrill he recalled from childhood filled him now. The terminal building vibrated as if at the onset of an earthquake. He shielded his eyes from the blinding, actinic glare as the sleek ship powered into the lower atmosphere on the start of its journey to the orbitals.

He left the gallery and made his way through the crowded concourse of the terminal building, showed his pass to a security guard and stepped out on to the tarmac. He walked around the building, away from the ear-splitting roar of departing vessels, to the area given over to machine shops, repair yards and hangars. Various shipping lines and colonial companies hired compounds within the port, areas the size of football fields secured by carbon-fibre fences. Consulting the map he'd picked up from the information desk, Bennett moved through a maze of compounds to the lot on the map marked with the letter M shot through with an arrow.

To prepare himself, he had accessed GlobaLink and read more about the Mackendrick Foundation and Mack-endrick himself. The Foundation had been set up by Mackendrick senior, Alistair, at the turn of the century, as a learning centre for a diverse set of scientific discip-lines, all devoted to the discovery and understanding of other worlds. The initial idea was that the foundation should turn out multi-discipline scientists equipped to work on the many habitable planets of the Expansion. Over the years the aims of the foundation had broadened: under the direction of Charles Mackendrick, the founda-tion bought out a small shipping line in '56, and so the exploration arm of the company was founded.

The biography of Charles Mackendrick himself read like

the synopsis of some improbable holo-vision adventure story for kids. Trained at the Space Academy on Mars, Mackendrick had graduated as a light-drive engineer at nineteen, specialising in the then recently developed Schulmann-Dearing propulsion systems. For five years he worked for various lines servicing the colonies, along the way picking up a pilot's diploma. At twenty-five he'd become the youngest chief pilot of an exploration vessel, in the employ of the Trans-Planetary Company. He had served on teams that had discovered and opened up a dozen worlds for colonisation, and in '50 had been among the first party of humans to locate and make contact with sentient extraterrestrial life-forms, the aliens known as the Phalaan. Six years later he had taken over the directorship of the Mackendrick Foundation and initiated the interstellar explorations, for which it was now principally known.

Mackendrick himself was portrayed as a restless work-aholic who until recently had lived for the exploration of uncharted space. A billionaire, he had retired from active planetary exploration just five years ago at the age of seventy.

He sounded, Bennett decided on finishing the hagio-graphic biography, just the type of person he'd rather avoid: thrusting, dynamic and aggressive. Bennett had never met a successful businessman he had actively liked, but perhaps his opinion had been negatively tainted by the influence of his father. Admittedly, his preconception of Mackendrick had been formed by reading between the lines, and watching the tape Mackendrick had sent last night, in which he'd come over as loud, overbearing and confident of getting what-ever, and whoever, he wanted.

Bennett was unsure whether to be alarmed that the billionaire tycoon had singled him out for attention, or flattered. He did know that he was not exactly looking forward to the forthcoming meeting with Mackendrick.

A chain-link carbon-fibre fence enclosed the Mackendrick Foundation compound, a sunken repair yard littered with various bulky machine tools, heavy lifting equipment and ship parts. In pride of place in the centre of the pit was the silver stylised arrowhead of a Cobra-class exploration vessel.

Bennett gave his name and showed his pass to a guard at the gate. The guard clicked his jaw to open communications and spoke quickly, seemingly to himself. Seconds later he nodded and allowed Bennett through.

He took a zig-zag flight of steps down into the sunken compound, inhaling a heady stench of air fouled by the mixture of test-fire ionisation and laser welding. Pre-fab offices occupied the far end of the pit, but they appeared to be empty.

'Hello down there! Can I help you?'

He looked up. High above, leaning over the gantry that surrounded the Cobra, a small figure in engineer's overalls waved down at him.

'I'm looking for Charles Mackendrick,' Bennett called.

'He won't be long – should be back any time now. Care to come up?'

Bennett climbed up the gantry, passing the ship's silver-muscled hydraulic stanchions, its curved flank excoriated by a million micro-meteorite impacts. The engineer was kneeling beside the swollen cowl of a booster nacelle, peering into its depths and periodically consulting a lighted com-board.

The engineer looked up. 'Bennett, isn't it? The pilot?'

Bennett nodded, surprised by the appearance of the engineer. From below, he had been unable to determine the man's age, but at close quarters he appeared to be in his eighties, a slight man with balding grey hair and a thin face.

'Mack's expecting you,' the engineer said. 'He's told me a lot about you. Hotshot pilot, by all accounts.'

'I wouldn't say that,' Bennett began, wondering how Mackendrick knew 'a lot' about him.

'What do you know about Dearing boosters, Bennett? Taught you mechanics and systems operations at pilot school, didn't they?'

Bennett wondered if this was part of the interview – to have a chief engineer grill him on basic mechanics. He entered into the spirit, knelt beside the engineer and peered into the nacelle.

'They're about the best, in my opinion, in terms of reliability and performance. The latest Mitsubishi might be faster, but I've heard rumours of poor stress analysis results. I prefer Dearings.'

'With Delta operating systems.'

Bennett nodded. 'Or the original Schulmann programs, especially for long-haul flights.'

'So what do you make of this?' The engineer thrust the com-board at Bennett. 'There, and there . . .' He pointed to read-outs flashing at the bottom right of the screen.

'That'd suggest an operating failure in the Delta relay. It can be remedied by inserting a Manx sub-routine. Of course, you wouldn't have this problem with a Schulmann program.'

The engineer nodded. 'That's what I thought.'

He stood and escorted Bennett around the cat-walk encircling the ship, stopping from time to time to point out some interesting addition or design feature.

They paused before the projecting nose-cone. Bennett peered inside at the spacious flight-deck, with wrap-around consoles and gimbal couches. Hell, there was room enough in there to contain his old Viper tug, and then some.

'I've heard about how you saved the *Northrop*, Bennett. Impressive piece of piloting. Saved . . . how many crew? Ten? And valuable cargo.'

Bennett shrugged. He hated it when people dragged out the old *Northrop* episode. 'It was a long time ago,' he said. 'Getting on for twelve years.'

In truth, he knew how lucky he'd been when the *Northrop*'s guidance system had packed up and he'd brought the ship down on manual. The weather conditions had been perfect and he'd had no time in which to panic.

'Quit the modesty, Bennett. You were a hero. If it wasn't for you, the ship would've smacked the tarmac good.'

'I think that whoever was on duty then would have done the same as me.'

'We'll never know – because they *weren't* on duty then. But you were. And you pulled out all the stops.'

It had been a strange time, the days following the near accident. The press coverage, the approbation of the Redwood high-ups . . . But his father had brought him down to earth. 'It's truly amazing what the involuntary responses are capable of when one's life is under threat . . .' It was his only comment on the affair, and Bennett had not forgotten his sense of crushing disappointment. All he'd wanted was a handshake and a simple, 'Well done.'

They strolled around the starship, chatting casually about every aspect of space flight and exploration. If this was a preliminary interview, Bennett felt that it was going well.

'Do you have any idea why Mackendrick wanted to interview me?' he asked. 'He mentioned something about a project.'

The engineer pursed his lips, considering. 'I do know that this ship's due out in two or three days, bound for an unexplored quadrant of the galaxy.'

Bennett smiled to himself. The kid in him would have loved the story-book adventure aspect of the 'project' . . .

At the far end of the pit, a woman emerged from one of the pre-fab offices and picked her way between discarded ion-drives and honeycomb radiation baffles. She paused beneath the gantry and looked up. 'Mr Mackendrick, there's a call for you.'

The engineer signalled down. 'I'll take it up here.'

He glanced at Bennett, as if to judge how he'd taken the deception, then moved off along the gantry.

Bennett watched him take a communicator from his breast pocket and begin a rapid dialogue, less annoyed than mystified by Mackendrick's duplicity.

The engineer he'd been talking to bore little resemblance to the man who had contacted him last night. The engineer was slight, thin-faced and balding, whereas the earlier Mackendrick had been broad and stocky, with a full head of grey curls. But, as Bennett studied the man speaking into the communicator, he discerned in the lines of the aged face a likeness to the Mackendrick of last night. It was as if he'd shed fifty pounds overnight, and aged thirty years.

Mackendrick returned the communicator to his pocket and rejoined Bennett. He held out his hand. 'Mackendrick,' he said. 'Call me Mack, though.' He regarded Bennett intently. 'I hope my little game didn't offend you?'

Bennett shrugged. 'I suppose you get a kick from playing the engineer?'

Mackendrick laughed. 'I don't make a habit of it, Bennett. But my reputation precedes me. People aren't themselves in the company of the billionaire director of the Mackendrick Foundation. They act, put on a show. I wanted to talk to you before you knew who I was.' He peered at Bennett, one eye screwed shut. 'I suppose you're wondering who called you last night?'

'Some kind of computer-enhanced image,' Bennett guessed, 'perhaps taken from a shot of you twenty years ago?'

'Right, Bennett. Or almost. Not twenty years ago – five. Why do you think I quit active exploration five years ago? It was my damned life, Bennett. Then wham! and I'm flat on my back in hospital with some damned viral complaint and my surgeons are running around like headless chickens thinking I'm going to kick it there and then. Well, they pulled me round – *I* pulled me round – but it left me looking like shit. And call me vain or egocentric or whatever the hell, but I didn't want Dan Redwood or Patel or any other of those bastards rubbing their hands and thinking I'm losing it, so I conference now via the comlink, and I look like a million dollars.'

Bennett listened to Mackendrick and knew he should have felt awed in the presence of the eccentric tycoon, but the fact was that something about the man put Bennett at ease.

'Can I ask you something, Mr Mackendrick?'

'Fire away. And it's Mack, for Chrissake.'

'What's going on here? I mean, why me?'

'Why you? Because you're a good pilot—'

'Redwood suspended me yesterday—'

'Redwood!' Mackendrick almost spat the name. 'Listen to me.'

He clapped Bennett's shoulder and led him on a lap of the gantry. Bennett found the intimacy of the gesture at once intimidating and confiding.

'What I'm telling you here is strictly confidential, between you and me. The simple fact is that you and

Ten Lee were fall guys. Redwood have a deal ongoing with Consolidated Colonial for three hundred Viper-class tugs and shuttles, and their operating systems. The deal's worth billions. But, you see, the Viper's operating systems are shot. There's a major glitch in there that their computer whiz-kids can't work out.'

'You sound pretty sure about that.'

'Pretty sure? Listen, kid, I'm one hundred per cent sure. I *know*. I have spies in Redwood. I know more about what's happening in the computer labs than Dan Redwood himself, because my spies'll tell me, but his men are shit scared of telling him the truth. That the programming systems are crap and if Consolidated Colonial gets wind of the stink, then the billion-plus deal is off.'

'So the other day . . . ?'

Mackendrick was nodding. 'You almost total the tug, and a starship into the bargain, and you swear it's an operating system, but does Control listen? You bet your ass they don't. It's Bennett and Theneka with red faces before the disciplinary committee, and believe me, if you stayed with Redwood you'd be kicked so far away from the Vipers your butts would still be smarting come Christmas.' He waved a hand in a disgusted gesture. 'Screw Redwood. My people've been telling me for years that you're a damned good pilot, so when the opportunity arose, I took it.'

They paused beside the twin exhaust vents of the Schulmann-Dearing boosters. Mackendrick leaned against the rail, staring down into the pit.

'You mentioned a project?' Bennett said.

Mackendrick nodded, glanced at him. 'How would you like to pilot the Cobra here, interstellar?'

Bennett wondered if his sudden sweat was wholly a result of the sun. 'Exactly where to?'

Mackendrick looked at him. 'We're heading so far

across sidereal space, Bennett, that it's totally off the usual exploration vector.'

Bennett had a dozen questions he wanted to ask, all at once.

'I'm interested,' he said. 'But why me? You've got a hundred pilots just as qualified—'

'That's debatable, Bennett. I wanted someone who's good in the gravity well, in adverse weather conditions. Your handling of the *Northrop* back in sixty-eight proved you're more than capable.'

'When's the planned flight date?'

'Later,' Mackendrick said. 'I'll answer that and any other questions when the systems analyst arrives. I'll go through the project then and we can talk it over.' He glanced at this watch. 'She's due pretty soon. In the meantime, how about coffee?'

He led the way back down the gantry and across the pit to the line of offices. Bennett followed Mackendrick into a plush chamber fitted with mock-wood panelling and hung with moving 3D images of planetary panoramas. The tycoon gestured to a suite of sofas and prepared the coffee. Bennett sat down, noticing as he did so a pillow and blanket stuffed into a storage unit against the far wall. So Mackendrick, like the workaholic of repute, slept *in situ* while working in the compound.

On a desk in the corner of the room was a pix showing a younger and healthier Mackendrick with a striking Indian woman in a sari. Mackendrick was cradling a baby in his arms, something proud and proprietorial in his pose.

Mackendrick passed Bennett a cup of coffee and lowered himself into an armchair.

'I heard about your father,' Mackendrick said. 'I'm sorry.'

'News travels fast.'

'I have my contacts.' He paused. 'I take it you weren't close?'

Bennett smiled. 'That's something of an understatement. We didn't see eye to eye, I suppose you might say. On anything.'

'Join the club,' Mackendrick said, indicating a pix on the wall above the desk. It showed a suited, middle-aged man clutching the hand of a small, stocky boy on the steps of some imposing building. 'My father, Alistair Mackendrick, founder of the foundation. Now he, Bennett, was a bastard of the first water. He wanted me to join him in academe, but I wasn't having it. You don't know how satisfying it was to open the foundation up to the actual exploration of space, not just the theory.'

Bennett sipped his coffee, wondering if Mackendrick's little speech was another trick to win him over. His gaze wandered back to the pix of Mackendrick and the Indian woman. The tycoon noticed.

'Naheed, my wife,' he said. 'We met while I was working at the Calcutta shipyards. She was the daughter of a well-to-do merchant. I never believed until then that I could fall in love. Didn't believe I had it in me, and was determined to remain single. And the thought of having children . . .' He paused and smiled sadly. 'It's amazing how your views change when you meet someone you feel you want to be with for the rest of your life.'

Bennett recalled no mention of his wife in the biographical essay he'd read that morning.

Mackendrick looked from the pix to Bennett. 'Naheed died almost thirteen years ago,' he said quietly. 'Leukaemia. There was nothing we could do. For all my wealth . . .'

Bennett looked away from the tycoon. To change the subject he indicated the pix and said, 'You had a son?'

'A daughter. Sita.' Mackendrick shook his head. 'Sadly, I no longer see her.'

Perhaps, Bennett thought, this explained Mackendrick's single-minded dedication to his work.

Mackendrick looked up, through the window overlooking the pit. 'And at last the tardy analyst decides to honour us,' he said.

A small figure, reduced by the distance, was making its way down the zig-zag steps. Minutes later Mackendrick's secretary knocked and opened the door. A tiny woman in a bright red flight-suit, barefoot as on the first occasion Bennett had made her acquaintance, stepped into the room.

'Ten Lee . . .' Bennett said.

'Joshua.' The Viet-Zambian inclined her head but did not smile. 'Mack told me last night that I might be working with you again, if you decided to join us. I resigned from Redwood immediately.'

Bennett nodded. 'I just might be joining you.'

He was surprised again by her diminutive stature. As she stood before him, her head barely reached his sternum. A small rucksack was strapped to her shoulders, its weight giving her back the pert curve of a reed.

'We need a first-rate analyst along,' Mackendrick was saying. 'My people recommended Ten Lee. How about coffee, Ten? A refill, Josh?'

While Mackendrick busied himself at the percolator, Bennett said to Ten Lee, 'It's good to see you again.'

Ten Lee blinked up at him, her expression blank. It seemed to take her a while to consider her reply. 'Yesterday I told you that my Rimpoche stated that my destiny was ever outward, Josh. It seems that he was right. When Mack contacted me last night, I had no hesitation in accepting his offer.'

'Has he told you where exactly we're going?'

'Only that it is further than any exploration vessel has gone before. It will give me plenty of time to meditate.'

Bennett smiled. 'I think the ship'll be fitted with suspension units, Ten.'

'Since when was their use declared obligatory, Joshua?'

'Touché. But rather you than me.'

She gazed up at him, her thoughts unreadable behind the mask of her expressionless features. 'Perhaps a period of contemplation would do you good,' she said.

'Well, maybe . . .' Bennett shrugged. 'What's in the rucksack?'

'My possessions. A change of flight-suit. Toiletries. And the *Book of Meditation*, the Bhao Khet book of philosophy.'

'You travel light, ' Bennett said.

She inclined her head. 'We all begin the journey light, Josh, but some of us burden ourselves on the way.'

Bennett gave a slow nod of feigned understanding. 'Right, Ten.'

Mackendrick passed them cups of coffee. 'Now that you're here, Ten, we can get down to business. As I've already mentioned, we're lighting into uncharted space. The fourth quadrant, and, to be even more precise, the Rim. If you'd care to sit down I'll show you some video and computer imagery.'

While Mackendrick tapped the touch-pad of the com-screen on his desk, Bennett eased himself on to the sofa. Ten Lee took off her rucksack and sat cross-legged on the floor. Mackendrick sat side-saddle on the edge of his desk, as his computer-enhanced alter ego had done last night. On the screen beside him was the still image of an unfamiliar solar system.

'A few years ago one of my uncrewed reconnaissance ships relayed some footage from a star system known only as G5/13. It was the furthest any vessel, from any line, had ventured, by some thousand or so light years. As you might know, the remit of the Expansion, which makes sense in the circumstances, is to explore space in an ever-widening cone along the spiral arm. This is merely in the interest of economic viability – it's good business sense to open colony worlds closer to known, inhabited space.'

Mackendrick paused.

'I like to do things differently. Call me a maverick, but I don't like running with the herd. There's all the sprawling universe out there, and I'm damned if I'm going to restrict myself to crawling around in our back yard like some helpless ant. So I take risks. I send out ships where other companies are too scared to go. Sometimes I draw a big fat blank. Sometimes I come up trumps. Some of my most successful ventures have discovered planets rich in valuable ores and metals, plant life indispensable in the production of pharmaceuticals. Over the years I've always gone that little bit further.

'As I said, one of my ships started sending interesting footage back from the Rim. The ship received information from one of its probes, processed it and relayed the results back to our receiving station on Mars. This is what one probe discovered.'

He turned and tapped the touch-pad. The scene began rolling, speeded up faster than real-time. It showed the system from the point of view of the survey probe. Ice-bound outer planets flashed by. Then came a collection of smaller Earth-sized planets, orbiting their primary at a distance of some twenty million miles, according to Mackendrick. The angle of approach turned, veering off towards the sun and a gas giant that rapidly filled the screen. The banded stripes of blue and green gaseous light filled the room with an aqueous glow.

Mackendrick paused the film.

Bennett leaned forward. 'A gas giant?' he said. Why

80

would the survey probe find a gas giant of particular interest?

Mackendrick smiled. 'I've named it Tenebrae,' he said, 'but it's not the planet I'm interested in. The planet in question is hidden by Tenebrae's bulk, almost indiscernible in this shot.' He pointed to a small disc, a coin held at arm's length, silhouetted against the broad, bright bulk of the gas giant. 'I've called the world Penumbra, for obvious reasons. Watch.'

The film continued, speeding up as the probe fell towards the tiny planet. Soon the planet filled the screen: a cloud-whipped, pale mauve world which resolved itself, as the probe plummeted through a storm-racked atmosphere, into a landscape of mountains and plains and long blue lakes, the vegetation predominantly a covering of purple and violet grassland and forest.

'The following footage is edited from over four hours of reconnaissance, so it's jerky and unconsecutive. The planet is prone to violent storms, which accounts for the poor quality of some of the shots. Also, the planet is predominantly in the shadow of Tenebrae, which radiates only about a third of the light of our own sun. Hence Penumbra. We should see the features of interest in a minute or two.'

Bennett sat forward, his curiosity piqued.

The rilled and rucked surface of the land, where foothills buttressed high mountains, passed beneath the eye of the probe. A valley flashed by, and Mackendrick paused the film. At first Bennett could see nothing, and then he made out two rows of orderly shapes in the valley bottom. Mackendrick magnified the image, and Bennett told himself that the shapes were clearly buildings.

'There,' Mackendrick said. 'What do you think?'

'It could be some kind of village or settlement,' Bennett ventured. 'It certainly looks too ordered to be an accidental collection of rocks or boulders.'

'Ten Lee?'

She inclined her head. 'Probably,' she said. 'They certainly look like constructed artefacts.'

'This is the only glimpse we get of such features,' Mackendrick said. 'The signal was lost soon after, probably due to storm damage. When I saw this I realised that I had to investigate. Not just send some of my men along, but actually go myself.' He stared from Ten Lee to Bennett. 'You do realise what this might mean, I hope?'

Bennett said, 'Sentient extraterrestrial life. Only, what, the second or third discovered?'

'It depends whether you class the cetaceans of Sirius VI as intelligent,' Mackendrick replied. 'I think the jury's still out on that one. So, if they are what I think they are, the work of intelligent beings, and if they're not extinct, then we might have ourselves some discovery here.'

'That's a lot of ifs,' Ten Lee pointed out.

Mackendrick shrugged. 'I'm willing to take the risk. Are you willing to join me?'

Bennett looked at Ten Lee. Her expression evinced no sign of having witnessed footage that might go down as significant in the history of stellar exploration.

At last she blinked and asked, 'How far is Penumbra from Earth?'

'Almost two thousand light years.'

'So it will take us three, four months to reach?'

Mackendrick nodded. 'About that. Of course, the ship is equipped with suspension units. By subjective elapsed time it'll take us no more than a day or two.'

Ten Lee blinked up at Mackendrick. 'May I ask another question?'

'Go ahead.'

'What I fail to understand,' she said, 'is why you don't send a fully equipped exploration team.'

Mackendrick nodded. 'Valid point, but an exploration

ship and team takes months, sometimes over a year, to equip and crew, especially for a haul as far as this.'

'No one's likely to discover Penumbra in that time,' Bennett pointed out, reasonably.

'No, but then I haven't got a year.' Mackendrick paused, then went on. 'Five years ago when I fell ill my doctors gave me four, five years at best. I'm living on borrowed time. I'll be lucky to last another year. I want to discover intelligent life on Penumbra more than anything else, even if it's the last thing I do. I need to assemble a small crew on a ship I have ready and waiting, and get there as fast as possible. Does that answer your question?'

Ten Lee inclined her head minimally. 'My Rimpoche forecast an outward journey. I will come with you.'

'Bennett?'

'Union rates?' Bennett asked, watching Mackendrick.

The tycoon smiled. 'Damn union rates – a hundred thousand a month. How does that sound?'

Bennett stared at the stilled image of what might have been an alien settlement. 'Count me in.'

Mackendrick switched off the com-screen and slid from the edge of the desk. 'We'll be lighting out on the twenty-sixth, three days from now. Until then we'll meet every day and go through the usual systems checks and routine maintenance. Any questions?'

The twenty-sixth, Bennett thought. My father's funeral. The townspeople of Mojave were going to think him crass and insensitive for not attending. Twenty years ago he had missed Ella's funeral, too – and he tasted again the bitter tang of guilt at the thought. He tried to push the feeling to the back of his mind.

'Right,' Mackendrick was saying. 'Let's call it a day. I need my rest. I'll see you here at ten tomorrow.'

Bennett stepped out into the bright sunlight with a sense of having entered a new chapter of his life. He thought of his father, of Julia . . . At last he was doing something to take himself away from a way of life he had wanted to escape for such a long time, but had been too craven to attempt. He never liked to look too far ahead, or to dream, but at least now he told himself that he just might be able to stop looking back and regretting.

He followed Ten Lee up the steps out of the pit. 'Can I give you a lift anywhere, Ten?'

'Thank you, but I prefer to walk.'

He shrugged. 'See you tomorrow, then.'

He gave a wave and was heading towards the parking lot when Ten Lee called to him.

'Joshua . . .'

He returned to where Ten Lee stood, watching him.

'Joshua, I've been thinking over what Mackendrick told us.'

'And?'

She blinked. 'Why do you think he chose you and me for this mission? He has many good pilots and analysts he might have selected.'

Bennett shrugged. 'Like he said, he thought we were the best. We were available at short notice.'

'Perhaps it has something to do with the fact that this is a dangerous mission. Penumbra is a stormy world.'

'Perhaps. Who knows? I can handle those weather conditions.' He smiled. 'Hey, don't worry, Ten.'

Ten Lee regarded him blankly. 'I'm not worrying, Joshua – just wondering.'

'Whatever you say. Sure I can't offer you a lift?'

But she had turned and was walking off towards the terminal building, a tiny barefoot figure with her rucksack secured on both shoulders.

Over the next couple of days Bennett, Mackendrick and Ten Lee worked on the Cobra, running maintenance checks and systems analyses. On the eve of departure

Bennett recorded a short message of resignation and sent it off to Redwood Station. He expected an immediate reply – Matheson threatening him with legal action for breach of contract. When his com-screen chimed five minutes later, he touched SECRECY. It was not Matheson, but Julia. He elected not to reply.

Just before sunset he steered his car from the garage and drove across the desert. He parked outside the dome where he had grown up and walked around the decrepit habitat to the memorial garden. He thought about summoning Ella's image and talking to her, telling her about the latest turn of events, but he had a better idea. He crossed to the mock-timber bench, knelt and lifted the lid of the seat. Secreted inside was the simulated identity hologram's memory circuit. He lifted it out and moved around the garden collecting the miniature projectors and receivers. Rather than leave Ella here and be without her company for who knows how long, he would take her with him, allow her to share the experience.

When he returned to this dome, he found that Julia had left a recorded message.

'Joshua . . .' She stared out at him, biting her lip. 'I've only just heard about your father. I'm sorry. You should have told me when we met the other day. Look, about what I said. I don't know . . . perhaps I was too harsh.' She paused, considering her words. 'I was wondering . . . can we meet sometime? Perhaps after the funeral?'

Bennett stopped the recording before she finished, wiped the memory and deactivated the screen. Then he sat for a long time in silence and stared out across the darkening desert.

8

Seven days into her new job Rana Rao was still familiarising herself with the ways of the Homicide Division.

For the first five days she had worked noon till ten, going through standard practice and routine with Varma Patel, a sergeant in her fifties who had been in the department for ten years and knew the answer to everything. Varma seemed content to be office-bound, doing her investigations via powerful computer networks and her com-screen. After three days of Varma's company in the stuffy offices, Rana had had a waking nightmare: this would be her in another ten years, gone to fat and happy to see out the rest of her police life working in the claustrophobic confines of the eighth floor. Varma had laughed when Rana admitted that she would find just one year of this kind of work more than enough. 'Don't worry,' the sergeant had confided. 'Vishwanath has you marked out for better things. Investigations, so I'm told.'

'He has? Does that mean I'll get out of this prison some day?'

'Be patient. Learning the ropes takes time. You need to walk before you can fly.'

It seemed that some of her desk-bound colleagues on the eighth floor had hard about Vishwanath's plans for her; either that or they resented her because she was a woman.

A couple of officers made it known that they found her attractive. One afternoon Varma had nudged her and said,

'What do you think of Naz over there? I think you'd make a fine couple, and I'm not the only one. Naz thinks you're the best thing to happen to the department in years.'

Rana had sighed. 'I'm not interested in anyone at the moment. I'm too young to think of anything like that. I need to concentrate on my work.'

A couple of days later Naz had found an excuse to talk to her. It wasn't long before he asked her out to dinner. He was sneering and arrogant even before she refused his offer. 'So it is true what the boys in the computer room say. You really are the virgin queen. Or perhaps you prefer women, ah-cha? What a waste!'

The best course of action, she knew from the past, was to ignore him. She had concentrated on the new computer systems she had to learn, the system of filing and cross-referencing she had had no need for in her old job. Indeed, the more she learned of her new posting, the more she realised it had nothing at all in common with her previous police work. In Child Welfare she had been left alone to get on with her own projects; she had been her own boss with no one constantly looking over her shoulder to check if she was following orders. Here, it seemed that she had to have her every breath okayed by her colleagues. She could not open a file without being briefed by the officer working on the case. It was daunting to have her every idea and initiative stifled by authority. She felt like a schoolchild who would never be allowed out into the real world.

She had spent her third day in the shooting range beneath the police headquarters, learning how to use a handgun on a variety of targets, stationary and moving. At the end of the day she had been handed a body-holster that fitted beneath her jacket, and a small pistol. Despite its size, the gun felt bulky next to her ribs. She had never carried a weapon in Child Welfare, and the thought of actually using it filled her with dread.

On the morning of the sixth day she had attended a seminar on interview technique on the tenth floor. She'd sat through a fascinating two-hour talk on how to go about extracting information from a murder suspect. In the afternoon she'd been ordered down to the fifth floor where a technician was giving a demonstration on what he called the 'crawler', the latest model of forensic robot which investigating officers took with them to the scenes of crime. She'd been picked out to recite what she had learned and to demonstrate the new model, and after initial apprehension she had performed reasonably well. Rana felt that at last she was getting somewhere.

Halfway through her shift on the seventh day, Investigating Officer Vishwanath emerged from his office, made straight for her desk and pulled up a chair.

He was a tall, imposing figure in his sixties, with an eagle's beak of a nose, thin lips that seemed cynical and eyes that had seen everything. He was feared by Rana's colleagues on the eighth floor, and something of their trepidation when in his presence – though Rana had yet to speak to him – had rubbed off on her.

She felt her mouth go dry and her face burn as he regarded her.

'Lieutenant, you come highly recommended from Commissioner Singh. I hope you accord to expectations. How are things at the moment? Settling in?'

She managed barely a nod and a meek 'Yes, sir.'

'Very good. Things a bit different from Child Welfare, no doubt.'

'Very different. Of course the work here is more pressing, but I'm learning.'

'Very good. Oh, and if Naz and his cohorts bother you again, tell them that I'll have them back in the basement quick sharp, ah-cha?'

She nodded, suppressing a smile of delight.

'Have security checked your apartment yet, Lieutenant?'

'No. I didn't know they had to—'

Vishwanath waved. 'Routine procedure. I have the premises of all my staff swept every few months. We're dealing with killers here, don't forget that. In the past, criminals have been known to bug the homes of investigating officers. The next security sweep will be in about a month's time, so your apartment will be searched then, ah-cha?'

Rana nodded.

Vishwanath slapped the desk and stood. 'Oh, and one more thing. There are a few files I'm too busy to look over at the moment, concerning cases I think might be connected. Could you go through them, correlate likely significant factors, and download the files and your report to my terminal before ten?'

'Ah-cha, sir. Right away.'

Vishwanath called over to Naz to send the files to Rana's terminal, nodded at her and strode away. Rana watched him go, aware of the flutter of her heart. Now if someone as mature and polite as Vishwanath were to ask her to dinner . . . She dismissed the thought. She was being stupid, indulging her fantasy of being swept away by a surrogate-father figure.

She glanced across the room at Naz, who looked as if he'd just bitten into a rotten mango.

For the rest of the shift she concentrated on the files describing the investigations, in minute and stomach-turning detail, of eight murders committed within the city limits over the past ten years. In each case the murder victim had been lasered in the head at point-blank range. On the cheek of each victim had been scored a crucifix. The dead were all businessmen – in one case a minor politician – who had been investigated on suspicion of corruption, bribery and drug trafficking.

Rana pored over the reports, downloading data on the

dead men from outside sources for factual corroboration, and made her report two hours later. 'Though it would seem at first glance that these cases are obviously linked,' she began, 'there is the very real possibility that because the second murder was reported in great detail – i.e. the cruciform cutting was mentioned – the third and following murders might very well fall into the category of copy-cat crimes. However, examination of the case material suggests that all the murders are connected . . .' She went on to list her reasons, and only when she completed, signed and downloaded the report to Vishwanath did she wonder if she had come down too vehemently in favour of the single-killer hypothesis.

That night she was unable to sleep for worrying that Vishwanath had found her report shallow and facile. It occurred to her that the notes were old cases presented to her as an initiative test.

The following day she began a new shift pattern: from eight in the evening through to six the following morning. To her dismay there was a message from Vishwanath flashing on her screen when she began work that night. She accepted it with a heavy heart, expecting a reprimand. She read, with relief: 'Excellent report re. the crucifix killer, Lieutenant. We must discuss the details when I have the time.'

It was a quiet shift. The office was all but empty, only Rana and one other officer working at the files. Midnight came and went and Rana experienced the strange isolation of working the night shift. Beyond the long windows of the eighth floor a vast ad-screen floated by, exhorting night-workers and insomniacs to try an ice-cold bottle of Blue Mountain beer.

She worked through the files that had built up over the past few days, assigning them to various desks. For the past week she had promised herself that she would slip down to Howrah bridge after work and look in on Vandita and the others, see how they were keeping and how Private Khosla was getting on with his new posting. But always at the end of every shift she had gone home and slept – or, in the case of last night, not slept – too exhausted to brave the crush and look for her friends. Tomorrow, she told herself. In the morning I'll leave here, keep myself awake with a strong coffee, and go see the kids.

Her thoughts were interrupted by the main door crashing open and Vishwanath running across to his office. He emerged seconds later carrying a com-board and speaking hurriedly to forensic, head cocked to one side, for all the world as if he were talking to himself. He paused long enough to gesture impatiently at Rana. 'Ah-cha, you, Lieutenant. Come with me!'

Rana stood and crossed the room, then dashed back to her desk for her com-board, grabbed it and gave chase, disbelieving. She hurried down the corridor and joined Vishwanath, Naz and the forensic team in the elevator.

Vishwanath nodded at her from a great height. 'Pleased you could make it, Lieutenant,' he said, but his acerbity was sweetened by a smile.

Naz pointedly ignored her.

'It seems as though we have another crucifix killing,' Vishwanath continued as they descended. 'The governor is getting impatient to have the crimes cleaned up. He says it "doesn't reflect well on the image of the city". Personally speaking, I am more concerned about catching the killer in order to save lives in future.'

They stepped from the elevator and into the underground car-park. The transport situation was a far cry from what she had been used to in Child Welfare. Two new squad cars were waiting, engines running. Vishwanath signalled for herself and Naz to join him in the first car, while two forensic officers took the second.

As the driver swept them up the ramp and on to the midnight streets of Calcutta, quieter at this time but still busy by the standards of most cities, Vishwanath turned in the passenger seat. 'I hope your com-boards are loaded with the details of the previous crucifix killings?'

Rana held up her board in reply.

Something in Naz's hesitation gave her an exquisite surge of cruel pleasure. 'I . . . was in the process—'

Vishwanath gave Naz a look that cut him dead. 'I don't want excuses, Lieutenant. Copy the details from Rana's board. On second thoughts, I think Rana should do it for you.'

Uncomfortable with her commanding officer's overt favouritism, but at the same time enjoying Naz's discomfort, Rana took his board and connected it to her own. Seconds later she had downloaded a copy of all the relevant data on the murders, plus a copy of her own report for good measure.

'The killing occurred in Pathan,' Vishwanath said, 'north of here at the Hindustan Plaza hotel. We have yet to learn the identity of the victim.'

Rana entered the details into her com-board, then sat back as the squad car carried them into the exclusive district of foreign embassies and consulates. They passed grand colonial buildings of white brickwork, like so many wedding cakes, set in lawns as vast as cricket pitches. There was so much unoccupied space in this suburb that Rana found it hard to believe they were in the same city; just two miles south of here was the teeming, chaotic heart of Calcutta. This place filled her with an uneasy feeling, like agoraphobia. She much preferred the familiar hurly-burly of the city centre and the surrounding slums, where she had spent so much of her life.

The Hindustan Plaza was a fifty-storey obelisk of sheet obsidian reflecting the distant lights of central Calcutta and the occasional floating ad-screen. There was much frantic activity in the forecourt: local police cars, beacons pulsing, an ambulance, redundant in the event, all watched by a gaggle of curious guests and uniformed staff.

Rana followed Vishwanath, aware that the little group of investigators and forensic scientists was the centre of attention. A local sergeant rushed up to Vishwanath, almost doubling himself up in obeisance, followed by the hotel manager who gabbled something about an 'unfortunate incident' and how 'this had never happened under my managership before'.

'I'm delighted to hear it,' Vishwanath replied. 'Now if you would show me and my team to the room in question . . .'

They rode in the elevator to the fourth floor. Rana stepped out on to a plush red carpet and followed the dancing manager and the sergeant along the corridor. They came to an open doorway. A pulsing low-powered laser cordon barred the way.

Vishwanath said, 'Who discovered the body?'

'The maid, sir,' the sergeant replied. 'She noticed that the door was slightly open. When she looked in . . . This was at eleven.'

'No one else has entered the room since then?'

'Only the hotel manager and my constable, sir. He confirmed that the victim was dead and contacted me immediately.'

Vishwanath nodded and signalled to the two forensic officers. They knelt before the open doorway and removed two crawlers from silver sterile bags, then placed them on the carpet. The crawlers dashed off into the room like hyperactive turtles.

'Do you have the name of the victim?' Vishwanath asked the hotel manager.

'Ah-cha. He was one Ali Bhakor. He was an eminent businessman of my very own acquaintance, sir.'

Rana entered the dead man's name into her com-board and peered through the doorway. She could see along the corridor into the lounge, and the chair upon which the late Ali Bhakor slouched. Only the man's left arm could be seen, hanging limply over the side of the chair.

'Have you accounted for Bhakor's movements last night?' Vishwanath asked the sergeant.

'Ah-cha, sir. I've detailed his known actions since six. Also I've interviewed the maid and bell-boy.' He proffered his com-board, and first Vishwanath, then Naz and Rana downloaded the relevant file.

While the crawlers gathered forensic evidence, Rana took the opportunity to read the meagre file. Bhakor had arrived at the hotel at six the day before, had dined alone at seven and returned to his room at eight. He had spoken to no one during that time other than hotel staff.

The crawlers scuttled back over the threshold and were retrieved by the forensic scientists. They examined the read-outs and then passed the crawlers to Vishwanath, Naz and Rana. Rana downloaded their findings into her com-board and cross-referenced the data with that compiled by the crawlers from the scenes of the other so-called 'crucifix killings'. She detected a number of possible correlations. Identical cloth fibres had been discovered at three of the crime scenes.

She reported her findings to Vishwanath.

'It's a slim connection, Lieutenant. The fibres might be of a cloth commonly worn. I want them checked and a full forensic report on type, origin, availability, et cetera.' He killed the laser cordon. 'Ah-cha, let's take a closer look.'

They passed into the room.

The forensic officers filmed the scene and the murder

victim and then examined the body, taking tissue samples and readings with instruments unfamiliar to Rana.

Ali Bhakor sat slumped in the armchair, arms dangling over the side, legs outstretched, his fat chin resting on his chest. There was something pathetic and undignified about his posture that was even more grotesque than the wound that had killed him. The right side of his face was blackened with the impact of the laser charge, but the left side was unburned and wore a strange expression of startled surprise. Rana had expected to be repulsed by the sight, but the strange fact was that it seemed no more sickening than the cosmetic effects of a hundred sensational holodramas.

Carved into the padded flesh of his left cheek was the bloody shape of a crucifix. Something about the mutilation, perhaps the sight of the blood or the fact that the crucifix was the killer's cynical calling card, seemed to Rana more ghastly than the laser burn.

She noticed the com-screen in the corner of the room. After receiving clearance from forensic, she accessed GlobaLink and typed in her commands. Ten minutes later she had compiled a file of news reports and court cases concerning the dead man. She downloaded the file into her com-board and returned to Vishwanath.

'I've found out a little about Ali Bhakor, sir.'

'Go ahead.'

'Like all the other victims of the killer – if they do share a common killer – Bhakor had a criminal record.' She passed her com-board to Vishwanath. 'Two years ago he was implicated in the import of illegal substances from Burma – heroin-plus and slash. Ten years ago he was jailed for a year for smuggling precious gems from a colony world.'

'Do you draw any inferences, Lieutenant?'

'Well, obviously the branding of the corpse with the crucifix . . . Perhaps the killer sees himself or herself as taking part in some kind of moral crusade to clean up the city.'

'That's certainly a possibility.'

'Or, perhaps these are vengeance killings. All the victims might have opposed the killer in some way in the past, perhaps with business deals.'

'When you get back to HQ I want you to check all the business dealings conducted by all the victims over the past ten years – and if you find nothing, go back twenty years. Also, if these are vengeance rather than morally motivated killings, reconsider the implications of the crucifix. It'll be a complex, time-consuming task, but this is priority, Lieutenant. Drop everything else and concentrate on this case.'

'Ah-cha, sir.'

A forensic officer stood up after examining the corpse. 'Standard 100 laser charge, sir. Might have been any one of a dozen types of weapon available over the counter. Just like all the charges used on the other victims. We estimate that he died between eight and eight-thirty yesterday evening.'

Rana moved to the window and stared at the screen of her com-board, reading through her notes on the other killings. She knew that somewhere among the morass of data and evidence were the facts that would lead to the solution of the puzzle. They would not leap out at her, but had to be considered minutely from every angle.

She looked up from the board. 'Sir.'

Vishwanath lowered his own board. 'Lieutenant?'

'It just occurred to me. The scenes of the crimes – there is a link.'

Across the room, she noticed Naz look up with irritable curiosity.

Vishwanath fingered the touch-pad of his com-board, frowned at the screen. 'I don't see . . .'

Rana wondered whether she had been mistaken in mentioning this. 'Well, the connection is tenuous, to say the least. There were three hotels, three parks, a public toilet, a nature reserve and a golf course.'

'And the connection, Lieutenant?'

'None of the victims was killed at home or at their offices. Maybe—'

She stopped. She had just called up a street map of the city, and positioned the crime scenes on the map. She stared at the screen of her com-board.

'What is it, Lieutenant?'

Silently, Rana held out her com-board to Vishwanath, who considered the revealed pattern on the street map. The locations of the murders, joined like a dot-to-dot, formed a crucifix spanning the city limits of Calcutta.

'So, it looks like they're connected, Lieutenant.' Vishwanath paused, staring at the screen. He handed it back to her. 'What do you notice about the crucifix?'

She stared at the cross, laid over the city on a roughly north–south axis. She shook her head. 'I'm sorry . . .'

'It isn't complete. Look – the vertical bar is made up of six points. The lateral bar comprises two points to the left, but only one to the right. There is a point missing, to the right.' He stabbed a forefinger at the place where the next point should logically follow. 'A region of slums to the east of the city, Lieutenant. If our killer has a symmetrical mind, then perhaps this is where he will strike next.'

'And if he isn't symmetrical,' Rana added, 'then it might be anywhere at these three points, north, south or west.'

'I'll have patrols concentrate on those areas,' Vishwanath said. He stared at the screen. 'Also, for the killer to form this crucifix suggests that he arranged to meet his victims at the various locations. It's hardly likely that he'd just happen upon people he considered evil-doers at these points.

Which suggests that he must have known, or at the very least had contact with, the victims to arrange a meeting.'

Rana nodded. 'I'll run checks and interviews with the victims' contacts to see if they received calls from a common acquaintance.'

'Excellent, Lieutenant.' He gave a slight smile, and Rana felt as if she had received a medal of honour from the president himself.

Ten minutes later Vishwanath decided that they had done all they could at the scene of the crime. The body was loaded on to a stretcher and taken away, the room sealed for a more thorough forensic examination later.

As they left the room, Vishwanath said to Naz, 'I want you to stay here, Lieutenant. Interview the staff. The usual routine. Download the file to my terminal by noon.'

Naz saluted, trying not to let his disappointment show at being given the donkey work.

Vishwanath and Rana descended in the elevator, moved through the crowd still gathered outside the entrance and climbed into the squad car.

Rana's shift was due to end shortly after she arrived back at headquarters. She spent a further hour making her report, downloaded it to Vishwanath, and asked if she could leave. She was tired after the long shift and the mental effort of collating her report. Seconds later the reply flashed on her com-screen: 'Off you go, Lieutenant. Well done.'

She took the elevator down to the ground floor and paused on the steps. She recalled her earlier resolution to visit Vandita and the other kids when her shift ended. But the sun was rising, burning up the grey mist of dawn, and the kids would be up and at work by now. She would call on them tomorrow.

She left the police headquarters and began the short walk home through the rapidly increasing heat of another Calcutta day.

9

Bennett and Mackendrick were checking supplies and equipment in the cargo hold when the Cobra gave a sudden jolt. The sensation of riding an elevator indicated that the floor of the repair pit was rising to meet the deck of the spaceport. Bennett grabbed the tail-gate of the open-topped transporter, swaying with the motion.

'If that's it down here we'll join Ten,' Mackendrick said.

They took the lift-plate to the upper deck, standing side by side in silence. Mackendrick was wearing a black flight-suit, so tight that it shrink-wrapped his thin frame, emphasising his prominent rib-cage and scooped pelvis. Since learning of the tycoon's illness, Bennett had never been able to look at Mackendrick without thinking that soon, perhaps within a year, the man would be dead. He wondered how one could go on living with the knowledge that death was imminent. He thought of his father, and how he had coped with the fact of his approaching end. Then he realised that right at this minute, in Mojave Town, the remains of his father were being interred in the grave garden. He recalled his father's eyes, as he died, accusing him, and he felt a sudden and painful stab of guilt.

The flight-deck was finished in ubiquitous regulation black: jet carpet, couches and curving walls, the better for the pilots to apprehend the dozens of illuminated read-outs and screens. Through the delta viewscreen Bennett watched a tug reverse towards the nose of the Cobra, engage grabs and take the weight of the ship. Slowly they trundled forward, past the terminal building, towards the vacant blast-pad and posse of waiting technicians and mechanics.

Mackendrick lay on the engineer's couch to the rear of the flight-deck, and carefully buckled his thin frame into the safety harness. Ten Lee was already strapped into her couch, the wraparound command console pulled close. Her face, surrounded by a bulging flight helmet with the visor screen down, was a study in emotionless concentration as she cycled through the pre-flight programs.

Bennett took his helmet from the pilot's couch and pulled it down over his head, feeling the familiar comfort of its snug fit. The irritating chatter of a flight controller played in his right ear; he modulated the noise below the threshold of audibility. They were still one hour from lift-off. He would rather be alone with his thoughts until then.

He climbed into his couch, sinking into its padded depths. Everything about the Cobra, from major mechanical specifics right down to minor design features, was superior to anything else he'd flown over the years. Mackendrick had spared no expense when fitting and equipping the ship.

He pulled the horseshoe console towards him, locking it in place. He flipped down his visor and went through the running program with Ten Lee. This was, he realised, more a routine process to soothe his pre-flight nerves. During his fifteen years in space he had never flown trans-c. In fact, the furthest he had ever travelled was to Mars on a short vacation ten years ago. He had every confidence in his own ability to fly the Cobra, especially when they arrived at Penumbra and he had to take them through the storm-riven atmosphere – and he knew that he could not hope for a better ship or operating system. But the fact remained that they were embarking on a faster-than-light voyage through two thousand light years of unexplored space. He found it hard to grasp the enormity of what was about to happen. The fact of the flight alone was mind-numbing, without considering what they might find when they finally made landfall on Penumbra.

He raised his visor and glanced across at Ten Lee. She was reading off a string of equations with the calm of someone to whom this reality was nothing more than a passing illusion.

They reached the blast-pad and the tug disengaged. Hydraulic gantries took the weight of the ship and eased it to the vertical. Bennett tipped, staring up through the viewscreen at the bright blue sky.

He opened communications with the control tower and for the next half hour went through the process of program checks and data monitoring. Through the side-screen he noticed the bowsers and trucks carrying the mechanics and technicians beetling away across the tarmac. The sight filled him with a feeling of isolation he recalled from ten years ago, when he regularly piloted shuttles from ground to orbit.

One minute before lift-off the main engines engaged. Control counted down. Bennett laid his head back against the rest and gripped the arms of the couch. He glanced back at Mackendrick, strapped into the engineer's couch. The tycoon sketched a brief smile and gave a thumbs-up gesture.

Seconds later the Cobra surged from the blast-pad, the pressure of ascent pushing Bennett further into his seat. His head rattled with the vibration of the rapid climb, blurring his vision. He thought of the sightseers in the observation gallery, the kids gasping at the spectacular pyrotechnics of blast-off.

In his helmet the tinny voice of the controller signed off. 'Good luck Bennett, Theneka. She's all yours.'

They climbed and turned. Through the sidescreen Bennett made out the vast sweep of the western seaboard, and then the great ochre plain of the Mojave, punctuated with the verdant circles of a dozen townships and settlements. From this high it appeared so artificial, impossible to conceive that down below normal people were conducting normal, everyday lives.

He turned his head and smiled at Mackendrick. 'You okay, Mack?'

It was all the old tycoon could do to lift a hand in silent assent. Bennett hoped Mackendrick would be equal to the stress of the take-off.

Ten Lee's voice interrupted his thoughts. 'Twenty seconds until phase-out.'

'Check,' he said, glancing at his screen. The system was running smoothly.

'Ten . . . nine . . . eight . . .'

They were almost at the altitude where it would be safe to effect the transfer. Then the Schulmann-Dearing would cut in, tearing the fabric of localised space with such concentrated energy that, had the phase-out been effected on the ground, the area of the port around the ship would have been destroyed.

Bennett felt a stab of apprehension. Hell, but in seconds he would be travelling faster than the speed of light, this tiny shell-like vehicle cancelling the laws of physics and hurtling three frail human beings to the very edge of the galaxy.

He thought of Julia. He almost wished he was with her now, suffering her barbed recriminations.

'Two . . . one . . . transition,' Ten Lee said.

The deafening rumble of the main engines cut out suddenly, to be replaced with an eerie almost-silence. As his hearing adjusted he was aware that the ship was ringing with a low, almost subliminal hum, like the constantly dying note of a struck tuning fork.

He peered through the viewscreen. Where the thin blue of the stratosphere should have been, or the familiar scatter of stars, the scene was unique and strange: the stars had turned to streamers and were hosing towards and around the ship like a bombardment of polychromatic flak. He was aware of a sensation of abstraction; he felt at several removes from the reality around him, like a patient in a post-operative daze.

Ten Lee pulled off her helmet. She stared through the viewscreen in silent wonder, her open-mouthed regard unusually expressive. 'Some scholars say that the void is the physical embodiment of the state to which we all aspire, Joshua.'

'Josh,' Mackendrick said from behind them. 'If you and the Dalai Lama wouldn't mind helping me to my unit . . .'

Bennett unfastened himself and moved over to Mackendrick. The old man looked pale, as if the stress of take-off and phase-out had been too much. He could hardly stand, and it took Bennett and Ten Lee supporting each arm to assist him from the flight-deck. They moved down the corridor to the suspension chamber. The three suspension units – long silver containers resembling nothing so much as coffins – stood side by side in the centre of the room.

Mackendrick lay down in the form-shaped padding and sighed as sub-dermal capillaries eased themselves into his flesh. The transparent cover hummed shut over his unconscious body. In four months, when phase-out of the void was accomplished, he would be woken up.

Bennett was due to come out of suspension at the mid-point stage of the voyage, to assist Ten Lee in routine systems checks. Ten Lee had requested that she remain unsuspended for the duration of the flight. She wished to meditate. She had even brought along meagre rations to last her until landfall, vegetarian fare consisting of lentil bread and soya cakes, even though the ship was equipped with pre-packed food supplies.

Bennett left the suspension chamber and moved along the corridor to his berth. He lifted the simulated identity hologram from his bag and placed it on the bedside unit. He had never talked to Ella's ghost anywhere other than the memorial garden; it was strange to think that he could commune with her so far from home. He moved around the small room, setting up the projectors and receivers at strategic positions. Then he sat on the narrow bunk and placed his finger-tips on the touch-sensitive module.

She appeared before him, sitting cross-legged in the middle of the room, and his heart lurched. The SIH had assessed the passage of time and changed Ella's style of dress accordingly. It must have been evening back on Earth, bedtime, for his sister was wearing her crimson pyjamas.

She leapt up and stared around the room. She looked at Bennett and beamed. 'Hi, Josh.' A frown. 'Where are we?' She ran to the viewscreen, reached up on tip-toe, leaned forward and peered out.

Bennett watched her, some unnameable emotion, poignant almost beyond endurance, swelling in his chest. The sight of her here, out of the usual context of the memorial garden, served to heighten the reality of her image and so emphasise the fact of her non-existence. Bennett was reminded of the many places she had never been, the many experiences she had never lived to enjoy.

She turned to him, a look of wonder transfixed on her pretty features. 'Are we in space, Josh? Are we?'

'We're aboard a Cobra lightship, Ella. You always said you wanted to go into space.'

'Hey!' she exclaimed, turning to the viewscreen and staring out at the flickering tracer of starlight streaming around the contours of the ship. 'This is fantastic, Josh! Thanks a million times!'

She jumped on to the padded seat before the viewscreen, turned so that she could stare out at the void and glance from time to time at Bennett. She hugged her legs and gave a conspiratorial grin. 'Is this my birthday present, Josh?'

'Your birthday?'

He smiled, caught. Her birthday was on the twenty-seventh, tomorrow, and in the past he had always avoided communion with Ella on her birthday, the anniversary bringing to mind thoughts and memories too painful to relive. The SIH was programmed so that it would present a never-ageing Ella, an Ella forever ten years old and full of health. Shortly after her tenth birthday, more than twenty years ago, she had died.

Bennett remembered the birthday party at the hospital, the forced cheer of the occasion, the almost desperate desire of his mother and father to celebrate the day as if nothing was amiss. But Ella had been woozy with powerful sedatives, increasingly fraught from having to endure the protracted, almost desperate festivities of parents too scared to admit to themselves that this birthday would likely be her very last. Bennett had bought her a present, spent much of his savings on a small computer diary, perhaps with the subconscious hope that she would be able to complete the year's entries. But she had been too tired to open it. A few days after her death, Bennett had walked out into the desert and buried it in the sand.

'This is the best birthday present I've ever had, Josh! Are we going to Mars?' Her eyes widened at another thought. 'Are we going to Jupiter, Josh? All the way out to Jupiter!'

Bennett smiled. 'Even further, Ella. We're travelling faster than light towards the Rim of the galaxy.'

'Far out!' she breathed, fingering a strand of hair from her eyes and gazing out at the light show.

Bennett watched her, understanding now why he had summoned her.

'Ella.'

She turned, still smiling.

'The last time I spoke to you . . .' he began.

She frowned with the effort of recollection. 'Oh, four days ago – you'd just got back from Redwood Station, hadn't you? And you said Daddy wanted . . . euthanalia?'

'Euthanasia,' Bennett said. 'I visited him that day at the hospital. I was with him when he died. I . . .' He knew why the admission was so hard to make. 'I didn't go to his funeral, Ella. It was today, the day we left Earth. Do you understand, Ella?'

She nodded, very serious. 'Of course I do. It's okay, Josh. Daddy would have understood.'

'Do you think it matters, if you miss a person's funeral?'

She pulled her thinking-cap face. At last she smiled. 'I don't think so,' she said, and with what might have been little-girl logic or computer sophistry went on: 'I mean, the person doesn't know you weren't there, do they?'

He stared at her. He recalled what had happened, all those years ago, when he had returned from the desert after burying her stupid, useless diary. His mother had given him a suit to change into and told him that they were to attend Ella's funeral, which seemed to Bennett in his youthful ignorance an event that could only compound his sense of loss. How could he have known

106

that the funerary ritual was a necessary part of the grieving process, a cathartic experience that had to be endured?

Now he reached out to the touch-pad. Ella, in the process of swinging down from the seat, froze in mid-leap, one leg pointing to the floor, her mouth open to speak to him.

He stared at her suspended image and, involuntarily, found himself telling her: 'The day of your funeral, Ella . . . It was so hot. I still couldn't believe you were dead. I mean, I knew, intellectually. I knew I'd never see you again, but something inside me just couldn't accept the fact. I suppose it was too terrible an idea to grasp.' He paused. 'It was so hot and the thought of you in that coffin . . . They were going to cremate you, and I couldn't take it. I'm sorry, Ella. I'm sorry I didn't go to your funeral.' He paused again, wondering why he had waited until now to admit the guilt he had kept buried for years.

They had driven to the grave garden in Mojave, and followed the procession as Ella's coffin was carried on an electric bier to the crematorium. At the sight of the building, pumping out the smoke of the previous crema-tion, something had snapped within him and he had vomited down his suit. He had complained of stomach pains and doubled over for effect, anything to be spared the trial of experiencing the funeral, the scattering of his sister's ashes in the pit where a tree would be planted in her name. It had worked: a family friend had rushed him to her nearby house, where he had washed himself and changed into clothes too big for him, and said that he needed to lie down. From the settee in the lounge of the stranger's house he had watched the smoke rise above the tree-tops.

He looked up, suddenly aware of a presence. Ten Lee was standing in the open doorway, staring at him. He wondered how long she had been there, how much she had seen.

'I'm sorry,' she said. 'I was passing . . .'

'It's okay.'

With her diminutive stature and scarlet flight-suit, she was a strange mirror image of Ella in her bright red pyjamas.

Ten Lee was staring at the image of Ella, frozen mid-leap. 'Who is this?'

Bennett stared at Ten Lee, challenging. 'She was my sister, Ella.'

Ten Lee nodded, the composure of her features suggesting neither censure nor comprehension. 'Was?'

'She died a long time ago, when she was ten.'

He reached out to the touch-pad. Ella completed her leap and landed on the floor before him. She saw Ten Lee and smiled. 'Hi there. Who are you?'

Ten Lee regarded Ella, considering her response. She looked past the image at Bennett. 'Joshua, please turn it off.'

'Ella,' he said. 'I'll see you later, okay?' He reached out and touched the pad and the image of his sister winked out of existence.

'What?' he said to Ten Lee, his aggression anticipating her criticism.

She gestured at the SIH unit. 'Why, Joshua?'

'It helps,' he told her. 'We were close when we were kids. Ella was a good friend. When she died . . .' He paused, gathering his thoughts. 'I know she isn't really Ella, but she's the next best thing. Over the years we've developed a relationship that I value.'

'Even now?'

Bennett nodded. 'Even now. She reminds me of the times we had together.'

'Joshua, we all live in the shadow of the fact of death. It

108

is the purpose of one's life to come to some acceptance of its inevitability, so that the idea of it does not destroy us. We must come to some accommodation of the fact of our own mortality.' She paused, her tipped eyes regarding him. 'Joshua, you can't accept the idea of your own death if you fail to accept the death of loved ones, if you cling to this . . . this fantasy.'

'It's all I have,' he whispered, staring at her.

'It is all you have because you have never given it up.'

Seconds elapsed, and when next Bennett looked up he saw that Ten Lee had slipped from the room, leaving him to contemplate the meaning of her words, as a disciple tries to unravel the conundrum of a *koan*. In the past he would have wished for sleep to claim him, the refuge from contemplation of his failings and weakness. Aboard the Cobra there was a means of oblivion far more effective than mere sleep.

He quickly left the room and moved to the chamber containing the suspension units. At his touch the lid slipped open and he lay down inside. His flesh crept to the touch of the sub-dermals. He might have felt apprehension had he given himself time to contemplate the fact of this, his first time in suspension, but all he sought was peace from his thoughts, and in seconds he was unconscious.

Later he thought that he had dreamed, but in suspension dreams were impossible. The workings of the mind were effectively stopped, metabolic processes halted. What he did recall were the memories and images that flooded his mind once the unit returned him to semi-consciousness; the dreams that filled the hours as he slowly became aware of himself, some two months later.

In this waking period he experienced a series of fractured images: his father, bizarrely dressed in the grey VR suit, walking through the grave garden behind Ella's coffin; then Ella herself, in pyjamas, running into the desert and frantically scrabbling through the hot sand in search of her buried diary. The pain of this final image tore a scream from his throat. He sat up quickly, shrugging the massage pads from his arms. He swung his legs free of their soothing ministrations and sat on the edge of the unit, holding his head in his hands and breathing deeply.

Two months had elapsed, he knew, but it seemed no more than minutes since he had left his room and given himself to the suspension unit. He felt an ache in his bones and he was overcome with a terrible weariness.

He stood, reaching for the wall to support himself. His vision swam and his head pounded with a severe, persistent throbbing, like migraine. He staggered from the room and crossed the corridor to the shower units.

Hot needles of water restored sensation to his body. He stretched, easing the pain from his muscles. He became aware that he was hungry and thirsty. After standing below the drier, he dressed in a fresh flight-suit and fetched a self-heating tray of food from storage. He ate in his room, wanting the reassuring company of Ella, but telling himself that he would appreciate her more if he waited until he had run through the checks with Ten Lee.

After eating, feeling better for the shower and the meal, he made his way to the flight-deck. Ten Lee was seated in the lotus position before the viewscreen, staring out at the streaming stars.

He tried to detect any change in the void surrounding the ship; he wondered if perhaps the elongated lights of the stars were less tightly packed here, the multi-colours fainter. It was hard to tell. The almost inaudible bass note still filled the ship, noticeable more in his solar plexus as a constant low vibration.

Ten Lee saw his reflection in the viewscreen and without turning said, 'Joshua.'

It seemed just two minutes since they had spoken in his room; he wondered if she would mention his reliance on the holographic Ella. Then he reminded himself that for Ten Lee two months had elapsed. She would have had much more to occupy her mind during that time.

'I checked on Mack from time to time, Joshua.'

'How is he?'

She smiled. 'Sleeping peacefully.'

She unfolded her knotted legs, stood and climbed into the co-pilot's couch. 'We're over halfway to the Rim, Joshua.'

'How's it been?'

'Peaceful. I have learnt much. I think the practice of meditating in the void can be recommended. I seemed to attain a greater appreciation of sunyata.'

'I'm pleased for you,' Bennett muttered. 'Shall we get this over with?'

For the next hour they cycled through the series of checks, calling off figures and read-outs to each other. Everything was going according to plan: they were on course, ahead of schedule, and the Schulmann-Dearing propulsion unit was performing at optimum. They were due to phase into the G5/13 star system in a little under six weeks.

The checks over, Bennett pushed the wraparound console away and stretched. 'Sure you're okay here on your own, Ten?'

She blinked at him. 'Why shouldn't I be?'

'I don't know. Don't you get lonely?'

She shook her head. 'I never get lonely, Joshua. Loneliness is just another one of your strange Western concepts.'

'You don't need anyone?'

111

'I am trying to go beyond need.'

Bennett thought of the times in the past when loneliness had suffocated him with a feeling of inescapability like claustrophobia. He recalled the years after Ella's death, when there had been no one out there who understood or sympathised. He wondered how he had survived without going mad.

He stared at Ten Lee. 'I'll leave you to it,' he said. 'See you in six weeks.'

She made no response. Her gaze was fixed on the void.

He moved down the corridor to his room. He sat on his bunk, staring at the touch-pad. He would talk to Ella for a while, then catch some regular sleep for a few hours before returning to the suspension unit.

He reached out and pressed the touch-pad.

Ella appeared in the middle of the floor, lying on her back and staring up at the ceiling. She was wearing a pale green gown, which Bennett was slow to recognise. A hospital gown, he realised with bewilderment.

'Joshua,' she said in a small voice.

'Ella?'

'I don't feel well.'

He stared at her. She was no longer the impossibly pretty, elfin-faced creature the hologram usually projected. Her face was pale and elongated, her eyes large, staring.

'Joshua . . .' she said, a note of appeal in her voice.

'Ella, get up. Stop playing games.'

His mind was racing. The module had never done this before. Always Ella had been radiantly healthy, full of energy and optimism. Then he noticed her hair. It was thin, straggling. Her pale scalp showed through the threadbare tresses.

Bennett slipped off the bunk and sat on the floor beside her. More than anything he wanted to reach out, take her

112

hand and comfort her. Emotion blocked his throat, hot and raw.

'I know what's happening, Joshua. We can't live for ever, can we?'

'Ella . . .'

'I've enjoyed our times together. We've had some good fun, haven't we? All those talks. Your stories of space. And coming here, for my birthday. That was really good.'

'Ella. You'll be fine, really. You'll get better.'

She gave a weak smile. 'Not this time, Joshua,' she said, staring at him. 'You see we all must accept death, our own, those of the people we love.'

Only then did he begin to understand. He stared at her, tried to protest.

'You'll soon be on your own, Josh. You must accept what is happening to me. Let go and lead your own life.'

She smiled and reached out, and Bennett lifted his own hand and reached for her, and their finger-tips met and meshed, and Bennett felt nothing.

As he watched, Ella's narrow rib-cage ceased its steady rise and fall, and her mouth opened with a final sigh, and her head slipped to one side.

Bennett wanted to cry out, in anger and grief.

He stared. Something was appearing around the still, silent image of Ella. He made out the steady upward growth of plush pink padding, of polished rosewood. The hologram of the coffin soon enclosed the body of his sister, pale now in death.

As he watched, the coffin and the body burst into bright flame, which grew and flared and then died, and soon exhausted itself, guttering out to leave nothing.

He closed his eyes, too drained even to weep. He experienced a surge of anger, directed at the young boy he had been, the coward who had missed his sister's funeral.

At last he stood, wondering how he might face Ten Lee, what he might say to her. He left his room and made his way down the corridor.

She sat on the floor of the flight-deck in the lotus position, the soiled soles of her feet upturned, thumbs and index fingers forming perfect circles. Her eyes were open, watching him.

He leaned against the wall, slid down and sat on his haunches. He felt unutterably weary, drained of all emotion. He tried to detect in Ten Lee's pacific visage some trace of censure or compassion.

'What now, Ten?' he asked.

She lifted her shoulders in an expressive shrug, maintained her posture. 'You have a choice, Joshua. We always have choices. It is the choices we make that determine how we regard ourselves.'

He shook his head wearily. 'I don't understand what the hell you're talking about, Ten. What choice do I have?'

'I made a copy of the old Ella program. You can have it, and resume your relationship with the hologram. Or you can leave it in my keeping to dispose of later. The choice is yours. I am saying nothing to persuade you one way or the other, and I will abide by your decision.'

He hung his head. 'I don't know. I just don't know.'

'Then go, Joshua, and make your decision later,' and she closed her eyes and resumed her meditation.

After perhaps a minute, Bennett pushed himself to his feet and hurried down the corridor to the suspension chamber. His thoughts rang with her words, the need to decide. He knew what he should do, he knew very well, but the spirit was weak and habit was hard to break.

He lay down in his unit and closed his eyes, and oblivion claimed him.

This time, upon awakening, he was beset by images of

114

flames, and beyond the flames Ella's face staring out at him and calling his name. He reached out for her, towards her illusory fingers, but as fast as he approached her she seemed to retreat, smiling sadly at him.

He awoke in a sweat, her words ringing in his ears. He swung himself upright and sat on the side of the unit, massaging sensation back into his arms. As the minutes elapsed, so the images faded, became nebulous and increasingly more difficult to recall. He was left, as he made his way to the showers, with an elusive sensation of loss somewhere deep within him.

After showering he moved to the flight-deck, expecting to find Ten Lee there and not relishing the encounter. He found only Mackendrick, lying on the engineer's couch. He looked frail; the months in the suspension unit seemed to have aged him, even though Bennett knew that the tycoon had aged not one second during the flight.

'Where's Ten?' Bennett asked.

'In her room.'

Mackendrick eased himself into a sitting position and Bennett sat down on the end of the couch.

'How do you feel?'

Bennett shook his head. 'I never realised how much suspension takes out of you. I feel like I've just had major surgery.'

'What happened to your body was even more radical than surgery, Josh. We were cryogenically suspended, maintained on a sophisticated life-support system for almost four months, and then revived. No wonder we feel like shit.'

Bennett smiled. 'You okay?'

'I'll live.' Mackendrick glanced at him and laughed. 'For a little longer, anyway.'

Bennett saw that the old man was holding a pix; he'd

been staring at it in silence when Bennett entered. Now Mackendrick passed it to him. The pix showed Mackendrick's wife, Naheed, sitting on the porch of a big colonial house, smiling at the camera. Bennett passed it back.

'I miss her, Bennett. Even after twelve years. When we knew there was nothing we could do, I financed research into how the suspension units might be utilised to preserve life. Sustain terminally ill people indefinitely, until a cure was found. Of course it can't be done. Oh, my scientists pushed the boundaries back a bit – the units can be used on trans-c flight for up to a year now, before living tissue starts to corrupt. Twelve years ago it was only six month, but that was a small gain. Nothing could be done to help Naheed, or the millions like her.'

'You never remarried?'

'Too busy, Bennett. Threw myself into my work. Never met the right woman. No one could replace Naheed. I suppose I shouldn't have compared, but . . .'

Bennett found himself saying, 'We can't hold on to the past, Mack.'

'Suppose you're right, but sometimes it's the only thing to hold on to. Sita, my daughter . . .'

Bennett glanced at the old man. He was pulling something from the breast pocket of his flight-suit. He passed a second pix to Bennett. This one showed the head and shoulders of a young woman, presumably Sita, very much like her mother.

Bennett recalled that Mackendrick had said he was no longer in contact with his daughter.

Mackendrick was shaking his head. 'When I said that the past is the only thing to hold on to, I meant that sometimes things happen, things that are hard to understand or believe. They leave you wishing that it might have happened somehow differently. You hold on to the past you knew before *it* happened.'

116

Bennett waited, not wanting to force the old man to talk of things so obviously a source of pain and regret. Filled with a sense of foreboding, he returned the pix of the young woman.

Mackendrick smiled. 'This isn't an actual image of a real person, Bennett. It's computer-generated, taken from pix of Sita when she was nine. It's how she probably would look now.'

Bennett found his voice. 'You mean, your daughter died?'

He wondered why Mackendrick had kept computer-aged images of Sita. Perhaps, he thought, for the same reason that I rely on the hologram of Ella.

Mackendrick was shaking his head. 'It was thirteen years ago, a year before Naheed passed on. I was working at my offices in Calcutta. Putting in a lot of time. Looking back I realise I neglected Sita. I hardly saw her during that period. She was looked after by a nanny. She was just ten at the time.'

Mackendrick paused there, staring through the viewscreen at the flickering void.

'I was at the office when the break-in happened. Sita was in her room, her nanny asleep in another part of the house.' He paused again. 'They took some things from the safe in my study – nothing that valuable, as it happened. The shortest way from my study to the grounds of the house was through Sita's room. They broke in through her bedroom window on the first floor. We don't know what happened exactly . . .

'When I got back early that morning I found the safe opened and Sita missing. I . . . I couldn't live through that discovery again, Josh. Finding evidence of robbery, thinking only of my daughter. Rushing to her room . . . There was evidence of a struggle. Things thrown around the room. But there was no trace of . . . no sign that she'd been injured. We think they took her because she saw them, might've been able to identify the intruders. Rather than kill her they took her and . . . .

'At first we assumed she was dead, killed and dumped somewhere. It was a nightmare period, Bennett. I couldn't help but think of the worst, that they'd sold Sita to surgeons for medical experiments, or for spare parts surgery, or to other evil bastards. Then, a month or so later, sightings of a young girl fitting Sita's description started coming in. I was filled with hope, convinced that she was still alive, living on the street, unable to find her way home. I thought perhaps she'd lost her memory.' He shook his head. 'That was thirteen years ago. The terrible thing is not knowing. I keep having these pix updated, in the hope that some day . . .'

He returned the pix to his breast pocket.

'We live in hope, Bennett, and I don't know whether that's an admirable thing or not. Perhaps I should have reconciled myself to the worst-case scenario long ago, and tried to forget.'

A silence came between the two men. Bennett wanted to say something, to find words of consolation. Instead, inadequately, he just nodded.

Footsteps sounded along the corridor. Ten Lee entered the flight-deck.

'We're due to phase from the void in one hour,' she said. 'Will you run through the systems with me, Joshua?'

Bennett nodded, relieved that she didn't mention the SIH. He needed time to think about what she had said.

He left Mackendrick on the engineer's couch, strapped himself into the pilot's couch and for the next hour concentrated on the familiar routine of checks and analyses. He felt a tension tight within him. Soon, in a matter of minutes, he would be experiencing for the first time the light of another sun.

Ten Lee nodded. 'That's it, Joshua. Phase-out in two minutes and counting . . .'

Bennett looked up from the control console and through the viewscreen, ready for the first sight of the star system.

'One minute . . .'

The void seemed to coagulate around the ship, the stars no longer streaming in towards them. The scene stilled, became a static slab of grey marble.

'Three . . . two . . . one . . .'

They phased out.

The void was replaced by a regular spacescape: a scatter of distant stars, the sun in the mid-ground and the orbiting planets diminishing in perspective. They were coming in on a ten-degree angle to the plane of the ecliptic, the sound of the ion-drive like an explosion after the relative quiet of trans-c flight.

He transferred the Cobra to the program system Mackendrick had written for the approach to Penumbra, and the ship accelerated through space.

'Estimated arrival time, four minutes and twenty seconds,' Ten Lee said.

Bennett concentrated on the read-outs scrolling down his visor screen, only occasionally looking through them to admire the view. The gas giant, which shielded Penumbra from the direct light of the sun, swelled alarmingly, a vast rolling orb of pastel green and ochre gas bands. Bennett made out the coin-like disc of Penumbra against the upper hemisphere of the giant, minuscule by comparison. The Cobra swooped ever closer and Penumbra grew, took on definition as a separate planet.

Ten Lee said, 'Entry into planetary atmosphere in ten seconds . . . eight . . .'

From his position on the engineer's couch, Mackendrick said, 'My God, it's beautiful . . .'

The planet became a broad, curved bow that spanned the width of the viewscreen, purple land showing through swirls of mauve cloud. The Cobra bucked as they hit the troposphere. Bennett slowed their descent, trimmed the angle of entry. Rags of cloud beat against the viewscreen. The ship rumbled like a toboggan, Bennett and Ten Lee swaying in their couches. In a split second they dropped through the floor of the cloud, from a realm of muffling opacity to a brighter scene of rearing purple mountains and vein-like rivers. They hit another stratum of cloud, this one the periphery of a storm front. Bennett disengaged from the pre-programmed flight-plan and took control of the Cobra, trying to veer around the edge of the storm pattern.

'We're three degrees off course if we want to come down in the vicinity of the geographical features,' Ten Lee reported with calm efficiency. 'Three-and-a-half degrees and increasing . . .'

'There's nothing I can do about that,' Bennett said. 'I'm not taking us through the storm, Ten. This is bad enough.'

Even as he spoke the Cobra was batted about the sky like a storm-tossed leaf. Bennett accelerated, trying to outrun the storm front. The vibration increased as the storm chased them and caught up, rattling Bennett and Ten Lee in their couches. He had no time to check how Mackendrick was coping. He fought with the controls, feeling the weight of the craft responding sluggishly.

At one point he gave a manic laugh, and earned a quick glance from Ten Lee. 'What, Joshua?'

'It's like . . . it's like the craziest roller-coaster ride in all creation!' he yelled.

'This is nothing compared to Bhao Khet,' she responded.

Cloud ripped against the screen as the Cobra dived

through the storm. Ten Lee called out a constant string of co-ordinates, her anticipation lightning quick. If anything, the storm seemed to be getting worse. To get this far, he thought with increasing dread, only to crash-land and . . . He grunted as he wrestled with the controls, the ship responding like a reluctant animal.

At one point, as if sensing that he was losing control, Ten Lee took over. Something seemed to side-swipe at the Cobra, and Bennett yelled in sudden fear as he felt himself losing control.

'It's okay, Josh!' Ten Lee shouted.

She sequenced a flight-pattern through the high-pressure area and took them through. Then, without a word, she disengaged and handed the ship back.

Bennett smiled to himself. 'Thanks, Ten. Where'd you learn to sequence like that?'

She just smiled to herself and stared at the figures scrolling down her visor screen.

The Cobra screamed low over violet snow-capped peaks and planed down towards a spreading purple plain.

'We're heading ever further from our destination,' Ten Lee said.

'So I'll bring us down here. Mackendrick?'

'How far from the features?' the tycoon asked.

Ten Lee consulted her screen. 'Two hundred and ten kilometres and counting.'

'Then land,' Mackendrick ordered. 'We'll ride the transporter back to them.'

They came down blind, the land obscured by driving rain and cloud. Bennett burned the vertical jets and the Cobra hovered, buffeted by the wind, and then came down slowly. Landfall arrived with a gentle bump and Bennett cut the jets. The Cobra ticked and clicked in the silent aftermath of descent.

'Well done, Bennett, Ten Lee,' Mackendrick said. 'How

does it feel to know you've come further than any crewed expedition before?'

Bennett sat in his couch and considered the fact. It was, he thought, hard to believe.

Ten Lee was going through the post-flight checks, having given the scene outside the ship barely a glance.

As Bennett stared, the storm abated and sunlight – no, not sunlight, Bennett reminded himself; the light from the gas giant – illuminated the land with an aqueous glow.

Mackendrick stepped between the couches and stared through the viewscreen. 'Jesus Christ,' he said. 'How beautiful.'

They had come down on a plain of short purple grassland between two long mountain ranges. Ahead, the serrated peaks of the northern range stretched off to left and right like massed scimitar blades. Beyond, dominating the landscape with its vast and brooding presence, the banded upper hemisphere of the gas giant – what had Mackendrick called it? Tenebrae? – swelled to fill half the sky.

Bennett reached over and touched Ten Lee's arm. She looked up, and he was pleased to see an expression of wonder cross her face.

10

One month had passed since the last murder, and Vishwanath, Rana and the rest of the homicide team on the eighth floor were making little headway on the case of the crucifix killings.

After all the progress she had made on the night of the last murder, she had expected some breakthrough before now. She had checked all the leads she and Vishwanath had made on the case, but had drawn a blank with each. For the past two weeks she had spent every shift tracking down the friends and acquaintances of the dead men. She could have contacted these people via her com-screen, but she had wanted to get away from the confines of the eighth floor, where Naz had initiated a hate campaign against her.

She suspected it had something to do with the fact that Investigator Vishwanath consulted her on most cases now, valuing her opinion. Naz had had his nose put out in a big way, and hated her in consequence. He made jokes at her expense – the old one about her lack of boyfriends, which she could handle – and other hateful jibes about her lowly origins. 'Is it true you were a street-kid, Rana?' he had asked in the staff canteen, surrounded by friends. 'But you look too fair to be a Dullit.'

'I am not ashamed of where I come from, Naz,' she had replied with civility. 'And if I were a Dullit I would be proud of the fact.'

'But that fair skin,' Naz had persisted. 'I've seen no street-kid so pale! Perhaps you're a half-caste? Is that it, Rana? Was your mother a whore and your father a European tourist?'

She'd considered telling him the truth, but knew that he would only ridicule her.

'That must be it!' Naz had declared with delight. 'Your mother was a drunken whore. You know what they say – like mother, like daughter.'

She'd stared at him. 'What do you mean?'

'She asks me what do I mean? What do you think I mean, Rana? How did you get to the eighth floor so fast? What was the reason for your meteoric rise? Of course, how stupid of me! You slept with Commissioner Singh, and now you're screwing Investigator Vishwanath. No wonder you have no boyfriends – you have no time.'

She was pleased, in retrospect, that her coffee cup had been empty, because Naz might have earned himself a scalded face and Rana a reprimand, no matter how bad the provocation.

She'd considered telling Vishwanath of Naz's continued baiting, but decided against that course of action. It would only fuel Naz in his belief that she had a special relationship with her commanding officer. She could take his immature jibes; they were, after all, the result of envy.

That afternoon Rana clipped her com-board to her belt, told Vishwanath that she was going out to interview an acquaintance of the last murder victim, and rode down to the underground car-park. She had requisitioned a squad car, and it was awaiting her when she stepped from the elevator. She gave the driver the address and, as the car made its way through the noisy crowds that flowed down the streets with little regard for their safety, she sat back and regarded the screen of her com-board.

She had checked on the origin of the cloth fibres

discovered at three of the crime scenes. Of course, there was always the possibility that the fibre had nothing to do with the killer, but, as was the nature of homicide investigations, that possibility had to be positively disproved before being dismissed. She had discovered that the cloth was imported from the colony planet of Madrigal, that it was made into expensive suits by an esteemed firm of Bombay tailors, and that both suits and cloth were extremely rare. She made a note to remind herself to look into the possibility that the killer was an off-worlder with a taste for designer clothing.

The car plunged into shadow as it eased down a narrow alley in the old sector of the city. Rana switched off her board and peered through the side window. The buildings on either side of the alley were ancient concrete tenements connected by illegal electricity leads and washing lines flying pennants of old clothing beaten colourless in the shallows of the nearby Ganges. Pot-bellied infants in nothing but shorts stared at her with kohl-rimmed eyes, and the occasional stoic cow barred the way, watching Rana with eyes just as devoid of curiosity.

At the third bovine obstruction, she leaned forward and tapped the driver on the shoulder. 'Ah-cha. I'll walk from here. No problem.'

She squeezed from the car and eased her way past the stolidly chewing cow, peering at the grey walls for the street names stencilled in sky-blue Hindi script.

She had extracted the name of Mohammed Iqbal from an acquaintance of Ali Bhakor. Iqbal, she had been told, was a business associate of Bhakor's. The acquaintance would say no more. Further enquiries from police records elicited the fact that Iqbal was a known small-time drug dealer who had worked for Bhakor from time to time. His was the very last name on Rana's list of people to interview.

Iqbal lived on the fifth floor of a crumbling grey tenement. The building was so old that it had no elevator, and Rana had to walk up the five flights of concrete stairs. She eventually found Iqbal in a room barely big enough to contain his bulk. Fortunately the rickety door was already open, for Rana was sure he would have refused to let her enter.

He was sitting cross-legged on a soiled white mattress on the floor, smoking what smelled like hashish in an ornately painted water-pipe. His eyes, already squeezed between rolls of fat, narrowed even further when he saw Rana. 'Who are you?' he snapped. 'What do you want?'

'Are you Mohammed Iqbal?' she asked. His over-filled face resembled the pix Rana had copied from records.

He muttered, 'What if I am? What if I'm not?'

'If you're not, then you must be his twin brother.' She tossed the pix into his lap.

He glanced at it and grunted. 'What do you want?'

She pulled off her boots, stepped over the threshold, and seated herself on the mattress before him. 'The answers to a few questions. I have no interest in whatever business you're conducting here—'

He spread gargantuan palms in a pathetic pantomime of innocence. 'For one full year I have touched nothing more than hashish, and then only for medicinal purposes. I am asthmatic.'

'My condolences. As I said, I'm not interested in drugs.'

'You are not another crawling narcotic agent who wants rupees to keep her silence?' Watching her, he took a deep lungful of hashish, retained it and then exhaled a dragon's breath of grey smoke towards her.

Rana was determined not to cough. 'I'm from Homicide, Iqbal, and I can't be bought off.'

His hooded eyes regarded her as he lazily scratched a nose the size of a samosa. He grunted a laugh. 'They send

126

a young girl to question me now! I am insulted. What do you want?'

'I understand you knew the businessman Ali Bhakor?'

'What of it?'

'When was the last time you spoke to Bhakor?'

He turned his palm in a lazy gesture of consideration. 'Now let me see . . . it would be, yes, perhaps five weeks ago. He came around to share a pipe.'

Five weeks ago . . . one week before his murder.

'Can you tell me if he had arranged to meet anyone at the Hindustan Plaza hotel on the evening of the sixth of July?'

Iqbal shook his head. 'He does not discuss his business deals with me.'

'Did he mention making any new acquaintances of late?'

Iqbal regarded her, something unpleasant in his eyes. He gripped his obscenely fat big toes and used them to haul himself forward. 'Officer, Bhakor is a man who juggles many fire-brands. He does not shout about his business for fear of dropping them, or burning his hands.'

Rana watched Iqbal as she said, 'Ali Bhakor was murdered on the evening of the sixth of July at the Hindustan Plaza hotel. He was shot in the head with a laser charge.'

She disliked the way his every movement, his every gesture, was conditioned and limited by his corpulence, but she was sure his reaction, minimal though it was, was genuine: his slit eyes widened fractionally. He had not known before now of his friend's death.

'I was expecting a call . . . We meet every five or six weeks for a pipe and conversation.'

'I'm sorry I had to break it to you like this. It is an unpleasant affair. I'm doing my best to get to the bottom of it. I would appreciate every little bit of help I can get.'

Iqbal inclined his elephantine head. 'Ah-cha. Of course.'

'Did Bhakor mention anything, anything at all, that might suggest who he was meeting that night?'

Iqbal leaned forward and stanchioned his head on all ten fingers and thumbs, a dramatic gesture of total concentration.

He looked up with a swiftness totally out of character. 'Why . . . he did say something. I am sure it meant nothing.'

'Let me be the judge of that,' Rana said.

Iqbal adjusted the white lace skullcap on the summit of his bald head. 'I don't know if it will help, but he did say that he might have an interesting business deal with a certain . . . contact.'

Rana stared at him. 'A contact?'

'That is what he said. He had met him once. The man was offering to supply Ali with a quantity of high-grade slash at a cut-rate price. He referred only to the dealer as the Man in the Black Suit.'

'The Man in the Black Suit,' Rana repeated.

'A very expensive black suit, woven from a bright material Ali had never seen before. The man looked rich. Ali said that he was considering the deal.'

Rana stared at the bulbous water-pipe standing between the callused soles of the man's feet. She felt something flutter in her chest, told herself not to feel too excited, yet. It was nothing more than another lead, one of many.

'Are you sure he said nothing else about this man? How old he might be? His nationality?'

Iqbal shook his head. 'I am truly sorry. He mentioned the man briefly in passing, and then only as the Man in the Black Suit.'

Rana nodded. 'That might be helpful, anyway.' She stood and paused by the door. 'Thank you for your time.'

'Would you care to join me in a pipe, officer?'

Rana smiled. 'While I'm on duty, Iqbal? I think not.'

Iqbal gave a sly smile of disappointment. 'So goodbye, and may Allah go with you.'

Rana hurried down the narrow staircase and made her way to the car. She slipped into the back seat and said to the driver, 'Do you know a good tailor?'

'Excuse me?' The driver looked at her in the rearview mirror.

'Please take me to Calcutta's most expensive tailor.'

He gave Rana an odd look and spoke hurriedly into his communicator. Seconds later he turned to her. 'Ah-cha. I'll take you to Nazruddin's, yes?'

The car started up and edged through the alleyway. Monsoon clouds were gathering to the east, great blue thunderheads stacked over the sea. Seconds later the deluge began, drumming on the roof of the car.

Rana sat back and considered what a break this might be, so early in her career on the eighth floor. But no, it was too much to hope for – that her last interview should provide the clue. But wasn't it often the case? The very last key of a bunch was the one that opened the door; the last bazaar tried had the finest papayas – as if all along fate had been tempting you to give in and abandon your search.

They entered the relatively new district of the city, the business sector boasting skyscrapers and the latest poly-carbon architecture, domes and ziggurats and pyramids, like something from a travel brochure for the colonies. The driver parked the car outside a double-fronted store with a platoon of mannequins in the window dressed in the latest fashions.

Rana jumped from the car and sprinted through the downpour and into Nazruddin's.

At the sight of her uniform, the manager ushered her

into a back room, fearful of what his customers might think. 'How might I be of help?'

'Do you stock sabline, a material produced on Madrigal?'

The manager blinked. 'You wish to make a purchase?' he asked. 'You see, I'm sure that on the salary of' – he glanced at her stripes – 'a Lieutenant—'

'I'm here on police business.' She showed her ID card. 'Rana Rao. Homicide. Now—'

'Sabline. Of course. We are the oldest established tailors in Calcutta, after all.'

'Have you recently sold suits made from the material?'

The manager laughed. 'Suits? My dear, we have *never* sold suits of sabline. Do you have any idea of the expense? Please . . .'

He gestured for her to follow him, and moved along an aisle between racked garments. He came to a series of thin drawers extending all the way up the wall, positioned a pair of step ladders and pulled out a drawer high above Rana's head. He descended with a slim box perhaps the size of a pix album. With a flourish he lifted the lid. Within folds of tissue was a cravat or neckerchief with the lustre of midnight made tangible.

The manager said, 'Go on, feel it.'

Rana reached out and touched the sabline neckerchief. It was as soft as down, finer even than silk. She wanted to lift it from the box and bury her face in its heavenly folds.

'Sabline is manufactured from the pelt of an animal native to Madrigal,' the manager told her. 'These animals shed their pelts only once a lifetime – the sabline is damaged if taken from a dead animal. It is ludicrously expensive. For example, this cravat . . . what do you think?'

'A thousand rupees?' Her wage for a month.

'Six thousand would be nearer the mark. A suit . . .' He shook his head. 'There is no demand for sabline suits, unfortunately. You would be talking about a figure approaching two hundred thousand rupees. The material is hard-wearing. A suit is guaranteed to last the lifetime of its owner without deterioration.'

Rana ran her fingers through the material for the last time. 'Do you know if any tailor in India sells sabline suits?'

'Well, the tailors of Bombay have manufactured sabline suits in the past, but only for the fabulously rich.' He shook his head. 'I haven't heard of one being made for years.'

He replaced the lid and slipped the box back into its drawer, and Rana thanked him and returned to the car.

She arrived back at headquarters as the monsoon rains were letting up. The sun was setting in glorious strata of tangerine and jade green, like an aerial representation of the Indian flag, and the ad-screens were climbing into the dusk sky. Vishwanath was off duty and so, thankfully, was Naz.

Only Varma was at her desk, like some overweight Hindu deity guarding the amassed knowledge of the files. She glanced at her watch as Rana passed her desk. 'I thought you went off duty two hours ago?'

'Working on a lead, Varma,' Rana said and hurried on.

At her desk she activated the com-screen and wrote a report detailing her findings: the discovery of traces of sabline at three of the murder scenes, and Iqbal's testimony that Ali Bhakor was dealing with a man in an expensive black suit. Tenuous, she thought, but at least it was a lead.

She put out a priority call to the Bombay, Madras and Delhi police forces to forward details of the manufacture and sale of sabline suits over the past ten years. Then she downloaded the report of her findings to Vishwanath's terminal, marked URGENT.

She sat back and considered what to do next.

Rana went through, step by step, what she had done so far, the leads she had examined and the people she had interviewed. The computer system, programmed to flag any significant correlation of fact, no matter how coincidental, had come up with nothing. It was down to the power of the brain, an individual's ability to think laterally, to move the case forward. That, or pure blind luck.

She sat up. She recalled her earlier thought that the killer might be an off-worlder. If the sabline came from Madrigal, then perhaps – it was a long shot, she knew – perhaps so did the killer. If, that was, the killer was the Man in the Black Suit.

She opened her com-screen and accessed internal files. She logged on to the colonial crime file and typed in the key words: Madrigal, Laser Charge, Crucifix. She gave a fifteen-year remit and waited, expecting to be deluged with thousands of files that would take hours to sift through.

Minutes later her screen flashed with the message that only ten murder files awaited her inspection on-line.

She downloaded them into her com-screen and called them up one by one. Madrigal, it appeared, was a tiny planet with a population of only three million citizens, mainly miners, space line workers and scientists. Seven of the ten murders involving laser charges had been solved, the perpetrators tried and sentenced. Two cases were awaiting trial, with the accused pleading guilty. That left one case, the seemingly motiveless murder of a psychiatric patient almost fifteen years ago. The killer had never been apprehended, even though an eye witness to the killing had provided a description of the alleged murderer.

Now this was more interesting. Rana requested the computer-generated image of the suspect, sat back and waited.

A minute later the image filled her screen. Rana stared at the thin-faced, dark-haired man, something sickeningly confident and self-assured about his expression, though she reminded herself that it was only a computer-generated image. He was Caucasian, aged perhaps thirty in the pix – which would make him forty-five now – and other information supplied by the witness suggested that he was just under six feet tall and of athletic build. The witness had not noticed the suspected killer's clothing.

Rana sent a copy of the pix through to Vishwanath's terminal, suggesting that they should put out a request for a search and detention order to all forces.

She made a copy of the pix, propped it on her desk and stared at the dark, handsome face for a long time. She wondered if the reason she thought the face looked familiar was because, to her, Western faces did tend to share certain similar characteristics. How many bronzed, finely chiselled male faces had she seen on holodramas over the years?

But there was something about this face . . .

She told herself to be sensible. She had concentrated on the crucifix killings so intently over the last month that she was becoming obsessed.

She looked at the big digital clock on the wall. It was nearly ten o'clock, way past the time her shift finished. She killed her screen, said goodbye to Varma, and left the building.

The orange glow-tubes of the street-vendors illuminated the rain-slicked street. A constant procession of traffic surged back and forth, horns blaring in a mindless concerto of futility. Rana walked briskly through the humid night. She was still energised from concentrating on the case, and she knew that sleep would be a long time coming.

She hadn't seen the kids down at the Howrah bridge for over a month – what better way to empty her mind of the day's events than to chat with Vandita and her friends over a chai?

She took a cab to the Ganges, paid the driver and crossed the pavement to the railings overlooking the broad sweep of the water. The tide was out, revealing a slick expanse of mud-flats. Stick-thin figures in dhotis and vests waded up to their knees in the estuarine silt, poking about with long poles for who knew what. From beneath the arching span of the Howrah bridge, Rana heard the echo of children's voices and laughter, and she was reminded of the spirit of community and camaraderie she had missed for so long.

Of all the children she had worked with over the years, in every part of the city, she had an affinity with the Howrah bridge kids most of all. There were many reasons for this: the self-help and co-operative scheme she had set up here a couple of years ago was still running successfully; the twelve-year-old Brahmin girl who organised the children, Vandita, reminded her so much of herself; and once she too had made her home between the steel pillars on the bridge's northern bank. Now the kids would be gathering there after a hard day's work, pooling their money, sending out for daal bhat and chai, gathering around the fire for a few hours of chatter before one by one they fell asleep.

Rana moved to the bridge and peered into the shadows. A flickering fire illuminated a circle of brown faces and bright eyes.

Vandita saw her and leapt to her feet. 'Rana-ji!' she cried. 'Where have you been?'

Rana felt a stab of guilt. 'I've been promoted, Vandita. I didn't want the job, but I couldn't refuse.'

Soon they were milling around her. They touched her uniform and the polished butt of her pistol protruding from beneath her jacket, as if it were some kind of talisman or good luck charm. Vandita took her hand and dragged her into the makeshift home beneath the bridge. They had laid boards on stones clear of the mud, covered the wooden slats with scraps of carpet and cloth, and had even found mattresses and old charpoys to sleep on. The three enclosing sides, two steel pillars and the brick wall, were hung with garish pix of Hindu gods, Shiva, Vishnu and Ganesh, alongside holodrama stars and skyball players. They even had a big, battered tea pot bubbling on a brazier.

Rana removed her boots and sat down on a mattress, her back against a pillar.

'Chai, Rana?' Vandita asked.

A chipped mug was pressed into her hand, full of sickly sweet, spiced chai. She looked around the beaming faces. 'I'm sorry I haven't called for such a long time,' she said in Hindi. 'Any problems?'

'The people who clean the bridge want us to move,' Vandita reported. 'We said we'd move out until the bridge is cleaned, and then move back in. But they're not happy with this. They want us to go for good. They say we dirty the bridge, but this isn't true.'

'Have you told Private Khosla?' Rana asked. 'He'll talk to the authorities and come to some arrangement.'

Vandita avoided her gaze. The other children looked unhappy.

'What? You have seen Khosla, haven't you?'

'He came once only,' Vandita said, jogging her head

from side to side. 'He told us that the money for our cleaning equipment – the subsidy you gave us – is to be cut. Now we get twenty rupees per month only, instead of fifty.'

'But he can't do that!' Rana looked around the staring faces, feeling guilty herself for Khosla's duplicity. 'I'll talk to him immediately, Vandita.'

A young boy in soiled shorts and a small vest said, 'When the officer came down, he had his nose in the air. We invited him in for chai' – he put his thumb to his lips in the gesture for drinking – 'but he wouldn't join us. The look on his face said that we smelled. He's like all the other cops.' He looked away from Rana's gaze.

She pulled a fifty-rupee note from her pocket and passed it to Vandita. 'For food,' she said. 'I'll talk to Khosla and get your money restored, ah-cha?'

Khosla was doing what officers had done for years before him: appropriating funds meant for elsewhere. If he was taking over fifty per cent of all the money spent on schemes meant to help the street-kids across the city, then he would be earning more than his actual wages. Khosla had probably assumed that she would cease her association with the kids as soon as she was promoted; no doubt he could not conceive of why anyone might seek their company. She would quietly tell him that she knew what he was doing, and that if it didn't stop she would inform his superiors.

'But you, Rana!' a young girl called Priti asked. 'Tell us about all your adventures!'

'How many murderers have you caught? Tell us!'

So she made up stories of car chases and shoot-outs, evil gang-lords and robbers, rather than disillusion them with the truth, that ninety-nine per cent of police work was boring administration.

She sipped her third cup of chai and listened to their

136

stories. Each child had a tale to tell, exaggerated epics of how they had been chased, robbed, beaten – but she knew that most of these adventures were imaginary. She had told the same tall tales years ago to while away the hours before sleep.

One small boy said, 'A holostar outside the Tata studios gave me twenty rupees! But then a drunken yar came and snatched it from me! I yelled and screamed, but where are the cops when you need them?'

The children laughed. They were forever complaining about the police, with justification, and smiling at Rana as they did so. She took as a compliment the fact that they no longer saw her as an officer of the law.

Midnight came and went and the brazier burned low. The children slipped quietly to sleep, the younger ones first, curling up where they lay on scraps of carpet or, if they were lucky, on old mattresses. The older children fought to keep awake, but long hours working on the streets, and the prospect of early starts at dawn, soon had them snoring.

Rana shifted her position on the mattress. She was warm and comfortable, and enjoyed the strange feeling of being safe among people she knew and trusted.

Carefully, so as not to wake the sleeping children, Vandita moved to her side and leaned against her. Rana stroked the matted tangle of the girl's rosewater-scented hair.

'Are you happy, Vandita?' she whispered.

The girl nodded beneath Rana's hand. 'I have friends, now, Rana. Life is hard, but I have friends.'

'At first it is hard,' Rana said. 'Everything is new, and you are never trusted because of what you left behind. They say, "How can you want to live like us? How can you turn your back on what you had?" But they don't understand that sometimes wealth and privilege can be terrible for the heart. In time things get better – you win their trust and they see you are just like them.'

She looked down at the girl curled by her side, but Vandita was asleep.

Rana stretched comfortably on the mattress and stared out from under the bridge at the silvered expanse of the Ganges, the ripples from the wakes of passing boats slicing the reflection of the full moon into shimmering ribbons.

It seemed such a long time ago now, a lifetime away, but at the age of ten she had been so unhappy. She had attended an expensive school with pupils from all over the world, and in a class of fifteen girls she had not one friend. She supposed it was her fault. She was small and quiet and cripplingly shy; in company she would have to screw her courage up to speak, and then it would come out too quickly, or the timing would be wrong, so that by the time she had thought of something to say the topic of conversation had moved on. She was never bullied, but sometimes she wished she had been, because then someone might have stood up to protect her, and she would have had a friend.

But if school was bad, then her life at home was even worse. She lived in a big house to the west of the city, with a big garden, and she had her own rooms and all the latest toys. She was looked after by an unsmiling nanny, a big woman with rough hands who hurt her when washing her hair or scrubbing her back, and showed her not the slightest sign of affection, or even friendship. She had heard other girls at school talk about how their nannies took them to holodramas and restaurants, but her nanny performed the bare minimum of duties for her weekly wage, and then abandoned her to her own devices.

Perhaps she could have tolerated the apathy of her nanny if her mother and father had shown her any affection. They were distant, monarchic figures she saw briefly – perhaps once a week. Her father was something to do with space exploration, and was often away in the colonies. He was like a stranger to her, and when he did return from the stars and pick her up and play with her briefly and insist she call him by his name, the forced and artificial quality of his affection pointed up the total lack of it the rest of the time. As for her mother . . . She had hated her mother even more, because there was no excuse for her lack of love. She was always somewhere in the house, arranging parties or working on this or that committee matter. She seemed to go out of her way to ignore Rana. She was not actively cruel – Rana had no stories of sadistic torture or punishment – but in a way her lack of connection was crueller still.

She had known at ten that she could not continue this way of life, but an alternative seemed impossible. She lost herself in books and holodramas, but these were temporary respites from a way of life she wanted to escape totally.

She had the idea one day when, driven by the family chauffeur to school, she had seen a gaggle of street-kids, scruffy tousle-haired urchins, playing kabbadi on the pavement. When eliminated from the contest they sat watching the game, arms about each other with unforced affection, laughing. They had nothing, she realised, and yet they had everything that she did not.

Two days later she joined them on the streets, having discarded her new clothes for a patched, thin dress belonging to her nanny's daughter and rubbed soil into her face and hair. They had asked her name, and rather than say that she was Sita Mackendrick, daughter of the millionaire owner of the Mackendrick Foundation, she had made up a name on the spur of the moment: Rana Rao.

They had been suspicious of her, of course, wary of her

precise way with words and her command of English, her fair skin that came as a result of having an American father, and the first few days had been hard. She had had to face taunts and jibes about her prissy manners and fastidiousness when it came to eating whatever scraps the others brought back, but she had found even in their laughing criticism a vital contact she had never known before. And in time, when they came to trust her and rely on her quick wits and even quicker tongue, they had shown friendship that made her weep with the joy of belonging.

She knew she had found true friends when, after perhaps a week of living in a derelict factory, the kids made her stay behind one day rather than join them begging on the streets. They had showed her a pix of herself – a prim, privileged self she hardly recognised – and said that police patrols were looking for her. They even moved themselves to another, distant part of the city for a month, until the search abated. Life was difficult: she often went hungry and was sometimes cold, and the ground made a hard and uncomfortable bed. But she became accustomed to hardship in time, and it was a small price to pay for the constant companionship of her new family.

One day, begging on the streets, she had caught sight of her mother through the window of an expensive restaurant, and this vision of a rich, sophisticated woman inhabiting another world had made her realise how right she had been to get away.

Now, Rana sat up, dislodging Vandita, and stared out into the darkness. That day her mother had been with another man, not her husband. The man had seemed to be comforting her. Her mother had been weeping, and he had reached out and touched her hand.

The man, Rana thought now, looked very much like the

computer-generated image of the killer from Madrigal – but then so did many other handsome, dark-haired Westerners. She knew that the similarity in this case had to be a coincidence. She lay back and closed her eyes.

She had lived with the street-kids for four years – the last year spent under this very bridge – until begging for food became more difficult: people were reluctant to give money to older children, who they thought should be working for a living. Some of her friends had drifted into prostitution, but Rana had seen how abused these kids were, how their pimps took most of their money and their customers beat them.

One day Rana had read an advertisement requesting students to sit a police academy examination. Thinking only of the rupees she might one day earn, Rana had bought forged high-school certificates and enrolled. To her amazement she had passed the examination, and one year later began working as Calcutta's only Child Welfare officer. For eight years she had worked to improve the conditions of the kids who made the streets their home, give them skills, in some cases professions, so that when they reached puberty they might find other means than prostitution to earn a wage.

Rana lay on the mattress beside Vandita. She was ten again, and living on the streets . . . She wondered where those kids were now, her friends for brief months or years. They had all grown up and drifted apart, in adulthood. She considered these children her friends, now.

Rana smiled to herself and wondered what some casual observer might make of the tableau, as she drifted to sleep beside Vandita and the other kids in the fading glow of the brazier.

11

Bennett and Ten Lee loaded the transporter with provisions and scientific equipment, Mackendrick supervising. He seemed to have gained strength since landfall, after the rigours of suspension. He was moving more easily, restored to his old ebullient self, as if looking forward to the exploration of Penumbra.

Bennett packed the containers of food on the flat-bed. Ten Lee fastened the inflatable dome with polycarbon ties and Mackendrick checked that the water canisters were full. At last they stood beside the cab of the vehicle, preparatory to driving from the Cobra's hold. Bennett let out a breath; the gravity of Penumbra was slightly higher than on Earth, and the effort of loading the transporter had tired him. He felt the tug of the planet's gravity pull on his entrails, making his limbs heavy and sluggish.

'We'll need these as a precaution,' Mackendrick said, handing out facial masks. 'The air's breathable, but we won't know about any possible dangerous micro-organisms until the tests come in.'

Bennett took his mask and slipped it over his nose and mouth, feeling it seal itself to his skin like something alive. Mackendrick and Ten Lee did likewise.

Mackendrick opened a container on the side of the truck and passed a short, bulky rifle to Bennett. 'Pulsers, for our protection.' His voice was muffled by the mask.

Ten Lee regarded Mackendrick, declining to take the rifle he held towards her. 'Why do we need weapons?'

Mackendrick sighed. 'We don't know what's out there, Ten. It's merely a precaution.'

She shook her head, her eyes watching Mackendrick above her mask. 'I could not bring myself to kill.'

Bennett said, 'They're pulsers, Ten. You can turn down the charge to stun. Look.' He adjusted the slide on his own weapon.

Her eyes pulled into a dubious frown, Ten Lee took the rifle from Mackendrick and pushed the slide down to its lowest setting.

'We'll take it in turns to drive,' Mackendrick said. 'Anybody for first shift?'

Bennett volunteered and climbed into the driving seat. Mackendrick sat beside him, plugging a com-board into the console on the dash. On a command from Mackendrick, the hatch of the cargo hold slowly lowered, forming a ramp.

A plain of purple grass stretched away from the ship, bejewelled with the result of the storm: diadems of captured rain-water scintillated in the half-light of Tenebrae, the gas giant, turning the grass into a shimmering, sequinned haze.

Bennett fired the engine and edged the vehicle forward, down the ramp and across the purple plain. The atmosphere of Penumbra invaded the cab, increasing the temperature with its cloying, sticky humidity.

The mountains on either side came into view, and Bennett made out the monstrous bulk of Tenebrae. It had risen since his first glimpse of it at landfall, and he had to tip his head back to stare through the clear roof of the transporter at the great bulging underbelly of the giant. There was something almost impossible about its

143

vastness, like an optical illusion the brain knows to be a fact and yet cannot visually accommodate.

Mackendrick tapped the com-board with a gnarled finger. 'This is our present position, this the location of the possible settlement, and the red line is our intended route.' The com-board showed a computer-simulated aerial view of the mountains and the central plain, and the flashing points denoted the transporter and the settlement. All Bennett had to do was keep the first flashing light on the red line. 'It's merely a case of following the lie of the valley plain,' Mackendrick said.

Their destination was just under three hundred kilometres distant. The com-board told them that at their present speed of thirty kilometres an hour, they would reach the settlement in approximately ten hours.

'But that doesn't take into account stops we might make,' Mackendrick added. 'I want to get out from time to time, see if there's any evidence of habitation. Also, it'll be getting dark in five hours. We'll stop and pitch camp, prepare a meal and grab a night's sleep.'

Shortly after landfall, Bennett had studied the original probe's astronomical report on the characteristics of Penumbra. The planet was unique. It turned on its axis in just sixteen hours, creating two fairly regular periods of night and day. The main source of light was that provided by Tenebrae, both the steady glow of its superheated gas and a more fitful illumination created by the electrical storms which raged in its upper atmosphere. The system was part of a stellar binary; the light of the major sun never reached Penumbra, hidden as it was behind the bulk of Tenebrae. A distant sun provided Penumbra with a secondary source of light, so that even during the night, when the planet turned away from Tenebrae, the minor sun would ensure that Penumbra was not in total darkness.

From time to time, as the belly of the gas giant overhead coruscated with storms, light pulsed across the surface of land around the transporter. The purple plain brightened perceptibly, and the shadows of rocks and plants fell in darker relief.

At one point Ten Lee pointed at something. 'Look . . .'

Bennett slowed the transporter. Five metres ahead, a raft of vegetation was undergoing a transformation. As they watched, a patch of deeper purple grass sprouted a thousand bright yellow flowers, tiny blooms that winked open and stretched towards the electric illumination of the distant lightning. All over the plain, in fact, a constellation of tiny flowers was blossoming.

Seconds later Bennett made out what at first he assumed was some kind of dark mist, hovering over the land. Then he realised that the mist was shifting, lifting from the land and moving on, then descending. It *was* a mist, he decided – a great pall of iridescent sapphire insects feasting on the flowers.

For perhaps three minutes the flowers remained open, a vast bright carpet, and then disappeared as quickly as they had arrived as the pulse of light from Tenebrae abated. Just as rapidly, the cloud of insects disappeared, as if absorbed into the land.

One hour later the storm arrived.

A driving wind hit the transporter head on, and low cloud swirled and swelled around them, driving a battering front of raindrops the size of golf balls. Muffled thunder sounded a distant, stratospheric cannonade. Seconds later the surrounding clouds pulsed with opalescent lightning. Bennett slowed the transporter and proceeded with caution.

Mackendrick doubted that it was a result of the lightning storm on Tenebrae they had just witnessed. 'Too soon for that,' he said. 'But I've no doubt that they're linked. What we're seeing now is probably the result of an electrical storm on the giant a day or so ago.'

The transporter rocked like a cradle in the wind.

Despite himself, Bennett experienced a surge of elation. He laughed, earning odd looks from Mackendrick and Ten Lee. 'It takes me back,' he said. 'You know, the storms when you were young, the sense of comfort from knowing you were safe.'

Ten Lee shook her head. 'On Bhao Khet the storms frightened me,' she replied. 'The typhoons killed thousands of people. I had an aunt who claimed they were avenging spirits. Of course that was nonsense, but I didn't realise that at the time.'

As abruptly as the storm began, it ceased. First the wind flagged, and then the rain stopped its noisy pounding on the roof of the transporter. The cloud lifted in minutes, revealing a land washed clean and sparkling in Tenebrae's milky light. A sea of rainwater coruscated across the plain, and another raft of tiny flowers, red as well as yellow this time, snapped open and drank in the light and the moisture. As before, a swarm of insects appeared to take advantage of the evanescent blooming.

Bennett was the first to witness the fauna of Penumbra. At first he thought that the movement to his left, on the periphery of his vision, was no more than a trick of the light, the shadow of a windblown stand of grass. The shadow continued its motion across the plain, though, and Bennett turned his head to see a long-legged animal, frail and skittish as a deer, halt in its sprint and regard them with intense suspicion. He slowed the transporter and pointed. The creature had a jet-black pelt as sleek as an otter and a thin wedge of a head. It was the improbable angularity of its head, and its massive bulging eyes, that marked it out as alien.

He realised, with amazement, that it was the first non-Terran animal he had ever seen in the flesh.

'And there are others,' Ten Lee said. 'Hundreds of them.'

Beyond the first animal, Bennett saw others, a great stilled herd watching the progress of the transporter with minute attention. Seconds later they had seen enough; as if at some signal, they turned as one and flowed off down the valley away from the vehicle. Bennett estimated they were moving at close to fifty kilometres an hour. In seconds they were lost to sight.

As the day progressed, Tenebrae moved from its oppressive position directly overhead and slipped towards the mountains to the east. It lowered itself slowly over the horizon, its progress visible behind the silhouetted mountain range, and the light dimmed. The sky to the west became a wash of indigo; a scatter of faint stars, the constellations unfamiliar, appeared above the plain. High in the sky the faint yellow beacon of the minor sun materialised, the night star that ensured Penumbra would never know total darkness.

On Bennett's reckoning they had covered some hundred and fifty kilometres – they were almost halfway to their destination.

Mackendrick suggested that they halt for the night. 'Don't know about you two, but I'm hungry. Let's move into the lee of the hills over there and call it a day.'

Bennett turned the transporter and tracked across the plain, approaching the gentle rise of the foothills. Trees came into sight, a forest of dark shapes covering the hillside in the light of the stars and the distant minor sun. He braked the vehicle and stared out. In the sudden silence, the rearing trees seemed an eerie presence. They were branchless for much of their height, and near the top sprouted long, dangling fronds. Some of these fronds

147

had connected themselves to neighbouring trees. Small dark shapes scurried from tree to tree, and occasional calls, piping ululations like the urgent shrilling of a piccolo, pierced the silence of the night.

Mackendrick touched the screen, and the computer graphic of their course was replaced by lines of text. 'The air's safe, according to the analysis,' he said. 'We can take these damned masks off now.'

Bennett peeled off his mask and massaged his face. He glanced at Mackendrick, who nodded that he should open the door and climb out. As he did so, swinging down into the humid twilight, it occurred to him that he was setting foot on the most distant planet ever explored by humankind.

The grass was springy underfoot, the warmth cloying. The animals in the tree-tops high above called out with shrill urgency.

They expanded the dome, set up a perimeter alarm to alert them to unwelcome nocturnal visitors, and carried inflatable mattresses and food trays inside. The dome was transparent, and they ate their meals – Ten Lee preferring her own vegetarian fare – in the half-light of the distant second sun. Later, Bennett and Ten Lee sat cross-legged on the floor while Mackendrick stretched out on his mattress, hands lodged beneath his head. They chatted among themselves, Ten Lee contributing only occasionally.

'So now that we're here, Josh,' Mackendrick was saying, 'how do you feel about things?'

He thought it best not to give the smart-ass answer that life was pretty much as it had always been. Mackendrick was trying to gauge the morale of his team.

He shrugged. 'I . . . I suppose I expected it to be more . . . I don't know – *alien*. I've never been out of Sol system before now. It's spectacular, I suppose. But perhaps not as threatening as I thought it might be.'

He realised he was saying the first things that came into his head. He could not tell Mackendrick and Ten Lee how he was really feeling.

When he had looked ahead at the start of the voyage, he had envisaged a strange new world with himself, his thoughts and emotions subtracted from the equation. He had imagined a wondrous, totally alien world, but the reality of being here was that he was slightly disappointed – because he was himself and had not been changed by the experience. He still carried his old worries and disappointments: his guilt over his father and what Julia had said to him at their final meeting.

Hell, he thought, we can go halfway across the galaxy and never really get anywhere.

He shrugged. 'I'm looking forward to reaching the settlement,' he said, which was true, even though he knew that once he was there he would inevitably feel some sense of dismay, no matter what they discovered. He recalled telling Ella's ghost that reality was never as bad as you expected it to be; but, at the same time, it was also true that no experience was ever as good as you hoped it might be.

Mackendrick turned and propped himself on one elbow. 'What do you think we'll find?'

'Well, we keep calling it a settlement. It certainly looked like one from the shots we've seen. Of course it'd be great to discover evidence of sentient life . . .' Even as he said the words, he hardly believed they would. 'I really don't know what to think until we reach our destination. I don't want to hope for too much in case we find nothing at all.'

Mackendrick nodded. 'Ten Lee? Any thoughts?'

'I cannot guess what we might find. Speculation is useless.' She paused, blinking down at her plate of half-eaten food. 'I am pleased to be here. It is *right*, destined.

149

My Rimpoche said go outwards. I am about as far out as it is possible to be in this galaxy, and for the first time I have the feeling that I am in the right place.' She turned a serious gaze on Mackendrick. 'I feel that Penumbra has at its heart a great secret.'

Mackendrick raised his eyebrows and lay down again, staring up at the ceiling of the dome.

Bennett watched the strange woman as she prepared her mattress and settled herself upon it in the lotus position. She closed her eyes and made circles with her thumbs and index fingers, then seemed to slow her breathing. There were times when he felt in awe of Ten Lee Theneka, her composure and certainty of thought. He sometimes wondered if she regarded everyone around her as shallow, mere puppets of conditioning, jerking to the meretricious dance of life's music.

He prepared for sleep, unrolling his mattress and lying down on his back. Mackendrick sat up, tipping a dozen small white pills into his shaking palm and swallowing them with a draught of water. There was something about watching someone taking their medication that filled Bennett with a sense of trespass. He recollected once or twice accidentally coming across Ella as she administered her own injections; he had always quickly retreated, as if the healing might in some way prove less efficacious if he was around to witness the ritual.

Surprisingly, he slept well that night. He awoke feeling refreshed and invigorated seven hours later. The milky light of Tenebrae filled the dome, along with the odour of freshly brewing coffee.

Mackendrick was kneeling before the microwave. 'Breakfast'll be ready in ten minutes.'

Bennett sat up and stretched, peering around. 'Where's Ten?'

Mackendrick pointed through the wall of the dome.

Ten Lee was a childishly small figure standing on a hillside fifty metres away, silhouetted against the light of the rising gas giant.

He felt a sudden pang of alarm at the sight of her. He looked around and saw her rifle lying beside her mattress.

'Is she safe out there alone?'

Without waiting for a reply he grabbed his rifle, found his boots and hurried from the dome. He was surprised at the quality of the air, how fresh it was despite the warmth, and scented with a perfume suggesting pine, but sharper. He jogged across the purple grass and climbed the hill to where Ten stood. The view was spectacular from the summit: the dwindling plain shimmered with haze in the light of Tenebrae, its girth straddling the entirety of the horizon.

'Ten!'

She turned and glanced at his pulser.

Bennett shrugged. 'I don't think you should be out here without this.'

He held up the rifle, but she ignored the gesture, took a deep breath and swept her gaze around the view, suggesting without words that he was being needlessly apprehensive.

He smiled. 'Beautiful morning.'

She ignored the observation and said, 'Have you thought about the SIH disc, Joshua?'

The question surprised him. He had wanted to let it ride, maybe assess how he felt about things later, at the end of the mission.

'I . . . no. That is, I know what I should do.'

She turned to him and stared. 'Then do it.'

She opened her palm before him, and upon it was the small silver disc from the hologram module.

He regarded it for what seemed like minutes.

'Joshua, you must let go. Accept what happened. In

151

letting go we free ourselves, open ourselves and admit that new experience is possible.'

'You don't know what it is like to lose—'

She blinked at him. 'Joshua, when I was eighteen I lost the man I loved. He was killed in the War of Independence. I know what it is like—'

'Is that why you . . . why you turned to religion? To get over the loss?'

'Of course not. I always believed in the Path. My belief helped me, when he died.'

'Have you had anyone since?'

'Not a lover,' she said. 'A few casual encounters . . .' She smiled at him. 'I am passing even beyond that, now. I need nothing, only the peace that meditation brings. Here, I feel as though I need only to meditate to be close to the essence.'

Bennett regarded her. She was still proffering the disc on the palm of her small hand. He thought of Ella, and then Julia, and then the other women he thought he had loved over the years.

'I wish I could do without people, Ten. They seem only to bring me pain.'

She shook her head. 'Perhaps you seek too much in others, Joshua. Perhaps you seek that which they are not, instead of that which they are. Accept them for themselves, not that which you wish them to be.' She stared at him. 'Now take the disc and throw it as far as you can.'

He realised that, if he hesitated any longer, he would disobey her command – and he knew that then he would hate himself.

On impulse he snatched the disc and drew back his arm. He launched the disc high, watched it go spinning through the air and catch the light once or twice, then fall on a long, slow arc into the valley bottom.

He thought of Ella, and felt a quick stab of guilt he knew to be irrational.

Briefly, in a gesture valuable because of its rarity, Ten Lee reached out and touched his hand. Then she left him and walked back down the hillside to the dome.

After a breakfast of coffee and fruit bread, taken outside the dome on the purple grass, they packed up and boarded the transporter on the final leg of the journey. Ten Lee drove and Bennett sat beside the open window next to Mackendrick.

They made good time as Tenebrae moved from west to east. It seemed less to rise than to roll with vast majesty across the valley. When Bennett tipped his head and stared through the roof of the vehicle, the giant filled his field of vision, blotting out the starfield and provoking a stifled sense of claustrophobia. Great flashes of lightning pulsed within the gaseous bands, sending floods of opal illumination across the plain before them.

They sighted more wildlife as the short day progressed. Ten Lee was the first to spot the flying creatures. She leaned forward, clasping the wheel in both hands, and peered through the windshield. 'Look,' she said. 'There. Straight ahead.'

At first they appeared as a flock of jet specks in the air at the far end of the plain. Seconds later they were overhead and silhouetted against the belly of the gas giant, creatures with sickle wings and great scythe-like beaks, not unlike pteranodons from the Cretaceous period. So vast was the flock that they took fully minutes to pass overhead.

'We can safely say it's looking a viable habitat for fauna at the top end of the food chain,' Mackendrick commented. 'I wonder what's at the very top?'

His words set Bennett to seriously contemplating the possibility that a sentient alien lifeform might inhabit

Penumbra. Certainly the aerial video of the so-called settlement seemed to indicate that some form of intelligence had been at work on the planet. The thought that, if this intelligence still existed, then sooner or later they would come across it . . . Bennett laughed to himself. It was one of those concepts – like the apprehension of infinity – just too vast to grasp.

Only three planets had been discovered to harbour sentient life from the hundreds so far explored on humankind's expansion along the spiral arm. Bennett had seen the usual documentaries about the alien races, and read a couple of books and a few articles documenting the story of the first contact and subsequent relations.

One race was humanoid, the Phalaan of Arcturus V, who were at a stage of evolution comparable to that of Neolithic man. After the discovery of these Stone Age people, and initial mutually incomprehensible contact, it was considered best for the future development of the Phalaan if they were spared relations with their more technologically sophisticated neighbours. The planet had been designated out of bounds for all but authorised scientific investigation teams.

The Kreyn of Betelgeuse XVII were an ancient race of starfarers who discovered humankind when one of their ships landed on the colony world of Bethany. They were crab-like beings, and about as far in advance of humanity as humanity was in relation to the Phalaan. It was they, the Kreyn, who decided that for the good of humankind contact between the races should be kept to a minimum.

The dominant lifeforms on Sirius were great sea-living cetaceans, and the jury was still undecided as to whether these aliens were sentient or not.

Humankind had yet to discover a race with whom they were on an equal footing, beings with whom they might come to some understanding in the many realms of endeavour: cultural, scientific, philosophical. The chances were that such a race was unlikely to be found on Penumbra. The planet was not developed globally as was the Earth; there was no evidence of cities or roads or other signs of civilisation, as such. But, Bennett told himself, perhaps Penumbrians lived underground, and had no need of cities in the Terran sense. It would be rash to discount any possibility so early in their explorations. Still, the thought of encountering intelligent extraterrestrial life, at any stage of their evolution, seemed improbable to Bennett.

They halted at midday to take a meal break, and it was shortly after they had finished their food trays – when Ten Lee slipped from the cab to stretch her legs – that she made the discovery.

She was gone perhaps thirty seconds when Bennett heard a shout. 'Joshua! Mack! Here!'

Something about her tone, an uncharacteristic urgency, alerted Bennett. He jumped from the cab and looked about for her. She was twenty metres from the transporter, kneeling and reaching out to touch something in the short grass.

She looked up as he approached at a run, an expression of surprise and delight on her face. 'I've found something, Joshua, Mack. Look.'

Bennett knelt beside her, joined by Mackendrick, and stared at the square, grey stone object in the grass. It was perhaps twenty centimetres high and a metre square, a slab of stone as dark as iron. It was not the uniformity of the object that was surprising, however, but the fact that inscribed into the surface of the stone was a series of neatly chiselled hieroglyphs.

Mackendrick stood and hurried back to the transporter while Bennett ran a hand over the stone's surface. The inscription was worn, and filled in places with lichen. A series of small circles, in various stages of completion, contained a number of dots, stars, squares and smaller circles. Each character was perhaps the size of a coin. Bennett counted a hundred such on the horizontal plane.

Mackendrick returned, burdened with equipment. He unstrapped an analyser from his neck and placed it on the stone plinth, kneeling to get a closer look.

Ten Lee was moving away, drawn like a somnambulist to something she had spotted a few metres away. Bennett watched her as she knelt, reached out and pushed aside the obscuring purple grass.

She looked up. 'Over here, Josh. Another one.'

He ran across to her. This stone seemed identical to the first in dimensions, but instead bore a series of square hieroglyphs. The markings within these characters, so far as he could make out, were identical to those on the first stone: dots, stars, squares, small circles. He looked more closely at the stone, and noticed that it was not perfectly square. The top and bottom edges, as seen from above, sloped minimally towards the left. He returned to the first stone. The edges of this one, too, were angled in the same direction as the second.

'A form of ironstone,' Mackendrick told him. 'Initial analysis measured the degree of wear of the various hieroglyphs – those in the middle and those at the southernmost edge, in the teeth of the prevailing winds. The read-out suggests they've been worn over a period of ten thousand years, so the stones in their chiselled state are that old at least.'

'Measurements?'

Mackendrick nodded and read off the dimensions.

'Could you do the same with the second?' Bennett asked.

They made their way to where Ten Lee was kneeling, and placed the analyser on the face of the stone.

Mackendrick read out the results. 'This one is smaller, but only slightly. It's as if it's cut out of the same length of receding block . . .'

Bennett was already on his feet and striding to an irregularity he'd spotted in the grass five metres away. There was another stone. He looked up, across the plain, and made out a series of similar slabs marching away across the grassland. He guessed, then, that each one would be smaller than the last, diminishing like the head of a giant arrow, as if pointing . . .

Only then did it occur to him to look up, all the way, to where the foothills began some two or three kilometres away.

What he saw there made him laugh out loud. They were like short-sighted ants wondering at the footprints of an elephant, when all along the elephant itself was just metres away.

'Ten Lee!' he called. 'Mack!'

They hurried to his side, looking down at the grass for another stone block.

'No,' he said. 'Not down. Up. Take a look at that.'

He pointed. In the distant valley, the great stone columns of a vast and ancient ruin brooded in the light of the gas giant overhead.

12

Ezekiel Klien ducked from the taxi, ignored the gaggle of beggars calling to him from the gutter, and crossed the monsoon-washed pavement. He made his way up the steps and into the police headquarters, then took the elevator to Commissioner Singh's office on the tenth floor.

Klien had known Singh for almost five years, at first seeking his acquaintance in a professional capacity, and then coming to appreciate a certain quality in the man's make-up: his cynicism. Commissioner Singh was corrupt, and what Klien most liked about him was that he made no effort to conceal the fact from those he trusted; instead, he rationalised his corruption with the conceit that by judiciously apportioning his favours he could better control law and order in the city. There would always be corruption, he claimed; the real sin of corruption was when one accepted largesse from the wrong people. Klien liked that. He understood Commissioner Singh. To do good in this world, one was forced also to do a certain amount of what might be considered bad.

Singh looked up when Klien knocked and entered the office. His face broke into a genuine smile of welcome. He stood and they shook hands.

Singh gestured to a seat. He touched his com-screen. 'Suran, two black coffees, please, and I don't want to be disturbed for an hour.'

They talked business for a while. The coffee arrived and Klien sipped the hot, bitter liquid. He told Singh the latest news on the smuggling ring he'd broken up after finding a tonne of high-grade slash in the hold of a Luna–Earth cargo ship.

'It was manufactured legally enough on Luna, but stolen from the labs. We've arrested the people responsible at the Luna end, but not down here. I've reason to expect that the drug was to be distributed by known Calcutta dealers.'

Singh gestured. 'Is there any way I can help?'

'I'd appreciate an hour looking through the files,' Klien told him. 'I have a list of people who might be linked, but nothing like as comprehensive as your records.'

'By all means. I'll have Suran take you down later.'

'I owe you one.'

Commissioner Singh's chestnut eyes twinkled beneath the swathes of his turban. 'When are you running your next training course?' he asked.

'Not for a couple of months, but as soon as it starts I'll notify you.'

For serviced rendered, Klien found places for Singh's officers on the security courses he ran a couple of times a year. They were strictly for spaceport personnel, but Klien was well placed to bend the rules occasionally.

'I have an officer who would benefit from a little training. Brilliant prospect. Young woman with a mind like a razor. In fact I'll get her down here to meet you.' He leaned towards the com-screen and got through to the eighth floor. 'Vishy, is Lieutenant Rao available?'

Klien sat back and wondered if this was another ploy by the commissioner to try and fix him up with a woman. Singh seemed overly concerned that Klien was over forty and still single. 'You need a good woman,' Singh had told him more than once. 'You haven't lived until you've experienced the love of a good woman!' Klien could debate the point, but for the sake of his relationship with the commissioner had declined to argue.

Now Singh spread his hands. 'Lieutenant Rao is out on a case,' he said. 'Perhaps some other time.'

'I'll tell you when the course is enrolling,' Klien promised. He changed the subject. 'Any luck lately with the crucifix killer case?' He liked to keep abreast of how the investigations were going. He was always cheered by Homicide's spectacular lack of success.

Singh grunted. 'Between you and me, Homicide is baffled. There was another killing last month bearing all the hallmarks of the same killer. I don't know the full details, but Vishy will fill you in if you go up and see him.'

Klien gestured that it was only a passing interest. 'Another criminal victim?' he asked.

'As ever,' Singh replied. 'To be perfectly honest I'm not that worried. I know, they are murders all the same, and the press are shouting about the unacceptability of vigilante killings, which they seem to think they are, but the fact is that these people are known drug dealers and criminals. For the good of society they are better off dead. I'm treating the case as experience for some of my younger officers under Vishy's tutelage.'

'So you don't hold out much hope of finding the killer?'

Singh smiled. 'Sooner or later we'll get him.'

Klien returned his smile. 'I'm sure you will,' he said. He finished his coffee and stood up. 'Thanks for your time.'

'I'll get Suran to take you down to files.'

Two minutes later Singh's secretary – yet another available young woman the commissioner had tried to interest him in – escorted him down to the first floor and a private terminal booth. Klien accessed the files containing the pix and information of all known drug dealers and associated criminals in Calcutta's teeming underworld.

He appreciated the fine irony of Commissioner Singh's allowing his access to these files. It was from here that Klien selected the criminals upon whom he would visit his retribution.

To do good in this world, one had also to do a little bad.

One hour later he copied the pix and personal details of half a dozen likely candidates. Over the next few weeks he would investigate these people, assess their undesirability and award them marks from one to ten on the scale of evil, and then chart their movements and security arrangements.

He closed the file and accessed another containing the pix and details of everyone with a criminal record in the sub-continent of India. He entered in the vital statistics of the person he was seeking and waited until the program trawled through the file and assorted sub-files. It was a long shot, he knew. Sita Mackendrick had disappeared over thirteen years ago and not a trace of her had been seen since.

For almost that long, Klien had built his career in Calcutta, and visited his vengeance upon those he judged deserving, but all the while he had worked at finding the girl. He had used the privileges of his position at the port to access files usually closed to the layman: government documents, business profiles and security records all of which contained pix of individuals, often without their knowledge. He had found nothing. It was as if Sita Mackendrick had disappeared from the face of the Earth. Which, of course, was entirely possible, but it would be a monumental task to look for her on every colony world in the Expansion. Of course, there was always the chance that she was dead, but Klien did not like to dwell on the consequences if this were so.

At noon he closed the file and left the police head-quarters. He dined at an expensive Japanese restaurant in

161

the city centre, and after the meal sat back with a glass of sake. It was the one day away from the port that he allowed himself every week. This afternoon he had arranged to meet a nasty individual known as Raja Khan, supposedly to talk about a consignment of stolen gold that Khan wanted to offload. Klien was posing as an interested potential buyer. In fact he would be deciding if he would be victim number . . . what was it now? Nine? Ten?

He ordered another sake, took the pix of Sita Mackendrick from his pocket and spread them on the table. They showed her as she was at the age of nine and as she would be now, a slight, intense woman with a pretty face and intelligent eyes. He wondered how many times he had looked upon these computer-generated images, dreaming of the day when he would at last find her.

It seemed a very long time since he had started out on the trail that had brought him eventually to Earth. He thought back to when he had traced Quineau through space to the planet of Madrigal, all those years ago. He relived again his disappointment on discovering that his one-time colleague no longer possessed the softscreen. It was, according to Quineau, in the hands of one Charles Mackendrick, who had taken the screen to Calcutta, Earth.

Klien had killed Quineau then – his very first killing – for the good of Quineau himself, for the good of humankind. It was God's will, he knew. He had shot Quineau in the head, and the traitor died instantly, without protest and, one could say, almost peacefully. Then Klien had knelt over the body and, like a priest bestowing benediction, traced the shape of a cross on the side of Quineau's face not blackened beyond recognition.

He had left Madrigal, and three days later arrived on Earth.

It seemed such a long, long time ago. He smiled as he recalled his assumption, when he stepped off the shuttle at Calcutta spaceport, that his mission was drawing to an end. If only he had known that it was only just the beginning.

He glanced at his watch. It was almost two – time for his appointment with Raja Khan. He paid his bill, left the restaurant and made his way to an underground bar a hundred metres along the street. In the lavatory he pulled the capillary net from his jacket and slipped it over his head. He looked in the mirror. A thin-faced, silver-haired man stared back at him.

He returned to the bar, ordered a beer and carried it to a private booth at the far end of the low-lighted room. Five minutes later Raja Khan entered, a giant of a man in a voluminous shalwar kameez, who had to stoop to allow his full head of oiled black hair safe passage through the doorway.

Klien lifted his glass in a salute, and Khan joined him.

'Have you decided yet?' Khan asked.

Klien had to control his reactions. He felt nothing but revulsion towards this man. He had read his file, his extensive criminal record. He would have taken great delight in eliminating him right now. But he had to be careful.

'Have you decided?' Khan asked again, greed evident in his insistence.

Klien looked away from the Indian, finding the oversized features of his face gross and displeasing. Two young women were leaving the bar, and Khan mistook Klien's gaze.

Khan reached across the table and tapped the back of Klien's hand. 'You like, hey? If you like, I can supply, ah-cha? Or perhaps you prefer boys?'

Klien realised, then, that he had decided. Raja Khan had just signed his own death warrant.

163

For the next hour they discussed the details of the transaction.

'We need to meet again,' Klien said. 'I must show you where the gold is to be delivered.'

Khan gestured. 'Ah-cha. Fine. You tell me a place, a time.' Klien smiled to himself. Very soon, he knew, the world would be a fractionally better place for honest citizens.

13

Bennett touched Mackendrick's arm and indicated the view through the transporter's side window. 'Another line of markers.'

They passed down an avenue laid with the arrow-like stones to either hand, as if to guide visitors towards the ruin. It had appeared massive enough from a distance; only as they drew into the valley did its true size become apparent. It receded in perspective, a series of tall columns and ornately carved cross-pieces.

When the transporter came to a halt, Bennett climbed from the cab and walked into the shadows of the ruin. Mackendrick followed with a shoulder-mounted camera. Ten Lee came last, even her usually immobile features registering something at her awe.

Bennett gestured to Mackendrick. 'How come this wasn't picked up on the satellite shots?'

'There was only one probe, remember, Josh? It made a single orbit and a lot of the planet was obscured by storms. It was a miracle it picked up what it did.'

Bennett nodded and moved off by himself, walking further into the valley between the columns. There was something about the scale of the ruin that demanded quiet and solitary contemplation. Each fluted column was perhaps a hundred metres high and five broad. Time and the storms had brought a number of columns and cross-pieces tumbling down. Their remains lay on the floor of the valley, claimed and covered by the pervasive purple grass. Bennett scrambled across the overgrown mounds, staring ahead at the columns marching off into the valley.

Ten Lee called from behind him. 'Over here!'

He jumped down and joined her. She was examining a carving at the foot of a column. It showed circles within circles, a concentric series of symbols and hieroglyphs.

Ten Lee was shaking her head. 'It's a mandala, Joshua. Look, these are the nine spheres of existence. In here, this garden at the centre, this is the symbolic representation of Nirvana. It is very much like the mandalas of the Mahayana school.' She fell silent, her small fingers tracing the weather-worn grooves.

Mackendrick lowered his camera. 'Must be a coincidence, Ten. Humans can't have built this. It's made from the same stone as the markers out there. At a rough guess I'd say it's at least ten thousand years old.'

'Humans had nothing to do with this,' Ten Lee said. 'The truth must be even more amazing.'

Bennett looked at her. 'What do you mean?'

'Don't you see? If aliens built this, then they too must have followed a philosophy similar to Buddhism. Do you understand the implications of this? It means that a second race has developed the same philosophy, arrived at the same universal truth.'

'If,' Bennett pointed out, 'this is indeed a mandala; if it meant the same to the aliens as it does to us.'

Ten Lee nodded. 'Of course. We must be cautious in ascribing motives and methods.'

They split up. Bennett resumed his walk along the boulevard of columns. Tenebrae was setting, lending a soft opalescent light to the ruinous scene. He noticed movement at the top of a column and froze with involuntary surprise. He relaxed – one of the great birds they had seen earlier, the pteranodon equivalent, was roosting in a messy nest, stretching its awkward sickle wings and cawing from time to time.

Bennett checked the foot of each column, looking for mandalas or other carvings. He came across one or two similar designs, and many more carvings similar to those on the markers on the plain: square tablets covered with the familiar hieroglyphs. He looked back the way he had come. The others were tiny figures lost in the perspective of the receding columns. He should, he knew, be feeling wonder now, a sense of the awe of discovery, and while he did feel something of the intellectual *frisson* at the consequence of this find, another part of him recalled what he had thought earlier: that no matter what they discovered, it would be an anti-climax. He, the observer, would still be aware of the fact that, at base, he was still himself, flawed and weak and full of self-doubt and worse.

So five minutes later, when he came across the first of the statues, he was thinking of Julia and Ella and still experiencing a residuum of pain, and at the same time he was staring up at the carved image of a being that was not quite humanoid, yet not quite insectoid, but something of an eerie amalgam of the two. There were other statues positioned between the columns, a whole series of them receding further into the valley.

It was a good thirty seconds before he remembered himself and called out. 'Ten, Mack! Over here!' Even then he could not stop himself thinking how Ella would have loved hearing about this.

Mackendrick and Ten arrived by his side, breathless. They stared up at the figures, each one perhaps three metres tall. Mackendrick swore to himself and Ten murmured something in her own language.

The statue was carved from white stone, and showed a bipedal, thin-legged creature, bent of knee, with a long torso consisting of too many ribs. Its head was attenuated with something of a horse about it, and at the same time a locust, its eyes large and staring. On the plinth beneath its feet was a series of hieroglyphs, as if the being depicted was a famous alien and this was some form of commemoration.

'Do you think they're life-sized?' Bennett said.

Mackendrick squinted up at the statue. He shook his head. 'In this gravity, and as thin as they are? No way, Josh. I'd guess that they'd be not much taller than us.'

'I wonder,' Ten Lee added, 'if they still exist.'

Bennett stared into the face of the statue. He was on a Rim planet two thousand light years from home, had just discovered incontrovertible evidence of alien life on Penumbra, and the fact was still to hit him. He wished he could forget himself and feel the sense of wonder Mack and Ten Lee were obviously enjoying.

'We're just an hour away from the settlement,' Mackendrick was saying. 'There's a couple of hours of daylight left. Should we press on to the settlement, or stay here the night?'

Ten Lee said, 'I would like to investigate the settlement, see what is there.'

'Me too,' Bennett said. 'Let's move on.'

They left the statues and made their way back down the avenue of columns to the transporter. Mackendrick drove from the valley and turned to the north, accelerating along the plain of purple grass.

They made the journey in silence, each unwilling to break the mood of expectation – and not a little apprehension – that had settled over them. Bennett considered what lay ahead, if indeed the settlement was a settlement and was inhabited. Would a confrontation with an actual living alien, not just a frozen statue, shake him from his apathy?

'We've been lucky,' Mackendrick said at last, breaking the tension. 'We haven't been caught in a storm today.'

'And it was fine during the night,' Ten Lee said.

It was as if they had to fill the silence with small talk in a bid to shut out what lay ahead.

'We'll probably experience the storm of all storms tonight,' Bennett added.

An uneasy silence followed. The transporter bucketed along at speed, as if it too was impatient to reach the settlement. Tenebrae descended with immense ease towards the mountains in the east. Overhead, in the rarefied dark blue of night, the minor sun beamed weakly among the scatter of distant stars.

'I was wondering . . .' Mackendrick began. 'When we get to the settlement, do we go in armed?' He glanced from Ten Lee to Bennett.

'If they're Buddhists,' Ten Lee replied, 'they'll be a peaceable people.'

'And if they're not Buddhists,' Bennett pointed out, 'and that mandala of yours was the symbol of a warring clan, they might butcher us first and ask questions later.'

Ten Lee gave him an unreadable look. He sensed her disdain.

'I'm sorry, Ten, but I don't think we should assume too much from symbols that just happen to look like something we know and understand from Earth.'

'Why don't we wait until we get there,' Ten Lee compromised. 'If you wish, I will go in first, alone.'

Mackendrick nodded. 'We'll assess the situation when we arrive – but there's no going in alone. We're in this together.'

The plain rose before them and the transporter laboured up the incline. At the crest, Mackendrick slowed and then cut the engine. They stared through the windshield at the revealed panorama.

169

The land fell away towards a narrowing of the two mountain ranges, and situated in a dipping saddle of land were the structures the probe had filmed on its fly-by. There were perhaps thirty constructions, small square cabins built of timber, in two orderly lines in the centre of the valley. To one side, overlooking the settlement, was a peculiar rise in the plain, an irregular hump like a low earthwork or tumulus.

'There doesn't seem to be anyone at home,' Bennett said. 'Unless they retire early.'

'We'll go in with the transporter,' Mackendrick said. 'As a precaution, keep your rifles at the ready.'

Bennett raised his pulser as Mackendrick powered up the transporter. They moved slowly down the incline, passing the earthwork and approaching the first of the cabins at a crawl. Mackendrick cut the engine and, in the sudden silence, they sat without a word and stared down at the settlement of crudely built huts.

It occurred to Bennett that the aliens, if they were also responsible for the settlement, had certainly devolved from the mighty race which had constructed the columned temple or museum.

'Okay,' Mackendrick said in a hushed voice. 'We'll get out and walk in together.'

Bennett jumped from the cab and clutched his rifle, apprehension creating a tightness in his chest. With Ten Lee and Mackendrick he walked slowly towards the first timber cabin. It appeared, he thought, little different from a crude shack in backwoods Oregon.

The first cabin was clearly derelict. The door hung on one hinge, and likewise the shutters on the glassless window. Purple grass and a form of bind-weed had climbed the outer walls. Bennett kicked open the hanging door and peered into the dim interior. The little light cast by the setting gas giant revealed bare boards and a broken chair; the sound of scurrying suggested that the cabin's only occupants were small animals.

Bennett backed out, shaking his head. 'No one at home, Mack.'

They moved to the next cabin in line, identical in design to the first and, it seemed, all the others. This one was empty even of broken furniture. They conferred outside the door.

'How long do you think they've been deserted?' Mackendrick asked. 'Fifteen, twenty years?'

'Or fifty, a hundred?' Bennett added. 'Much of the timber's rotting, but we're on an alien world. How long does wood take to rot on Penumbra? It's hard to tell how long they've been empty.'

'Do you think the same beings built the columned structure and these shacks?' Ten Lee asked.

'If the ruins are at least ten thousand years old,' Bennett said, 'a race can go a long way downhill in that time. They entered a dark age, lost their collective ability to design great architecture – or their need to build it – and resorted to these.'

'Okay,' Mackendrick said. 'Let's split up and search each cabin. If you find anything, shout.'

Bennett moved to the third shack, ducking past what remained of the door. He looked around the single room. The skeleton of a bunk bed occupied one corner. There was no sign of personal effects or possessions of any kind, no tools or utensils that might have been left behind when their erstwhile owners moved on.

He walked from cabin to cabin along the row, finding much the same in each: the odd scrap of broken furniture, or nothing at all. In the last cabin he recognised the shape of an infant's cot, made from the same timber as was used on the huts, rotted through and lying on its side. It spoke to him more eloquently of a lost race than had the statues in the ruin, carved with care and skill for posterity. He considered the similarities in such diverse races. He had travelled thousands of light years to the Rim, and here was something constructed for an alien infant, recognisably a cot.

He was stepping from the cabin, about to find Mackendrick and suggest they pitch camp for the night, when Ten Lee's muffled voice sounded from the second row of cabins. He walked around the shack and looked up and down the length of what once might have been the main street. Ten Lee was a tiny figure standing outside the last cabin in the row, waving frantically.

'Joshua! In here!'

Mackendrick appeared from a nearby hut and hurried over to Ten Lee. She was leaning against the jamb of the door, wearing an expression of shock.

'Ten?' Bennett took her shoulder. 'Ten, are you okay?'

She shook her head. 'I honestly don't know.'

'What is it?' Mackendrick snapped.

She indicated over her shoulder. 'In there. On the far wall. I don't *think* I was seeing things . . .'

Bennett hurried into the shack, Mackendrick behind him. The last light of Tenebrae sent a pale searchlight through the window and illuminated a square patch on the wall, and in the illuminated square was a picture, an old pix crudely framed with four lengths of the ubiquitous timber.

'I don't believe it,' Mackendrick whispered.

Bennett reached out, lifted the pix from the wall and carried it outside so that the brighter light might confirm what he was seeing. He sat on the step, Ten Lee and Mackendrick beside him. He understood, now, Ten's strange reaction. He was experiencing it himself. The pix showed a view, faded with time, of the Eiffel Tower.

'Paris,' Mackendrick said, needlessly. 'Paris, France.'

Bennett turned the pix over, as if looking for something to confirm its authenticity. He laughed. What confirmation did he need? He was holding – there was no doubt about it – a pix of the Eiffel Tower.

Even though he knew it was impossible.

Ten Lee, sharper-eyed than Bennett, pointed to a detail in the pix, a tiny automobile beneath the tower. 'Look, isn't that an electric Volvo? That model went out with the ark. It must be a hundred years old.'

Speechless, they stared at the pix of Paris a century old.

'Okay,' Bennett said. 'Silly question: how the hell did it get here?'

Mackendrick said, 'Let's go through the cabins again. Check everything. There must be something else that might explain what the hell's going on here.'

For the second time they searched the deserted settlement.

Bennett had no idea what made him look up, back towards the transporter and beyond. He stepped from the first cabin, having found nothing other than the broken chair, and glanced at the distant mountains, then the transporter reflecting warped highlights of the gas giant. Behind the vehicle was the long, low rise of the earthwork. His heart hammering, hardly daring to hope that he was right, he set off up the hillside. Mackendrick and Ten Lee were going through the second row, and he didn't want to alert them in case he was mistaken.

He passed the transporter and ran the last fifty metres. The ground underfoot became soft, waterlogged. The hill rose before him, the purple grass covering the shape of something long and low, and strangely familiar.

He knelt and tore away a handful of purple grass, revealing a section of silver metal.

He stood and walked along the length of the sunken structure. He pulled at the vegetation, which came away

173

easily, and peered down. This section of the upper body-work had been removed, no doubt in the process of cannibalisation, and only the struts and spars of the framework remained. He climbed down, using the frame of the skeletal ship as a ladder, and found himself in the hold of a colony liner, a vast central chamber like the nave of a cathedral, illuminated by the pale light of Tenebrae falling through the rent he had made high above.

He stepped forward, moving down the length of the ship. He imagined its final descent, the inability of this cumbersome, clumsy craft to negotiate the storms that lashed the planet. He saw it ploughing into the plain, nosing up a bow wave of soil. He considered the terror of the thousands of colonists as they imagined death on an alien world so far from home.

There was very little of the ship left other than its shell and framework, and much of that had been removed, no doubt taken to help with the construction of a more permanent settlement elsewhere. The settlement of cabins had been a temporary measure, makeshift accommodation for colonists while they dismantled and transported parts of the ship to a more viable site. This completed, they had departed the cabins, leaving only broken furniture, and the tantalising pix of the Eiffel Tower. And over the years the starship had slowly submerged into the bog, and the vegetation of Penumbra had gone to work and reclaimed the land ploughed by the starship.

He paused beside a flange of outer panelling that had come loose from the framework of the flank and fallen. On the panel, excoriated by its transit through the void and faded by the storms, he could just make out the red, white and blue logo of the François Aeronautics Line.

He wondered how it had found itself so far off course, on the Rim of the galaxy instead of in the safe cone of inhabited space known as the Expansion. Unless, of course, they had set out deliberately to explore this far afield. It would be just like the French, with a gesture combining bravery and bravura, to flout convention and head for the Rim.

He considered the events of the short day, the discovery of the ruins and the wreck of the liner. It was ironic that, of the two finds, it was that of the old liner from Earth which had filled him most with wonder, made him forget for however brief a moment the fact of himself, his cares and concerns. He turned and made his way back along the length of the ship, hurrying to tell Mackendrick and Ten Lee what he had discovered.

He was climbing up towards the rent he had made in the grass when he heard the sound of laser fire burning through the air. His heart kicked. Laser fire . . . not pulser fire. Which meant that someone other than Mack and Ten Lee was doing the shooting.

He reached the hole in the grass and peered through.

Down below in the settlement a cabin was burning, filling the twilight with its garish illumination. He tried to make sense of the scene. He saw two vehicles bounce to a halt outside the settlement, absurdly spindly contraptions with balloon tyres and next to no bodywork. Perhaps a dozen men – small dark figures at this distance, but obviously human – poured from the vehicles and ran towards where Mackendrick and Ten Lee stood with their arms above their heads. One of the humans fired again, setting to flame a nearby cabin, a display of blatant overkill given that Mack and Ten had already surrendered.

The humans swarmed around their prisoners, old-fashioned laser rifles levelled and ready, and gestured for

Mackendrick and Ten Lee to move towards the closer balloon-tyred vehicle.

Slowly, arms still in the air, they obliged.

Bennett watched, considering his options. If he attacked now, attempting to free his friends, he would be hopelessly outnumbered. He wouldn't stand a chance, and his actions would probably get Ten and Mack killed as well as himself. It would be wiser to wait, bide his time. He'd remain in hiding until the humans left the settlement, and then follow at a safe distance in the transporter. At some point he would leave the vehicle and continue on foot. He was armed. He would have the advantage of surprise. He would find where Ten Lee and Mack were being kept and attempt to effect their rescue.

The humans boarded their vehicles and drove off, bouncing over the purple grass. They moved quietly, obviously electric-powered, their wide tyres leaving helpful tracks in the vegetation.

Then the transporter started up, and he told himself that he should have known they were hardly likely to leave behind such a valuable resource as a fully equipped transporter.

Okay, a slight change of plan. He would follow on foot, find where Ten Lee and Mackendrick were being held, and get them out.

He watched the transporter and the balloon-tyred vehicles pass into the glare behind the burning cabins. He waited long minutes, aware of the laboured thudding of his heart. There were no signs that the humans had left any of their party. The only movement was the dance of shadows as the cabins burned themselves out.

Heart racing, he climbed from the starship and ran towards the settlement, feeling suddenly vulnerable out in the open. He passed the burning cabins and paused behind the last shack in the row. After the brightness of the flames, it was some time before his vision adjusted to the twilight. The distant minor sun provided meagre illumination, perhaps twice that of a full moon on Earth. He made out the mountains narrowing on either side, the plain sloping off to the left and eventually, a kilometre or so away, ending in a pass between high foothills. In the pale starlight the tracks of the vehicles showed as dark parallel lines of flattened vegetation.

Bennett left the sanctuary of the last cabin and jogged across the plain to the three sets of tracks in the grass. He slowed to a walk, his breath coming with difficulty. He had tried to work out on Redwood Station, using the gym every other day, but he had only maintained a low level of fitness. It was no preparation for a long-distance run.

He peered ahead. Far away, on the pass between the enfolding foothills, he could just make out the three small shapes of the beetling vehicles.

He combined jogging with long stretches of walking, taking deep breaths through his nose. Soon the weight of the rifle became a burden. The absurd notion of ditching it brought to mind the very real fact that soon he might have to use it to free his friends. The thought of killing people, even those who had captured Ten Lee and Mack, filled him with dread. He set the rifle to stun.

Perhaps an hour later the plain narrowed and rose towards the pass high above. He paused, knelt and regained his breath. He looked up at the crest of the incline, wondering what he might find beyond. Christ, but there might be kilometres to go yet, before he came to the humans' permanent settlement.

Bennett stood and set off, refusing to contemplate the possibility. The climb was enervating after the distance he had already covered. He stopped often, kneeling to rest his legs and fill his lungs. The crest was elusive, an optical illusion that seemed never to get any closer.

At last he slowed and moved to the rugged ground where the hillside rose in a tumble of rocks. He would proceed with caution from here; he had no desire to walk straight into trouble. He crept over the uneven terrain, keeping his gaze fixed ahead, alert to the slightest movement. He came to the highest point of the pass, stood and peered down.

The land fell away acutely from here, forming a vast valley lodged between the converging mountains. On the near slope of the valley, Bennett made out perhaps a hundred dwellings: domes perched on broad bands of terracing, timber lodges, more substantial villas made from stone, all illuminated by the light of the stars and the minor sun. Then he saw, on the distant far terraces, yet more dome habitats and villas. Stationed on the mountainside at strategic positions around the valley he made out the tall, slender shapes of wind turbines – perhaps a hundred in all. No doubt the balloon-tyred vehicles were powered by electricity generated by the turbines.

He wondered at the population of the settlement. Star liners held five thousand citizens, and they had been here for perhaps a century. The vast scatter of dwellings and the proliferating turbines suggested that they had prospered. The growth of the colony also suggested that they had managed to utilise and maintain the manufactory with which all colony ships were equipped.

The pass became a track that extended high above the settlement, following the contours of the mountain. In the distance Bennett made out the last of the vehicles, the transporter, as it disappeared behind the bend. His heart sank. He had kilometres yet to traverse. He was about to set off when he saw, in the distance, the reappearance of one of the balloon-tyred vehicles; the track evidently curved back on itself, following a zig-zag route to negotiate the steep slope of the valley wall. The vehicles carrying Ten Lee and Mackendrick were now coming back towards him.

He ran along the track, then turned down the incline, moving through a field of some kind of wheat. He passed a dome habitat, the hemisphere darkened, and paused on the edge of the farm above the road. He crouched behind a dry-stone wall, his pulse racing, and peered over. One by one the vehicles passed a matter of metres from where he was concealed. He made out, on the leading truck, the crouched form of Ten Lee. The vehicles turned, easing around a bend on to another stretch of lower track. He saw the first vehicle stop before a big timber lodge, built out over the drop and supported on pillars. As he watched, Ten Lee and Mackendrick were manhandled from the vehicle and marched into the building. The vehicles started up and moved off. Half a kilometre away they turned into an area beside one of the farm buildings.

Bennett climbed over the low wall and ran across the track. He moved through another field, bent double, and stopped beside the retaining wall. Fifty metres away was the lodge in which Ten Lee and Mackendrick were imprisoned. A light showed in one of the long side windows.

He waited. At last the light went out. He jumped over the wall, crossed the track and approached the building, feeling conspicuous with his rifle. If anyone should look out and see him now, in his distinctive flight-suit, carrying a rifle . . .

He made the building and crouched in its shadow, aware that he was shaking with uncontrollable fear. He tried to work out what to do next, to form some kind of plan. Try to enter the building without alerting the colonists, obviously. Easier said than done. They were unlikely to leave the door obligingly open. So break in, without making a sound. A tall order. He was not a house breaker. Storm the place, then. But nor was he a commando.

The decision, in the event, was taken from him. He stood, intending to move around the building to a window where he might see what was going on inside. He had hardly taken two steps when a voice rang out, challenging him: 'Stop!'

He turned in time to receive the full force of a rifle butt on the side of his head. The assault was so sudden that he had no time to dodge the blow or catch sight of his attacker. His head seemed to explode with pain and he fell to the ground. He tried to gather himself, get up and fight, but after the initial anger at being caught, he thought again. The man was armed and there might be more than one of them by now. He should stay down and bide his time.

He felt hands grasp his body, lifting him. He was carried, perhaps by two or three people. He opened his eyes to see where he was being taken, but he was face down and could make out only the shadowy gravel of the pathway. He closed his eyes as his head throbbed painfully.

Bennett heard a door opening, then closing, footsteps on timber. He was dropped without ceremony to the floor. He was aware of people in the room, perhaps two or three others; small movements and whispers gave them away. He kept his eyes shut, feigning unconsciousness.

He heard two people conduct a hurried conversation. He tried to appreciate the melodrama of the situation. If this was not actually happening to him, he would have found it hard to believe. He told himself that things like this only happened in holodramas . . . then the pain in his head informed him otherwise.

'They're not terrorists as we first thought, sir, they're off-worlders.'

A pause, then: 'But how did they find out?'

Another voice answered, deep and richly textured. Bennett imagined a silver-haired patriarch. He tried to work out the meaning of their dialogue.

'Perhaps Quineau did reach Earth, after all?'

'But Klien was confident of stopping him.'

'Then perhaps their arrival here is purely accidental. They know nothing – they're explorers, prospectors.' A pause. 'I want them questioned. Subtly, of course.'

A brief silence. Bennett felt himself drifting, the pain in his skull almost too much to bear. He tried to concentrate.

The first colonist said, 'We can't let them go back, sir.'

'What are you suggesting,' the deep-voiced patriarch replied, 'that we kill them?'

'Precisely. Then they're out of the way. Alive, they're dangerous.'

'If they are scientists and have nothing to do with Quineau, then they might prove a benefit to the colony. They might be just the type of people we need.'

'But if they find out?'

The patriarch replied, 'We will have to ensure that they *don't* find out – as simple as that.'

'How do we keep them here? What about their ship?'

'Have someone question them as to where they landed. Then send out a team to destroy it. When they find out, we'll blame it on the terrorists.'

'I don't know . . .' The first colonist sounded uneasy. 'It would be far easier if we just killed them.'

'You worry too much,' said the patriarch. 'Trust me.'

Bennett felt himself losing his grip on consciousness. He tried to concentrate on the voices, but they faded, became no more than background noise.

At last, mercifully floating free of pain, Bennett passed out.

181

14

Klien stood before the full-length mirror and dressed with care. Tonight was to be a killing night, when he would do his microscopic bit to make this corner of the Expansion a better place. As ever on these special occasions, he wore his sabline suit.

He moved to the lounge with its sunken sofa bunkers, its *objets d'art*, an aria by Verdi playing softly. He stood for a long time, staring at the room until he no longer saw it as a physical location, but as an abstract idea – the one locus of the universe where he was safe, his refuge from all the corruption and the evil out there. He steadied his breathing, tried to control the crazy thudding of his heart. He knew that he had to leave now, to walk off his nervous excitement. He ensured that he had his capillary net and laser pistol and then walked from the house and through the quiet streets.

The monsoon rain had refreshed the trees and shrubs in the gardens and parks. The rising moon and the lights of the high orbitals reflected in rain droplets on leaves and flowers. It was like, he thought, the garden of Eden. It was hard to believe that this idyllic corner of Calcutta, the meanest city on the meanest planet of all, was surrounded by so much evil. He thought back to his time on Homefall; it had been a period of innocence, or perhaps ignorance. He had been privileged to live on such a haven, without knowledge of what existed outside. And people like Quineau, they wanted to open up the planet, allow the evil of the Expansion to inundate paradise.

He walked quickly past the overblown residences of millionaires, many of the houses, like his own, styled upon the grand buildings of history. He was often sickened by the profligacy of wealth, and nowhere was such excess more evident than the country where abject poverty was still a fact of life for many. Oh, dear God, how he missed Homefall. He told himself to concentrate, to think only of the job ahead. If he were to allow his mind to stray, his thoughts to dwell on anything other than his mission, then disaster would befall him.

He stopped when he came to a com-screen kiosk, stepped inside and pulled on the capillary net. A silver-haired stranger regarded him in the blank screen. Satisfied, he left the kiosk, a new man.

He wondered, as he strode through the gathering darkness, if the officers of the Homicide Division had worked out the pattern of his killings yet. It had come about quite accidentally, eight years ago after his third killing. A newspaper report carried a map of the district, with stars to locate the positions of the murders; they happened, he noticed, to form a straight line running approximately north to south. Into his head came the sudden and blinding vision of a crucifix, and he was struck by the notion of how appropriate, how fitting, the symbol would be. The brand of God, eradicating evil, upon the face of the city.

With each execution, he realised, he ran the increased risk of the pattern being discovered. One day, he knew, some observant officer in Homicide would notice the partly formed crucifix, and stake out the areas where he had yet to commit a killing. He admitted to himself that the chance of being apprehended added a certain *frisson* of risk to his self-appointed mission of cleansing the city.

He wondered if, on some subconscious level, his decision to commit the murders in the design of a great cross was a desire to be apprehended and punished? Perhaps, in lieu of returning to his planet of birth, to paradise, he would rather die the death of a martyr on Earth? Whatever, he hoped that his day of judgement would be suspended for a short while yet. He had three more killings to accomplish before the crucifix would be finished: one at the very end of the right crossbar, and one beneath each crossbar, to represent the moons of Phobos and Deimos.

Klien smiled to himself. They would be puzzled by the location of tonight's killing, no doubt. This one would represent Phobos, for the crucifix he was carving across the city was the cross of the Church of Phobos and Deimos, formerly of Mars, but no longer existing anywhere but on his birthplace of Homefall.

He was safe for a while yet, at least.

And after that, when the crucifix was completed? What then? Then, he would sit back and consider his options.

He crossed a quiet residential street and cut down a tree-lined footpath. At last he came to a small square of grass, an area of parkland where during the day the children of the rich played, watched over by their nannies and bodyguards. Tonight the park was quiet.

He paused at the end of the pathway. He looked at his watch in the light of the moon. It was almost eight o'clock. He realised that his hands were shaking, his heartbeat thumping. At times like this, when he was about to end the life of another, he felt most alive himself.

He looked out for the arrival of Raja Khan. He scanned the area for any sign that Khan had disobeyed his instructions and brought along accomplices – but Khan knew that if he did so, Klien would cancel the deal. It was in Khan's interests to follow Klien's instructions to the letter.

Seconds later he saw a shadowy figure at the far end of the park. Khan, his great bulk eclipsing the coachlight of a house done in the style of an English Tudor mansion, moved across the park towards Klien. The man was alone.

'Where are we?' Khan asked. 'Where's your warehouse, Smith?'

Klien gestured in the half-light. 'Down here. A hundred metres to the left.'

Khan sounded unsure. 'In this neighbourhood? Are you sure?'

'What are you frightened of, my friend?' Klien said. 'You want the money, don't you?'

This shut him up. 'Ah-cha,' he said at last. 'We go.'

Klien led the way back down the footpath. He judged that the nearest residence was perhaps fifty metres away. The crack of a laser charge would go unnoticed. He reached into the jacket of his sabline suit and caressed the butt of his laser pistol.

He paused in the silver illumination of a streetlight, and half turned. He wanted to look upon the face of the criminal as Khan realised that he was about to die, see the surprise in his eyes.

'What?' Khan said. 'I don't see—'

Klien withdrew his pistol, took aim and fired. By some fluke, Khan anticipated the shot and ducked to one side. The charge missed the man's head by a fraction and, screaming in panic and pain, he turned and staggered off along the footpath. Klien gave chase, his stomach churning. Khan fell to his knees, then slumped on to his side. Klien stood over him, kicked the giant on to his back. Khan stared up at him with terrified eyes, the flesh of his forehead and a great chunk of hair burned away.

'Why?' Khan managed in a whisper.

Klien knelt, aware of the overwhelming feeling of exultation coursing through him. He was being presented, on this occasion, with the opportunity always denied him: to inform his victims why they were about to die, to make them face the ultimate consequence of their ways.

'Do you repent?' Klien almost spat, his face inches from the dying man's. 'Do you recognise your sins and are you truly sorry?'

'I . . .'

'What? Say it! Say you repent!'

'You're . . . you are mad.'

'Verily I am angry, Khan. I am angry on behalf of God. You' – he pointed the pistol, almost firing then – 'and people like you deserve no more than summary execution. Criminals, drug dealers, pimps and murderers, you bring misery to the innocent, the blight of evil into the lives of those who have done you no harm! Do you repent?'

'I . . .' Khan spluttered, a mere gasp of pain. 'I was doing what I had to do to survive.'

Klien almost wept with rage. 'You brought pain and misery to the innocent,' he said, 'and for this you must die!'

'No!'

Klien fired, the charge frying the right side of Khan's face, causing instant death by massive neural dysfunction. Kneeling over the body, crying quietly to himself, Klien reached out with his razor and sliced the sign of the cross into the ample flesh of Raja Khan's left cheek.

He stood and hurried from the body, enraged still by Khan's defiance in the face of death. Perhaps, he thought, as great an evil as one's original crime was the inability to see it as such and admit to one's sins.

He heard a noise to his right, movement in the garden beyond the hedge. He stopped and listened intently, but no further sounds came. Perhaps it had been an animal, or in his anger he was becoming paranoid. He hurried on,

186

almost running in his haste to gain the sanctuary of his home.

Ten minutes later he locked his front door on the world. He put his pistol and capillary net in the safe behind the Vermeer print, moved to the bathroom and showered. As the hot water massaged his tired skin, he felt the tension drain from him. It was a mistake, he realised, to have tried to extract some admission of sin from Khan. Evil men would never admit to the errors of their ways. He would not make the same mistake in future. He would merely carry out the killing and rest assured in the knowledge that the world was then a little safer.

He moved to the lounge, poured himself a large brandy and lay in one of the sunken bunkers. For the next hour he closed his eyes and concentrated on the taste of the brandy, riding the wave of exhilaration surging through him. It was at times like this, when he seemed to be most alive, before, during and immediately after a killing, that he was reminded of why he came to Earth.

From a drawer in the table in the middle of the sunken bunker he withdrew a stack of pix. He spread them on the cushion beside him and sipped his brandy.

On arriving on Earth almost fourteen years ago, Calcutta had struck him as a hellish congestion of humanity, traffic and constant noise. He had literally stopped in his tracks on stepping from the spaceport at midnight. He had never before seen so many people. They flowed down the streets in never-ending waves, thousands of people of all types: Indians in strange clothes, more familiar Europeans in suits and dresses, tall jet-black Africans in robes and djellabas. He'd thought that perhaps this area was so congested for being so close to the spaceport, but when he caught a taxi to the city centre he'd stared out in horror: the entire city was a mad-house of crowds and deafening traffic and strobing lights and vast nightmarish screens that hovered over everything and exhorted the populace to buy. He had booked a room in a hotel and did not venture out for two days.

Then, the urgency of his mission spurring him on, he'd emerged on to the crowded streets. The city was a curious mixture of the ultra-modern and the old, with the soaring polycarbon structures of the city centre overlooking a sea of slums patched together from scavenged carbon-fibre scraps and polythene, the rich commingling with the poor. His first experience of beggars, their tenacity some measure of their desperation, had shocked him profoundly. He'd wondered how a rich citizen of the city could exist without being tortured by guilt and shame.

Klien had located the headquarters of the Mackendrick Foundation, and Mackendrick's private residence to the west of the city, and considered how he might go about obtaining the softscreen. To his surprise he'd discovered, over a period of days of surreptitious surveillance, that Mackendrick's mansion was not only inadequately guarded, but lacked security cameras. He'd considered the possibility of breaking in and locating the softscreen by chance, but dismissed the idea. He would stand a better chance of finding the softscreen if he could by some means gain legitimate admittance. He'd been considering this when he heard on a news report that the house had indeed been broken into. A safe was robbed and Mackendrick's daughter had been kidnapped.

Klien saw his opportunity and had moved quickly to set up his own security and investigative company. He sent com-messages to Mackendrick's business headquarters and private mansion, detailing his spurious expertise in the field of security and private investigations.

About ten days later he'd received a summons to an exclusive city centre restaurant, not to meet Charles Mackendrick, as he'd expected, but his Indian wife,

Naheed. She had explained that Mackendrick's own security firm was handling the investigation into the theft and the kidnapping of their daughter, and that Mackendrick did not want outside concerns working on the case. Naheed had argued that surely two sets of people working on the same case would be an advantage, but Mackendrick had been adamant. Therefore, for the sake of her daughter, Naheed was willing to pay him a considerable sum to track down the kidnappers and return Sita. He'd asked if he might be able to visit the mansion at some point, but Naheed Mackendrick had been unsure.

'Is it absolutely necessary? I mean, if my husband found out . . .'

'It would help in my investigations, madam,' he'd said.

'What do you need to know? I have pictures of Sita' – she'd given him half a dozen pix of a shy-looking girl in a blue knee-length dress – 'and if you need to know what was stolen . . .'

Klien had frowned, wondering how he might gain admittance to the mansion. 'It might help.'

'All that was in the safe at the time was a small sum of money, and something belonging to my husband – an old softscreen entertainment.'

Klien remembered feeling the bottom drop from his stomach. He'd looked up at Naheed to see if she had noticed his reaction.

'A softscreen entertainment?' he'd said. 'What exactly . . . ?'

Naheed Mackendrick had waved dismissively. 'Oh, it was some old screen thing that Charles brought back from one of the colonies. He seemed to think it was valuable.'

'What did the . . . the screen show? What kind of entertainment?'

189

'I only glanced at the thing. It was some adventure story, set on a mountainous planet. Three explorers were looking for alien artefacts or some such.'

'I see,' he'd said, at first elated that he had made the breakthrough, and then immediately daunted at the prospect of having to find the kidnappers and the soft-screen in a city as populous as Calcutta.

'Do you think you'll be able to find my daughter, Mr Klien?'

He had reached across the table and touched her hand. 'You have my word that I will do my very best.'

From that day he had devoted his time to finding Sita Mackendrick. If he could locate the girl, and find out from her the identity of her kidnappers, then he would be that much closer to finding the softscreen. If, of course, she was still alive. For the first few weeks he had told Naheed Mackendrick to expect a ransom demand, but when no demand was made and Naheed came to him distraught at the thought that her daughter was dead, he had comforted her with the idea that perhaps she might have escaped.

'In that case, why hasn't she returned home?' she'd asked him.

He had wondered how to phrase it diplomatically. 'Was your daughter happy at home?'

Her silence, her avoidance of his gaze, had told Klien more than enough.

Klien had taken to the streets then, making enquiries, talking to people who had contact with street-kids, befriending the kids himself. At the same time he had scoured second-hand electrical stores and auction houses. In itself, the screen was not that valuable; perhaps the kidnappers had sold the softscreen, or even discarded it. All the while he had kept himself alert for news that an exploration company was heading for a hitherto uncharted planet out on the Rim, prompted by the discovery of an intriguing softscreen recording. No news had been forthcoming, and as the months progressed he convinced himself that the screen had been discarded or lost.

A year after the kidnapping of her daughter, Naheed Mackendrick had succumbed to leukaemia, so Klien's monthly stipend was curtailed. To earn a living and to keep abreast of developments in space, he had applied for a job as a security guard at the spaceport. His rise since then had been, as they say, meteoric. He had even accustomed himself to the squalor and poverty of Calcutta. He had become, without really realising it, one of the rich who deigned not to notice the poor.

But all the time, down all those years, he had not relented in his search for Sita Mackendrick. It had occurred to him, as he considered the many possibilities that surrounded the case, that she had not been kidnapped at all. He knew it was a wish-fulfilment fantasy, but what if it had been Sita Mackendrick herself who had stolen the contents of her father's safe and run away from home? What if she had the screen in her possession, after all these years?

He stared at the pix of the pretty young woman, wondering where she was now, wondering if the truth might ever be known.

He realised that his search had become an obsession, and he wondered what his reaction might be when, if, he finally did locate the girl. If she did indeed possess the screen, or knew of its whereabouts, and his search came to an end, then perhaps he would be unable to stop himself, and he would kill her as he had killed all his other victims over the years.

He reached out and drew, over the image of her face, the sign of the cross.

15

Rana was woken early by the chime of the doorbell. She fumbled her way out of bed, pulled on her wrap and moved to the speaker by the inner door of her new, spacious apartment.

'Who is it?'

'Security, Lieutenant Rao. Investigator Vishwanath sent me.'

'Oh . . . yes. Of course. Come on up.'

A minute later a spry Tamil sergeant stepped into the lounge carrying a case of equipment and a com-board. 'A small matter – I'll be no more than ten minutes,' he said. 'First I'll install an alarm pad in case of emergencies.'

She rubbed her eyes. 'Emergencies?'

The Tamil bobbed his head from side to side. 'Standard procedure,' he said. 'We've got to protect our officers. I'll make a sweep for bugs and other electronic surveillance apparatus.'

He set to work installing the alarm. 'I'll put it in here, behind this picture,' he said. 'In case of emergencies, all you need to do is press it lightly. This will activate alarms at the local station.'

Rana sat on the arm of a chair, watching him attach the small, flat rectangle to the wall behind the picture, a Chinese landscape inherited from the apartment's previous occupant.

He replaced the painting and looked around the room. 'Now I'll sweep the apartment for electronic listening devices and suchlike.'

He opened his case and took out an instrument like a communicator, switched it on and turned in a circle, directing the device at the walls.

He examined the screen and frowned. 'I'm getting something.'

Rana rubbed her tired face. 'You mean the place is bugged?' She was unconvinced.

'No, not bugged. There's a homing device in the apartment, a very crude affair. It's . . .' Like a diviner seeking water, he moved the device back and forth. 'It's in that drawer,' he said, pointing to her desk.

Her only possession worth locking away was the softscreen. She unlocked the drawer and lifted it out. Wafer thin, perhaps half a metre square, it was blank until pressed. Then it showed a fictional narrative set on some colony world, a drama featuring intrepid explorers battling through mountainous terrain.

'Do you mean this?'

The sergeant nodded. 'Can I examine it?'

Rana passed him the softscreen. He turned it over, minutely examining the weave of the fabric. 'It's very old,' he said. 'Perhaps a hundred years old?'

She nodded. 'It's an antique. It was . . . my father gave it to me when I was young.'

She could hardly tell him the truth, that she had taken the softscreen from her father's safe, along with a few hundred rupees, all those years ago.

The sergeant was frowning. 'It's implanted with a primitive homing device. Did your father put it there, to trace it in case it was ever stolen?'

Rana shrugged. 'I don't know.'

But her father could not have known about the homing

device, or he would have used it to trace her when she ran away from home . . .

The sergeant looked up. 'Can I take it back to the lab, Lieutenant? I'd like to examine it more closely. The homing device is embedded very skilfully into the fabric of the screen. I've never seen anything like it before. I'll issue you with a receipt.'

'You'll bring it back when you've finished with it?' she asked.

'I'll bring it back in a week, Lieutenant.' He folded the softscreen into his case and wrote out a receipt.

'The rest of the apartment is clean?'

He smiled. 'You've no need to worry, Lieutenant. I'll be back in a few months to run another check.'

The sergeant packed his case and saluted as he left. Rana closed the door behind him, then made herself a cup of coffee and drank it slowly, sitting by the window and staring across the mist-shrouded Nehru park.

A week had passed since Rana had reported to Vishwanath about the Man in the Black Suit, and the killer from Madrigal whose computer-generated image was now with every police station in the city. She had expected, in her naivety, to hear about the apprehension of the suspect within days, but there had been no progress at all on the case of the crucifix killer. Vishwanath had counselled confidence, and told her to try another lead. He had praised her initiative so far, but told her that in all likelihood the black suit had been just another one of those lines of enquiry that resulted in a dead end. Homicide work, he said, was full of them.

Rana had worked on other cases, murders she had had no real involvement in, and therefore could not feel as enthusiastic about. She knew they had to be solved, and she worked hard on them, but they would never have the appeal of her first investigation.

The chime of an incoming call sounded in her ear. She clicked her jaw to activate the communication. 'Rao here.'

'This is Lieutenant Nazeem.' His voice sounded loud in her ear. 'Vishwanath wants you quick sharp.'

'What is it?'

'The crucifix case you're working on.' He emphasised the 'you're', as Vishwanath had reassigned him shortly after Rana's arrival in the department. 'Something's happened.'

'What? Have they caught—'

But Naz had cut the connection.

She hurried from the apartment and caught a taxi to the police headquarters. She still had an hour to go before her shift officially started, so to be called early like this must mean that something important had occurred. She tried to control her excitement as she dashed into the building and rode the elevator to the eighth floor.

She unlocked her desk and retrieved her com-board, then made her way to Vishwanath's office.

'They've caught him?' she asked when she got there.

Vishwanath shook his head. 'I'm afraid not. Far from it, Lieutenant. That was forensic. It appears that our man has struck again.'

Rana felt as if a punch had knocked the wind from her. 'But I thought we had extra patrols—'

He nodded. 'We did. But he didn't strike where we thought he might.'

'Are you sure it's the same killer?'

'Forensic seem pretty convinced.' He picked up his com-board and stood wearily. 'Shall we go and take a look, Lieutenant?'

She followed him into the elevator and then out into the underground car-park. They climbed aboard a squad car and accelerated up the ramp and into the street. The morning mists had lifted and sunlight filled the bustling streets with its harsh glare.

'Where did he strike, sir?'

'Somewhere in the Raneesh suburb.'

Rana accessed the city map on her com-board. 'Below the left-hand crossbar of the crucifix. Do you know the identity of the victim?'

'One Raja Khan. He's known to us – he's a smuggler and extortionist. It would seem that the killer is continuing his moral crusade.'

Rana watched a food market flash by in a kaleidoscopic blur of reds and greens. She felt suddenly depressed at the thought of another murder, and it came to her that it was not the loss of life that was dispiriting – the dead men were, to a soul, evil-doers after all – but the fact that the killer could so easily get away with his crimes. Every new murder pointed up her department's, and her own, inefficiency.

Raneesh suburb was a modern, rich residential area of habitat domes and state-of-the-art polycarbon structures. The squad car halted by one such, a building tastelessly styled on the pyramid foyer of the Louvre. Rana followed Vishwanath past the house and down a tree-shaded footpath.

The usual activity surrounded the scene of the crime. Officers had erected low-powered laser-cordons to keep away the gaggle of sightseers, curious children and rich citizens out walking their dogs. Crawlers scurried back and forth across the path like oversized beetles. A forensic officer knelt by the corpse, entering data into his com-board.

Raja Khan had been a big man in his fifties, his size emphasised by his voluminous shalwar kameez. He was ying on his back, arms spread in an accidental gesture of appeasement. The right side of his face had been charcoaled by a laser charge, and cut into his left cheek was the usual bloody cross.

'He died between eight and eight-thirty last night,' the forensic officer was saying. 'It's a quiet area – the body wasn't discovered until this morning.'

Rana entered the data into her com-board. She looked up at Vishwanath. 'All ten murders were committed between eight and nine, sir.'

'So perhaps the killer works regular office hours . . . though a big help that is.'

'There is a very interesting feature,' the officer went on. 'The victim has obviously been shot twice, unlike all the other victims. The first shot narrowly missed his forehead – note the burned skin and hair. Then came the *coup de grâce* to the right side of the face.'

'You think he survived the first attack and tried to get away?'

The officer nodded. 'Very possibly.'

'So the initial attack might not have happened here,' Vishwanath mused.

Rana asked, 'Do we know Raja Khan's address?'

Vishwanath passed his com-board to Rana and she downloaded the information. Khan had an address in an exclusive city centre apartment building.

'Sir, seeing as how the location of this killing doesn't conform to the crucifix, I was wondering if this was perhaps a preliminary meeting set up by the killer to lure Khan to one of the four locations. But it went wrong. Khan got suspicious and tried to run. So the killer struck then.'

'Where does that leave us, Lieutenant?'

Rana shrugged. 'Perhaps the killer lives in the area.'

'It's a long shot. Contact Naz and have him organise a house-to-house in the district.'

Rana contacted headquarters and relayed Vishwanath's order.

The forensic officer was downloading the data gathered by the crawlers into his com-board. He shook his head. 'Nothing, sir. Lots of information, but precious little of any use.' He consulted the screen of his com-board. 'There's no correlation between data picked up here and that at the other crime scenes.'

Vishwanath turned to Rana. 'I want you to compile the usual list of the dead man's family, friends and acquaintances. Interview them all – you know the routine.'

Rana was staring at her com-board, and the crucifix pattern that overlaid the city map. 'One thing, sir. Perhaps the location of this killing *does* conform to some kind of crucifix.'

Vishwanath regarded her down the stern length of his aquiline nose. 'Do you mean something like the cross of Alsace?'

Rana shrugged. 'Maybe.'

'Then why,' he said heavily, 'isn't the crucifix cut into the victim's cheeks the cross of Alsace, Lieutenant?'

'Because it isn't exactly the cross of Alsace. It's . . . I don't know . . . perhaps something that's harder to carve.'

Vishwanath pursed his lips and finally nodded. 'Ah-cha. It's worth looking into, Lieutenant.'

'I'll check it when I get back to HQ, sir.'

The corpse was lifted into the back of an ambulance, the lasers dismantled and the crowd told to disperse. Rana rode back in the squad car with Vishwanath. He sat in the passenger seat in silence, watching the passing scenes with eagle-eyed intensity.

Ten minutes later she sat down behind her desk and dealt with the incoming calls. She accessed the messages from duty officers doing the footwork on the Khan murder. They had searched his apartment and come up with a list of addresses. Rana downloaded them and, over the course of the next four hours, got through to over twenty citizens in and around the city. She went through a routine series of questions, establishing each individual's connection with the dead man, and then made appointments to interview them face to face.

Raja Khan had had contacts in many walks of life, from characters with criminal records to well-positioned state politicians. It spoke volumes for the probity of elected representatives that they kept company with such low life, but then that was the way of the world. Often during her six weeks in the Homicide Division, Rana had wished she was back in the safer, simpler world of Child Welfare.

The monsoon deluge began on time just before five, beating on the windows with the percussive music of relief after another sweltering day. The sun was going down when Rana finished speaking with the last of the dead man's listed acquaintances and sat back. Her next two shifts would be spent interviewing petty criminals and politicians. For the past two weeks she seemed to have done nothing but conduct fruitless interviews with reluctant citizens.

She remembered the pix of the suspected killer from Madrigal; the day before she had requested further visual enhancement from the computer division. She accessed the file and downloaded a dozen pix of the computer-generated image. These showed different versions of the same man, aged so as to appear in his forties. In one the passage of time had treated the man well: his face was flushed and well-fed; in another he was thin and worn. There were pix of him bald, and with hair in various styles and degrees of grey. Rana printed out copies of each pix and slipped them into the breast pocket of her shirt. She would take them with her when she conducted the interviews tomorrow.

She consulted her com-board and read through the

notes she'd made at the scene of the crime. The more she considered her suggestion about the crucifix, the less viable the idea became. She wondered if she had been merely throwing out off-the-wall ideas in an attempt to impress Vishwanath.

Nevertheless, she accessed GlobaLink on her com-screen and entered the data bank of symbols and logos. She sketched a representation of a cross of Alsace, with a dozen or so variations, and gave the search command. As she waited, she knew that this would be yet another dead end, another hopeless lead she could forget.

Thirty seconds later the screen flashed with the message that half a dozen crucifixes resembling the image she had requested were ready to be downloaded.

Rana touched the command. Instantly, the six crosses appeared on the screen. Five of them resembled the cross of Alsace, to varying degrees. The sixth crucifix was of the regulation Christian type, but with a small circle beneath each arm. Rana sat up, suddenly interested. What if this was the cross the killer had scored on the cheeks of his victims, but he had been unable to carve a representation of the two small circles? Tenuous, she knew, but worth looking into.

She requested information about the crucifix. Seconds later the screen filled with text. Rana read the article, digested the information, then went through it a second time.

The crucifix was the symbol of a Martian Christian cult known as the Church of Phobos and Deimos, hence the stylised representations of the moons. The church had been founded almost one hundred and twenty years ago by French settlers on the red planet, when two young girls belonging to a traditional Christian order claimed to have seen the image of Christ on the faces of the orbiting moons. Furthermore, they said that they had been told by

God to leave Mars and settle the newly founded colony of Columbus, Sirius III, which like Mars had two small moons. Almost a hundred years ago the Church of Phobos and Deimos had raised sufficient funds to expedite the venture. They had sent their disciples to the various space academies, and in time had the expertise to crew their own colony liner. Ninety years ago the entire church, some five thousand citizens in all, had boarded the starship *New Hope* and embarked on their God-given quest.

They had never arrived. The liner was reported missing, presumed destroyed, a month after phase-out from Olympus spaceport. No trace of the ship was ever discovered, either in normal space or in the void. The disappearance of the *New Hope* and its five thousand passengers remained a mystery to this day.

Rana sat back, digesting the implications.

She accessed GlobaLink and requested every last scrap of information concerning the Church of Phobos and Deimos, existing branches, chapters and off-shoots of the church, no matter how small or removed from the original doctrine of belief. A minute later she had a lot of information concerning the church's dogma, but nothing at all about extant chapters. The church had effectively ceased to exist with the disappearance of the *New Hope*.

She sent a message to Vishwanath: 'I've come across something to do with the Christian symbol, but I don't know how relevant it might be.'

Seconds later Vishwanath emerged from his office. He pulled a chair up to Rana's desk and stared at the screen, minutely going through the article about the Church of Phobos and Deimos.

He shook his head. 'The very fact of the church's demise would suggest that there's no link to the killings.'

Rana shrugged. 'What if there were some church

members left behind? Their descendants might have secretly carried on the traditions . . .' She stopped, realising how far-fetched it sounded.

'I don't know, but we can't dismiss it out of hand. Check with the victims to see if they had any links with Mars.'

'Yes, sir.'

'Of course, all this is pure speculation, based on the presumption that the location of last night's murder was a part of this old symbol.'

Rana felt herself redden. 'Yes, sir.'

'But I'll put an extra patrol out in the area of the other side of the arm, where the second circle would be, just in case.'

Rana sighed. 'I don't seem to be getting anywhere fast, sir.'

Vishwanath gave a paternal laugh. 'You're doing fine, Lieutenant. You can't expect instant success. Homicide work involves much unrewarded speculation. But speculation has to be worked through and dismissed.' He smiled. 'Often the breakthrough comes from the most unlikely of sources. Keep at it, Rana.'

Rana, now . . . She smiled as she watched him stride back to his office.

Five minutes later her screen flashed. She accessed the call. The face of a receptionist stared out at her. 'We have a private outside caller wishing to speak to you, Lieutenant.'

Rana frowned. She knew few people outside the force who might want to contact her at work. 'Fine,' she said. 'Put him through.'

She was surprised to see a street-kid's frightened face fill the screen.

'Vandita – this is a surprise. Is everything okay?'

The girl was in a public com-screen kiosk, obviously

unaccustomed to using the technology. Rana wondered if this might account for her cowed expression.

'Rana, I need to see you.'

'Vandita? What is it? Is something—'

'I need to see you. Please, will you come right away? I'll be by the bridge.'

And without further explanation she cut the connection.

Rana tidied her desk, deactivated the com-screen, and locked away her com-board. She was due to leave in one hour, but Vandita had sounded desperate. She could always come back here and put in the hour when she'd talked to the girl.

She hurried from the building and took a taxi to the Howrah bridge.

Vandita was squatting on her heels by the railings, a tiny figure obscured by the passing crowds, when Rana climbed from the taxi. She pushed her way through the press to the girl, who looked up at her with a timid smile.

'Vandita . . . ?'

'We can't talk here. Come with me.'

She stood and gripped Rana's hand, pulling her along the street to the steel pillars of the bridge. Rana's mind raced through the possibilities. She wondered if one of the kids had done something wrong, which might explain the girl's anxiety.

Vandita kicked off her plastic sandals and climbed on to the timber platform, squatting on a mattress and not meeting Rana's gaze. Three candles provided fitful illumination. The other children had not yet arrived home. Rana removed her boots and sat cross-legged before the girl. She reached out and took her hand.

'Vandita, please, what's wrong? I'll do everything I can to help. You know that.'

The girl was clasping her hands around skinny shins.

203

Her eyes finally focused on Rana. 'Last night, Rana, someone I know . . . he saw a terrible thing.'

'Tell me,' Rana said.

The girl remained silent.

'Do I know him? Does he live here?'

Vandita shook her head. 'He lives near the spaceport, in the old scrapyard. But last night he was somewhere else, in a rich area. He saw something and told his friends, and I found out.'

'Tell me what it was, Vandita. What are you frightened of?'

The girl looked pained. 'This boy, I know him only slightly. He won't be happy if police are involved.'

'What was he doing in the rich suburb last night, Vandita?' She squeezed the girl's hand. 'I can guess, but tell me.'

'He was stealing – robbing a house.'

'And he saw something, but was too scared to tell the police because of what he was doing? Vandita, if you tell me what he saw, I'll ignore the fact that he was burgling a house, ah-cha?'

Vandita shrugged unhappily. 'He won't like me telling you.'

'There's no need for him to know that it was you who told the police. Now . . .'

For long seconds Vandita looked at Rana, and at last she whispered, 'He was robbing a house in the Raneesh district—'

Rana stopped her. 'Raneesh?' She was aware of her hammering heartbeat.

Vandita nodded. 'He was coming from the house when he heard two men talking on a pathway nearby. One of the men tried to run, but the other man fired a laser at him. The man fell over and the other man fired again, at his face. Then the man walked away. After a few seconds the boy followed the man, perhaps a kilometre, and saw him go into a house. Then he left quickly and went home to the scrapyard near the spaceport.'

Rana swallowed. She tried to marshal her thoughts.

'Vandita,' she said at last, 'do you know where the killer lived? Did the boy say?'

Vandita shook her head. 'I didn't talk to the boy. A friend of his told me. He didn't say where the killer lived, but the boy saw the house he went into.'

Rana was nodding. Shiva . . . after all the work she'd done, all the complex reasoning, she might solve the case thanks to the testimony of a chance eye witness.

'Vandita, this is important. Can you tell me the boy's name? I swear to you that I won't tell him who told me. You've no reason to be afraid.' She paused. 'You've got to tell me. We've got to stop this man killing again.'

Vandita nodded. 'Ah-cha. The boy is called Ahmed Prakesh. You will find him in the old Tata scrapyard.'

Rana reached out and stroked the young girl's cheek. 'Vandita, you don't know how important this is. I'll see you later.'

Rana left the makeshift dwelling beneath the Howrah bridge and took a taxi to the spaceport. She considered contacting Vishwanath about the latest development, but decided against it. She would have to be very careful in her dealings with the boy. The presence of more than one police officer might provoke Ahmed to flight. She would handle this interview herself.

The Tata scrapyard was a vast area of tangled carbon-fibre parts neighbouring the spaceport. The mammoth carcasses of decommissioned spaceships reared against the lights of the port, arranged like the exhibits in some forgotten museum. Rana paid the taxi fare and squeezed through a rent in the polycarbon fencing. In the glaring overspill of the spaceport halogens, the scrapyard was transformed into a landscape of dark shadow and high-lighted carbon fibre. Rana walked between the sliced and sectioned remains of ships that had once proudly made their way through the void, sad chunks of machines bearing the faded livery of lines long defunct.

She halted, stood quietly and listened. The only sound was from the port itself, the roar of a tug as it hauled a spaceship across the tarmac to a blast-off pit. The noise faded, replaced by silence. To her right, Rana detected the faint sound of music. When her eyes adjusted to the dark shadows, she made out movement – the figure of a young boy or girl, running towards the source of the music, no doubt to tell his or her friends of Rana's intrusion.

Rana walked towards the bulbous shape of a derelict space-tug. The music stopped. Rana imagined a gang of street-kids, holding their breaths, watching each other in alarm.

She ducked through the entrance hatch of the old tug. Before her, half a dozen big-eyed urchins sat around the bulky shape of an ancient radio. A defective glow-tube provided stuttering half-light. A drooping stick of incense filled the old cargo hold with a sickly sweet stench.

Rana squatted on her heels and looked about the group of boys and girls. She smiled at the chubby, frightened face of a small girl. 'Amita? Is that you?' she asked in Hindi.

The six-year-old smiled timorously. 'Officer Rao,' the girl said. 'We thought it was a security guard!'

Rana smiled. 'Aren't you going to introduce me, Amita?'

She glanced around the group, trying to detect the boy called Ahmed from his guilty expression. The difficulty was, their suspicion of the police gave them all expressions of guilt.

Amita looked at her friends. 'Officer Rao works with children,' she explained. 'Last year she gave me rupees for a new dress.' She glanced at Rana, smoothed her palms down the front of a dirty blue smock, and smiled proudly.

'Who are your friends, Amita?' Rana asked.

'This is Nadeen, and this is Sumar, and Kal, and Ahmed, and Ashok . . .'

Ahmed . . . a tiny boy in shorts and a ripped T-shirt that once upon a time might have been white. He was no older, Rana thought, than six or seven. He stared at Rana, a rabbit mesmerised by a cobra.

Rana nodded. 'The thing is, you see, I came here hoping that you might be able to help me. I have a hundred rupees to give to anyone who can tell me something.' She paused and stared at the children. Their eyes bulged at the thought of so much money. 'Last night a terrible murder was committed in the district of Raneesh, three kilometres south of here. A man was shot dead with a laser.' She glanced at Ahmed. He was staring at the ground. 'I need information about this killing. I need to know where the killer lives, so that I can lock him up and stop him from killing again.'

The children looked at each other. One or two glanced furtively at Ahmed. The others, clearly not in the know, looked disappointed that they would be unable to claim the rupees.

'If anyone can tell me where the killer lives, they can have . . .' She reached into her pocket and counted out five twenty-rupee notes, laying them one by one on top of the old radio. The children stared, transfixed.

Rana picked up the notes and slipped them back into her breast pocket. She stood up and said, 'I'll be waiting outside. If anyone can tell me what I want to know, come and see me and I'll give them all the rupees, ah-cha?'

She looked around the group of staring faces one last time, before ducking out of the old spaceship and standing, heart hammering, in the dazzling glare of a halogen spotlight. She could hear the frantic babble of high voices from inside. Then silence.

A minute later, appearing timidly like some hibernating animal fearing the presence of a predator, Ahmed emerged through the hatch. He stood shivering in the humid night before Rana, staring up at her with massive eyes.

'I . . .' He could hardly speak for fear. He gulped 'I know someone who saw the killing,' he stammered. 'The boy . . . my friend, he told me where the man lives.'

Rana knelt and took his hand. 'Can you remember what your friend said?' she asked. 'Can you remember where the man lives?'

Ahmed nodded, his Adam's apple bobbing. 'Ah-cha. My friend said he lives on Allahabad Marg, near Raneesh.'

Rana nodded. 'Can you remember the number of the house?' Allahabad Marg was a long street that stretched for over a kilometre through the exclusive western suburbs.

The boy looked crestfallen. 'No . . . my friend, he cannot remember.' He brightened. 'But the house, it's strange. It looks like this.' He moved to the flank of the tug and, in the dust that covered a domed engine nacelle, drew the shape of the house with his forefinger.

Rana watched the collection of odd shapes appear in the dust, a series of almost semi-circular cowlings. It was not exactly an architect's scale drawing, but she recognised the shape. In the rich suburbs it was fashionable to have one's house styled in polycarbon after famous world buildings.

This one, she knew, was the old Sydney Opera House.

She felt her stomach tighten in excitement. From her breast pocket, along with the rupee notes, Rana took the dozen pix of the computer-aged Madrigal laser killer.

'Ahmed, did the man look anything like any of these men?'

She showed him the pix one by one.

Ahmed frowned and shook his head. 'I think he had a thin face, and silver hair.' He stopped, realising his mistake, and looked up at Rana. 'I won't be arrested?' he pleaded.

'Ahmed . . .' She took his fingers and kissed them. 'I promise you that nothing will happen, ah-cha? Look, here are the hundred rupees.'

He reached out, slowly, and took the red notes. He held them before his eyes as if disbelieving his luck. Then he darted back inside the ship, chattering excitedly to his friends.

Rana slipped the pix back into her pocket. So the killer was thin-faced, with silver hair. It could still be the Madrigal killer, she realised, though prematurely aged. He might even have been in disguise.

She resolved to go immediately to the house on Allahabad Marg that looked like the old Sydney Opera House. She would claim that she was conducting routine enquiries, question the man about the recent killing in the area, and assess his reaction.

As she left the scrapyard and made her way to the spaceport taxi rank, she wondered whether correct procedure would be to contact Vishwanath first. But, she reasoned with herself, he had given her permission to follow her own initiative. For the past two weeks she had conducted her own interviews, followed her own hunches. Why should this case be any different?

As she climbed into the taxi and gave her destination, she found it hard to believe that soon she might be confronting the man known as the crucifix killer.

16

Bennett woke by degrees, his memory returning in disordered fragments. For some reason he recalled the ruin of the alien temple first, and then the crash-landed starship. Only then were these images superseded by the events of the night before: Ten Lee and Mackendrick's capture, the blow to his head and what he had overheard before passing out.

He opened his eyes, expecting a renewal of the pain, but he felt only a dull throbbing where he'd been struck. He was in a wood-panelled room, fragrant with a scent like that of pine. He was no longer lying on the floor but in a comfortable bed. He sat up and stared down the length of his body. He was wearing clean undergarments, not his own. His flight-suit was folded over the back of a chair next to the bed.

There was no guard in the room with him, no interrogator.

He swung himself out of bed and pulled on his flight-suit. He stood and walked to the end of the room and stared through the floor-to-ceiling picture window.

The view was spectacular in its alien beauty. Tenebrae was half risen, its equatorial diameter spanning the entire length of the near horizon. Its opal light spilled over the terraces that marked the various levels of the valley like contour lines. A hundred domes sparkled like beads of dew made monstrous. Above them, lining the far side of the valley, was a forest of wind turbines. As he absorbed the scene he made out the tiny figures of people working on the narrow, stepped fields, and vehicles making their slow way up the switchback track that climbed from the valley bottom.

Only then, as if in reaction to the idyllic scene before him, did he recall what he had heard the night before. He recollected the voice that had wanted them dead, the other, patriarchal voice that counselled less severe measures. Well, he was relieved that the patriarch had won the day, but something was not right on Penumbra. They had matters they clearly wanted to keep hidden, and would even consider murder to do so.

He turned at the sound of a door opening, expecting a colonist. Ten Lee peered through, her face brightening when she saw him. She padded across to Bennett, pressed her head to his chest and held him in an uncharacteristic embrace.

'Joshua, we didn't know what happened to you! The attack was so sudden.'

She pulled her head away and looked up at him, frowning at the bruise on the side of his head.

'I'm okay,' he said. 'I followed you here.' He smiled. 'So much for my attempt to free you.'

She looked up at him like a frightened child. 'They were human, Joshua. I'm sure they were human.'

'Colonists,' he said. 'They crash-landed.'

'They told you?'

'I . . .' He paused and considered telling her about his discovery of the liner. 'Later, Ten. Where's Mackendrick? We need to talk over what happened.'

'In the middle room, along the passage.'

She took his hand and pulled him from the room and along a corridor. She knocked on the next door and pushed it open.

Mackendrick was in the process of zipping his flight-suit. He looked up as Bennett and Ten Lee entered, came forward without a word and embraced him. He felt the wiry old man in his arms, emotion constricting his throat.

'Thank Christ you're okay, Josh!'

'The feeling's mutual,' Bennett said.

Mackendrick saw his bruised head. 'What happened, Josh?'

Bennett sat on the bed between Ten Lee and Mack. 'I followed you here. Someone saw me and gave me this.' He fingered the bruise. 'Before I passed out I heard them talking. They didn't know who we were, or rather they thought we were terrorists.' He looked from Mack to Ten. 'Something's going on here. They talked about killing us, but decided against it. Instead they're going to destroy the ship and keep us here – they said they need scientists. They'll offer us places in their community.' He told them what he'd overheard, the mention of people called Quineau and Klien, the cryptic line about their not finding out.

'Who are Quineau and Klien?' Ten Lee asked.

'I've no idea. They didn't say. I got the impression that Quineau had left Penumbra to tell Earth what was happening here, and that Klien had tried to follow and kill him. I think they assumed we came here because of Quineau.'

Mackendrick was staring through the picture window at the bulk of the gas giant lifting itself through the morning sky.

'We'll tell them we crash-landed in the mountains north of here, okay?' he said. 'We'll say the ship was destroyed. That way they might not look for it. We'll make no mention of trying to get away from here.'

'And what is our story when they ask why we came to

Penumbra?' Ten Lee asked. 'They might be suspicious. If they think that this fellow Quineau sent us . . .'

Mackendrick considered, and said at last, 'We'll tell them a version of the truth, that we were on a survey/ exploratory mission, charting the arm. They should have no reason not to believe us.'

'And then?' Bennett asked.

'Then we try to find out what's going on.' He looked from Bennett to Ten Lee. 'You don't want to run back to the ship at the first opportunity, do you?'

Bennett was the first to reply. 'I don't want to be stranded here, Mack. The longer we hang on, the more likely they are to locate the Cobra.'

'Not if we tell them that we crashed in the mountains,' Ten Lee said.

'But the grass of the plain shows our tracks. All they have to do is follow them back to the ship.'

'There was a storm last night,' Mackendrick told him. 'Our tracks would've been obliterated. I say we hang on, find out what's going on here. Ten Lee?'

She nodded, her expression serious. 'I too think we should wait and investigate this place.'

Bennett said, 'Okay. But we've got to be careful. Some of these people would gladly kill us without a second thought.'

'That's settled, then,' Mackendrick said. 'We play the innocent, stranded scientists. We accept their invitation to become part of their society. All the time, we keep our eyes and ears open.'

They talked on, going over what Bennett had over-heard, trying to piece together a view of this society from mere fragments of arbitrary information.

Perhaps an hour later they heard a door open in the corridor.

'This is it,' Mackendrick reminded them. 'From now on we play dumb.'

They stood and faced the door, Bennett unsure what to expect.

A woman knocked and entered the room. She was in her fifties or sixties and wore a simple brown frock, belted at the waist, and sandals. Bennett noticed that affixed to the collar of her frock was a metal brooch in the shape of a cross.

She smiled disarmingly. 'Here you are.' She looked at them each in turn. 'Sabine Deauchamps, representing the Council of Elders. I'd normally extend a warm welcome to our planet of Homefall, but after your treatment last night I suspect any overtures of hospitality would fall on deaf ears.'

'You can say that again,' Bennett said.

The woman adopted a pained expression. 'Please, allow me to explain. A terrible mistake was made. We've been suffering an increasing frequency of attacks from . . . I suppose you would call them terrorists. They are a faction who oppose the governing body of Homefall. We are a peaceable community, averse to violence, but when our opponents resort to criminal tactics we find ourselves in the position of having to defend ourselves.'

'Hence our arrest and detention,' Mackendrick said.

Deauchamps gestured. 'Please, if you would look at the situation from our point of view,' she said, with a reasonableness that Bennett found almost convincing. 'Our patrol came across armed strangers who we knew were not of our community. What was the likelihood of these strangers having arrived from off-world, after we've endured almost a hundred years of seclusion? The patrol did what it had been trained to do: detain these armed strangers who they assumed, wrongly in the circumstances, could only be terrorists. It was not long before the mistake was realised.' She looked at Bennett. 'I can only apologise on behalf of the guard who attacked you.'

She paused, then went on. 'We don't know the reason for your arrival on Homefall, of course – we assume you are an exploration team – but we'll aid your stay here however we can. There's just one precaution we must take. We're concerned for the safety of your ship. The terrorists will take the first opportunity to attack and disable it as their cause wouldn't be helped if we established trading links with the rest of the Expansion. If you could tell me of its present whereabouts, I'll immediately despatch a patrol to ensure its safety.'

Bennett glanced at Mackendrick.

'I'm afraid that won't be necessary,' the old man said. 'We were caught in a storm on entry and came down in the mountains to the north. Our ship was irreparably disabled. We managed to salvage supplies and the transporter, but little else.'

Deauchamps considered his words, nodding with concerned understanding. 'I'll tell the council,' she said. 'We'll be convening a meeting this afternoon. My fellow elders would like to question you about your mission, and your long-term plans. I hope you don't consider this an imposition. We've been isolated for so long, and suddenly to have visitors from our homeworld . . .

'You must be hungry. You'll find a meal prepared in the dining room. In one hour I'll send someone to escort you to the council chambers. Until then . . .' She inclined her head in farewell and left the room.

'I can see why they elected Madame Deauchamps to make the overtures,' Mackendrick declared. 'One smooth operator. If I didn't know better, I would've swallowed her little speech whole.'

'She gave the game away by asking about the ship,' Bennett said. 'You could almost smell her need to get her hands on it.'

'I want to know more about the so-called terrorists,'

Mackendrick said. 'In all likelihood, these are the people we should be dealing with. The friends of our enemies, et cetera. If something is rotten in this society, then they'll know all about it.'

'She didn't ask if we'd been contacted by Quineau.'

'Probably didn't want to sound too inquisitive. They'll no doubt get round to it at the meeting later.'

Mackendrick led the way along the corridor to a comfortably appointed lounge overlooking the stepped terraces. A table was laid with a colourful array of food: great cobs of white bread, various cheeses, sliced meats and native fruits. There were even pots of what turned out to be a passable imitation of coffee.

Bennett helped himself to a plate of bread and cheese and a mug of the coffee substitute. He moved to a window seat with a view of the steeply descending valley, spectacular in its breadth and depth. Only from very close to the window could the valley bottom be seen, the sparkling filament of a silver river twisting its way through a series of green fields.

The few people tending the nearby terraces were dressed simply, the women in pastel-coloured one-piece frocks, the men in lightweight trousers and smocks. The garments were obviously of man-made, manufactured material, and other aspects of Homefall – the wind turbines and crawlers – suggested a well-developed manufacturing industry somewhere. Bennett guessed that this valley was not the extent of the colony.

He finished his breakfast and tried the door leading outside. To his surprise, it was open. He had expected it to be locked, the three of them to be under benign but strict house arrest. He stepped outside. There were no guards in sight. It occurred to him with sudden alarm that the casualness with which they were being treated was a result of the colonists having already located, and disabled, the Cobra.

216

The door opened and Mackendrick joined him, taking a deep breath and staring down into the valley.

Bennett said, 'A worst case scenario, Mack. The colonists find the ship and destroy it, blaming it on the terrorists. What do we do then?' He considered the irony: just four months ago, on Earth, he had been dreaming of life on a colony world.

'What do you suggest, Josh? That we should make a run for it? Take the transporter, or sneak out on foot at night?' He shook his head. 'How far do you think we'd get? If they haven't found the ship, then we'd be leading them straight to it. It'll be far safer if we lie low, let time pass, find out what's going on here and then make a break for it.'

Bennett nodded. 'Put like that it does make sense. It's just that the thought of being stranded here . . .'

Mackendrick smiled. 'I suppose there are worse places to spend the last year of my life.' He looked at Bennett. 'But don't worry, Josh. I've arranged for a back-up ship to set off here in a year, if you haven't arrived back by then.'

Bennett nodded, at once relieved at the thought that there would be another way off the planet, and disturbed by the reminder of Mackendrick's illness.

Five minutes later the small figure of a young woman made her way up a winding footpath, raising a hand in greeting as she reached the garden. 'Miriam James,' she said. 'If you're ready, I'll show you to the council chambers.'

Mackendrick moved back inside to tell Ten Lee.

Bennett watched the woman as she strolled to the edge of the terrace. Miriam James was small and tanned, with cropped black hair. Unlike the other colonists he had seen today, she was dressed in green combat fatigues and carried a rifle. He wondered if she had been part of the patrol that had fired on the others last night. On the lapel

217

of her combat jacket was a small silver crucifix, with a tiny circle beneath each crossbar.

'Why the armed guard, Miriam?' he asked now. 'Are we under arrest?'

She turned to him, smiling. She seemed an unlikely combatant. 'Of course not.' She patted her rifle. 'This is for your own protection. The terrorists have been known to strike at the heart of the settlement. If they decide that you might have information valuable to them . . .' She nodded up the incline to the terrace that overlooked the building. 'That's why you've been under armed protection all night.'

Bennett looked up and saw two green-uniformed guards standing on the road and watching the building.

'Just who or what are the terrorists?' he enquired.

She opened her mouth to say something, but thought better of it. She shook her head. 'Later,' she said. 'The Council of Elders will answer all your questions.'

Mackendrick and Ten Lee stepped from the building. Miriam James led the way from the terrace and down a tortuously winding footpath between serried fruit brushes and terraces of a wheat analogue.

The council chamber was a dome so big that the hillside had been excavated to accommodate its diameter. It was surrounded by a plinth of timber steps, and as Bennett followed the others around the walkway, he recognised the dome as the old astrodome cannibalised from the liner. The lower metre of its curving flank was banded with the red, white and blue tricolour. Above the entrance hatch was a large silver crucifix with a circle beneath each crossbar.

They stepped into the chamber, fitted out with rising tiers of timber seats for the assembly of the council. In the middle of the floor a hexagon of benches had been arranged informally. Six colonists, three men and three women – Bennett recognised Sabine Deauchamps among them – were already seated and awaiting their arrival.

Miriam stood guard at the entrance.

Deauchamps stood in greeting. 'Welcome to the Council of Homefall,' she said. 'I trust you ate well? If I might introduce my fellow elders . . .'

As their title suggested, Bennett estimated that all six men and women were over fifty, some as old as eighty. They regarded their visitors with hospitable smiles and nods. They seemed, he thought, about as threatening as the activities committee of an old people's home.

He reminded himself that appearances were often deceptive.

A small, portly red-faced man stepped forward and shook them by the hand. 'Welcome to Homefall, messieurs, madame. I'm Edward De Channay, elected chairman of the council. Please, be seated.'

It was the voice, rich and cultured, of the man Bennett had last night termed the patriarch. He had expected someone tall and silver-haired, not dumpy and balding.

He sat down on one of the benches between Ten Lee and Mackendrick.

Deauchamps said, 'This is by way of welcoming you to Homefall, an informal meeting to acquaint you with our society, and to allow us to get to know you.' The other council members nodded in agreement. 'There'll be a more formal welcoming in a day or two, a dinner at which you'll get to meet the citizens of the valley. I know that Chairman De Channay has one or two questions, as well as many answers to your own questions, no doubt.'

De Channay cleared his throat. 'Thank you, Sabine.' He looked from Mackendrick and Bennett to Ten Lee. 'Of course, your arrival here has been as much a surprise for us as I suspect it has been for you. A pleasant surprise, might I add. For over ninety years we've gone about our

219

lives on Homefall with little hope of establishing contact with the rest of the Expansion. We came here by accident, a fortuitous accident, as it turned out.'

'The Rim wasn't your destination?' Bennett asked.

'Far from it. Our ancestors were members of the Church of Phobos and Deimos, founded on Mars in the last century. They elected, more than one hundred years ago, to start a colony on a planet where they might practise their religion without outside influence. To this end they set off for a newly discovered, habitable planet in the Sirius system. The details are vague, as the accident happened so many years ago, but an error in the navigation system resulted in the ship being flung far off course. Our ancestors emerged from the void many light years from here, with insufficient energy supplies to effect a return to inhabited space. For two years they explored the few star systems in the region, before chancing upon Homefall, as they christened their new home. In attempting to land they crashed, suffering many casualties. However, they rallied and founded the settlement you see here. For ninety years we've prospered, thanks to the will of God, with only occasional setbacks along the way.'

'The terrorists?' Mackendrick observed.

'The terrorists being a case in point.'

'What exactly,' Bennett asked, 'are they opposing?'

He tried to discern discomfort in the manner of De Channay, but the elder was practised in the ways of duplicity.

'They're anarchists and troublemakers opposed to the rule of the council. For almost fifteen years they've mounted an armed war against society. The precise politics of the situation need not concern you at this time.'

He paused and changed the subject. 'Fellow Elder Deauchamps told me that your ship came down in the mountains. I only mention it as it might be a wise move if we sent out a team to salvage the wreckage, before the terrorists locate the site and destroy what we might be able to use.'

Bennett was aware of the eyes of the elders fixed on Mackendrick, who nodded in broad agreement. 'I don't have the precise co-ordinates to hand, but I know the general whereabouts. I doubt, though, that the terrorists would easily locate the wreckage.'

'You are unaware of the resources of our opponents,' De Channay replied.

The man seated next to De Channay, dark-haired and younger than the others, spoke up. 'Your transporter was in remarkably good condition considering that it had suffered a crash-landing.'

Bennett's throat went dry. He recognised the voice. It was the man who last night had wanted them killed.

Mackendrick nodded. 'It was practically the only thing we could salvage from the wreckage, and then we had to cannibalise it from the three other transporters we carried.' He looked up, staring De Channay in the eye.

The chairman nodded. 'I take it that you are a scientific survey team? Were you sent here, by any chance, as a result of Quineau?'

Mackendrick repeated the name. 'I'm sorry . . . the name means nothing. Who is Quineau?'

Bennett and Ten Lee looked suitably blank.

De Channay said, 'In the crash-landing our ancestors suffered extensive damage to the two scout ships we carried aboard the liner. For many years we didn't have the technological or industrial expertise and resources to repair them. Only twenty years ago were we able to begin the necessary repairs. Then we sent a council elder, Pierre Quineau, to attempt to establish contact with Earth or the colonies and tell of our survival. We've heard nothing

221

since, and had given up hope of ever receiving word from or contact with the Expansion.'

Mackendrick was shaking his head. 'We came out to the Rim on an independent scientific survey mission, charting new stars and prospecting potentially habitable planets.'

'So the Expansion is moving out to the Rim?' the elder asked.

'I'm afraid not. We are an independent company working outside the jurisdiction and remit of the Expansion. Scientific curiosity, the spirit of adventure, brought us this far out.'

'You're not part of a concerted exploration of the arm? Can we hope that your loss will be noted and a rescue mission set up?'

'As I said, we are an independent company. Or should that be, we were? There is little or no hope of rescue.'

De Channay spread his hands. 'Then I'm afraid, as we do not have the capabilities to manufacture void-going ships ourselves, that until such time as the next ship does happen this way, you are stranded on Homefall with us.'

Mackendrick nodded. 'It would seem that way.'

'Then all I can do in the circumstances is avail you of the hospitality of the Council of Elders,' De Channay said. 'We can find you suitable positions in the manufactories on the coast, or if you would prefer to farm . . .' He gestured. 'But you have hardly arrived here and I am talking of employment! You'll need time to settle in, become accustomed to the ways of society on Homefall. I'm afraid that after the sophistication of Earth you might find us somewhat lacking, but I'm sure that in the circumstances . . . If you have any questions we might be able to answer, my council is at your disposal.'

Mackendrick nodded. 'From orbit we detected spectacular ruins to the south of here,' he said.

'Ah, the ruins of the Ancients, as we call them. When we discovered the ruins, and others in the vicinity, we assumed that we were not alone on the planet.'

'But the aliens are extinct?' Ten Lee asked.

De Channay nodded. 'We've found evidence that there was a great civilisation spanning the globe, intelligent but never industrial. We assume some catastrophe befell their race. Archeological records date their fall to around five thousand years ago. Perhaps, once you've settled in, you'd like to visit the various ruins along the coast?' He looked around at his colleagues. 'If there are no more questions? Very well.' He addressed Mackendrick. 'For the next few days we'd be pleased if you'd make yourselves at home in the valley. Unfortunately it will be necessary to have armed guards accompany you at all times, in the interests of security and your own safety. Perhaps after lunch you'd like to visit our settlement on the coast? Until then . . .'

They exchanged handshakes, and the Council of Elders bowed and left the dome.

The guard, Miriam James, appeared at Bennett's side. 'If you'd like to return to the lodge . . .'

They followed her back up the twisting path, attracting the attention of colonists who paused in their work in the fields and watched them pass. Bennett looked into their faces and saw only expressions of wariness and suspicion.

James remained outside on the lawn, rifle braced across her chest, while Bennett followed Mackendrick and Ten Lee into the kitchen. They found the table set for lunch, a tureen of steaming soup awaiting them, alongside plates of bread and cheese. Bennett sat down and helped himself to a cup of the coffee substitute.

'So . . .' he said. 'What did you make of that?'

Ten Lee sat on the window seat and hugged her shins.

223

'If we didn't know they were keeping something from us,' she said, 'I'd say they couldn't have been friendlier.'

Bennett grunted. 'The friendship of necessity, Ten. I wouldn't trust them as far as I could spit.'

Mackendrick looked up from his coffee. 'But do you think they believed us?'

'About the ship?' Bennett shrugged. 'Going on what I heard last night, they wouldn't take any chances. I can't imagine they'd sit back and quietly accept that we crash-landed. They'll be scouring the area for the Cobra right now.'

'And the terrorists?' Mackendrick said. 'De Channay seemed pretty reluctant to fill us in on that front.'

Bennett said, 'I'd like to know what they're trying to keep from us.'

They stared at each other in silence.

'All we can be certain of,' Mackendrick said, 'is that they want to keep us here, and that they want to keep the rest of the Expansion out.'

'What about Quineau?' Ten Lee asked. 'They said they sent him to make contact, but last night you thought that they sent someone called Klien to stop him?'

'They're lying,' Bennett replied. 'They obviously want us to think they sent Quineau, that they want to be found.'

Ten Lee smiled to herself. 'I'm sure my Rimpoche didn't send me all the way out here to play detective,' she said. 'But now that I am here, I admit I'm intrigued.'

'You're becoming too involved in this illusion, Ten,' Bennett warned.

Ten Lee gave him a pleasant scowl.

'So we sit tight and see what happens,' Mackendrick said.

Bennett nodded. 'As you said earlier, there's little else we can do. At least,' he added, 'the coffee substitute is drinkable.'

224

After lunch Miriam James collected them for their journey to the coastal settlement. 'We'll be travelling in a convoy of crawlers,' she said as they left the lodge and climbed the hillside to the track.

Tenebrae hung overhead, gales swirling the bands of its gaseous fleece. The day was humid, an electric charge in the air filling the valley with an atmosphere of pre-storm expectancy.

Three balloon-tyred crawlers were waiting on the track above the lodge, the first and last vehicle swarming with green-uniformed guards. De Channay was standing beside the middle crawler.

Ten Lee climbed on to the flat-bed with Miriam James and another armed guard, while Bennett and Mackendrick occupied the front seat next to De Channay.

'We're going to the settlement of New Marseilles on the coast,' he said. 'A journey of some twenty kilometres.'

De Channay started the motor and the crawler purred into life and accelerated down the rough track. Instead of descending into the valley, they took a turning through a high pass. On the crest of the rise, Bennett stared at the revealed scene. The mountainside fell away steeply, the incline striped with cultivated terraces. Ahead and far below, between an embrasure of headlands, the sea shimmered like silver lamé made liquid. The first balloon-tyred vehicle bounced ahead of them, the half dozen guards staring up the mountainside, rifles at the ready.

'Three years after the crash-landing,' De Channay was saying, 'our forefathers moved to the valley. The land was fertile and sheltered from the frequent storms. Over a period of years, as we expanded and developed our manufacturing industries, we settled the coast. Now New Marseilles is Homefall's largest centre of population, home to some ten thousand citizens.'

225

'Are you anywhere near building further starships?' Mackendrick asked.

De Channay glanced at him, shaking his head. 'Sadly, no. Perhaps in twenty, thirty years . . .'

'And yet you repaired a shuttle twenty years ago?'

De Channay nodded, staring ahead. 'Unfortunately, we don't possess the mining capabilities to extract the necessary materials to produce more ships.'

'About the power structure of Homefall,' Mackendrick said. 'You said you were an elected Council of Elders?'

'I used the term "elected", I must admit, only loosely. We are not a democracy as such. The population doesn't have a free vote in anything other than the equivalent of local council affairs. The Council of Elders is a self-elected body of members of the Church of Phobos and Deimos—'

'A meritocracy?' Mackendrick suggested. Bennett detected a certain irony in his tone.

De Channay pursed his lips. 'More of a theocracy. The power structure is based on the system of rank that maintained among the church officials who crewed the liner before the crash-landing. It was only ever meant to be a temporary affair, until such time as the colony found its footing, but as things turned out it proved successful and we've never seen any reason to change to another form of government.'

'Convenient for the self-elected members,' Mackendrick commented.

De Channay shifted uncomfortably. 'The population is happy with the system,' he said. 'They've had no complaints.'

Bennett refrained from mentioning the terrorists.

So, whatever it was that Homefall did not want known to the Expansion at large, the duplicity was sustained by the system of self-electing its ruling members. The Council of Elders of the Church of Phobos and Deimos, quite

226

apart from running the affairs of the colony, was also in a position to ensure that the colony remained isolated.

No wonder, Bennett thought, that they had over-reacted when we arrived on Homefall.

They edged around the flank of the mountain on a track barely wide enough to take the crawlers. Bennett glanced down to his left, saw the vertiginous drop, then looked away and kept his eyes fixed ahead.

Perhaps one hour later, still clinging to the high track like tiny insects, the first balloon-tyred vehicle came to a halt. De Channay braked, muttering with impatience. One of the guards on the first vehicle jumped down and examined the battery beneath the hood. A minute later he stood and waved his arms over his head to De Channay.

Something in the posture of the guard and the attentiveness of the others on the back of the vehicle filled Bennett with a sense of foreboding. He was aware of movement behind him. He glanced back and saw Miriam James on the flat-bed. As he watched, she lifted her rifle.

De Channay sighed and made to climb from his seat. Oddly, Bennett wanted to say something to stop the elder, delay him from whatever was about to happen. He said nothing, and watched with appalled fascination as De Channay climbed from the crawler and walked towards the stalled vehicle.

He was halfway between the crawlers when the firing began.

Miriam James fired the shot that hit De Channay between the shoulder blades. Bennett ducked, the blue light of the laser blinding him. He heard James grunt with satisfaction, and when his eyes adjusted he saw the elder's body fall in slow motion. A silence stretched and no one moved, as if the players of the drama were too stunned or disbelieving to take in the consequences of what had happened – and then all hell broke loose.

The guards on the first truck sprinted towards Bennett's crawler and, using it as cover, began firing at the third balloon-tyred vehicle. Fire was returned, lasers and conventional projectile shots which narrowly missed the crawler. Bennett was aware of fire from above; he saw dark shapes in the mountain appear and disappear as they fired down on the third crawler.

He tried to make sense of what was happening. Obviously some of the guards were in on the ambush; the figures on the mountainside were terrorists; and the guards in the third crawler? They were evidently militia loyal to the elders.

Miriam James screamed, 'Out! Climb down!' her face transformed into something ugly, an adrenalin-charged mask of terror and delight.

She almost dragged Mackendrick from the crawler. Bennett dived after him and followed as they staggered across the track and behind the cover of a rock. The air sang with the sound of the fire-fight – the burn of laser charges and the ricocheting whine of bullets. Bennett looked around for Ten lee. A guard was pushing her from the back of the crawler. She landed nimbly, crouched to gain her bearings, and then launched herself across the track towards the cover of the rock.

The bullet hit her with a spectacular force, all the more dramatic for being unseen. One second she was sprinting from the crawler, the next she was sprawling across the track. She hit the ground hard and lay very still, a small red shape on the sandy ground, bullets chipping spurts of dust all around her.

Bennett screamed and ran from the cover of the rock, ignoring shouts from Mackendrick and Miriam James exhorting him to get back. He reached Ten Lee and scooped her up, aware only of the pumping of his heart, the rattle of bullets against the nearby vehicle. He hugged her to him like a child and staggered back to the rock, James dragging him to safety amid the din of the fire-fight.

He scanned Ten Lee in panic, trying to assess the extent of her injuries and fearing the worst. Her torso was fine – no blood! – and her head . . . no blood there either. Then he saw the stain spreading through the fabric of her flight-suit. She had been hit in the upper leg. He felt a wave of relief, followed by panic at the amount of blood she was losing. The material of the legging had been ripped by the bullet. He tore it the rest of the way and used it as a tourniquet to staunch the flow of blood. It seemed, though he was no expert, to be only a flesh wound. Ten Lee was staring up at him, childish disbelief in her big eyes. Bennett stroked her cheek. 'You'll be fine, Ten. Stay calm. Chant a mantra or something.'

He looked up, praying for an end to this hell.

The guards from the third truck were being picked off by the terrorists high above. Their bodies littered the track, blood soaking into the dust. Still the survivors exchanged fire, bobbing up from behind the truck to loose off more laser fire.

Miriam James jumped up to fire at the third truck, and then slid down behind the rock again. Her eyes found Mackendrick. She said something to him, and at first Bennett failed to register the words. They seemed divorced from the fact of the battle raging around them.

'So Quineau got through?' she said.

Bennett heard the words, but had difficulty under-standing their significance. Only slowly did he begin to comprehend what James was talking about.

'We met,' Mackendrick replied, glancing at Bennett. 'He told me.'

James grabbed Mackendrick's arm. The old man winced at the force of the gesture. 'But did he give you the softscreen? Have you got it with you?' There was something close to desperation in her voice.

'He gave me the softscreen. But' – and here Mackendrick looked up at Bennett again, as if apologising for his deception – 'it was stolen from me.'

'Jesus! You haven't got it? Christ!' She hit the rock with the palm of her hand, tears streaming down her face.

Bennett looked at Mackendrick. 'Mack . . .' He shook his head. 'What's going on? Why didn't you tell us?'

'Josh, I couldn't. Please believe me. I'll tell you later, explain everything, okay?'

Bennett closed his eyes. He wanted to believe Mackendrick, but at the same time could not quell the sour feeling of betrayal rising in his throat like bile.

17

The muffled crump of an explosion shattered Bennett's thoughts. He looked back along the road. The third crawler was a twisted mass of metal and rubber engulfed in roaring flames. He saw militia-men running, human torches cavorting in pain, and looked away.

Miriam James kicked him. 'Get up! Back to the crawler. It won't be long before they send out a patrol.'

'What about Ten? She's injured!'

'We have medics where we're going,' James said. 'She'll be well looked after.'

Bennett stood, lifting Ten Lee. She was no weight at all as he carried her at a run to the crawler and eased her on to the flat-bed. He climbed up after her, holding her head in his lap as the crawler started up and tore off down the track, Mackendrick in front with James. Other green-uniformed guards had started the first vehicle and it accelerated ahead, away from the scene of death and conflagration.

Ten minutes later they slowed. Bennett peered ahead. The first truck was turning off the track, seemingly into the very face of the mountain itself. Their crawler followed and plunged into darkness. They were passing through a tunnel bored into the mountainside. Bennett closed his eyes and sat back in the padded seat, holding Ten's head. Her small hand found his fingers and squeezed.

They seemed to travel through the pitch black of the mountain's heart for long, uncomfortable hours. Bennett nodded off, but came awake often when the crawler jolted over uneven rock. He lost all sense of duration. Ten Lee's fingers were still clutching his, and from time to time he heard her soft moans of pain.

Ahead, at last, he made out a source of faint light. They emerged from the mountain, into the pale opal glow of the setting gas giant. They trundled along another narrow track, the land falling away precipitously to the right. All around, rearing craggy rock filled Bennett with a sense of lifeless hostility. They seemed to be moving ever higher, climbing through an endless series of sweeping tracks carved laboriously from the side of sheer cliff faces. Bennett closed his eyes and considered the terrible irony of surviving the fire-fight only to die when the transporter plunged into a ravine.

They came to yet another bend in the track, but beyond this Bennett made out the purple sweep of a small vale dotted with habitat domes and A-frames. The crawler slowed, skirting a road that hugged the face of the mountain.

Beneath a great sheltering overhang Bennett saw a ragged collection of old vehicles, antique transporters and automobiles. Other vehicles were drawing up beneath the crag, armed men and women jumping down and embracing each other.

The crawler passed into the shadow of the rock, slowed and came to a halt. Wearily, Bennett lifted Ten Lee from the flat-bed and, carrying her in his arms with Mackendrick beside him, walked out of the shadow of the overhang towards a group of men and women climbing the incline of the valley to meet them.

'Mack,' he said. 'What the hell's going on? Who are all these people?'

Before Mackendrick could reply, a tall, bearded man stepped forward with outstretched arms. He embraced Mackendrick, touched Bennett on the shoulder and called for assistance for Ten Lee.

'Welcome to Sanctuary,' he said. 'Hupcka. Hans Hupcka. Please, come this way.'

Bennett followed Hupcka down the sloping sward of purple grass, Ten Lee in his arms. Something in her eyes as she stared up at him, her lips pursed to fight the pain, reminded Bennett of a child's trusting gaze.

'Where are we, Josh?' she said in a small voice.

'Wish I knew, Ten. They must be terrorists.'

But what Bennett could not work out was the nature of Mackendrick's involvement with them.

They came to a large A-frame and Bennett climbed the steps into a spartanly furnished lounge. Mackendrick and Hupcka crossed the room and stepped out on to a veranda overlooking the slope of the plain, the two men deep in conversation. Bennett laid Ten Lee on a foam-form and within seconds a medic was in attendance, peeling away the makeshift bandage of her flight-suit legging and cleaning the wound. Bennett knelt beside her, holding her hand and smiling encouragement rather than view the bloody gash.

'You're lucky, girl,' the medic said. 'The bullet went straight through. An inch to the right and it would've hit a major artery. We'll have this fixed up in no time.'

He gave her an injection in the thigh and stitched the gaping hole. Bennett had expected the medic to use a plasti-skin sealant, but they were not on Earth, now. An antiseptic needle and thread was about as good as they could expect.

Ten Lee squeezed Bennett's hand. 'I heard what Mack said back there, Joshua. Why did he lie to us?'

'I don't know. He must have had his reasons.'

'But why didn't he tell us that he knew Quineau?'

Mackendrick came from the veranda and sat next to Ten Lee on the foam-form. He looked at Bennett. 'I couldn't tell you anything. I'm sorry. I didn't know what the situation was here. For all I knew the elders might've taken us into custody and tortured us for information. I couldn't risk that happening.'

'They might have tortured you,' Bennett said.

'Of course, but that was a risk I had to take.'

Ten Lee tried to sit up. 'What's happening?'

The medic finished applying fresh bandage and Bennett eased Ten Lee into a sitting position. Others came up the steps and into the A-frame, Miriam James and four other green-uniformed guards. They were joined by two men and a woman in civilian dress, ragged and soiled versions of the simple fashions worn by the farmers Bennett had seen earlier. There was a hushed sense of anticipation about the group as they quietly settled themselves around the room, their eyes taking in Mackendrick, Bennett and Ten Lee.

Hans Hupcka pulled up a three-legged stool and sat before the gathering. He was a big man, perhaps in his late twenties, his beard and broad lintel brow giving him an imposing air of authority.

'We've waited a long time for your arrival,' he said, nodding at each of them in turn. He spoke English with the precision of someone to whom it was an acquired language. 'We often despaired that you'd ever arrive. For fifteen years we've planned for this day. We planted sleepers in the militia; for a time we even had a man on the council itself, until he was discovered. In the interim, waiting for help from outside, we have waged a war with the regime known innocently as the Council of Elders.' Hupcka indicated James and the other men and women. 'This is my own council. They might call us terrorists, but we prefer to call ourselves rebels.'

234

Bennett leaned forward. 'We've been hearing a lot about someone called Quineau,' he said. 'The elders said that he left Homefall to get word of the colony to the Expansion. But the council sent Klien to eliminate him.' He looked at Mackendrick. 'I presume Quineau reached Earth, where he contacted you?' Bennett considered the many questions he wanted to ask, not the least of which was why Quineau had sought out Mackendrick.

What Hupcka said next cleared up that mystery. 'Quineau didn't head specifically for Earth – anywhere in the inhabited Expansion would have done. He went with the intention of locating the representatives of one of the big shipping lines or exploration companies – Patel or Redwood; we were not aware of the Mackendrick Foundation at the time – who might view the fact that Homefall was Earth-norm and inhabitable as a reason to open up lines of trade and communications. He obviously achieved this, though not quite as fast as we hoped.'

'It's fortunate that Quineau reached the cone of Expansion at all,' Mackendrick added, 'and pure luck that he came to my attention. His ship was poorly equipped, in a bad state of repair. It was a miracle he achieved transfer to and from the void in one piece.'

Hupcka smiled. 'He departed in somewhat hurried and dangerous circumstances,' he said.

'How did you find Quineau, Mr Mackendrick?' Miriam James asked.

'I didn't,' Mackendrick answered. 'One of my exploration vessels came across a small scout ship becalmed in regular space just inside the limit of the Expansion. They took the ship on board and found someone in the suspension unit. We learned that his name was Pierre Quineau. The ship had suffered massive systems failure in trans-c flight through the void; only an automatic eject program had brought it back into regular space. One of the systems failures meant that Quineau had been in suspension for over a year as the ship floated in space. When my men found him and gave medical assistance, he was irreparably brain-damaged.'

Hupcka shook his head. 'But was he able to tell you about the expedition to the interior?'

'I was on Earth at the time of the discovery, and I wasn't immediately notified of his rescue. I had many other matters to attend to. My engineers and computer specialists had been working to find out where the scout ship had originated as the systems failures had all but destroyed the record of its flight-path. The information they did find suggested that the ship had phased into the void at some location far out on the Rim, which they couldn't believe. Ships didn't explore that far afield, and as there were no colonies out there . . .

'This is when I was told of the mysterious star traveller. I was intrigued enough to travel to the colony world of Madrigal, where he was undergoing psychiatric treatment at a foundation medical centre. I found a man . . .' Mackendrick paused and looked around the group of staring faces. 'He could only be described as not being in his right mind. At the time of our first meeting he was extremely violent and had to be forcefully restrained. I tried to talk to him, but his rantings made little sense. No one had ever survived more than a year in suspension, and the psychiatrists diagnosed his symptoms as those produced by chronic suspension trauma.'

'Did he recover?' Hupcka asked.

Mackendrick shook his head. 'I saw him three more times during the week I was on Madrigal, and he showed no signs of recovery.'

Miriam James said, 'What did he tell you, Mr Mackendrick?'

'You must understand that he was barely coherent at

the time. He ranted for hours in a mixture of French and English. He couldn't even tell me the name of his planet. All he said was that he came from a world on the Rim, and that he'd been on an expedition, a long trek with two other men. He said that they'd walked into mountainous country and descended into a deep underground chamber. There he claimed that they'd discovered an alien race. He told me that the Ancients, as he called them, had incredible healing powers.' Mackendrick smiled. 'Of course, I was far from convinced. I took his story for the rantings of a madman.'

'But didn't he have the softscreen?' James asked.

Mackendrick nodded. 'He told me about the screen. He'd told no one else, he said, because he could trust no one. Secreted aboard the scout ship was a softscreen recording of the exploration he undertook with his colleagues, Klien and Carstairs. I had my engineers search the ship. I was still on Madrigal when they found the screen. I watched it with Quineau in his hospital room.

'It showed the first week of the expedition, the long trek through high mountainous terrain, much of it through snow blizzards. They reached the entrance of the underground chamber and descended, but then the quality of the recording deteriorated drastically. There was very little light down there, and only shadows could be made out. The recording actually ends before Quineau and the others make contact with the aliens, if of course he was telling the truth. I left for Earth, taking the softscreen with me. I wanted to get it analysed, the underground shots computer-enhanced.'

Mackendrick stopped there, staring at his hands. He looked up, at Hupcka and the other rebels, and shook his head.

'When I reached Earth, I was contacted by the police

authorities on Madrigal. Pierre Quineau had escaped from the grounds of the hospital while taking exercise, and had been found murdered in a public park a kilometre away. A woman had witnessed the shooting, and I requested a copy of the police computer-visual of her description of the killer. To my amazement it bore more than a marked resemblance to Quineau's fellow explorer I'd seen on the softscreen recording, Klien. I began to wonder if there might be a grain of truth in Quineau's story.'

Miriam James said, 'You told me that the softscreen was stolen.'

Mackendrick nodded. 'Shortly after I arrived on Earth, a thief broke into my house in Calcutta and stole it.'

Hupcka said, 'So Klien killed Quineau, came to Earth and took the softscreen.'

Mackendrick was shaking his head. 'That wasn't possible. Quineau was killed on the twenty-fifth of May, and the softscreen was taken from my safe just two days later. It takes three days by starship to reach Earth from Madrigal. There was no way Klien could have murdered Quineau, boarded a ship and stolen the screen in Calcutta. Hard though it is to believe, the theft was just a terrible coincidence.'

'And it's never been discovered?' James asked.

'I hired private detectives to hunt both Quineau's killer and the softscreen, with no luck.' He paused. 'So I decided to set about exploring the Rim for Quineau's planet. I sent out uncrewed exploration ships to the sector of the Rim adjacent to where his ship was discovered, but of course the area we were searching was vast. It was no wonder it took us more than twelve years to locate Homefall.' He looked around the staring faces. 'The rest you know.'

Hupcka smiled, almost regretfully. 'We had hoped that Quineau would get through to the inhabited sector and alert Earth to the fact of our existence.' He looked from Bennett to Mackendrick. 'I didn't know Quineau, but he was a friend of my brother. Just over fourteen years ago he returned from the expedition to the interior alone, without Carstairs or Klien. The story was that Carstairs had died on the way back; we suspect that Klien killed him, though what exactly happened has never come to light.

'Quineau told Jan, my brother, an engineer working on the reconstruction of the scout ships, that he had to get off the planet, alert Earth to the fact of Homefall and what he'd discovered in the mountains. At that time on Homefall, the council was divided as to whether to re-contact the Expansion. Some wanted to, while a more conservative element was violently opposed to the idea. They had founded a viable community on Homefall, away from the perceived sins of the Expansion, and they didn't want their Eden invaded. The pro-contact faction had held sway for some time, hence the rebuilding of the scout ships, but the anti-contact faction was gaining power. There was talk that the ships were to be destroyed. Quineau convinced Jan and others to help him flee the planet aboard one of the ships. It was pre-programmed with the flight-path to take it in the approximate direction of the Expansion. My brother planned to take the second scout ship and follow Quineau. He'd manufactured a device . . . I suppose you would call it a homing device, a small receiver designed to pick up a signal, and implanted it in the softscreen recording Quineau was to take with him. Quineau left Homefall aboard the scout ship one night a few weeks after returning from the interior.'

Hupcka paused there. He considered his words, then continued.

'The following day, my brother was arrested as he

tried to board the second ship. Over a dozen other sympathisers were also arrested. They had copies of the softscreen recording made by Quineau, and these were taken and destroyed. Fortunately they did not find the receiver – Jan gave it to me shortly before his arrest, told me to bury it where it wouldn't be discovered. Jan and the others were interrogated and tortured. They were never seen alive again and their bodies were never discovered.'

Hupcka fell silent. He looked up at last.

'Two days later Klien was despatched in the second ship to track down and kill Quineau. The conservative element of the Council of Elders gained ascendancy and routed the liberal forces. The rumour was that Quineau, Klien and Carstairs had discovered something in the mountains, something that the conservative elders didn't want the Expansion, or the people of Homefall, to know about. They began rounding up everyone associated with Quineau and his sympathisers, and I managed to escape with a few others. We formed the resistance movement with friends and sympathisers of the men and women killed by the Council of Elders. We knew nothing of what Quineau and the others had discovered, just rumours that they'd come upon evidence that the Ancients, once thought to be extinct, actually still existed. We organised expeditions to the interior, trying to trace the route Quineau had taken to the underground caverns, but without a copy of the softscreen to guide the way, we had no luck. The land to the west is hostile and inhospitable – we lost many men and women in the search. For the past decade the elders have waged a ruthless war against us, and we have fought back as best we can, while continuing the search.'

Hupcka looked up and smiled at Mackendrick. 'You can

have no idea the joy we felt on hearing that people from Earth had landed on Homefall.' He gestured. 'We are devastated that Klien achieved his aim of killing Quineau. That the softscreen should be lost . . . what a terrible irony.' He smiled sadly. 'Your crash-landing here is the final cruel twist of fate. We had hoped that you might be able to return to Earth, with the receiver, and locate the stolen screen.'

Bennett felt something kick within him, a surge of excitement and at the same time fear. He looked across at Mackendrick.

'Perhaps you had better tell them, Josh' Mackendrick said.

Hupcka looked up, alert. 'Tell us what?'

Beside Bennett, Ten Lee gave a small laugh of delight.

'We didn't crash-land,' Bennett said. 'We told the council that so they wouldn't go looking for the ship. It's actually in full working order on the plain three hundred kilometres south of here.'

Hupcka stared, his expression shocked. 'So perhaps we can defeat the council at last,' he said. 'First, we've got to get you to the ship. Miriam, gather six of the fittest men and women. Ready two ground effect vehicles and report back to me in one hour.'

When James jumped up and hurried from the room, Hupcka turned to the other freedom fighters and issued orders in rapid French.

Bennett said to Mackendrick, 'Ten's in no fit state to travel, Mack. And with respect, I wouldn't put you through another four months of suspension.'

Ten Lee touched his hand. 'Can you pilot the ship alone?'

'I'll just take twice as long with the checks,' he said. 'Don't worry, I'll get to Earth and do my best to trace the softscreen.'

Ten Lee squeezed his fingers. 'I want to see the Ancients,' she said, determination in the set of her features.

Bennett looked up suddenly at Mackendrick. 'Good God. You knew you were dying . . . Quineau told you that the Ancients had healing powers.'

Mackendrick gave a sad smile. 'I hope you understand why I put you all at so much risk,' he said. 'When I first heard Quineau's story I was intrigued, and then I was diagnosed five years ago, and I knew I had to come here. It's a long shot, Josh. Perhaps Quineau's story really *was* nothing more than the ravings of a lunatic. But I want to find out for myself.'

Bennett thought of Ella, and how modern medicine had been unable to heal her, then he cursed himself for trawling up memories and emotions he should have worked through long ago. Hell, for the past day or so he had been so consumed by the rush of incidents that he had hardly had time for self-pity.

He looked ahead, to the void-flight to Earth, the search for the softscreen. Soon he would be consumed again, with little time to consider himself, and the thought was like a balm.

Two hours later he said goodbye to Mackendrick and hugged Ten Lee. 'I'll see you in . . . Good God, eight months seems like such a long time.'

Ten Lee smiled. 'For you it will pass in an instant.'

Bennett strode up the incline towards the overhang where Hans Hupcka, Miriam James and half a dozen others, all armed, waited in two balloon-tyred vehicles. Hupcka passed him a silver oval device the size of a cigar case: the receiver. Briefly he instructed Bennett in its use.

They set off minutes later. Mackendrick and Ten Lee were small figures on the veranda of the A-frame, and

Bennett raised his arm in a farewell salute. They headed out of the valley on a different route from the one they'd used to get here, going around the mountain to avoid the long road above the inhabited valley. This track would bring them out on the purple plain well south of the deserted timber settlement and the remains of the sunken starship.

Hupcka sat beside Bennett and steered the bouncing vehicle. 'In four hours we'll be out of the mountains, Josh. Perhaps six hours after that we'll reach the ship.'

'I only hope the council militia hasn't found it before us.'

'They had a patrol scout on the plain yesterday,' Hupcka said. 'But they only got as far south as the ruins. I know because we have a man in their ranks.'

They had left the valley far behind and were travelling down a boulder-strewn ravine. Ahead, the first crawler bounced like a child's toy, a comically frail structure rocking this way and that over the uneven terrain.

Tenebrae slipped down behind the mountains as they travelled, and the stars appeared in the strip of sky high above the gorge. The minor sun shone like a distant orange lantern, providing sufficient light to illuminate the track ahead. The balloon tyres of the crawler came into their own, climbing over boulders and across pot-holes, the suspension creaking in protest. Bennett held on as the vehicle bucketed along, Hupcka laughing into the headwind like a madman.

They passed from the protection of the mountains and descended on to the purple plain, the first crawler racing ahead. Bennett had not slept for what seemed like ages, and as the vehicle rocked back and forth he took the opportunity to doze.

He was awoken, hours later, when the crawler lurched, tossing him between Hupcka's bulk and the door. He rubbed his eyes and looked around. It was dawn. The bright ellipse of the gas giant's upper hemisphere spanned the far horizon, casting its opalescent light across the plain. He must have been asleep for almost six hours. They had climbed from the plain and were skirting the foothills to the west, the purple grass spreading like a sea far below.

Hupcka glanced at him. 'I didn't want to worry you unduly, Josh. But a couple of hours ago we discovered we had company. Look.' He passed Bennett a pair of binoculars and pointed. 'Halfway across the plain, at about two o'clock.'

Bennett adjusted the focus. At first all he saw was a dancing blur of purple grass. Then he caught a flash of something. He steadied his hand and centred the speeding object. It was a balloon-tyred vehicle like their own, swarming with green-uniformed militia.

'A council patrol,' Hupcka said. 'Perhaps they're taking your crash-landing story with a pinch of salt, checking further afield for the ship.'

'Where's Miriam's crawler?'

'When we saw the council militia we decided to take action. The other crawler moved down to the plain to follow at a safe distance. If the militia looks like getting anywhere near the ship, they'll attack and provide a decoy.'

'And if the militia see us?'

Hupcka nodded. 'It's a possibility. If they move our way, or start firing, then Miriam and the others will move in.' He smiled. 'Don't worry. This is routine stuff. We'll get you to the ship in one piece.'

Bennett nodded, fear tight within him. He was, he realised, not cut out for the role of a man of action. He liked the mentally anaesthetising effect of living on the edge of his wits, but when things got out of hand – like the fire-fight yesterday, or the possibility of conflict now – he had to admit that he wished he was elsewhere.

But do I wish I was back on Earth, with Julia, he asked himself? It came as a surprise to realise that he would rather be in the thick of the action.

Hupcka glanced at him. 'Once we reach the ship, how long will it take you to lift off?'

'Five, ten minutes. No more.'

Hupcka nodded. 'Okay.' He lifted a radio microphone and shouted into it in French. A crackling voice replied. Hupcka shouted again, clearly issuing orders.

'We're getting close, Josh. I've told Miriam to move in and attack the militia.'

Bennett turned in his seat, raised the binoculars and found the rebels' crawler far below. As he watched, it closed in on the militia crawler and opened fire with a hail of laser charges. Explosions bloomed in the plain around the first vehicle as it took evasive action and swerved from left to right. One green-uniformed militia-man tumbled, loose-limbed, over the side. They returned fire, and the lasers illuminated the dawn with quick flares of electric blue.

'Hold on, Josh! I'm going for it.'

Hupcka turned the wheel of the vehicle and they veered off down the incline, Bennett swaying in his seat. At this distance, without the benefit of binoculars, the militia crawler and the rebel vehicle were reduced to the size of scurrying insects.

Bennett held on as the vehicle bounced and juddered over the uneven terrain. Five minutes later they hit the plain and accelerated. Bennett turned and adjusted the binoculars. The crawlers were far behind, their progress lit by the bright flares of exploding laser charges.

'The ship!' Hupcka called, staring ahead. 'Two minutes, Josh! Get ready to board.'

Perhaps half a kilometre away, squatting on the plain where they had left it, was the slick tear-drop shape of the Cobra resplendent in the morning light of Tenebrae. Bennett turned and looked for the enemy crawler. He judged that the two vehicles were a couple of kilometres away, and closing.

They slewed to a halt in the shadow of the Cobra and Bennett jumped out. He took Hupcka's hand in a fierce grip, words of either encouragement or farewell beyond him.

'I'll see you in eight months, Josh. Good luck!'

Bennett ran towards the Cobra, slapped the sensor panel on the hatch and dived inside. Seconds later he was on the flight-deck, throwing himself into the command couch and touching the surrounding console to life. He typed in the command for immediate lift-off – he'd worry about the phase commands when he was in orbit. The main consideration was to get into the air and out of the range of the militia lasers.

The Cobra's take-off system cycled into life, seeming to take an age to process Bennett's commands. Through the viewscreen he made out two tiny vehicles on the plain, approaching at speed. As he watched, a third vehicle emerged from beneath the ship's nose: Hupcka. The rebel halted his crawler and stood, lifting a laser rifle to his shoulder and taking careful aim.

The militia crawler accelerated, heading straight for the Cobra. Seconds later the first explosion rocked the ship. A spray of soil erupted from pits gouged in the ground just metres away. He abbreviated the take-off program, dispensing with half a dozen checks. He would be airborne in a matter of minutes, with luck.

Below, Hupcka was firing at the militia. Their crawler swerved on a slalom run across the plain, miraculously avoiding Hupcka's laser charges. Only two militia-men remained alive and fighting. One of them stood and levelled a laser-cannon at the ship. Seconds before the Cobra lifted, the bolt exploded beneath the nose of the ship, swatting it with mighty force. Bennett yelled and closed his eyes.

The ship lurched, falling, and he could see how it would end in failure, the ship damaged beyond hope of repair. Then the boosters kicked in and fired, catapulting the Cobra forward, and it was all he could do to wrest the controls from the pre-programmed routine and direct the ship across the plain at a grass-cutting height. He swerved to avoid the militia's vehicle, and the crawler veered and rolled over as the Cobra swept into the sky.

He tried to regain his composure. He slowed his breathing and steadied the ship in a stable hovering attitude. Far below, Miriam James and the other rebels were running towards the last two militia-men. He made out Hupcka, raising a fist in a victory salute, and then he lifted the Cobra away from the plain. He let the program take over, relinquishing control with relief, and set the system for phase-out.

Five minutes later the roar of the engines ceased suddenly, and the milky light of the upper atmosphere was replaced with the grey marble effect of the void. Bennett sat and stared at the streaming stars, amazed at the fact of his escape in the quiet aftermath of the attack. He set the computer to revive him from suspension in a little under two months, so that he could make the necessary systems checks. Approximately two months after that, he would be on Earth.

He sat for a long time in the command couch, letting the shakes leave his body, his thoughts quieten. He had never really gained from looking ahead before now; the future had always promised nothing more than the same old events, reordered. But now he had a goal, and people

247

were relying on him to succeed, and he looked ahead to the search for the softscreen in Calcutta with confidence and hope.

18

Rana Rao stood for a long time beneath the cedar tree across the road from the luminously white, scaled-down copy of Sydney Opera House. It rose between a grand representation of the White House and a half-sized imitation of the Feynman dome on Mars. The street was lined with similar kitsch examples of architectural folly, a parade of tasteless ostentation Rana found sickening.

She moved from the shadow of the tree and into the glow of the street lighting. She found it hard to believe that she was, perhaps, just metres away from the man responsible for the crucifix killings. Soon he would become a real person, with a real identity: name, profession, perhaps even a family who loved him.

She stepped from the pavement and crossed the road, her hand straying involuntarily to the polished butt of the pistol beneath her jacket. The opera house was set in a couple of acres of landscaped lawn. As soon as she stepped on to the wide gravel path, spotlights activated to light her way.

She paused before the door and took a breath, then reached out and touched the door-chime. The soft notes of Beethoven's Fifth sounded from inside – appropriate, given the design of the house. She waited, conscious of the staring eye of a security camera positioned above the door.

A voice issued from a grille, rich and urbane. 'Good evening? May I help you?'

'Lieutenant Rao. I'm from the Calcutta police force.'

'One moment, please.'

Seconds later the door swung open automatically and standing perhaps two metres away, arms folded across an ample chest, stood a man who bore not the slightest resemblance, apart from being male and Caucasian, to Ahmed's description of the killer. He was not thin-faced and silver-haired, but had a well-fed face and a dark head of curls.

He gestured for her to enter and walked ahead of her. Rana followed, swallowing a sense of despair, and wondered how she should proceed.

'I've been expecting you,' he said, surprising her. He was crossing a large, circular lounge fitted with sunken sofas, throw cushions and discreet lighting. A soprano's voice quavered on a high C.

Rana blinked. 'You have?'

He reached out to the wall and the aria modulated. 'Please, take a seat.' He indicated one of the below-floor sofas.

Rana descended three steps and seated herself, feeling at a distinct disadvantage.

The man loomed over her, holding a com-board. 'I have the file here,' he said, 'but I'll fix you a drink first. Coffee, or something stronger?'

'Ah . . .' She was about to say that she thought there had been some mistake, but the man misinterpreted her hesitation.

'Of course. I'm sorry, I should have realised. You're on duty. Coffee it is, then.' He murmured into a wall-speaker. 'Two coffees, Raisa.'

Within seconds a maid entered the room bearing a silver tray and two small bone china coffee cups, a jug of milk and a bowl of sugar. She stepped into the sunken bunker and placed the tray on a small table in the centre.

'Thank you, Raisa.' The man joined Rana in the bunker, sitting across from her and pouring the coffees. 'White, sugar?'

'White, no sugar.' She could only watch the man in silence, wondering how to proceed.

'I was rather hoping that Commissioner Singh might have called for the report personally,' he was saying. 'We have a lot to discuss on the security front which I'm sure you'll understand I cannot broach with his staff.'

'As a matter of fact,' Rana began, 'I am not here to collect the report. You see, I am calling on residents in the area as a matter of routine.'

The man looked surprised, but made a sophisticated show of apologising. 'But my dear, I am so sorry. You see, I was expecting the commissioner or one of his staff. But allow me to introduce myself. I am Ezekiel Klien, chief of security at Calcutta spaceport. And you are?'

Rana swallowed. 'Lieutenant Rana Rao, Homicide Division, Calcutta police force.'

'Homicide? And how might I be of assistance?'

'It's just . . .' she began, falteringly. 'I'm making a series of routine door-to-door enquiries. Last night there was a murder committed a kilometre from here. The killer was seen leaving the scene of the crime.'

'How appalling. If I can be of any assistance, any at all . . .'

Rana took a breath to steady her nerves. The more she thought about it, the more she realised that there had indeed been some misunderstanding. Ahmed must have lied about seeing the killer enter this house, or mistaken the house itself.

'I was wondering if I might ask you a few questions, Mr

Klien? Routine things I've been asking everyone in the neighbourhood.'

'Of course. By all means.' He sat back and sipped his coffee.

Rana took a gulp of her own coffee to moisten her dry mouth. Her hand shook, setting up a nervous rattle of cup on saucer. She would have to drastically revise her questions. She had planned to ask him if he knew the identities of victims of the crucifix killer, and if he could account for his whereabouts on certain dates, but such a line of interrogation would hardly be appropriate in the circumstances.

'We have reports that a man was seen in the area last night.' She went on to describe the man Ahmed had seen enter this very house.

Klien nodded. 'As a matter of fact, yes. At perhaps ten last night someone did come to the door. It was a man very much fitting your description. He was lost, had no money, and asked if he might call his wife to pick him up. I was busy with the report at the time, so I gave him ten rupees and directed him to a public com-screen kiosk. He left and I thought no more about it. You don't think . . . ?'

Rana shrugged. 'We'd like to question the individual to eliminate him from our enquiries,' she said. 'I wonder if you'd allow a computer artist to come round and take your impressions of the man?'

Klien gestured, the very epitome of accommodation. 'By all means. I'm in most evenings after eight.'

Rana finished her coffee. 'Thank you for your time and the coffee, Mr Klien. I hope I haven't disturbed you.'

'Of course not. I'm delighted to have been of some assistance. I only wish that I could help you further.'

Before Rana could protest that she really must be going, he leaned over and poured her another cup of coffee. He poured himself a second cup and sipped delicately.

'Tell me, Lieutenant, if you don't mind my asking, how long have you been with the force?'

She smiled, pleased at the change of subject. 'Almost eight years now. Most of the time working with street children. I was promoted to Homicide a few weeks ago.'

'Homicide . . . Isn't that Vishwanath's department now?'

'Do you know him?'

'We've worked together in the past. I rate Vishwanath very highly, Lieutenant.'

'I'm enjoying working with him.'

This time when she finished her coffee she placed a hand above the cup. 'I'm afraid I must be getting on, Mr Klien. Thank you again.'

'Not at all. I'll show you out.'

He rose and escorted her from the lounge and into the hall. The door swung open automatically. He placed a hand on her elbow as she stepped through the door. 'Good night, and take care, Sita.'

She stopped, her stomach lurching. She turned and stared at him. 'What did you say?'

He was smiling, as if mystified. 'I'm so sorry? It was Sita, wasn't it? Or Rita?'

'Rana,' she murmured, 'Rana Rao.'

'Of course – Rana. Well, good night, Rana.'

He stepped back, still smiling, and the door swung shut after him.

Rana made her way slowly away from the house, trying to regain her composure. She had been sure, for a second, that his slip had been deliberate. He had intentionally said her old name, to see how she might react. But how was that possible? How might he know of her old identity? He was head of security at the port, though. Perhaps, when she ran away all those years ago, he had worked for her father? But how did he know now, having never met her, that she was the person once known as Sita Mackendrick? She told herself that she was being paranoid. There was a very simple explanation. He had misheard her name, as he claimed. He had made a genuine mistake, thought she had said Sita. It was a common enough name, after all.

She made her way to the main road and caught a taxi home.

Back at her apartment, she considered her meeting with Klien. After expecting so much to come from her investigations, she felt disappointed. At least, she told herself, there was the lead of the silver-haired man to follow up. She would tell Vishwanath, when she started her shift at twelve tomorrow, that her interviews had elicited descriptions of a silver-haired man in the vicinity of the murder scene last night.

She went to bed but could not sleep. She tried to work out how Klien might have recognised her, and known her true identity, after all those years.

At dawn she got up, tired and frustrated, her mind still racing. She made herself a strong pot of coffee and sat by the window overlooking the park, huddling around the cup and taking the occasional sip.

The knock on the door startled her; she jumped, spilling coffee over her bare knees. All visitors should have buzzed her from the outer door; how had they entered without being let in? She wondered if it was one of her neighbours. Or maybe the security sergeant with her softscreen, entering at the same time as one of her early-rising neighbours left for work.

Pulling her wrap more tightly around her, she crossed the lounge and opened the door. She stared, surprised, and stepped back.

A thin-faced, silver-haired man stood on the threshold. He gave her a smile of disarming charm.

'What do you want?' The question sounded more brusque than she had intended.

He stepped past her, entering uninvited, and strode across the lounge to the window. He stood with his back to her, staring out.

'How can I help you?' Her voice faltered.

He turned, still smiling. She was suddenly aware of her nakedness beneath the wrap, and folded her arms across her chest.

'How did you get in?'

'That need not concern you,' he said.

Rana started. She recognised the voice, the soft, cultured tones. It was the voice of Ezekiel Klien – but how was that possible?

'What do you want?' she asked again. She knew that she must have presented a frightened sight, cowering with her arms crossed protectively over her chest.

'It's a very delicate business. You see, I've been looking for you for a very long time.'

Rana felt a sudden heat rise through her chest. She wanted to throw up. Something was happening here that she did not understand, and ignorance fuelled her fear.

'Consider the irony. For years I have been, on and off, scouring Calcutta for you. Of course, you might have been dead, but I had a hunch . . . a hunch that you were still alive—'

'Klien,' she said, before she could stop herself.

The man smiled. 'Very clever of you, Sita. The voice, of course.' He gave a quick, mocking bow. 'I am Ezekiel Klien.'

She closed her eyes, fear flooding through her. She had known, just as soon as she said his name, that she had made a mistake. He was the crucifix killer, disguised, and he would kill her just as he had killed all his other victims.

'How . . . ?' she said, staring at his face. 'How did you . . . ?'

He smiled. 'A simple capillary net,' he said.

'I . . . I didn't know . . . I didn't think it was possible . . .' She had heard that capillary nets were still at the prototype stage of development, still undergoing tests.

He ignored her. 'Thirteen years ago,' he was saying, 'I was a private investigator hired by your mother to find you.'

Rana recalled the man she had seen with her mother in the restaurant, all those years ago.

She stared at him. 'I don't know what you're talking about.'

She told herself not to panic. There was, after all, a simple solution to the situation. She clicked her jaw, opening communications with Control. Now they would hear her every word, discern that something was amiss. She waited for the voice of the duty officer to sound in her ear.

Klien was smiling at her, something almost playful in his expression. He smiled, and clicked his jaw in an arrogant, mocking gesture, and said, 'You didn't think for one second, did you, that I would let you get away with that?'

From the breast pocket of his suit he produced a compact silver oval, the size of a cigarette case. A scrambler.

'Nice try, Sita,' he said.

Rana had never felt more naked or vulnerable. This man, of all the people on the planet, knew her secret. He was in a position of inestimable power, and it was not knowing quite how he intended to use this power that was terrifying.

She glanced across the room at the Chinese print, behind which was the alarm. She would make her way very casually towards it, then lean against the print, and with luck security would arrive before he killed her.

'I know that you are Sita Mackendrick.'

He moved from the window and perched on the arm of a chair, something proprietorial and arrogant in his posture. He was a metre away from the picture. There was no way she might reach it, now, without arousing his suspicion.

He smiled at her. 'As I said, consider the irony. For so long I have been looking for you, and last night you actually found me. Remarkable . . . I could hardly believe my fortune.'

'How . . .' she began. The words, the admission of her true identity after so many years of denial, had to be forced out. 'How did you know . . . ?'

'Your mother made available a few pix of you, of course. Over the years I've had them updated, computer-aged. I knew who I was looking for . . . if, that is, you were still alive. It did occur to me that the people who robbed your father's safe might have killed you, but I hoped not. I assumed there might be a ransom demand, but when none came I began to worry. Perhaps they had killed you, after all. You saw them entering your house, you could identify them, and so you had to die. But I kept up my search. The consequences were too important not to.'

His smug expression, his assumption of superiority, was sickening.

'What . . . what do you want?' she managed.

Klien stood, moved away from the picture on the wall and strolled around the room. Rana's heart began a laboured pounding. This was her chance. She moved towards the Chinese print.

Klien stared at her. 'I want to know who they were, Sita,' he said.

'Don't call me that!' she cried.

She reached the wall, folding her arms protectively across her chest, and leaned back. She felt the picture give beneath her shoulder blades and at the same time experienced a terrible sense of anti-climax. She prayed that the alarm would be sounding loud and clear at the local police station.

'But Sita is your name, isn't it?' Klien paused, licked his lips. How he was enjoying this, his moment of victory after years of disappointment. 'I want to know the identities of the people who kidnapped you.'

She stared at him. Her one satisfaction, amid all her fear, was the knowledge that he was so wrong. She would play along with his little game.

She shook her head. 'I don't know who they were. They took me and locked me up. I managed to escape.'

Klien was shaking his head. 'It doesn't make sense, Sita. Why would they take you from the house and simply lock you up? They would either demand a ransom, which they didn't, or kill you, which they didn't. So . . . are you going to tell me the truth, Sita?'

'I don't know what you want from me.'

'Shall I tell you what I think happened?' he asked. 'I think they took you, locked you up as you said, and were going to demand a ransom, but something happened?'

She shook her head. 'What?'

'I think that, while they held you, a certain rapport developed. It often happens between kidnappers and hostages. You grew close to them, and they perhaps to you. They took you away with them, perhaps you even worked for them at, what? Thieving? Prostitution? For whatever reasons, you never returned home. Either they kept you captive for years, or you actually enjoyed the life you were leading.' He shook his head. 'But that is irrelevant. What matters is that you know the identity of the people who took you, and I want to know who they are.'

He was no longer smiling, and the sudden transformation, from condescending affability to controlled but obvious rage, filled her with fear. She stared at him, shaking her head. 'I . . . I don't know.'

He stood, and in one fluid menacing movement slipped a hand inside his jacket and produced a laser pistol. He held it almost casually at his hip, directed at her chest.

'Who were they? Where are they now? Tell me.'

'I don't know. I honestly don't know.'

He nodded with a show of reasonableness. 'Very well, I'll explain. They took something from your father's safe, something that is very important to me. It is called a softscreen, and it contains information that I need. Now do you understand, Sita? I need to know who kidnapped you so that I can trace them and locate the softscreen. Now, are you going to tell me, or should I resort to more than mere verbal persuasion?'

The softscreen . . . She wondered what information the softscreen might contain that was so vital to him.

'Now, Sita, tell me: who were they?'

The very fact that he wanted information from her, she realised, might prove to be her salvation. He would hardly kill her if he thought she might be able to lead him to the screen. She decided, then, to tell him the truth. She would tell him what he wanted to know, play for time, and hope that the security team would arrive before she had finished her explanation of the screen's whereabouts.

'Who were they?' he asked again, raising the laser.

She imagined herself as his latest victim, one side of her face burned beyond recognition, the other scored with a bloody crucifix.

No, she told herself. He needs me alive.

'I've killed many people, Sita,' Klien told her matter-of-factly. 'I would suffer no compunction at killing you, too.'

She wanted to call his bluff, then, tell him that if he killed her he would never know who kidnapped her. But something in his manner made her realise that this would be a mistake. He had lost his urbane charm, or arrogance, and he was close to breaking point. There was a light in his eyes that was almost maniacal.

She shook her head. 'You've got it all very wrong, Mr Klien. You see, there were no kidnappers.' String it out, she told herself. Play for time . . .

He barked a laugh. 'No? Then who robbed your father's safe? Who took the softscreen?'

'I took the softscreen, Mr Klien. I ran away from home, but first opened the safe and took some money and the screen.' She shrugged. 'People must have thought that I was taken by whoever stole the softscreen, but that wasn't how it happened.'

That gave him pause to consider. He watched her, his mind ticking over.

He nodded slowly and licked his lips. 'Very well.' His voice was no longer the sophisticated drawl. The words caught in his throat. He was so close, after all, to what he had sought for such a long time. 'Very well, Sita. Now tell me, what did you do with the softscreen?'

She smiled. 'I kept it, of course. I lived on the streets for five years and kept it with me. It was a source of great entertainment for me and my friends. We—'

He interrupted. 'Where is it now, Sita?'

She hesitated. She imagined the security team, hurrying towards the apartment. Play for time . . .

'Tell me why you need it, and I'll tell you where it is.'

His reaction scared her. He moved forward, jabbing the gun at her. 'Tell me!'

'Ah-cha, ah-cha . . .'

She glanced through the window. Shiva! In the street below she saw an unmarked truck draw up, half a dozen plainclothes men jump out. She thought she might pass out with fear and dread.

'Sita, if you don't tell me . . .'

'Ah-cha. It's . . . I sold it. I sold it to . . .' She bit her lip, feigning concentration. She heard footsteps on the stairs.

'Who? Who did you sell it to, Sita?' He stared at her, something insane in his eyes. He raised his pistol and directed it at her chest.

She heard a movement in the doorway. The door swung back, smacking the wall. The first shot turned the window behind Klien's head to molten, dripping slag. Rana saw a security marksman crouching in the doorway.

Klien ducked and swung his weapon, fired instantly. The marksman screamed and fell as the laser hit him in the head.

Rana watched with a sense of disbelief as Klien turned towards her. She could intuit his intentions from the look in his eyes. She began to plead with him, but, almost sadly, he shook his head. In the second before his finger pressed the trigger, she imagined that she saw something like pity in his eyes.

She screamed, and Klien fired.

The laser hit Rana in the chest and she fell back against the wall. She slid to the floor, staring at Klien in disbelief. The pain seemed to fill every cell of her body with agonising fire.

He fired again, this time at another security officer in the doorway. He dived across the room, sending a barrage of shots through the wall. He ran to the doorway and scanned the hall, firing all the time. Rana heard another cry.

He paused and looked back at her. His gaze fell to the hole burned in her chest. For a brief second she thought that he was about to fire again and finish her off, but instead he moved through the door and disappeared, and something in his confident dismissal of her fate frightened her even more than the thought of the *coup de grâce*.

Rana began to cry. She reached up and fingered the wound in her chest. The skin between her breasts was burned and blackened, and though the pain pulsed through her body in sickening waves, worse than the pain was the thought that she was dying.

It was this knowledge, that after such a short life, at just twenty-three, she was going to die so needlessly, that made her cry like a child.

Rana's vision blurred. Nascent in her thoughts, but cut short, was the satisfaction that at least Klien had failed to find the softscreen.

19

Bennett lay in the command couch and allowed the Cobra to fly itself through the upper atmosphere of Earth. He monitored the screens set into the console that surrounded him, vigilant without a co-pilot to back him up. The ship entered the upper cloud layer, the aluminium blue of the troposphere replaced suddenly by opalescent cloud whipping around the viewscreen. The Cobra hit turbulence and rocked solidly, Bennett swinging in his couch. Seconds later the ship dropped through a raft of cumulus and the desert of northern India seemed to extend forever far below.

He got through to Control at Calcutta spaceport. 'Ah, Bennett here. Mackendrick/Cobra/7–55.'

A tinny voice replied in the ear-piece of his flight helmet. 'Ah-cha, Mackendrick/Cobra. You are cleared to land. Please copy these co-ordinates . . .'

For the next five minutes, as the Cobra roared over northern India, Bennett programmed the approach flight-path in the Cobra, then lay back and closed his eyes. His effective involvement in the process of bringing the Cobra to Earth was over.

Twelve hours ago he had awoken for the second time from suspension and climbed from the unit, shaking off images of bloated gas giants, alien statues and militia racing across the purple plain towards him. He had showered and eaten, bringing his body slowly back to

263

life. When the ship phased from the void he had been greeted by a distant vision of Redwood Station, the dozen industrial orbitals winking silver in the sunlight, and he had to smile to himself. It seemed a long time since he had worked there; in real time it was over eight months ago, subjectively something like a week, though to Bennett it felt like years.

He had instructed the ship's navigation system to program itself a return trajectory, from Earth to Penumbra, ready for indefinite inception.

He considered Penumbra and the people he had left behind. Hopefully by now Ten Lee's leg wound would have healed and she would be up and walking. And Mackendrick? He had seemed well when Bennett left him with the rebels, but he had an amazing ability to hide the extent of his illness. Nearly four months had elapsed, and it would be at least another four months before he returned. Mackendrick had been given just one year to live, but that had been ten or eleven months ago, now.

He contemplated what Quineau had told Mackendrick, all those years ago. Was it possible that the Ancients had survived in an underground chamber, that they were in possession of some arcane healing lore? It sounded, he admitted to himself, like the stuff of legend. Only when he located the softscreen, and the rebels traced the underground chamber for themselves, would the truth be known.

The ship began the long deceleration burn as it came in on an oblique trajectory towards Calcutta spaceport. In a matter of hours he would be in the city, attempting to locate the softscreen with the help of Hupcka's receiver. Of course, the screen might be anywhere on Earth, and even if he did locate it, it might not be so easily recoverable.

A voice sounded in his ear: 'Mackendrick/Cobra receiving.'

'Ah-cha. Landing clearance, check. Mechanical maintenance and resupply authorised by Mackendrick Foundation, check. We will ready Cobra for immediate turn-around as requested. Ah, security will need to board ship for routine inspection. Also, they will need to interview you immediately after touchdown.'

'Fine by me, Control.'

'Ah-cha. Safe landing, Mackendrick/Cobra.'

Through the sidescreen Bennett looked down on the vast sprawling conurbation of outer Calcutta, sunlit beneath wisps of low-lying cloud. He seemed to take long minutes to fly over the city, a vast inland spread of crowded grey concrete. The Cobra banked north, tilting Bennett for a better view of the Ganges delta and the shimmering Bay of Bengal beyond.

The spaceport came into sight, the small shapes of other craft climbing slowly into space. The ship rattled as it decelerated and dropped steeply, giving Bennett a fullscreen view of the wide tarmac apron pocked with blastrings and stationary ships.

The Cobra levelled out and slowed dramatically, hovering for seconds on its vertical boosters. Bennett watched the control tower and terminal building rise around the ship as it came in to land with a loud impact of stanchions, a diminuendo of engines, and then a sudden and startling silence.

He pulled off his helmet and unstrapped himself from the couch, feeling the tug of the Earth's gravity as he walked from the flight-deck. He collected the holdall containing his scant possessions and palmed the sensor to lower the ramp and open the exit hatch.

He was greeted with the stench of India: dust and dung, the waft of spices. Strange, alien cries reached him from port workers, the engineers and grease monkeys swarming over the ship like parasites. A squad of blue-uniformed security officials was already striding up the ramp, pushing past him without greeting or acknowledgement before the hatch was fully open.

At the foot of the ramp stood a tall, overweight man in a similar blue uniform, his arms crossed over his chest. He wore his black hair in ringlets, tied back from a plump face glistening with sweat in the heat of the Indian sun.

'Bennett, isn't it? Welcome to India. Please excuse the haste of my team – pressure of work, as I'm sure you'll understand. I'm the chief of security here at the port. If you could spare ten minutes of your time, I'd like to ask a few routine questions. This is purely a formality I go through with all unscheduled landings. If you'd care to come this way.'

Touching the warm oval of the receiver in the pocket of his flight-suit, Bennett followed the perspiring security chief across the tarmac to the control tower. A ten-minute formality he hoped was all it would be; he was more than a little impatient to begin his search.

They entered a small room looking out over the port, furnished with comfortable sofas and chairs. The security chief gestured Bennett to sit, and he sank back into a ridiculously padded sofa. The officer himself elected to perch on the arm of a nearby chair, establishing a positional superiority. He glanced down at the comboard in his right hand. With his free hand he mopped his face with a red bandanna.

'You've come a long way, Mr Bennett.' He indicated his screen. 'All the way from the Rim. Do you mind describing the nature of your flight?'

Bennett wanted nothing more than to get away from here. He would answer the questions quickly – and lie, of course.

'Exploration,' he said. 'I work for the Mackendrick Foundation and I was prospecting a number of outlying systems for the usual mineral deposits.'

'Alone? Without even a co-pilot?'

'The Cobra's a good ship,' Bennett said, and added, 'and I'm a good pilot. I didn't need a co-pilot.'

'No doubt. But you would agree with me, wouldn't you, that solo flights so far out are a little unusual?'

Bennett shook his head. There was something about the chief of security that he didn't like, a presumed familiarity beyond the call of duty. 'I see nothing unusual in it at all. Many ships these days are flown solo.'

'Then perhaps I'm behind the times. Tell me, which systems were you prospecting on the Rim?'

'I looked at three systems in the G5 sector.'

'And you found?'

Bennett returned his stare, considering his reply. 'That information is confidential and between myself and my employers.'

'Of course.' The officer waved a feigned apology. 'You discovered no habitable planets?' His smile showed that the question was intended as his little joke.

Bennett played along. 'Unfortunately not.'

'And you have returned to Earth for what reasons?'

'To report to my employers with my findings.'

The officer nodded, stood and moved to a com-screen on a desk in the corner of the room. He considered the screen for a minute, lips pursed.

He looked up. 'My team informs me that the Cobra is programmed for a return flight to the G5 sector.'

Bennett tried not to let his surprise show. He wondered since when protocol allowed port workers, even those in security, to access the flight systems of privately owned starships.

'Well, Mr Bennett?'

'I wasn't aware that you'd asked a question.'

A look of impatience flashed across the security chief's face. He mopped his brow. Bennett noticed that his hand was shaking.

'Why return, Mr Bennett, if you have already prospected that system?'

'I don't see what that information has to do with the security of Calcutta spaceport,' Bennett replied. 'But for your information there are more planets in the systems to be explored.'

The officer waved a hand. 'It must be an interesting life, prospecting the stars.'

'It pays a wage. If that is all, I have a lot to do.'

'Why, of course, Mr Bennett. I do hope I haven't been intrusive, but one must be vigilant. India has many enemies and one can never be too careful.' He reached into the desk and produced a small polycarbon card. 'This allows you entry into India for a stay of up to three months. It is official authorisation of admittance, so please keep it about your person at all times.'

Bennett took the card and slipped it into the breast pocket of his flight-suit.

The officer held out a hand. 'My apologies if I have kept you, Mr Bennett. Enjoy your stay in India. If you will make your way round the tower to the terminal building, immigration will process your card.'

Bennett shook the proffered hand, found it warm and sweat-soaked. He was aware of the man's eyes on his back as he left the room.

He crossed the tarmac and entered the terminal building, and five minutes later he was through the checks. He crossed the foyer, bustling with the newly arrived and those come to greet them, and stepped through the sliding glass doors into the harsh sunlight of the subcontinent.

He took a taxi and they crawled down streets crowded with pedestrians, stall-holders and beggars not averse to thrusting their hands into the open window of the moving car. He closed his eyes, at least visually editing the strangeness of the country from his consciousness. The noise of the place, however, was not so easily ignored. The blare of horns set his nerves on edge, along with the cries of vendors and the occasional stentorian boom of a passing ad-screen.

He booked into a hotel close to the spaceport, drank a beer from the cooler in the room, then sat on the bed and pulled the receiver from his pocket. He stared at it for a long time, before touching the panel Hupcka had told him would activate the small screen set into the silver face of the device.

Only when the screen flashed on did Bennett realise that he'd been holding his breath. The screen was working, but there was no flashing arrow or numerical measurements to indicate the direction and distance of the softscreen. It was, he supposed, highly unlikely that he would have struck gold at first try. The screen had a range of ten kilometres. After a meal he would take a taxi and cross and re-cross the sprawling city.

If that failed, then he would reassess the situation.

He dined in the hotel restaurant – the first real meal he had eaten in weeks – then withdrew local currency on his credit card from the hotel bank. He left the building, ignored the press of beggars encamped on the steps, and boarded a taxi. He instructed the driver to take him to the city centre. There he would buy a map of Calcutta and block off the sections of the city as he searched.

He tried not to dwell on the awful possibility that the receiver might be defective.

As the taxi carried him from the hotel drive and gained speed along a busy main road, Bennett considered the events that had conspired to bring him back to Earth. The incidents on Penumbra, from the landing to his capture and subsequent escape, and his time with the rebels to the flight in the Cobra, had about them the quality of a dream. After the unspoilt vastness of Penumbra, the noisy, overcrowded streets of Calcutta seemed imminent and ultra-real. He found it hard to credit that on a distant world Mack, Ten and the rebels would be impatiently awaiting his successful return.

He pulled the receiver from his pocket, touched the control and stared at the screen. It was still blank. He watched it, expecting the arrow and numerals to appear at any second. When they did not, he took to looking away for long seconds at a time, staring through the window at the passing city, and then glancing almost surreptitiously at the screen, hoping each time to see the arrow.

The taxi was passing down narrow streets flanked by long, low lines of concrete shops, each unit open like a garage and stacked with goods: fruit and vegetables, bolts of cloth, household goods. Before most shops were beds without mattresses, dining chairs on which men sat in circles and smoked. Above each shop was a sign in Hindi, with the occasional English word appearing more alien for being misspelled. Ahead, Bennett made out the rearing polycarbon skyscrapers of central Calcutta, shimmering in the midday sun.

He was considering the daunting possibility of having to search the whole of India for the softscreen when he glanced down at the receiver and, to his disbelief, saw a flashing arrow, and beneath it the distance in jade green: 9 KILOMETRES, 500 METRES, and counting down.

The arrow was pointing in the direction of the city centre. He experienced a surge of relief, followed by a warning to himself that it couldn't be so easy. He had still to locate the screen. If it were in the possession of someone unwilling to part with it, for any amount of money, what then? Or what if it were part of an antique collection in some upmarket emporium, priced beyond his reach? There were, he decided, a hundred possibilities, all of which were futile to contemplate. He would simply have to wait and see where the receiver led him.

He watched the screen count down, the arrow shift fractionally as the road took a slight bend. It was pointing directly at the skyscrapers of the city centre.

7 KILOMETRES, 300 METRES, and counting down.

The Indian driver tried to engage him in small talk. Was this his first time in India? Was he here on important business? Bennett pointedly ignored him, watching the crowds stream by outside, and soon the Indian gave up.

4 KILOMETRES, 600 METRES, and counting down.

Soon, the fact of the human colony on Homefall would be known to the Expansion. Then would begin the opening up of the planet dreaded by the Elders of the Church of Phobos and Deimos. He considered the media coverage of the event, the story of the discovery of a lost colony on the Rim.

2 KILOMETRES, 100 METRES.

They were passing through streets lined with old Victorian buildings, which soon gave way to more modern structures, ugly concrete office blocks, then the sleek, soaring shapes of modern polycarbon architecture.

1 KILOMETRE, 200 METRES.

But now the arrow was turning to the left, and the counter was rising. They were moving further away from the softscreen. Bennett leaned forward. 'Left here . . .'

At the next intersection the car turned and joined a solid flow of traffic heading down a wide, palm-fringed boulevard. The receiver read 0 KILOMETRES, 900 METRES, and began rising again.

'Stop! Anywhere around here.'

The driver pulled into the side of the road, and Bennett paid the fare and climbed out. After the air-conditioned interior of the car, the humid air enveloped him in a viscous embrace. He unzipped the jacket of his flight-suit and glanced down at the receiver. He was 960 metres from the softscreen, and the arrow was indicating ten o'clock. He took a street at right angles to the boulevard, past a parade of plush shops lining the ground floor of a tall polycarbon skyscraper.

The counter fell with his every stride. The arrow indicated eleven o'clock – he was heading in the approximate direction of the screen. He moved through crowds of well-dressed shoppers, a multi-national mix of racial types, predominantly Indian and European, and tried not to make his glances at the receiver that obvious. His curiosity as to where he might find the softscreen was almost unbearable.

He was one hundred metres away when he came to a wide road that crossed the street at a sharp angle, and the arrow moved back to ten o'clock. Bennett turned left and watched the counter count down: 89, and, seconds later, 80.

He hurried along a wide pavement lined with stall-holders and food-vendors, their cries loud and incoherent. To his left was the façade of an ancient building, to his right the stalls of frying food, stacked fruit and vegetables set up in the gutter. He glanced at the screen: 25 METRES.

When he judged that he had walked that distance, he looked down at the screen again. The arrow had turned to nine o'clock, pointing towards the monstrous Victorian building to his left, and the counter read 10 METRES. He turned and stared up at the imposing stone façade. A flight of steps rose to the sliding glass doors, above which ran the legend: CALCUTTA POLICE HEADQUARTERS.

He stood and stared up at the building, buffeted by impatient passers-by, and wondered how to proceed. Nearby was a chai stall, a wooden table covered by a make-shift carbon-fibre awning. He ducked under the cover, sat down on a rickety wooden chair and ordered a chai.

He sipped a glass of the sweet milky tea and considered his options. The softscreen could be inside the police building for a number of reasons: it could be stolen goods, or lost property, or the possession of someone who had it adorning the wall of his office. How best to find out? There was one obvious course of action.

He finished the chai, crossed the pavement and climbed the steps into the police headquarters. He was gratified to see that he was not the only civilian in there: the corridors seemed to be home from home to half the city, squatting on their haunches and looking doleful. He glanced at the screen. Two arrows had appeared: the main one read 3 METRES and indicated two o'clock, and the new arrow in the corner of the screen was pointing straight ahead to the words: 6 METRES, UP. So the softscreen was located six metres above him and then three metres in the direction of two o'clock.

He noticed a flight of stairs to his right. Civilians seemed to be using them, so he joined the procession and climbed the steps. When he came to the first floor and glanced down at the screen, only one arrow showed. It indicated three o'clock, and below it 5 METRES.

He turned right and walked along the corridor. Offices opened off the corridor, each one bearing a sign project-ing from the wall at right angles to the open entrance. The signs were printed with two legends, one in Hindi and the other in English.

He came to an office beneath a sign saying: SECURITY. He looked at the screen. It was pointing into the office and reading 2 METRES.

A small man in a khaki uniform with sergeant's stripes sat at a desk behind a com-screen. What now? Before Bennett could think, much less move from the open doorway, the sergeant looked up and saw him. 'Yes?' he rapped in English. 'How can I help you?'

Bennett slipped the receiver into his pocket, took a breath and entered the room. 'I'd like to report the theft of a softscreen,' he said.

The sergeant stared at him. 'This is not the correct office to be reporting stolen property.' Then he blinked. 'What did you say has been stolen?'

'A softscreen, the recording of a mountain exped-ition—'

'Please describe the softscreen.'

'Well . . .' Bennett gestured. 'It's just an old softscreen, showing scenes of an expedition through mountainous territory.'

The sergeant stood. 'Please stay here. I'll be one moment only.' He moved around the desk and left the office.

Bennett slipped the receiver from his pocket. The screen indicated that the softscreen was located directly before him, and less than a metre away.

It was in the sergeant's desk, then.

He considered looking through the desk while the sergeant was away. But if he was caught . . . No, better to wait, as instructed.

Two minutes later the sergeant returned and took his seat behind the desk. 'If you would care to wait one moment, please. There is someone who would like to see you.'

Bennett nodded and sat back in his chair, confused by

274

this turn of events. The softscreen, which he had travelled from the Rim to find, was less than one metre from him, and he was absolutely powerless to do anything about it.

He wondered who, in Calcutta, might wish to meet him.

20

Rana Rao thought that there were three types of pain. The first was the dull pain of dying, when the injury was so severe that the body shut down and anaesthetised the senses. The second was the sharp pain of recovery, when you often wished that you had died. The third type of pain was the pain of betrayal, and perhaps that was the most agonising of all. She had experienced all three types of pain, from the second Klien fired at her all the way through to being discharged from hospital.

She'd lost consciousness soon after she was shot, then came awake – disoriented and confused – some unknown time later in a private hospital room, abstracted from sensation by sedatives and analgesics. At that first stirring of consciousness, at some lonely time in the dark early hours, she was ridiculously concerned about only one thing. She had never been vain about her appearance, but now she tried to reach up and touch her face. Her arms seemed to be tied down – no, not tied down, but restricted by tubes and catheters, their plastic loops and lengths catching a distant light. She pulled against them and the muscles of her shoulders protested, but she managed to bring her finger-tips up to her cheek and lean forward minimally. She almost wept with relief as her fingers encountered soft flesh. She tried the other side then, and discovered that that cheek was also unscarred.

Then she remembered the shoot-out. Klien had shot

the security officers and left her for dead. He'd had no time to scar her.

'You shouldn't do that.' She was aware of the face swimming into her view, gentle hands on hers, forcing her arms down by her sides. 'Close your eyes and rest,' the nurse said. 'There, try to sleep.'

When she awoke next it was to a searing pain in her chest, as if a burning arrow had lodged itself in her sternum. She screamed and opened her eyes and saw many green-smocked medics gathered around her bed, staring at her without expression above surgical masks. In that intense second of agony she wished that Klien had succeeded and killed her. Then the pain diminished, and she closed her eyes and drifted off into oblivion.

She seemed to wake up frequently after that, for short periods between long stretches of sedation, and always the pain was a little less intense. Always she tried to remain awake a little longer, without success.

She remembered fragments from these awakenings. Vishwanath sitting beside her, concern etched on his aquiline face, a hand on hers. He was saying something, asking her if she could recall anything, but when she tried to speak she found that the words would not come. The next time she opened her eyes she saw Naz standing next to the bed, a bunch of flowers in his hand. He reached out and took her fingers. 'Truce?' he asked, and this time she managed a few words: 'Ah-cha, truce.'

The next time she came to her senses, it seemed to her a proper awakening. It was morning, and she was in a different room, with sunlight spilling in through a window, illuminating her bed and so many beautiful, fragrant flowers. She was no longer attached to drips and tubes. She wondered if she were out of intensive care now, if she would live. She looked through the door of her

277

room. An armed guard was stationed there. She closed her eyes, against her will, and slept.

A voice came to her as if from a great distance. 'Rana?'

She tried to open her eyes, to focus. She recognised the voice. She smiled. It was her father's voice, and she was five again, and he was playing with her on the lawn of the mansion . . .

She opened her eyes.

'Rana?' Vishwanath said. He sat on a chair next to the bed, leaning forward and staring at her.

She turned her head slightly, managed a smile.

'I don't want you to speak if it's too difficult, Rana.'

She tried to lick her dry lips. She was aware that she was thirsty. 'I'm fine,' she murmured. 'Can . . . can I have water?'

He jumped up to fetch a glass of water, held it to her lips. The sensation of the cold, clear liquid wetting her lips and flowing over her tongue was a delight.

She dropped her head back to the pillow. The effort of drinking had exhausted her.

'You're lucky to be alive, Rana.' He squeezed her hand.

'How . . . how long have I been—'

'Almost a month, Rana. You were in a coma for two weeks, and then in intensive care on a life support machine for a week. You don't know how lucky you were. The laser missed your heart and spine by milli-metres.'

'A month . . .' She marvelled to herself.

'The killer got away, Rana. When the medics found you, they thought you were dead.'

She tried to return the pressure on his fingers. 'Did you . . . did you get him?'

Vishwanath shook his head. 'He killed three security officers and got away. But we have the description of a tall, grey-haired man leaving the apartment buildings.'

Rana tried to sit up, but Vishwanath restrained her.

'No . . . disguise. He was in disguise. He has *black* hair.'

Vishwanath frowned. 'Black hair?'

She tried to raise her head from the pillow, but fell back, exhausted.

'It was Klien,' she managed eventually. 'Ezekiel Klien.'

Vishwanath stared at her. 'Klien, the security chief at the port?' His tone conveyed disbelief.

'Klien . . . the crucifix killings. He did them all. I . . . I interviewed him. He knew I was getting close, so . . . so he came to kill me. He was in disguise.'

She remembered their confrontation, and his demanding from her the softscreen. But what did that mean? Why did he want the screen? Where did that fit into the scheme of things?

She was exhausted, too wrung out to say another word or even to remain awake. Her last sight was of Vishwanath staring down at her incredulously.

When she came to her senses again, Vishwanath was sitting on one side of the bed, Commissioner Singh on the other. She assumed that minutes had elapsed, that Vishwanath must have called Singh. Then she realised that it was dark beyond the window. Hours had passed.

She blinked from Singh to Vishwanath. 'Two visitors now,' she managed. 'Must be getting better.'

Vishwanath pulled his chair forward. 'Rana, I want you to tell Commissioner Singh what you told me. About Ezekiel Klien.'

She turned her head to regard the overweight Sikh. She was aware of the weight of his regard, his reluctance to be convinced.

'Klien,' she said, her every word an effort, 'Klien is the crucifix killer. I . . . I interviewed him. He knew I was on to him. Someone saw him kill Raja Khan, then walk to his house on Allahabad Marg. Only he was in the disguise of the silver-haired man. Same man who . . . who came to kill me. It was Klien.' She paused, licked her lips. 'He has a . . . a capillary net. One of the prototypes.'

The words dried up. It was all she could do to look from Vishwanath to Singh, try to assess their reaction.

Vishwanath touched her hand. 'We're continuing our investigations, Rana. Rest, now. I'll see you later.'

The two men left the room. She watched them in the corridor, talking animatedly in low tones.

She closed her eyes and slept.

Soon her cycle of sleeping and waking regulated itself. She slept during the hours of darkness and woke in the morning. The last of the tubes, those inserted directly into her stomach, feeding her for the past month, were removed and she was allowed to eat small meals. Her first breakfast of fried egg, vegetable cutlet and sweet chai was the finest she had ever tasted.

She was allowed out of bed, but only as far as the chair facing the window. The short walk of half a dozen steps exhausted her, but at least there was no pain.

She was examined regularly by a doctor, and once her surgeon introduced himself. 'The laser went straight through your chest,' he said with matter-of-fact relish. 'A millimetre either way and you'd be dead. As it was, it just broke a few bones and nicked your right lung.' He reached out and rubbed the back of her hand. 'Touch you for good luck, Rana. We'll have you out of here in a week.'

She looked forward to Vishwanath's next visit. She did not want his praise so much as his acknowledgement that her investigations had borne fruit, that her work had led to Klien's arrest. Then, no doubt, would come his censure for her pursuing interviews without notifying him of her intentions.

The next time Vishwanath visited, Commissioner Singh was with him again. She was sitting up in bed, leafing through a holodrama magazine, when the two men entered the room. Vishwanath closed the door behind him. In silence they took their seats on either side of the bed.

She smiled from Vishwanath to Singh, but they did not smile back.

'Lieutenant Rao,' Singh said, 'the allegation you made against Ezekiel Klien is a very serious matter.' He watched her with an unflinching gaze.

'I know that,' she said. Something turned sickeningly in her stomach. 'Of course it's a serious matter. So is trying to shoot someone dead.'

Singh glanced at Vishwanath and sighed. 'The fact is that we've investigated your claims, Lieutenant, and we cannot find a shred of evidence to justify taking any action against Klien in regard of the so-called crucifix killings or your attempted murder.'

She looked from Singh to Vishwanath, wanting to laugh out loud and at the same time wanting to cry with rage at the injustice. Vishwanath was regarding her with the gaze of a disappointed father.

She shook her head. 'I know who shot me,' she whispered. 'It was Ezekiel Klien.'

'Lieutenant Rao,' Singh began with manufactured patience. 'We have questioned Klien as to what he was doing at the time of the killings over the past ten years. He has an alibi to account for his whereabouts on every single occasion.'

'What about the killing of Raja Khan?'

Singh glanced at Vishwanath, who said, 'Rana, we have three witnesses who will testify under oath that they saw him at the spaceport that night.'

'And the morning he tried to kill me? I suppose he's paid liars to testify for him then?'

Singh said, 'Lieutenant, I've had some of my best men

281

working on your claims. I'm sorry, but no evidence whatsoever was discovered to corroborate what you said.'

She fought to keep her voice calm. 'Are you calling me a liar, sir? I *know* who tried to kill me!'

Vishwanath said patiently, 'Rana, Klien was on duty in his office on the morning you were shot. We have witnesses who saw him.'

'But that's impossible. Please believe me, I know who I was talking to. I know it was him. He introduced himself!'

Singh shook his head. 'I can only assume that you were mistaken, Lieutenant. The alternative, that you are deliberately lying, is too offensive to contemplate. Ezekiel Klien happens to be an acquaintance of mine of long standing. Your bizarre claims have caused me severe embarrassment.'

He nodded at Vishwanath, who touched Rana's hand, almost apologetically, before rising and opening the door for his superior.

Rana lay back and stared at the ceiling, tears of rage and betrayal tracking down her cheeks. She had considered telling him that Klien had demanded to know the whereabouts of her softscreen, but they were determined to disbelieve her anyway. What difference would it make to their assessment of the case if she told them?

By keeping the knowledge to herself, she had her first lead in her case against Klien. He wanted her softscreen, and she had it; therefore she was in a position of power.

Over the period of the next two weeks she made a steady recovery, and just six weeks after the shooting she walked from the hospital. For reasons of security she was relocated to a police apartment in the city centre, a short walk from police headquarters, and a twenty-four-hour armed guard was posted on her door.

Rana was told by Vishwanath to take a holiday and not

to return to work for a month. She decided to stay in the city. She visited Vandita and the other kids, but said nothing about the shooting. 'But you haven't visited us for so long!' they complained. She smiled and made excuses, told them stories of car chases and shoot-outs. She wanted to hold them all, as night drew in, as if to protect them from the city and all the evil out there. The thought of Klien and his crimes filled her with a black depression. She considered taking a weapon herself and shooting him dead. The thought, if nothing else, was a catharsis.

After just one week of her month's leave, she contacted Vishwanath and begged to be allowed back to work. She told him she was fit and healthy and could work at her com-screen as well as the next officer. Vishwanath relented, allowed her to start work, but only at her com-screen; on no account was she to go out on a case. She wondered if this stricture was in view of her health, or on the orders of Commissioner Singh.

Varma gave her a great hug on her first day back, and a card from Naz stood on her desk among the others; it asked if she was free for a meal that evening. Smiling, she caught his eye across the room, tore the card in two and dropped it into the litter bin. It was back to business as usual on the eighth floor.

Rana was taken off the crucifix killings and given the files of other cases to analyse. Occasionally her curiosity got the better of her and she accessed the files on the crucifix case. She read through other officers' reports concerning Klien and his alibis, and sure enough on the date of every killing his whereabouts were accounted for by trustworthy witnesses. But the very fact that he had an alibi for every murder struck Rana as suspicious. He had friends who were willing to lie for him, or people whom he had bribed. She thought of Commissioner

Singh, who actually knew Klien, and she knew that the task of proving Klien guilty would be almost impossible.

One morning, as she was going through the files of the case yet again, it came to her that Commissioner Singh might actually be aware that Klien was the crucifix killer, that Singh was in fact protecting his friend. It made sense. Klien was, after all, ridding the city of criminal elements, saving Singh the work of investigating these criminals himself. She wondered if there was any shred of truth in her suspicion, or if she was merely taking out her resentment on Singh because he had refused to believe her. But, she asked herself, how else had Klien managed to produce so many alibis, convince so many investigating officers of his innocence?

The thought plunged Rana into depression.

Then, a few days later, something happened which put all thought of Singh's possible corruption from her mind.

Before she began work one morning, she stopped by the second floor and found the security sergeant in his office. He was apologetic. 'I still have your softscreen in my desk, Lieutenant. Unfortunately I've had no time to examine it.'

'Oh . . . I was hoping you could tell me something about the homing device, Sergeant. I want to know if the screen, or the device, is valuable or special in some way. Is there any reason that anyone might . . .' She was about to say 'kill' for it, but checked herself. 'That anyone might wish to steal it?'

'Ah-cha. I'll have a look at the first opportunity, Lieutenant. I'll be in touch.'

That day on the eighth floor, Rana worked half-heartedly on the cases given to her by Vishwanath, and hated every minute of it. She was depressed by the thought of Klien's freedom, mocking her. She wondered how many other criminals were walking the streets thanks to the corruption of those in power.

She entertained the fantasy of running away, of dropping the persona of Rana Rao, police officer, forgetting Klien and the terrible injustice of his liberty and starting a new life somewhere. But where, she asked herself? She knew only about life in Calcutta. She had run away once, but it had seemed so easy then – there had been the whole city to run to. Her gaze strayed unbidden to the travel article on her com-screen, advertising life on the colony worlds.

Someone approached her desk, startling her – the sergeant from security.

'Lieutenant Rao,' he said. 'There's been a development regarding the softscreen.'

She looked at him. 'There has?'

'A gentleman has come to my office in search of the screen,' he said. 'He is a Westerner, I think perhaps American.'

Rana felt her mouth go dry. Klien, she thought. But how had he traced the screen to security?

'Describe him.'

The sergeant blinked. 'He is tall. Perhaps thirty-five. Long-haired, down to here' – he touched his shoulder – 'and he is wearing the flight-suit of a space pilot.'

It didn't sound like Klien, unless he had disguised himself again.

Apprehensive, Rana told the sergeant that she would be down in five minutes. She closed the file she was working on, then made sure her holster was open and took the elevator down to the second floor.

Cautiously, she paused at the door and looked in. She released a relieved sigh. The man was sitting nervously in his chair, hunched forward. His flight-suit was scuffed, his long dark hair lank and unwashed.

Rana gestured to the sergeant, who joined her at the door. 'If you'd allow me a few minutes alone with him . . .'

The sergeant nodded. 'Ah-cha. I'll be next door if you need anything.'

She stepped into the room and closed the door behind her. The American swivelled quickly in his seat, regarded her with dark eyes that seemed at once suspicious and afraid.

She rounded the desk and sat down. 'I am Lieutenant Rao,' she said.

'Bennett,' he said. 'Josh Bennett.'

His face was unshaven and sallow, and there was a tiredness and grubbiness about the man that made her wonder what he had been through to get here. Also, there was a gentleness about his manner. He was a big man whose movements were slow and considered, as if conscious of forever trying to prevent himself from clumsiness.

Rana remained stern-faced. For all she knew, he wanted the softscreen for the same reasons that Klien did. She wondered, though it was hard to believe, if he would be as desperate as Klien to obtain the screen.

'Can I ask you why you are here, Mr Bennett?'

'I . . . I'm an employee of the Mackendrick Foundation, Lieutenant. A pilot—'

'The Mackendrick Foundation?'

She stared at him. So Bennett worked for her father, and was here in search of the softscreen . . . But how did he know that the screen was here, in this office? She felt dizzy with confusion.

Bennett was nodding. 'I work directly for Charles Mackendrick himself. Years ago an item of property belonging to Mackendrick was stolen from him. A soft-screen. It's vital that the screen is returned.'

'You . . . you're in contact with Mackendrick?' She felt as she had when awakening in the hospital, removed from the reality around her, watching proceedings as if at a distance. 'How do you know the softscreen is here?'

Bennett ran a big hand through his receding hair, beginning a combing motion on top of his head, finishing at the nape of his neck. His hand stayed there as he considered her questions.

'I'm in contact with him. Well, technically I suppose I'm not – he's light years away on a Rim planet. But I was in contact with him. I . . . I was given a device, a receiver, that would locate the softscreen.'

Rana shook her head, totally confused. 'But why didn't he use the receiver to locate the screen when it was originally stolen?'

'Because he didn't have the receiver then. He's only just found out about it. He sent me to Earth to find the screen and take it back to him. It's vital that he gets it. Look, if you doubt who I am, contact the Mackendrick Foundation, here in Calcutta. They'll confirm that I'm employed by Mackendrick, at least.'

'I believe you, Mr Bennett. Tell me, how is Mackendrick?'

He blinked. 'You know him?'

'I . . . I met him when he was resident in Calcutta,' Rana dissembled.

Bennett gestured. 'To be honest he's very ill. He has only months to live. I need to get the softscreen back to him.'

Rana closed her eyes. She recalled her father's voice, his smile as he played with her on the lawn of the mansion when she was five years old. She tried to assess her reaction to the fact that her father was dying. Shock, she supposed, even though she had not seen him in years, even though she could not claim to feel any degree of love for him, in the accepted sense of the word.

But he was her father, and he was dying.

She opened her eyes suddenly and stared at the pilot. 'Why does he want the screen?'

How many times had she watched the softscreen unfold the dramatic story of three explorers on some far-flung alien world, as they trekked through blizzards into a high mountain range? She had found it entertaining as a child on the streets, a window on to an unimaginably cold and hostile other world.

Bennett gave her a shy smile. 'Lieutenant, it's a long and improbable story. To be honest, I don't think you'd believe a word of it.'

'Tell me.'

'The recording was made by a man called Quineau, on a planet settled by the survivors of a crashed starship way outside the Expansion. The softscreen was . . . *is* . . . the only means by which anyone could find the way back to where he claimed he'd discovered a race of aliens known as the Ancients. After returning from the expedition, Quineau left the planet to tell the Expansion of the colony's existence. He was found by a Mackendrick salvage ship, which is how the softscreen came into Mackendrick's possession. Quineau was followed from Penumbra by someone from the governing council who didn't want the planet's existence known to outsiders, an assassin called Klien, who killed Quineau in order to silence him—'

Bennett stopped as he noticed Rana's expression. She stared into space, the pieces of the puzzle slowly falling into place.

'Klien . . .' she whispered to herself.

'You know him?'

She smiled at Bennett. 'We have met. He tried to get the softscreen from me.'

'You mean, you had the screen?' He looked confused.

'But it was stolen years ago. How did it come into your possession?'

Rana sat back in her seat and stared at the ceiling. Then she looked at Bennett and smiled. 'It's my turn to tell you a story that you might find hard to believe,' she said. 'You see, thirteen years ago I stole the softscreen, and I've had it with me ever since.'

Bennett massaged his tired face with both hands, finally parting them like shutters and staring out at her. 'This is crazy. I don't understand. His safe was raided, his daughter kidnapped—' He stopped, his eyes widening in sudden realisation. 'You . . .' he said at last.

'I took the screen from the safe, along with some money. I ran away and lived on the streets.'

Bennett stared at her in disbelief. 'To this day,' he said, 'your father grieves over losing you.'

Rana matched his stare. 'Perhaps, had he been more of a father to me back then, I might never have run away.'

Bennett was shaking his head. 'It's hard to believe . . .' He stared at her, then said, 'You're really Sita Mackendrick?'

'Not any more, Mr Bennett. I'm Rana Rao, now, and I have been since I was ten years old.'

'Okay. I don't know what you went through then. Who am I to opinionate?' He paused there, considering. 'But your father needs the screen, Lieutenant. He's dying, and he seems to think that maybe the Ancients – *if* they exist – might be able to heal him.'

'Are you returning to Penumbra?'

'Just as soon as I get the softscreen,' Bennett said.

It began as an absurd notion, fleeting and soon dismissed. Then it returned, not so easily dismissed this time, because Klien had to be defeated, the softscreen had to be taken to where it was safe – and it was time for Rana to run away again.

She thought of her father. This would be her very last chance to see him, to tell him that she was sorry.

Rana pulled open the drawer of the desk, reached in and produced the folded screen. She began to hand it across the desk to Bennett, then paused.

'I will give you the softscreen,' she told him, 'on one condition.'

His hand halted in the act of reaching. 'Name it.'

She looked into his eyes as she said, 'Take me with you, Bennett. I want to go to Penumbra.'

He smiled, accepted the softscreen, and said, 'You've got yourself a deal, Lieutenant.'

21

Klien had been waiting for this day for almost fourteen years, and when it came he was seized by a sensation of disbelief. He had marshalled his faculties and asked Control to corroborate what he was reading on his com-screen, and they had confirmed that a Mackendrick Foundation Cobra-class ship was indeed heading to Calcutta port from the Rim sector of G5.

Which meant that Mackendrick had at last discovered Homefall, and, for whatever reasons, the Council of Elders had allowed the ship to return. That, or the ship had been commandeered by the elders themselves. Klien knew that such speculation was useless. He had been away for many years. Anything might have happened in that time to change the situation on Homefall.

He had scrambled his top security team and had them ready and waiting when the Cobra made landfall. He wanted the ship searched from top to bottom, its flight system and programs analysed as fast as possible and relayed to his monitor. He had contacted Control and requested that, as the ship was making an unscheduled landing, it should be berthed within the secure com-pound beside the security tower itself. They had deferred to his seniority and experience.

Thirty minutes later he was waiting at the foot of the ramp. Control had informed him that the pilot's name was Bennett, an employee of the Mackendrick

Foundation. When the hatch had cracked, revealing a tall, long-haired figure, unshaven and dishevelled in a black flight-suit, Klien had gestured for his team to get to work, and greeted the pilot.

He had taken Bennett into the interrogation room, requesting that he answer a few routine questions. Klien thought he had been informal and amicable, despite the thudding of his heart and a sweat he had no way of controlling, but Bennett was tired after four months in suspension, uncommunicative and unforthcoming, suspicion manifest in his brooding eyes. He'd claimed that he had explored the G5/13 system on the Rim, and had discovered no habitable planets. Klien knew that he had to be lying.

It was Klien's one regret of the interrogation that he had been unable to ascertain whether the Mackendrick Foundation had possession of the softscreen.

As he was interviewing Bennett, a preliminary report came in from his team aboard the Cobra. The ship was pre-programmed for a return flight to the Rim and the G5/13 sector, departure indefinite.

Klien felt as if his innards had suddenly liquefied. So . . . Bennett was returning to G5/13. But what was he doing here on Earth?

There was, of course, one way to find out.

He passed Bennett an authorisation card, explained that he should keep it upon his person at all times, and watched the pilot stride from the room.

Klien smiled to himself. It had gone as well as could be expected, so far.

He seated himself behind his desk and inserted an earpiece. Seconds later he heard Bennett pass through customs, leave the terminal and board a taxi to a local hotel. Two hours later he took another taxi to the city centre. The sound quality was slightly muffled, as the card was in Bennett's breast pocket, but his ear-piece managed to filter out most of the background interference.

Thirty minutes later Bennett left the taxi and walked through bustling streets. The noise of downtown Calcutta filled Klien's head. He mopped the sweat from his face and neck.

Fifteen minutes later he heard Bennett order a chai and drink it noisily. Two minutes later the street noises diminished: he had evidently entered a building.

'Excuse me,' Bennett said in his American drawl. 'I'd like to report the theft of a softscreen.'

Klien sat up, galvanised by the word *softscreen*. Report the *theft* of a softscreen? Where was Bennett – in a police station?

He missed what someone replied. There was a period of silence lasting a good five minutes. Klien waited, his heart thudding with apprehension.

Then: 'I am Lieutenant Rao,' a familiar voice said.

Klien smiled to himself. Was the softscreen lodged at the police headquarters?

'Can I ask why you are here, Mr Bennett?'

'I . . . I'm an employee of the Mackendrick Foundation, Lieutenant. A pilot.'

'The Mackendrick Foundation?' She sounded surprised.

'I work directly for Charles Mackendrick himself,' Bennett was saying. 'Years ago an item of property belonging to Mackendrick was stolen from him. A softscreen. It's vital that the screen is returned.'

Klien leaned forward, listening intently.

'You . . . you're in contact with him?' A brief silence, then: 'How do you know the softscreen is here?'

Klien clenched his fist on the table top and almost wept. He listened to the conversation unfold, learned that Charles Mackendrick himself was on Homefall, terminally ill and wanting the softscreen.

He sat back and listened, his heartbeat loud, and knew that soon his mission would be over.

As Rana Rao's high, precise voice filled the room, he wondered if she realised how lucky she had been. The first he had realised that he had not killed Sita Mackendrick – or Rana Rao, as she liked to call herself now – was when Commissioner Singh dropped by to see him at the port. He had taken some time to come to the point, perhaps finding the matter a cause of embarrassment. The simple fact of the matter, he had said, is that one of my officers was shot recently, lasered in the chest and almost killed, and she claims – this is absurd – she claims that you were responsible. Of course the matter is outrageous, but there are formal lines of enquiry that protocol dictates I follow.

Klien had gone out of his way to accommodate the investigations of Singh and his team. He had nothing to fear. He might have killed the ten victims, but he had ensured that the crimes could not be traced back to him. He told Singh that he understood fully, and if he could help in any way, any way at all . . .

So Rao had managed to survive, and was obviously trying to persuade Singh that he, Klien, was responsible for the attack, and the so-called crucifix killings.

Klien swore to himself that she would not survive a second encounter with him.

Singh's investigations, as he had known they would, came to nothing. He had alibis for all the murders, friends in high places willing to vouch for him. The commissioner had been almost servile with his apologies.

Now Klien listened as the dialogue between Bennett and Sita Mackendrick wound up. He clapped his hands and laughed out loud. How perfect that they would be travelling together! He would soon kill two birds with one stone. He would make the woman regret that she had ever denied him, and Bennett that he had high-tailed it back to Earth on Mackendrick's errands.

And then, he would have the softscreen.

He listened as they made arrangements to gather a few of Rao's belongings and take a taxi to the port, then switched off the ear-piece.

He estimated that he had about one hour.

He set up his hologram projectors in the interview room, timed to start up in ten minutes and shut off in three hours, and gave instructions to Frazer that he was not to be disturbed until he called again. He contacted his team and ordered them to leave the Cobra and check another ship way across the port. Then he left the interview room and locked the door behind him. He took the elevator to the basement and unlocked the door to the armoury. He selected a pair of laser pistols from the rack on the wall, slipped spare charges into his pocket, and left.

Klien crossed the tarmac towards the Cobra, and paused to glance back at the tower. Through the window of the interrogation room he could see the holographic projection. For all the world it was himself, diligently working away at his com-screen. It was a foolproof method of providing him with an alibi. He had used it often in the past. Now, it would keep Frazer and his team from bothering him while he boarded the Cobra.

Ahead, the sleek silver ship squatted on the tarmac while the blue-uniformed resupply team ferried sealed containers up the ramp. Klien followed them into the hold and supervised them as they worked, relishing their palpable unease. He ordered them to leave a container on the tarmac to be checked over by his security team – it was, he judged, approximately his own body weight. He was probably being paranoid, but if Bennett checked the payload before taking off and discovered that he had a stow-away . . .

When the last of the resupply team exited the ship, Klien hurried to the storeroom behind the flight-deck, excitement coursing through him. He could hardly bring himself to believe that his time on Earth was coming to a close, at last.

He collected food-trays and canisters of water sufficient to last him four months, and then moved through the Cobra seeking a suitable hiding place in which to secrete himself when Bennett and the girl were not in suspension. He decided on the starboard engine compartment, a cramped space beneath the ion-drive booster. Unless something drastic happened during the flight, he judged that Bennett would not be using the compartment. He sat on the floor and switched on his ear-piece.

Ten minutes later Bennett and the girl arrived at the port and passed through security. They made their way across the tarmac towards the waiting Cobra. Seconds later Klien heard the hatch slide open and their footsteps moving through the ship.

He held his breath as they made their way along the main corridor to the flight-deck. Bennett was giving Sita Mackendrick a guided tour. The Indian girl could offer only monosyllables of wonder in response.

One hour later the ship was tugged across the port to a blast-pad. Klien braced himself in the cramped confines of the engine compartment and waited tensely as Bennett ran through the systems checks. The period of waiting seemed to last an age, and Klien closed his eyes as he considered the possibility that Bennett might find him. He told himself that he had nothing to worry about.

One hour after that he was deafened as the main drive engaged. The Cobra lifted, and Klien grimaced as he was forced against the floor. He experienced intense pain throughout his body as the ship vibrated, shaking him as he attempted to hold himself in place between two narrow metal spars. He felt as if a giant fist was squeezing his torso, and his lungs protested as he gasped for air. His vision swam and he cried out in pain.

He was wondering how much more he could take when the G-force abated. He opened his eyes and managed to fill his bruised lungs. Little by little the pain diminished, and he knew that the brief trauma had been worth the reward of escape.

Klien sat up and smiled at the thought of what Commissioner Singh might make of his disappearance, so soon after his questioning over the crucifix killings. The mystery would cause quite a stir among his former colleagues. He considered everything he was leaving behind on Earth, which was not, all things considered, that much: a house, a few possessions, his paintings and music collection. He considered the sacrifice with little regret. He had made no friends during his time in Calcutta, deliberately avoiding intimacy of any kind. He was leaving behind his old way of life, his old identity, after fifteen long and difficult years, and he had no regrets at all. At last, against all expectations, he had succeeded.

Minutes later the ship phased into the void and the roar of the engines was replaced with a strange and silent calm. He heard Bennett escort the girl from the flight-deck and explain the process of suspension. 'I'll be waking up halfway through the journey to run a few checks,' Bennett told her. 'See you in four months.'

Klien heard a suspension unit sigh open, and then close as the girl gave herself to the long sleep. Minutes later another unit opened and Bennett climbed in and laid himself out. He heard Bennett exhale as he lost consciousness, and then the hum of machinery go to work on the pilot.

Klien waited a further ten minutes, and then let himself out of the engine compartment. He moved to the suspension chamber, chastising himself for being so furtive. He had the ship to himself, and there was no way that Bennett or the girl might detect his presence.

He stood between the suspension units and stared through the clear covers at the sleepers. The corner of the folded softscreen projected from the pouch of Bennett's flight-suit. The girl lay frozen, as still and perfect in her beauty as some fairytale princess. Klien smiled to himself. They seemed so content, little realising that their mission would end in failure.

He considered killing Bennett and the girl while they slept, but decided against that course of action. He had examined the complex control systems of the ship. If he killed Bennett now he would effectively be signing his own death warrant, as there was no way he could pilot the Cobra safely through the turbulent atmosphere of Homefall. He would call a temporary stay of execution for the pilot and the girl. He would kill them later, when they had delivered him safely to the planet of his birth.

He made himself at home in the berth opposite the suspension chamber. During the following weeks he ate well and kept himself fit with regular exercise. He even found to his delight that the ship possessed an excellent library of classical music discs.

For long hours he sat in the pilot's seat as stirring symphonies swelled round him, staring out at the star-streaked void and contemplating his triumphal return to Homefall.

22

Bennett rocked in his command couch as the Cobra phased out of the void. Tenebrae filled the viewscreen, awesome in its breadth, and Bennett had to search its face for Penumbra. He found the planet at last, a minuscule violet coin silhouetted against a central streamer of pastel green gas. As the Cobra accelerated towards Penumbra, he checked the flight program one last time and unstrapped himself from the couch.

He moved to the suspension chamber. Rana Rao's unit was open, and she was blinking up at him. 'We're here?'

'Estimated time of arrival, one hour. Clean up and join me on the flight-deck. The view's spectacular.'

She struggled upright. 'It doesn't seem two minutes since I climbed into this thing.'

'No dreams?'

She frowned. 'No – yes.' She smiled at him. 'I dreamed of my father, when I was young. We were playing on the lawn. It's a recurring image. I'm—'

'Apprehensive about meeting him after so long?'

She jogged her head in that quaint Indian gesture that seemed to Bennett to signify a qualified affirmative. 'A little. So many things have happened, and the circumstances of our meeting will be so strange.'

He smiled. 'I'll be on the flight-deck. See you soon.'

As he strapped himself into the command couch, he looked ahead to the landing and reunion, the handing over of the softscreen to Mackendrick and the rebels. He wondered at Mack's reaction to being reunited, after so long, with the daughter he had lost.

Rana joined him fifteen minutes later, climbing into the co-pilot's seat and staring in wonder through the viewscreen.

Bennett told her about his involvement with Mackendrick and his mission, the landing on Penumbra and subsequent escapades. Then he asked Rana why she had run away from home, all those years ago. Reluctantly at first, Rana told him about her unhappy childhood, how running away from parents who seemed not to care about her had seemed the right thing to do at the time. She told him about her years on the street, and her rise to the rank of police lieutenant. Her manner of speech was quick and precise, her delicate articulate hands turning with a million gestures. He was mesmerised by her impossibly large eyes, which seemed to contain at once the dark shadows of experience and the light of hope for the future. He thought that there was something immensely strong about the woman, but that also within her was the vulnerable child who had run away from home so long ago.

She stared through the viewscreen at Penumbra turning slowly before them, and behind it the immense backdrop of the gas giant. 'It's hard to imagine that my father is down there.'

As they watched, Penumbra grew from the size of a coin held at arm's length, expanding like a ball thrown towards them in slow motion. Soon it filled the viewscreen, a rolling sphere wrapped in bands of cloud.

'Strap yourself in, Rana,' Bennett said. 'The ride down might be bumpy.'

They entered the cloud cover. For long minutes they experienced nothing but a glowing opalescence beyond the viewscreen, and vision-impairing vibration as atmospheric turbulence rattled the ship. Then they fell from the clouds, the sudden appearance of purple-clad plains and mountains startling to the eye. Rana gasped and leaned forward against her harness, staring down at the folded hills far below and the upthrust mountain ranges. They were travelling at a little over twenty-five thousand kilometres an hour, and the land below seemed only to be crawling by.

To their left, Tenebrae was rising slowly over the line of mountains. Another day was dawning on Penumbra.

Bennett had programmed the Cobra to approach the plain where they had originally landed, and then relinquish control to him. From there he would fly the Cobra up the valley and into the mountains where the rebels had their hide-out. He had copied their co-ordinates into his com-board; it would be a matter of seat-of-the-pants flying through the mountain peaks until they reached the valley. He smiled as he imagined the reaction when Mack, Ten Lee and the rebels heard the sonic booms announcing their arrival.

The Cobra screamed down the long valley plain at an altitude of five hundred metres. This low, with the mountains slipping by to either side, the sensation of speed was breathtaking. Rana gripped the arms of the couch like a child on a funfair ride.

'Down there to the right,' Bennett pointed out, 'you can just see the ruins we found the day after we landed.'

They appeared briefly, reduced to the size of a child's model, and then were gone.

Minutes before they came to the colonists' original timber settlement and the crash-landed spaceship, Bennett took control of the Cobra, decelerated and veered right, ascending over the foothills towards the western mountains. He glanced at the screen of his com-board, reading the distance they had to travel to the rebel valley. Two hundred kilometres and falling . . . estimated time of arrival, four minutes.

Bennett eased the Cobra between great mountain peaks, covered with blinding white snow at this altitude and whipped by raging winds. He slowed, banked around a clenched fist of rock, and planed down into the broad saddle of purple grassland.

'I can see buildings down there,' Rana reported. 'And people, Josh. They're leaving their houses and waving.'

Bennett felt a sudden tightness in his chest, an emotion he had not expected. He glanced down and saw a wide area of grassland beyond the last A-frame. Rana was right. Rebels, dozens of men and women, were streaming from the buildings and across the plain. He applied the vertical thrusters and brought the Cobra down slowly for the gentlest contact with the ground.

When they hit land he cut the engines, exhaled and lay back in the sudden and profound silence. Through the viewscreen he could see the A-frame and domes, and people running towards the ship. He hit the command to lower the ramp, then unbuckled himself from the couch and climbed unsteadily to his feet.

Hans Hupcka was the first aboard. He appeared at the top of the ramp and then burst into the flight-deck, more wild-looking and bearded than Bennett remembered. Others appeared behind him: Miriam James, and other rebel faces he recognised.

Hupcka halted before him, staring like a madman. 'You have the softscreen, Josh?'

Bennett tapped the folded screen in the pouch of his flight-suit and Hupcka enveloped him in a fierce bear hug.

'Incredible! We never expected . . . We thought you'd take a year at least, not just eight months.'

Eight months . . . To Bennett it seemed just like yesterday that he had left Penumbra.

'How's Mack?' he asked. 'Ten Lee?'

'Ten Lee's fine,' Hupcka said. 'Her leg's healed. She spends much of her time meditating. Mack . . .' He shrugged his huge shoulders. 'Mack's ill, but he's stable.' Hupcka's gaze slipped past Bennett to Rana, standing beside her couch. 'You have a co-pilot this time?'

He smiled. 'It's a long story.' He passed Hupcka the softscreen. 'I'd like to see Mack.'

Hupcka nodded. 'I'll take you straight to him. We'll study the screen and plot the position of the entrance to the underground caverns. Also, Mack isn't up to a trek. Can we make the journey in the ship?'

'If there's somewhere reasonably level to land, I can't see any problem.'

Hupcka nodded. 'I'll take you to Mack.'

Bennett turned and reached out for Rana. She took his hand and they hurried from the ship, past smiling faces, across the purple plain.

Hupcka indicated an A-frame. 'Mack is in there. Ten Lee is nursing him. See you in a while.'

Bennett and Rana climbed the steps to the veranda of the A-frame. He turned to her. 'Perhaps it'd be best if I saw Mack first, explain what happened. It's likely to be one hell of a shock.'

Rana nodded, her expression worried and apprehensive. 'Ah-cha,' she said. 'Okay. I'll wait out here.'

Bennett opened the door and ducked into the room. Ten Lee, tiny in her scarlet flight-suit, her skull clean-shaven, rose with fluid grace from a cross-legged position and hurried across to him. Her face showed no hint of emotion, but her embrace was greeting enough. He pressed her head to his chest, looking past her to the bed where Mackendrick lay, struggling to sit upright.

Ten Lee pulled herself away and looked up at him. 'You have the softscreen, Joshua?'

'It's with Hupcka. He's studying it now.'

'I want to find the subterranean chamber,' she said, staring at him but seeing much more. 'I want to find out if the Ancients are still in existence.'

He moved past Ten Lee and crossed to the bed, sat down and forced Mackendrick back into the stacked pillows. He seemed much older now, as if in the eight months he had aged a decade. The skin of his face was drawn tight and wax-like over prominent bones. In Bennett's arms he seemed light, reduced physically if not in spirit.

'Well done, Josh,' he said. 'You don't know how damned proud I am.'

'It must've been a hell of a wait, Mack.'

He laughed. 'Hell no! I assumed you'd be gone for ages. Times were when we even reconciled ourselves to the possibility that you'd never find the damned thing!' His voice, at least, was as strong as ever. 'But I want to know all about it! Everything!'

Ten Lee came and sat on the bed across from Bennett. 'How did you find the softscreen, Joshua?' she asked.

Bennett looked at Mack. 'I . . . to be honest I don't know where to begin. Mack . . . there's someone I want you to meet. I think she'll be able to explain about the screen better than I could.'

Mackendrick gave him a puzzled look. 'What the hell are you talking about, Josh?'

Bennett glanced at Ten Lee. 'Is he up to a surprise, Ten?'

She nodded and touched the old man's hand. 'He's as strong as an ox.'

'Josh?' Mackendrick growled.

'One minute.'

Bennett stood and moved to the door. He slipped out,

expecting to find Rana on the veranda, but there was no sign of her. Then he saw her, about ten metres away, standing alone on the purple plain, staring up at the lofty mountain peaks, at Tenebrae majestic overhead. He stepped from the veranda and crossed the grass, pausing beside her. He touched her arm.

'Rana . . .'

When she turned to him he saw that her eyes were glazed with tears. 'It is all so sudden,' she said. 'There are so many years, so many incidents that have made us both different people. We'll be strangers to each other.'

'He's your father,' Bennett said gently. 'Now's the time to get to know each other again.'

'We've so little time left, Josh.'

'All the more reason to meet him and say what you have to say.'

She smiled up at him. 'I know. You're right. It's just so . . . so very difficult. Ah-cha.' She took a breath and nodded. 'Okay, I'm coming.'

He walked with her back to the A-frame, up the steps and into the lounge. Rana was holding herself tensely, her small fists clenched. She paused across the room from the bed that contained her father. Mackendrick raised his head from the pillow, mystification in his eyes.

Rana stepped forward and approached the bed. She sat down on a chair and pulled it closer. Ten Lee stood and moved to Bennett, sensing their need to be alone.

Mackendrick was staring at the Indian woman. He glanced at Bennett, as if for confirmation. 'Josh?'

Rana reached out and took her father's hand. She lifted it and kissed the bony fingers. 'Father, I have so much to say, and I don't know how to say it.'

'Sita?' For once, Mackendrick seemed at a loss for words. In barely a whisper he said, 'Sita, is it really you?'

Rana held her father's hand in hers and touched it to her forehead. 'It is me,' she said. 'Sita.'

Bennett looked at Ten Lee and they moved quietly from the A-frame and sat down on the steps of the veranda.

From the beginning, the time he left the valley with Hupcka and the rebels, Bennett told Ten everything that had happened.

The gas giant rolled overhead, filling the valley with its vast creamy underbelly and effulgent glow. Someone brought them cups of the excellent coffee substitute, and plates of bread and cheese, then quietly left them talking. Ten Lee listened without expression, this strange distant woman he had come to respect over the period they had been together, even if he could not honestly claim to know her.

At last, after a long silence, Ten Lee said, 'There is a sense of perfection and closure to Sita Mackendrick's reunion with her father, as if it were destined.'

Bennett smiled. 'And you? Are you okay?'

She blinked at him. He had that feeling again, of wondering if she thought him crass with his need for superficial talk. 'I am at one with the essence,' she replied, making him smile. 'I, too, was destined to come here.'

Across the plain, Bennett saw Hans Hupcka, Miriam James and others hurrying towards them.

'We think we've located the entrance!' Hupcka called. He was waving a map, which he spread on the deck of the veranda. The contour map of the western mountains was marked with a thick red line. 'We're here,' Hupcka said, indicating a valley. 'The marked line is the route which Quineau and the others took. It twists and turns for over three hundred kilometres from a point ten kays north of here. This' – he brought a thick forefinger down on a point at the very western extreme of the map – 'is where

306

the entrance is located, at the very top of this valley, below an overhang.'

'Will I be able to land the Cobra?'

Hupcka stabbed the map. 'A matter of a hundred metres away, in the valley. We can land there and move on foot to the entrance. I've arranged supplies of food and water.'

'When do you want to set off?' Bennett asked.

'We've been ready for months,' Hupcka said. 'It really depends on how you're feeling. Are you up to an immediate start?'

'I can't think of any reason to wait.'

Hupcka folded the map and passed it to Bennett. 'Very well. I'll get the ship loaded with the provisions. We'll be ready in ten minutes.'

Bennett returned to the A-frame. Rana was sitting beside her father on the bed, holding his hand. She stopped talking when she heard Bennett, looked up and smiled.

'Sorry to interrupt – we're almost ready to go. There's a valley near the entrance, Mack. I can land the Cobra and we'll go on foot from there.'

Mackendrick looked at his daughter, and then at Bennett. 'Can Sita come too? I'd like her to be with me.'

Bennett nodded. 'Of course.'

Mackendrick closed his eyes. 'This is it, Sita,' he murmured.

Bennett and Ten Lee returned to the ship, followed a little later by Rana and Mackendrick. He walked slowly, like the old man he was, assisted by his daughter.

Hupcka and his men were carrying backpacks and thermal wear up the ramp. A crowd had assembled around the ship, watching in silence. As Bennett strapped himself into the command couch, he looked through the viewscreen at the faces of the gathered rebels. In their hardened expressions he saw the dawning light of hope, after so many years fighting a hopeless battle.

Ten Lee read the co-ordinates from the map and Bennett programmed them into the onboard computer. Five minutes later they were ready for lift-off.

Hupcka stepped on to the flight-deck. 'The provisions are aboard, Josh. Mack and Rana are in one of the sleeping chambers. We're ready when you are.'

Bennett sealed the hatch and looked at Ten Lee. Her eyes regarded him from beneath her bulky flight-helmet. 'Ready, Joshua.'

'Hold on, Hans,' Bennett said.

He touched the controls. The vertical thrusters fired, filling the ship with a concentrated roar. The crowd gathered on the purple plain quickly backed off. Bennett turned the Cobra on its axis, until they were facing west, and eased the ship forward, felt it surge with restrained power. They climbed slowly and banked around the enclosing mountains. Bennett relinquished control and set the Cobra on the pre-programmed flight-path, slabs of cold grey rock passing slowly by a matter of metres from the sidescreens.

He glanced across at Ten Lee, absorbed in the figures scrolling down the screen of her visor. On the engineer's couch, Hupcka was gripping the harness, staring through the viewscreen with an expression at once awed and alarmed.

Thirty minutes later the Cobra decelerated, and down below they saw the valley between two high summits of snow-covered rock. The valley, likewise, was covered with an undisturbed mantle of snow, blinding in the glow of the gas giant.

Hupcka pointed. 'There, the entrance is beneath the overhang to the right.'

'I'll bring the ship down as close as possible,' Bennett said.

He engaged manual override, decelerated and edged the Cobra towards the rock face. Perhaps twenty metres from it he switched to vertical thrust, lowering the ship gradually to the valley floor.

'There's a bit of a slope down there,' he warned. 'Hans, go warn Rana and Mack that we're coming down on a right-to-left incline. Tell them to brace themselves.'

Slabs of iron-grey rock rose around them as the Cobra descended and hit the ground. The ship tilted suddenly, and settled at an angle of fifteen degrees from the horizontal. Bennett cut the thrusters and the engines whined into silence. He peered through the sidescreen at the overhang, two hundred metres away through a deep drift of snow.

For the next thirty minutes they prepared themselves for the trek. Hupcka handed out thermal trousers and jackets, then distributed the backpacks containing food and water and flashlights. Bennett suited up, began to sweat immediately, and opened the hatch to admit cold air. Mackendrick and Rana emerged from their cabin, muffled beyond recognition in their thermals.

Hupcka looked at Bennett, then around at the others. 'So, if we are ready, my friends . . .'

Hupcka led the way down the ramp and into the snow, Bennett and Ten Lee following Mackendrick and Rana. The snow was a metre deep and concealed uneven terrain. They picked their way through the drift with difficulty, losing their footing and frequently falling. Bennett helped Rana with her father, and ten long minutes later they made it to the overhang. They rested, regaining their breath, while Hupcka scanned the wall of rock for the entrance.

Mackendrick held on to his daughter's arm, breathing heavily.

'You okay?' Bennett asked.

'Don't patronise me, Josh. I'll be fine.'

Bennett smiled and joined Hupcka in looking for the entrance. The rock at the back of the overhang was a seamless dark grey slab, with no sign of a break or inlet. He considered the awful possibility of coming so far and being unable to find the entrance.

Hupcka had moved up the incline, to where the overhang narrowed so that he had to stoop. At last he gave a cry and waved. 'Up here!' He indicated a narrow, dark shadow in the face of the rock.

They joined him and he stepped through first, soon disappearing from sight down the steep drop. Rana and Mackendrick went next, illuminating the way with their flashlights. Bennett stepped after Ten Lee, having to turn and force himself with effort through the crevice.

They were walking down a tight, sloping corridor cut into the rock. Within minutes Bennett was sweating, despite the cold. He unfastened his thermal jacket and cooled rapidly. He stopped and looked back up the way they had come. The entrance was a glimmering sliver of opalescent light high above. He continued walking, soon catching up with Ten Lee.

The corridor sloped through the mountain at an angle of thirty degrees, for the most part chiselled from solid rock, but occasionally following the contorted twists and turns of natural chambers.

Only when they had been descending for over an hour did Bennett notice the carvings. In square panels of rock to either side were chiselled hieroglyphs similar to the ones they had discovered on the plain, so many months ago: stars and circles and crosses, all enclosed within squares, triangles and ovals. He recalled the statues of the

Ancients they had discovered in the temple ruins. So far he had never really considered the possibility that they might still exist – it seemed too incredible a leap of faith to believe in the word of a single man, Quineau, deranged by too many months locked in a suspension unit. He wondered at Mackendrick's desire to believe in the remote possibility that, even if the aliens were still alive, they might just possess some form of remarkable healing power. As they descended, Bennett considered Mackendrick, and the desperate desire only the dying must know to go on living.

They had been walking for perhaps three hours, and Bennett was tiring, the muscles of his legs becoming tight with unaccustomed use. Even the appearance of the circular patterns on the walls, which Ten Lee said were mandalas – representations of the various stages on the path to nirvana – failed to divert his attention. He wondered how Mackendrick, ahead, was coping with the descent.

At last Hupcka called a rest halt. They sat down and passed a canteen of refreshing ice-cold water between them. Bennett played his flashlight up the natural walls, catching flashes of blue and turquoise veins rising in the rock like the ribs in a cathedral ceiling.

Rana sat cross-legged beside her father, holding his hand.

Bennett joined them. 'How are you feeling, Mack?'

Mackendrick waved away his concern. 'I haven't felt better for months, Josh.' He stared at Bennett, his gaze intense. 'I'll be fine.' In the glow of the flashlight, though, his thin face looked pared of flesh and his eyes bright with something like fever, or faith.

Bennett looked around at his travelling companions. 'How far can we go before having to turn back? What if we find no sign of the Ancients?'

Hupcka shrugged. 'We have supplies enough to last us six, seven days. If we find nothing in that time, we really should consider returning to the ship. We could mount a bigger, better-equipped expedition at a later date.'

'So we have a week,' Ten Lee said. 'If the aliens are down here, then in that time we will find them.' She looked around the group, something defiant in her expression. 'And I know we will.'

They fell silent. Bennett drank his share of water and passed the canteen to Rana. Her eyes shone like amber gemstones. She returned his smile shyly, accepted the canteen, and held it to her father's lips.

Ten minutes later Hupcka suggested they continue. He led the way, followed by Rana and Mackendrick, Ten Lee and Bennett. They made their way slowly into the heart of the mountain, the plummeting corridor becoming so narrow in places that they had to force themselves sideways to get through. Ten Lee, Rana and Mackendrick managed this without much difficulty, but more than once Hupcka and Bennett became lodged fast in fissures and crevices.

After a further hour of walking, the slope levelled out and they found themselves in a long, high corridor flanked by carved panels. They rested briefly and passed around the water canteens. The random beams of their flashlights illuminated an assortment of panels, and the scenes depicted were all the more stark and startling for being picked out in isolation. As he rested with his back against the rock wall, Bennett looked around at the bas-relief carvings. Among the mandalas were more graphic images: a scene depicting a line of aliens, arms raised; and individual Ancients, long and thin of arm and leg, their heads attenuated, almost equine.

Ten Lee pointed out a mandala to Rana and explained

what it represented. Rana gazed around at the alien carvings. She shook her head in wonder. 'Do you really think that the aliens – the Ancients – believed in Buddhism?'

Ten regarded her impassively. 'I think they believed, maybe even still believe, in the truth, the universal truth. I call that truth Buddhism, but what the Ancients called it doesn't really matter. What does matter is that they shared a common understanding with certain schools of human thought—'

'You can't be certain, Ten,' Bennett objected.

She turned her passionless gaze on him, and he felt involuntarily chastened. 'I've had eight months to meditate, Josh. I have come to understand that Penumbra is special.' With a small hand she indicated the mandalas carved on the walls. 'These are not the only signs that the truth is to be found here.'

Rana stared at her with massive amber eyes. 'Do you think the aliens still exist?'

Ten inclined her head minimally. 'I truly believe in my heart that not only do the Ancients exist, but that we've been called.'

Something about her calm certainty, her air of utter conviction, sent a cold shiver down Bennett's spine. He wondered at the chances of two races, separated by hundreds of light years, independently arriving at a similar system of belief. If so, then did it necessarily follow that that belief had its foundations in some form of universal truth, as Ten seemed to believe? For so long he had been comfortable in his belief of nothing, and the notion that there might be some real truth out there he found disquieting.

As if to lighten the atmosphere, Rana said, 'At least we know we're heading in the right direction.'

Bennett smiled at her. He didn't point out that there

313

was only one possible direction in which they could proceed.

'I reckon we've walked for something like five kilometres,' Hupcka said. He looked around him at the narrow corridor. 'This is obviously leading somewhere, chambers or living quarters where the Ancients gathered, or still gather.'

Put like that, in terms of this being the lair of aliens, the possibility, however slight, that the Ancients still inhabited this subterranean network made Bennett shudder. It was an involuntary sensation, a superstitious fear his rational self knew to be irrational, but which he could do nothing to banish.

'We'll go on for a few more hours,' Hupcka said. 'Then I suggest we stop and camp for the night.'

Everyone nodded. Bennett was tired and could do with a rest, though he guessed that sleep in the circumstances would be impossible.

They started up again. The corridor was perhaps two metres wide, four metres tall, and, like the incline they had left behind them, seemed chiselled from the rock but for occasional sections where the tunnellers had hit natural caverns. Here the tunnel-like aspect of the corridors ceased, along with the carved panels, and opened out into irregular grottoes, spiked with stalactites and stalagmites, echoing with dripping water. Then the corridor would begin again, along with the panels depicting Ancients in all manner of strange and unguessable rituals.

Hours later – Bennett had lost count; it seemed as though he'd been walking for days – Hupcka halted and pointed ahead. 'There! Look!'

Bennett peered. Beyond their flashlights' dancing cones of radiance, he made out a pale pink glow. They started up again and walked a hundred metres, and the corridor opened out into a cavern perhaps twenty metres wide by as many high, lit by a wan, pink fungus which covered the rock walls and high cave roof. They switched off their flashlights and were plunged into an insubstantial and eerie half-light. As they passed into the cavern, their course was joined by a stream of water pouring in from a mouth-like hole in the rock high above. They followed the burbling stream on a slight downward incline, the pink fungus reflected in surging and rushing high-lights.

They walked until the cavern widened yet again, and became a subterranean valley so vast that on either side the walls were hidden by pale wreaths of mist, and vaulted so high overhead that Bennett had to crane his neck to make out the fungi-shrouded ceiling. The valley dropped away at their feet, and far below they made out a forest of etiolated fungal trees, and great lianas or vines hanging from the ceiling. Closer to hand, Bennett saw tiny delicate flowers, pale pink and yellow, growing beside the widening stream.

Hupcka called a halt. Above ground, Tenebrae would be setting. He suggested that they keep to the natural rhythm of night and day and make camp. They pulled bedrolls from their backpacks and laid them side by side on the river bank. Their evening meals were pre-packed cobs of bread, tinned meat, hard cheese and fruit. They gathered in a circle while Hupcka brewed a pot of coffee on a portable stove.

Bennett ate his bread and cheese, surprised at how hungry he was. Hupcka refilled his mug with hot coffee.

Rana stared down into the valley. She caught Bennett looking at her and smiled. 'It seems like just yesterday,' she told him in a small voice, 'that I was working for the Calcutta police force.' She shook her head. 'How did I get here?'

Ten Lee looked at Rana above the rim of her mug. 'You

were called, Rana, as we all were called. We are here for a purpose.'

Rana looked up. 'What purpose?'

Ten Lee, sitting in the lotus position with her back as straight as a bamboo cane, looked as thin as Buddha after his period of denial. She blinked her canted eyes and regarded Rana evenly. 'I do not know. We will find out when the time is right.'

Rana half-smiled and looked at Bennett, who tried not to smile himself.

He finished his coffee, moved to the river and swilled out his mug in the water. He remained squatting on the bank, staring down into the valley. He tried to detect movement between the pale trees, the first sign of animal life down here, but saw nothing. When he returned to the camp, the others had bedded down for the night. He lay on his bedroll, closed his eyes and tried to sleep.

He must have succeeded, as he was awoken some time later by the murmur of voices. He rolled over and opened his eyes. Ten Lee was sitting cross-legged on her bedroll, eyes closed in meditation. Hupcka, Mackendrick and Rana were gathered around the stove, sipping mugs of coffee. He joined them, feeling surprisingly refreshed.

'How long have I been asleep?'

Rana passed him a mug of coffee. 'About six hours, Josh.'

Hupcka was staring down the valley at the fungal trees. 'I feel we're getting somewhere,' he said at last. 'The chamber is widening the further we go. Perhaps we're almost there.'

'There?' Bennett asked.

Hupcka shrugged. 'Wherever it was that Quineau claimed he made contact.'

They packed away their bedrolls and ten minutes later were ready to move on. Bennett and Hupcka led the way, striding down the gentle incline. They kept to the bank of the river which bisected the valley. On the far side was the forest of pale, leafless trees, as intricate and delicate as undersea coral. This side of the river was bare of vegetation save for a pale fungal growth which covered the ground and made walking treacherous. They made slow progress until the incline levelled out and the fungus gave way to bare rock.

Perhaps one hour later, as they were still trooping through the vast cavern, Bennett saw something. He happened to be looking to his left, to where the wan, ghost-like trees climbed the slope on the far side of the valley, when he caught a flash of movement from the corner of his eye. He turned and stared. He could have sworn that he saw a tall, upright figure move quickly into a stand of distant trees.

The others had halted. Mackendrick was pointing. 'There,' he said, his voice unsteady. 'I saw it too. It had . . .' He looked at Bennett. 'It was watching us. It had red eyes, and it was watching us.'

Perhaps, had he been alone, Bennett might have persuaded himself that he was hallucinating. Mackendrick's confirmation that he had indeed seen something filled him with unease.

They moved on. Bennett led the way with Hupcka, keeping close to the big man. The valley widened, and soon they left the forest in their wake. Now the terrain was flat on either side, a smooth expanse of dun rock stretching as far as the eye could see. At least here they knew that they were not being watched.

One hour later the ground began to slope downwards, and Bennett hurried ahead and then came to a halt as the valley floor dipped more dramatically. He caught his breath and stared, aware of the others pausing beside him and gazing in wonder at what stood before them.

They were standing on the edge of a vast amphitheatre, perhaps two kilometres across, though more amazing still was the structure that occupied its centre.

A towering, monolithic ziggurat rose in a great series of steps connecting the floor of the great hollow to the stone high above. It was as if the ziggurat had been laboriously wrought from the solid heart of the mountain, as if the chamber had been expressly excavated to produce this startling feat of architecture, and then the jet stone polished to create a lustrous, midnight gloss.

The others halted at the edge of the amphitheatre, staring down in silence.

Only then did Mackendrick speak. 'Christ,' he whispered. 'Christ almighty, look!'

He swung his arm in a gesture encompassing the entire circumference of the chamber which contained the amphitheatre.

The pink radiance was faint here, and the distant walls were in shadow, but even so the serried rows of hollows in the surface of the surrounding rock could be seen, and within their dark depths the twin ruby points of staring eyes.

Bennett tried to deny the fact of what his senses were communicating, but as he stared with a mixture of awe and fear, he made out more than just the staring eyes. It was, he thought, a vast gathering of the august beings, a convocation. He guessed that there were hundreds, maybe even thousands, of individuals stationed silently in their hollowed caves. They sat with their great shanks crossed, their backs ramrod straight, their heads held high and staring ahead.

Mackendrick looked at Bennett. 'Quineau said . . . over and over he said one word: temple. It didn't mean anything at the time, of course. I didn't give it a second thought.' He stared down at the polished jet ziggurat.

'I feel,' Ten Lee said in a whisper, 'I feel as if I am being drawn towards the temple.'

Bennett nodded. Perhaps it was nothing more than the knowledge of the aliens' massed regard that suggested to him, too, that they were being tacitly invited to continue.

He turned to Mackendrick. 'Are you sure it's safe?' he began.

'Of course it's safe!' Mackendrick almost snapped at him. 'You don't think I came all this way . . . ?' He gestured impatiently. 'Enough talk. Let's get down there.'

They set off again, slowly this time, moving in a group down the steep slope towards the rearing ziggurat. The slope eventually bottomed out and they stood in the great dish of the amphitheatre, still perhaps a kilometre from the first step of the ziggurat. Only when they began walking again, and the structure grew before them so that they had to crane their necks to make out its summit, did the ziggurat's true size become apparent. They were reduced to the size of ants as they stood in the shadow of the first step.

Before them, a long stairway was carved through the rock of the great step, leading to a shadowy archway high above, itself the size of a three-storey building. They began the steep ascent, the high steps – clearly not designed for human use – a final torture after so long a trek.

Perhaps ten minutes later they reached the top of the stairs. A wide apron of polished inlaid rock, as midnight dark as obsidian, stretched away to the arched entrance of the ziggurat proper. As one they made their way towards the awesome portal, their footsteps echoing on the burnished rock.

Bennett stopped suddenly. He made out movement in the shadow of the archway. The others came to a halt around him, staring.

A figure stepped from the entrance and paused before them, a human figure dressed in a simple robe and smiling at them with an expression of beatification.

'My friends,' he said, his voice as calm as his expression. 'Do you come in the name of peace?'

Mackendrick stepped forward. 'We come in peace,' he said. 'I . . . I knew Quineau. He told me of the Ancients.'

The man smiled. 'So Quineau made it back with word of the truth.'

'Carstairs?' Bennett said. 'Is it really you?' He shook his head. 'We thought you were dead.'

The gaunt, balding man, his face thin and pale from so many years spent underground, inclined his head. 'I *was* dead,' he said. 'A man called Klien shot me, many years ago.' He turned and gestured up at the ziggurat. 'Welcome to the temple of the Ahloi,' he said.

23

To return home after all those years, to leave behind the evil of Earth . . .

Ezekiel Klien sat on the floor of the engine compartment and listened to the slow burn of the vertical thrusters as the Cobra came in to land. The impact was gentle, followed by silence, and Klien closed his eyes. The descent through the atmosphere of Penumbra had been much less of a trial than the take-off from Earth, but he still felt shaken and bruised from the roller-coaster ride. He gave thanks that he was home at last.

He activated his ear-piece. Muffled voices came to him from the flight-deck. 'You have the softscreen, Josh?' someone asked.

A period of silence, then Bennett asked about Mackendrick and someone called Ten Lee. Klien listened intently, trying to work out precisely where he was, who Bennett was talking to.

'We'll study the screen and plot the position of the entrance to the underground caverns,' Bennett's contact was saying. 'Can we make the journey in the ship?'

Bennett replied that they could if there was a suitable landing place. Klien heard their footsteps on the ramp as they left the ship.

Bennett seemed to be in contact with people who wanted the softscreen as a guide to the subterranean cavern – obviously, then, opponents of the Council of

Elders, and therefore his own enemies. He guessed that they were somewhere in the mountains, in hiding from the council. Soon they would attempt to fly to the entrance to the underground lair of the Ancients.

He considered the wisest course of action.

It had been a strange four months for Klien, effectively alone as the Cobra lighted through the void. He had had the freedom of the ship. He had eaten well from the stores, and slept in the comfortable beds one at a time, for variety.

During that time he had contemplated the years since leaving Homefall. He was satisfied with his achievements. He had successfully eradicated Quineau, though the fact that the softscreen had remained at large had been a constant source of regret. His time spent in Calcutta he considered a success. He had worked hard to gain his position of eminence at the port, and he had done his best to eradicate evil from the city. Granted, the execution of those he considered unworthy had done little to undermine the rampant spread of evil, but the fact remained that he had done his best. Thanks to him, Earth was a better place, and it was his duty to do the same for Homefall.

He listened to Bennett as he spoke to Mackendrick. A period of silence was followed by Bennett talking to a woman called Ten Lee about how he had discovered the softscreen on Earth. Then they were joined by a number of the renegade colonists. Evidently they were looking at a map, charting the position of the mountain entrance.

'When do you want to set off?' Bennett asked.

'We've been ready for months,' a renegade said. 'It really depends on how you're feeling. Are you up to an immediate start?'

'I can't think of any reason to wait,' Bennett said.

Klien felt his pulse quicken. Soon they would be flying

to the entrance of the underground passage which, sixteen years ago he, Quineau and Carstairs had stumbled upon. He considered the fact that, but for that accidental discovery, the entire course of his life would have been completely different. He could only assume, in the circumstances, that his had been a God-given mission.

Thirty minutes later he heard the sounds of footsteps moving through the ship. The ramp was retracted and the engines powered up. He reached out for his laser pistols, reassured by their presence. Soon, he would be fulfilling the very last act of his long and arduous task.

The Cobra lifted. Klien closed his eyes and waited out the journey. In the warmth of the engine compartment, lulled by the vibration, he dozed. He was awoken, later, by the sound of voices. They had landed. Bennett and the others were preparing themselves for the descent into the subterranean caverns. He listened to their brief conversation, heard the ramp go down and the sound of departing footsteps. He waited ten minutes. Judging by the laboured breathing communicated through his ear-piece, Bennett and the others were climbing up the side of the valley.

Klien moved from the engine compartment and hurried to the flight-deck. Through a sidescreen he made out five tiny figures climbing towards the overhang. He considered what to do now.

If he could contact the Council via the ship's radio and tell them that he had returned . . . But how would that help the council? He had no idea of the position of the renegades' hide-out.

Then, on the console before the command-couch, he saw a folded map. With trembling hands he opened it out.

There were two red circles marked on the map, and a line marked in red which he judged to be the route he and the others had taken sixteen years ago. One circle was

323

situated high in the western mountains, and could only be the entrance to the underground chambers. The other was two hundred kilometres to the south. This southern-most circle had to be the position of the renegade camp.

He activated the radio and attempted to get through to someone, anyone, on Homefall. If he could contact the Council, inform them of the whereabouts of the rene-gades' camp . . .

He tried every wavelength, every band, but without luck. The receivers relayed only the white noise of static. Evidently he was too far away, or perhaps atmospheric conditions were scrambling the signal.

Very well, he would try later. He would follow Bennett and the others underground, choose his moment and kill them. He would take their protective thermals, return to the ship, and try to contact the Council again. If unsuc-cessful, he would make the long trek to home valley, equipped with supplies from the ship, and the map. He had done it once before; he would do it again.

First, though, he had to eliminate the enemy.

In his ear-piece he could hear the heavy breathing of Bennett, the sound of ringing footsteps on rock.

He lowered the ramp and left the ship with his laser pistols. The wind was biting, and he was hardly dressed for the conditions, but soon he would be in the caverns, warming himself with the thrill of the chase. He followed the trail of footprints through the snow to the overhang of rock. The sight of it, the grey slab jutting out over the valley, brought back a slew of memories. He moved from the snow and clambered up the slope, soon locating the narrow entrance.

He began a cautious descent, the sound of Bennett's breathing playing in his ear.

He removed the ear-piece so that he might hear his quarry naturally and so judge how far away they were.

Over the period of the next six hours, Klien followed Bennett and the others down the sloping corridor and the long, panel-flanked passage, until they came to the head of the natural valley. For the first time he caught sight of them as they stopped to make camp for the night. He inserted his ear-piece as they settled down to sleep, so that he would be alerted when they awoke and set off again. He found a natural mattress of fungus and napped.

Hours later they set off again, and Klien followed at a safe distance. Soon, he knew, they would be coming to the amphitheatre containing the ziggurat of the Ancients.

He recalled Carstairs, and what they had witnessed in the chamber so many years ago. He had not been able to let Carstairs go after that, could not let him spread the word of the Ancients. So he had killed him . . . and tried to kill Quineau as well. But Quineau had managed to flee the temple, escape the mountains before he, Klien, could silence him.

He tried to shut out the terrible images, concentrate on what lay ahead.

He realised that he could have killed Bennett and the others ten times over during the past few hours, but something had prevented his doing so. Not mercy, or anything like compassion, because he knew he would take great delight in eliminating Bennett and his cohorts, preventing their disseminating the evil ways of the Ancients to the universe.

No, something else had stayed his hand so far.

Only as he came to the end of the valley, and paused on the lip of the vast amphitheatre, did he understand. As he watched Bennett and the others climb the steps of the ziggurat, Klien knew suddenly why he had been brought to this place.

Not only would he kill Bennett and the other humans,

he would use his considerable firepower to rid Homefall of every last Ancient as well.

Filled with the fervour of the righteous, Klien activated his lasers and descended into the amphitheatre.

24

Bennett stared at the gaunt figure of Carstairs in the entrance of the temple.

'Welcome,' Carstairs repeated. 'We are preparing a ceremony of reception for you.'

'Klien killed you?' Mackendrick said, voicing Bennett's incredulity.

'We never really die,' Carstairs said. 'We merely relinquish our physical forms when the time is right, and, move on. When I died, the time was not right for me to move on. First, I had to learn.'

Bennett heard Ten Lee beside him. 'Yes . . .' she whispered to herself.

Carstairs lifted a hand. 'Come, I will explain. If you would care to follow me.'

Mackendrick looked around the group, his face frozen with shock and hope. He gripped Rana's hand and followed as Carstairs turned and walked into the shadowy portal. Bennett, Ten Lee and Hupcka joined them.

They passed down a wide, high corridor, leaving the pink fungal glow behind them. They switched on their flashlights and filled the corridor with a hundred dazzling reflections.

Carstairs turned. 'Please, in the temple, only the light of naked flames.'

Obediently they switched off the flashlights. Bennett walked on, blinded by the absence of light in this midnight tunnel. As his eyes became accustomed to the darkness, he saw a faint source of illumination far ahead. He felt a hand grip his, small and warm: Rana. They left the corridor and entered the great circular chamber, illuminated by the flames of perhaps a hundred tiny candles set high in the curving walls.

Mackendrick, Rana and Bennett were the first into the chamber after Carstairs, and they stopped and stared at what was revealed in the fitful candlelight. Bennett's pulse quickened and fear clutched at his chest.

Stationed like silent sentries around the circumference of the chamber, Bennett made out the tall and shadowy shapes of the Ancients – the Ahloi, as Carstairs called them. They stood unmoving, their long arms by their sides, even longer legs slightly bent at the knees. Rana almost collapsed against him in shock. He took her weight, wishing that someone would likewise support him.

Carstairs, ahead, turned to them. 'Please,' he said. 'Follow me.'

'Where . . .' Bennett began. 'I mean, where are we going?'

'There is much I must explain,' said their guide. 'This way.'

He turned and led them across the chamber, past a short, central stone, towards a dark square set into the floor. As they approached, Bennett made out a flight of stairs. He followed Carstairs down the steps, Rana supported between himself and Mackendrick. Ten Lee and Hupcka brought up the rear.

The meagre illumination from the candles in the chamber lit their way down the short staircase. Then they were in another wide, high corridor, receding into absolute darkness. Bennett heard Carstairs' footsteps ahead, checked that the others were with him, and followed.

They walked for perhaps ten minutes before the darkness was alleviated by a light in the distance. It appeared tiny at first, a mere speck like a star, but rapidly grew as they approached. At last they made out the shape of the tunnel ahead, the walls, floor and ceiling receding in perspective to form a square exit filled with a familiar opalescent glow.

Bennett knew where he had seen such light before, but he found it hard to believe that this was the same. Then he felt the lapping of a faint wind about his face, and knew that his eyes had not been deceived. They were emerging from the mountainside, into the light of Tenebrae.

They arrived at the end of the corridor, and Bennett halted and stared out. An ever-widening flight of stairs fanned out from the exit of the corridor and descended the flank of the mountain. Far below a vast sea was contained and encircled by a rearing rampart of cliffs like the inner wall of a volcano. Let into the almost sheer face of the rock were dark slits like windows, hundreds of them, thousands in fact, in serried rows one above the other. Bennett moved his gaze from the far wall of the mountain, around in a great sweep, to the sheer cliff faces on either side of the corridor's exit. Here he could see that each of the window slits was at least ten metres tall, carved into the mountainside to form great, cavernous chambers.

Carstairs made a sweeping gesture to encompass the whole spectacular design. 'Welcome to the monastery of Ahloi-tennay,' he said.

Bennett looked around at his friends. He knew that the expressions of wonder on their faces matched his own.

Only then did he see the statues, small compared to the great slit windows, that stood in a great phalanx on a ledge to either side of the exit and encompassed the entire sea. He could make out the details only of the first dozen or so. They were carvings from the natural rock of . . . at first he assumed they were animals, and then revised his opinion. Among the first few statues was that of an upright being, a humanoid with a regal bearing; it possessed a great domed skull, tiny childlike features, its body enveloped in a robe. Next to it was something very much like an upright scorpion, and next to this an ursine being, and then an arachnid with great faceted eyes and ferocious mandibles. Bennett began counting the statues, and reached a hundred before the diminishing perspective defeated his vision.

Carstairs turned to them, silhouetted against the opalescent dome of Tenebrae, and spread his hands.

'The Ahloi are an ancient race,' he said. 'They are *the* most ancient race in the universe. They are the only survivors among the many who inhabited the young universe, billions of years ago. They were once a materialistic race like any other, but while their fellows across the many galaxies wasted themselves in futile aggression or the hedonism that results from the pursuit of materialism, the Ahloi managed to survive this stage of their evolution. In time, over many millennia, they became contemplative beings.

'They crossed the universe by means of star-flight unimaginable to us and lost to the present Ahloi. They seeded many galaxies, and settled to fulfil their self-appointed roles of guardians, or teachers. Over time, over millions of years, many races came to the planets inhabited by the strange and wise beings, often accidentally, and then purposefully when they heard the Ahloi's message.

'Homefall, or Ahloi-tennay as we call this world, is where the Ahloi set up their monastery, their ministry, in this galaxy. We have received many novices in our time, as you can see.' Here Carstairs gestured at the statues to either side of the exit. 'They came, and we healed them, and in so doing they saw the light of the truth, and some remained with us in contemplation until they relinquished their forms and became part of the shannath, or nirvana, while others returned to their planets of origin.'

Mackendrick said, 'They were dying, these individuals, and the Ahloi cured them?'

'They were not dying, as such,' Carstairs replied. 'We cured them of the many ills the flesh is heir to, diseases if they were diseased, or merely the blight of ageing. You see, nature has imposed cruel limitations upon the life-spans of its many races. In the terribly short spans they were allowed to live – often only long enough to reach adulthood and reproduce – they were unable to mature spiritually. They were like fireflies; just as they begin to apprehend the wider world they are cruelly snuffed out. Humans, too, are such a race. We need more time, extra years, in which to contemplate the truth of existence. The Ahloi refuse no one in their desire to propagate contemplation of the truth.'

'But if all races came here,' Bennett said, 'then Ahloi-tennay would be overrun.'

Carstairs' calm smile halted his objection. 'But Josh, over the millennia, entire races *have* sought the ministrations of the Ahloi. Entire planets have passed through our portals, and been cured and informed of the truth, and returned to their own worlds to consider those truths. In time, of course, these individuals pass on, relinquish their physical forms, just as I will in years to come. The Ahloi have given them that most precious gift of all, that which normally cannot be gained: the gift of time.'

Ten Lee said, 'It is the belief of my people that,

although we do not have time to gain the truth in one life, we are reborn into others so that the quest for the truth can be continued. Like this, after many lives, we at last arrive and become at one with sunyata.'

Carstairs bowed his head. 'Your way is valid and true,' he said. 'But the Ahloi considered it a source of much misery and suffering, this endless cycle of rebirth. Our way is a short cut, if you like, a means of achieving what you call sunyata in one, albeit extended, lifetime. But each form is valid, Ten Lee. Follow your own path, if you wish. Or you may join with us.'

Into the silence that followed Carstairs' words, Mackendrick said, 'You refuse no one? You will take me?'

Hesitation showed on Ten Lee's face. Then she stepped forward. 'And me?'

Carstairs gestured at the group. 'We will take you all, if that is what you wish.'

'You say "we",' Mackendrick said. 'You sound as if you belong to the Ahloi now, as if you're a part of them?'

Carstairs nodded. 'That is true. When you apprehend a universal truth, when you share something as fundamental as the Ahloi's knowledge, then it is impossible not to become a part of what they are.'

'But they haven't taken you over?' he asked.

Carstairs laughed at this. 'You use the combative terms typical of the human race,' he said. 'In essence, of course, they have taken me over, for it is a fact that I now believe what they believe, and what is being "taken over" if not coming to believe in the truth as perceived by others? But I can assure you that it is an entirely passive and beneficial form of take-over. We share in the joy that contemplation affords, and if you wish to join us you are welcome.'

Mackendrick said, 'When you have cured me, then must I remain here?'

'My friend,' Carstairs said with patience, 'we make

332

you do nothing. We show you the light, that is all. However, once you have perceived the way, then you will be unlikely to want to return to the life and the world you knew. It will seem shallow and superficial. The ways of materialism will hinder your concentration. In all likelihood you will wish to remain here, with us.'

Mackendrick nodded. 'I am ready,' he said at last.

'Then, if you would like to return with me to the Chamber of Rebirth? Please,' he gestured to the others, 'you are welcome to observe, or even join, the ritual.'

He moved back into the tunnel, soon disappearing into the darkness. Bennett looked about him one last time, at the great circular sea and the encompassing mountains, the statues of the legion of aliens long since passed from this world. Then he followed Carstairs, Rana still holding on to him as if in fear.

On the long walk back to the chamber, Bennett considered the words of Carstairs, the convert to this strange alien belief system. He supposed the crux of whether or not one believed in the way of the Ahloi was how one viewed their power of bringing the dead back to life. Did their ability necessarily mean that their belief system was correct?

He stopped himself there. What proof was there that the aliens *could* bring the dead back to life? He wondered if he was being materialistic and crass in his analysis of something so amazing as the promise of rebirth.

They climbed the steps, and they saw that now the chamber was bathed in torchlight. The obsidian walls reflected the bright orange flares of a hundred flaming brands. As they emerged into the chamber, Bennett halted and stared about him. The Ahloi stood in a great circle, their gaunt forms thrown into stark relief by the flickering torches held aloft by every other individual.

Those without torches stepped forward to form a smaller, tighter circle. Carstairs moved to the central stone. He was joined by two of the tall, stiffly articulated aliens. The Ahloi bent their knees and lowered their long heads as if to speak to him. Bennett heard a rapid series of clicks and whistles. Then another Ahloi came hurriedly into the chamber, moving with the spry articulation of an insect. The alien approached Carstairs, bent and hurriedly addressed the human.

Carstairs swung around, facing the corridor down which they had originally entered the chamber. He hurried back to Mackendrick and the others.

'You have been followed,' he said. 'Already he has slain many Ahloi.'

They turned and stared. Bennett wondered what Carstairs was talking about. Who could have possibly followed them all this way?

Seconds later a figure emerged from the mouth of the opposite corridor. Bennett stared at the intruder, who paused on the threshold of the chamber. His face, in the light of the flames, was soaked in sweat and appeared just a little insane. He held a laser pistol in each hand and raised them as he took in the gathering.

Beside Bennett, Rana gasped. 'Klien!'

Bennett recognised the security chief who had interviewed him in Calcutta four months ago, and knew then how Klien had managed to follow them here.

Carstairs stepped forward, arms raised in a gesture of reconciliation. 'Klien?' he said. 'Is it you, Klien? I never thought we would meet again.'

'We watched their ceremony of rebirth, Carstairs,' Klien said, his voice cracking, 'and I couldn't allow you to spread the word. So I killed you, and then these . . . these *devils* brought you back to life!' He gave a terrible laugh and shook his head. 'I knew what I saw, but over the years

I began to doubt. I almost convinced myself that I'd been tricked.'

'It was no trick, Klien,' Carstairs interrupted. 'The Ahloi possess the ability to heal the sick, bring the dead back to life.' He paused, then spread his arms. 'Look at me, Klien. I live.'

'No!' Klien cried, raising a pistol and taking aim at Carstairs.

'Please!' Carstairs said. 'Please, no violence. I beg you.'

'I will kill you first,' Klien cried, 'and then dispose of the Ancients.' He looked around at the group of humans. 'You have been deceived by the ways of the devil and you will repent at your leisure in hell.'

Bennett almost wept. How banal Klien's punitive theology seemed in light of what he had heard from Carstairs. He would rather believe neither, in his ignorance and materialism, but if pressed he would have no hesitation in siding with Carstairs and his alien cohorts.

Carstairs took a step forward, and Bennett could only watch as Klien casually pulled the trigger of his pistol. The laser fire lanced instantly across the chamber, bright as lightning, and in the dark aftermath of the shot Carstairs crumpled to the ground.

Then Klien cried and began firing at random. The effect was gruesomely beautiful, as sapphire spears of laser light criss-crossed the chamber and illuminated the falling figures of the Ancients. At that second Hans Hupcka yelled out and charged. He was almost upon the assassin before Klien reacted. He fired, the bright flash dazzling Bennett. He grabbed Rana and dragged her to the floor. When his eyes adjusted, he saw Hupcka lying dead – obviously, horribly dead – beside the central stone.

Klien continued with the slaughter, and for long seconds a series of flashes snapped on and off around the chamber. Oddly, the Ahloi stood unmoving, facing

Klien's insane rage with the fatalism of true believers. Klien was turning like a homicidal dervish, crying out as he fired. One by one the Ahloi tumbled grotesquely, their cries high-pitched and inhuman, and hit the floor with a chitinous rattle of limbs.

Bennett shook Rana from him, but she grabbed his hand and would not let go. 'No!' she cried. 'He'll kill you!'

Brutally he pushed her away and scrambled around the chamber in the brief periods of darkness between the bursts of laser fire, attempting to get on Klien's blind side. He was overcome with the need for vengeance, a rage he had never before experienced.

He leaped towards Klien, and at that precise second the madman turned and fired. The charge tore past Bennett's head, the heat burning his hair, and a second later he impacted with Klien and knocked him from his feet. They struck the stone floor and rolled, Klien roaring with rage beneath him as one pistol skittered away across the polished stone floor. Bennett wrestled with Klien for the second pistol, pulled it from him and tried to roll away and shoot. Klien dived after him, pinning him to the floor and reaching for the laser.

Bennett felt a painful grip on his wrist, and then Klien was forcing the pistol little by little towards Bennett's head. Klien seemed possessed with the strength of the insane, and Bennett felt his resistance weakening as the bulbous barrel of the laser pistol moved closer to his face.

He closed his eyes, heard the quick hiss of a shot, and Klien spasmed on top of him.

When he opened his eyes he saw Rana standing nearby, frozen in contemplation of the enormity of her actions, the laser pistol Klien had dropped now gripped in her outstretched hands. Klien toppled from him, the lower half of his skull a shattered gourd spilling the viscous liquid of his brains.

Rana ran to Bennett's side and helped him to his feet. Mackendrick joined them, taking his daughter in his arms without a word. The humans huddled in a group in the centre of the chamber and watched the activity of the Ahloi all around them.

More Ancients were hurrying into the chamber, their clicking legs working like stilts; they gathered about the dead and fallen, lifting the lifeless bodies and carrying them down the steps and away. They seemed to approach Carstairs with especial reverence, half a dozen Ahloi lifting him with care, caressing his body with their long-fingered hands.

Bennett was aware of movement behind him. When he turned he looked into the attenuated, insectoid visage of an Ancient. Its swollen ruby eyes regarded him without discernible emotion. It opened its mandibles, and beneath its clicks and hisses Bennett made out the whispered aspiration of words.

'Bennett . . .' it said in a hot rushing breath. 'They will be taken . . . resurrected. In time they will live again.'

Bennett shook his head, turned and watched the dead as they were carried from the chamber.

Hupcka's great body was lifted by four Ahloi and borne away, his leonine head hanging lifeless, his chest a charred mess where the laser had impacted. Next came the perpetrator of the killings; three Ancients hurried away with Klien's macabre remains.

He looked at the Ahloi beside him. 'What will happen to Klien?' he asked.

'Like the others,' the alien breathed, 'he too will be brought back to life.'

'But he will be punished?'

The alien regarded Bennett with all the expression of a praying mantis. 'Punish?' it breathed, as if that word were missing from its vocabulary.

337

Perhaps, Bennett thought, an indefinite period in which to contemplate the error of his ways would be punishment enough for Klien. He checked himself. He was taking for granted something that hours ago he would have considered impossible.

'Is it really possible?' he asked. 'I mean, how can you . . . ?'

'No injury is beyond our ability to repair,' the alien whistled. 'It will take longer to effect their transcendence, but we have time in abundance. And now . . .' The tall Ahloi turned to Mackendrick. 'Carstairs informed us that you were ill, that you sought the truth.'

The alien moved to the centre of the chamber and stationed itself beside the nub of stone. It was joined by another, this one bearing a flaming brand. As Bennett looked about him, he realised that the Chamber of Rebirth was no longer a scene of carnage. As if nothing untoward had occurred, a circle of Ancients stood about its circumference.

The alien who had spoken to Bennett now lifted a long, skeletal arm and gestured to Mackendrick, who stepped slowly forward.

Rana moved from Bennett's side, rushed to her father and held him. For long seconds they embraced, Rana sobbing like a child, before Mackendrick released her, coaxing her with gentle whispers to rejoin Bennett. She nodded and stumbled across the chamber. Bennett pulled her to him, holding her as they watched with a sense of awe and disbelief.

Mackendrick took his place between the two aliens.

'First,' the Ahloi said, 'you will be touched . . . granted a glimpse of the way. You will make your decision, and if you wish salvation, then the ceremony will commence.'

Mackendrick raised his head. He seemed a small figure, reduced by age and illness. He stared back at Bennett, Ten

Lee and his daughter, something proud and at the same time apprehensive in his eyes.

'I'm ready,' he said at last.

The alien reached out, spanned Mackendrick's head with its long fingers, and Mackendrick staggered but remained upright. The alien lowered its long head and whispered to him. Mackendrick raised his face to the alien and spoke, then seated himself on the central stone.

The Ancient turned towards Bennett, Rana and Ten Lee. 'Mackendrick has perceived the way, and wishes to join us.'

At once, the Ahloi stationed around the chamber moved forward, causing great disorienting shadows to fly and flap around them. They surrounded Mackendrick in an orderly yet frightening melee, a ritual Bennett found dreadful in its similarity to nothing in his experience. It was as if the aliens were devouring the human, taking something from him instead of giving. For long minutes they reached out with attenuated arms and caressed Mackendrick with long fluttering fingers, obscuring him from sight. Bennett was aware of a charge in the atmosphere of the chamber, as if, truly, the miraculous was being performed.

Then the Ahloi backed off, resumed their silent stations around the chamber, and the Mackendrick seated on the stone seemed like a man transformed. His face glowed, Bennett thought, though it might only have been an effect of the torchlight, and his posture was that of a man years younger, no longer bent with age and pain.

He stood and walked to Bennett and Rana. He embraced his daughter, touched Bennett's arm in a wordless communication of his joy and transformation.

'Father?' Rana began.

'I must go now,' he said. 'I . . . there are many things I need to consider. In time we will meet again, talk . . .'

He staggered, almost fell. Quickly two Ahloi moved to his side, caught him under the arms and carried him from the chamber.

Bennett turned back to the central stone. Ten Lee squeezed his hand, then let go and hurried towards the Ancient pair.

'Ten!' Bennett said. He wanted to say something, a farewell that might fully express his sense of loss, but she was already stationed before the central stone.

The alien without fire reached out, spread its fingers across her shaven skull, and Ten Lee rocked and gasped at its touch. She took her place upon the stone, and again the ceremony was repeated. The Ahloi moved to her, enveloped her, two circles of dark and light, obscuring her from sight, and when they backed away she too had been affected, and the look upon her face, her expression of hallowed rapture, convinced Bennett.

She tried to stand, but collapsed, and was carried by two Ahloi from the chamber.

The alien stepped forward. 'Please, if anyone else . . .' It gestured to the stone.

Bennett took a step forward. He thought only of Carstairs' description of the Ahloi and their way, and it seemed so right to him. He felt Rana's hand in his, restraining him. He heard her say something, but her words were reduced, stripped of meaning, just so many sounds conveying emotions beyond his comprehension.

He stepped forward and moved slowly towards the waiting Ancients, then stood between them and turned, and across the chamber Rana seemed so small and vulnerable as she stared at him with tearful eyes. She reached out to him, pleaded with him to think about what he was doing, and in that second Bennett wanted to explain to her that he was trying to leave all the pain behind.

He inclined his head, trying to prepare himself for this foretaste of the universal truth, but he knew that preparation was impossible. The Ahloi reached out and touched his head with hard, cold fingers.

Instantly his awareness was transformed. He knew nothing of time. The concept of duration was meaningless. A part of him knew that Mackendrick and Ten Lee had experienced this foretaste for as long as the Ahloi's hand had spanned their skulls – a matter of seconds only – and yet it seemed to him that the time during which he experienced the wonder of the universal essence was limitless.

He was at once aware of himself as an individual identity, and aware too of the many other countless identities that constituted a whole; a kind of gestalt mind, and yet not a mind but an essence made up of every living thing that had ever been. It was an ocean of life that underpinned this reality, an essential ur-reality from which life as he had known it sprang and to which it would return. He seemed always on the verge of mentally apprehending this universal truth, this essence, but prevented from doing so by the fact that this was a foretaste only, that he had not yet relinquished his human form and joined the gestalt.

He knew that he was experiencing the truth not through any of his usual senses: he could not see the gestalt, or hear it, or even touch it. He sensed it, was aware of the fact of the ur-reality with a part of his mind he had never before been fortunate enough to use. Apprehending this, he *thought* his way into the ocean of universal life, wanting to become part of it and yet proscribed from taking that final step. A part of him reached out, searching for something, needing something he sensed was there, he knew *should* be there, but could not find.

With that same part of his mind, which he had never

before used, he asked for Ella. He discerned her essence on the very edge of his consciousness, a faint presence like an elusive ghost. And as he failed to make contact, as he felt within him an awful ache of loss, he heard a voice that was not a voice, felt an explanation enter his consciousness. He was told, or he was suddenly aware, that though the essence of Ella, and of his father and mother, and indeed everyone else who had ever existed, was maintained in this limitless ur-reality, they were now a vast and indivisible whole that could not be said to be made up of individuals, but which was something more. He understood that, because he was still an individual, still part of the realm of the physical; he could not truly apprehend the wonder of the truth, could grasp but a fleeting glimpse. Only when he relinquished his present material life would he conjoin with the ultimate, the infinite and eternal.

He understood then that human life was in some way an aberration, his existence like an individual drop of water thrown from an ocean, which would exist alone for a time before it was drawn irrevocably back into the body of the vastness to which it truly belonged. It was as if life was a travail of hardship through which one had to pass to truly appreciate the sublimity of the essence, and upon realising this the man who was Bennett was granted something of how it felt to be part of the whole. It was, he thought later, a feeling very much like, but greater than, the sacred experience of being loved, of being accepted and accepting and knowing only the rightness of belonging.

And then the Ahloi removed its hand from his head, and Bennett lost consciousness.

25

For a long time before he came to his senses, Bennett tried to regain something of the experience of the ultimate, the foretaste of the truth. Like an elusive dream, vanishing upon awakening, it would not be caught. He was aware of his body moving, of taking steps, of breathing, but the fact of his physicality seemed so distant and removed that it hardly mattered.

When he finally came to his senses and opened his eyes, he was no longer in the Chamber of Rebirth. He was blinded by a glare of whiteness, assailed by a cold wind that seemed to scour his very soul. He was aware of someone beside him, holding him upright.

'Rana?'

She looked up at him. 'We're almost there,' she said.

'Where . . . ?' he managed.

She pointed.

Through the flurry of a snowstorm he made out the silver teardrop shape of the Cobra.

He shook his head. 'What happened, Rana? I . . . the last thing I remember . . .' He caught a tantalising suggestion of the sublimity of the essence which awaited all living things at the end of their tenure of the flesh. 'Why didn't I join Mack, Ten Lee? The Ahloi would have let me join them.'

Rana urged him onward through the snow. He could not bring himself to argue. He lunged forward, almost falling through a deceptive drift. He stumbled and righted himself, the small Indian woman at his side gripping his arm. Together, slowly, they made their way through the whiteout of a raging blizzard. The cold clutched his face, squeezing feeling from his features, burning.

They made the ship and staggered up the ramp, hurrying through the Cobra to the warmth of the flight-deck. Bennett collapsed into the pilot's seat, exhausted. Rana pulled off her thermal jacket and sank to the floor with her back against the bulkhead. Her face was glowing, her brown eyes large and alive like burnished gems.

'Rana . . . what happened?'

'You didn't want to stay down there,' she said. He saw that she was crying, and he wondered why. 'Don't you remember? You said that you'd beheld a miracle, but that you weren't ready for it. You said that you could always make the journey later.'

He shook his head. 'How long was I out?'

'The alien touched you for about, I don't know, ten seconds, no more.'

He marvelled at what he had experienced in that short time. He recalled that Mackendrick and Ten Lee had elected to take the longer ceremony. What wonders during that mass laying on of hands had they been granted, what insights had they glimpsed?

'And I didn't want to undergo the full ceremony?' he asked now.

Rana shook her head. 'No. You told me what you'd experienced, but you said you wanted to leave, return to the ship. You said . . . you said that you wanted to live before you gave up this life. For the past ten, twelve hours we've been climbing back through the mountain.'

Bennett wiped the melted snow from his face. 'Did you . . . did you experience the truth?'

She shook her head. 'No. I . . .' She turned her beautiful

344

hands in a delicate, articulate gesture of doubt and circumspection. 'I too want to live before I die. I mean, we know what awaits us, Josh. There is enough time to be part of the whole. But all I want now is to be myself.'

She reached out, then, and took his hand.

Bennett stared through the viewscreen at the massive bulk of Tenebrae as it rose over the mountain peak. He felt within him something of the residuum of the love he had felt while experiencing the ultimate, and a part of him wondered at his decision, no doubt subconscious and out of his control, to forgo the way of the Ahloi. Another part of him wanted nothing more than to return to the temple, rejoin Ten Lee and Mackendrick and the others, and devote his life to the contemplation of that which he had experienced in the Chamber of Rebirth.

He wondered then if this desire to give himself to the Ahloi was merely a way of saving himself from the suffering, a way of avoiding all the usual emotional involvement that was an inevitable and irrevocable part of being human.

He helped Rana to her feet and strapped her into the co-pilot's seat.

Soon, Homefall and its secret would be opened to the Expansion. Soon Mackendrick's ships and scientists would arrive and transform the planet, and, in time, the Expansion and everyone in it would be transformed.

Rana must have been reading his thoughts. 'Things will be different now,' she said. 'It will never be the same. Change is on the way.'

Bennett looked into his heart and saw the truth. 'For the better,' he said. 'The change is for the better.'

She smiled, gazing out at Tenebrae. 'And now?'

He pulled the console array towards him and began powering up the ship. 'Now we return to the rebels' valley and await the arrival of Mackendrick's men.'

She turned to him and smiled. 'And then?'

And then? He looked at Rana. 'The outsiders will need guides,' he said, 'people to escort them to the Ahloi temple and the Chamber of Rebirth. We know the way, Rana. We can show them the way.'

Then Bennett lifted the Cobra, turned the ship slowly on its axis and accelerated down the valley, heading through the mountains towards the stronghold of the rebels.